Created with Vellum

WIND FLOWERS

LINA C. AMAREGO

A BABYLON NOVEL

Wind Flowers

A Babylon Novel

Lina C. Amarego

SILVER WHEEL PRESS

Personas Vitae

The Earth Kingdom of Dunyas

King Boris
Queen Vera
Princess Catirina
~~Prince Nikolaj~~
Lord Jakir
Lady Egrete

The Fire Kingdom of Jalta

King Odion
Queen Katia
Princess Naria
~~Prince Rashin~~
Duke Hizan
Duchess Asira
Lord Avi

THE WATER KINGDOM OF NEHIR

King Skifar
Queen Ecei
Prince Drakkar
~~Duke Enir~~
Duchess Ishta
Duke Samir

THE AIR KINGDOM OF SORA

King Lin
Queen Mina
Prince Haro
Princess Hana
Duke Askil

GLOSSARY OF TERMS

EASINIR

People born with the ability to affect an element.

TYPES OF EASINIR

Aquamentals: Water manipulators
Teramentals: Earth manipulators
Pyromentals: Fire manipulators
Aermentals: Air manipulators

OTHER VARIATIONS

Medementals: Any type of Easinir that uses their abilities to study and treat the human body.
Sanguimentals: A rare subtype of Aquamental with the ability to manipulate blood.
Vitamentals: An extremely rare type with the ability to manipulate life-force itself.

Levels of Easinir

Quantifiers: Easinir with the ability to manipulate the quantity and movement of an element, but not the properties of it.
Qualifiers: Easinir with the ability to manipulate the quality, phase, and properties of an element, but not the quantity or the movement.
Controllers: Easinir with full ability to manipulate the quality, quantity, properties, and movement of an element.

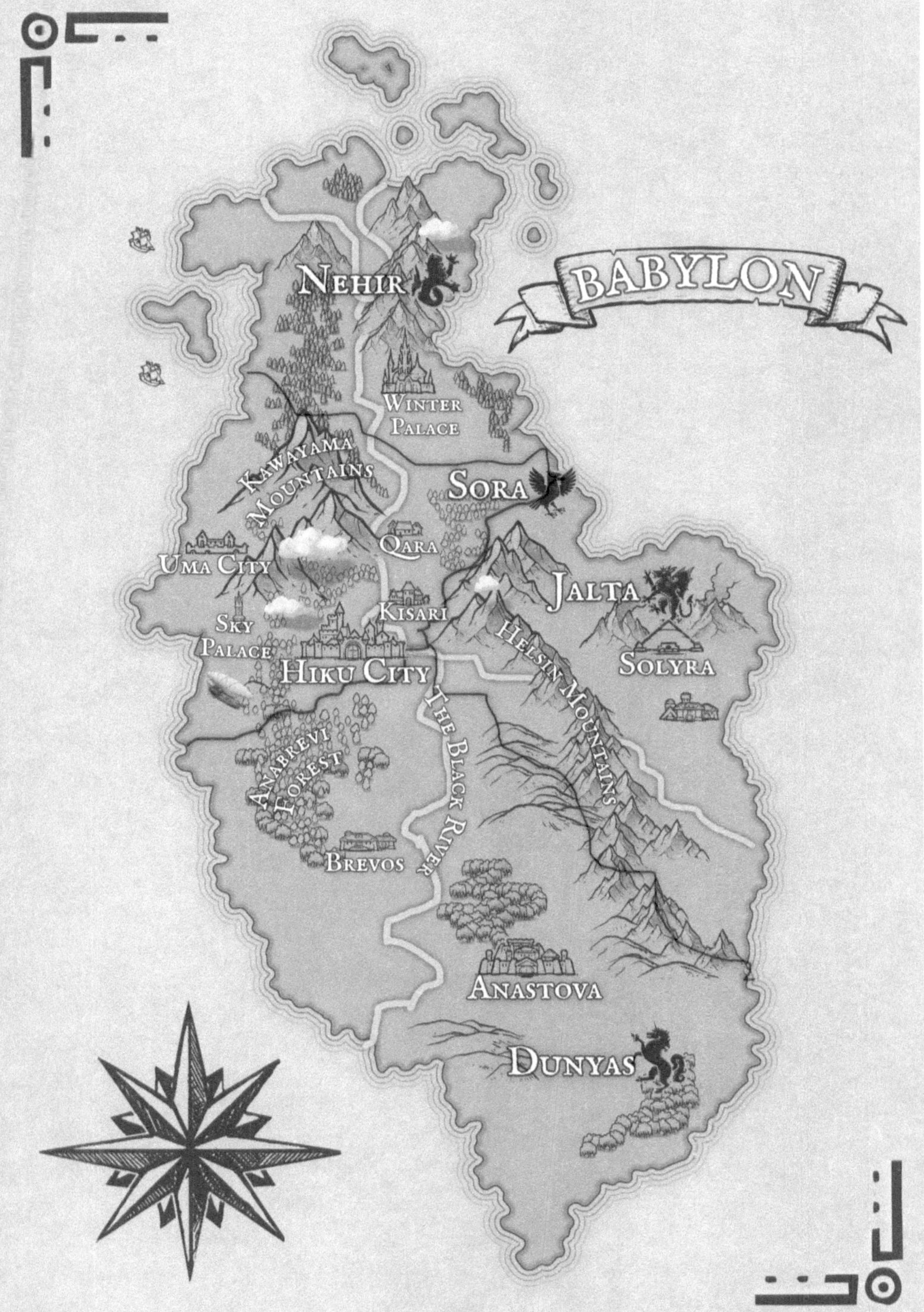

BABYLON
Nehir
Winter Palace
Kawayama Mountains
Sora
Qara
Uma City
Jalta
Kisari
Sky Palace
Helsin Mountains
Solyra
Hiku City
Anabrevi Forest
The Black River
Brevos
Anastova
Dunyas

WIND

ONE

The wind spoke the language of thieves.

It whispered through the overcrowded streets of Hiku City; through the hazy smoking dens and seedy game houses, in and out of frayed coat pockets and hungry bellies, finding its way into the ears of every lost soul stupid enough to listen.

One more hand of cards. One last puff of fragrant smoke. One final kiss.

Like a phantom, it worked its con, tricking the fools and failures into believing they were gods. And when the magic wore off and the luck ran out, the wind helped us rob them blind.

When I was a boy, long before my sister was born, I thought the wind wicked. Thought it lured men to their ruin, stoking the fire of temptation with its siren song.

Now, I knew better. *Men* were wicked. Men were their own ruination. They only needed the wind's permission as an excuse to let loose the blackness of their hearts.

Now, the wind was my greatest ally.

Tonight, as I crouched on the sharp, red incline of old Ms. Kusi the fortune teller's roof, waiting for Mal's signal, the wind sang me the song of the city. There was a melancholy to the tune, masking an underlying danger that beat like a drum. It was the song of change, the song of the wheel of fortune tilting.

I hoped it spun in my favor.

I didn't want to think of the alternative. I had too much riding on tonight's performance, too much at stake.

My thoughts drifted to Aya. She was only sixteen, but the bags under her eyes were old and deep enough to have seen the creation of Babylon. Her skin had waxed pale and pasty, her normally silky black hair dulled. It was early autumn, the leaves on the trees still clinging to their greens, but the coughs that wracked through her were enough to keep us all up every night. Sometimes, I sat at the corner of her cot, watching the rise and fall of her chest, holding my own breath as if it would spare some more for her.

It would be worse when winter settled, when the northern wind spoke the language of war, her frozen fingers around our throats.

A flash of red from the street pulled me back to where Mal dropped her handkerchief in front of five young men. The hair on my neck stood at attention, the song filling my veins with the same mix of danger and delight.

The mark—a young nobleman from Nehir, according to the crest on his expensive azure jacket with ridiculous gold buttons down the front and more laces than I had teeth—picked up the scrap of cloth, a wolf's grin spreading across his handsome features.

"Hello, precious. Drop this?" His thick northern accent was clunky as he spoke the common language with the grace of an ox trying to meow. His friends snickered behind him, a pack of dogs circling their prey.

"Oh, thank you, sir!" Mal blinked up at him with her doe eyes, tossing her wiry brown curls from one side of her head to the other, and she broke into a blush-tinted smile. "You're such a gentleman. Can I repay you?"

"Your smile is repayment enough." The man puffed out his chest as he handed her the trinket, and her giggle added to the sweet music of the night.

One last cheeky smile.

Typical Nehir wolf. The northern aquamentals were notorious for their tastes in all things beautiful and fragile—and for their uncanny knack for breaking them. I'd seen enough of the girls at Mrs. Tsojo's brothel after a night of northern revelry to confirm the unsavory stereotype.

And to paint Mal in the perfect image of a damsel in distress.

Had he met her as I did, the man would not have been so easily charmed.

I'd stumbled upon Mal in a western sewer, that same luscious head of curls matted with grime and dirt, those doe eyes wide with fear as she snarled at me, feral and untamed while she hid her toddler brother behind her. Only nine at the time, her parents had died in the Jaltan uprising, leaving her and her brother Kas utterly alone.

But even then—though she was but skin and bones and air, with nothing to call her own and a starving toddler at her back—I saw her for what she truly was:

Valuable. A diamond in the rough, forged under pressure and fire, waiting to be cut and shined into something hard and sharp. We'd been inseparable ever since.

Now, she reached out to squeeze the northerner's impressive arm, sinking into her hips. "Are you sure there is *nothing* I can do?"

The signal.

I kissed the delicate silver locket hanging around my neck once for luck before tucking it into my tunic, a prayer to a long-forgotten family. The wind let out a howl, the tune of the music shifting as I sprang into action.

Scurrying down the drain pipe, I pulled the slip of black fabric up over my face and drew my dagger, ready to play my part. I sucked in a breath, the wind surging through my lungs and soaking into every cell, transforming my very essence into the same intangible stuff as I ran toward them, swifter than an eastern zephyr.

This was the first game Mal and I learned to play, before we found the rest of the Lost Ones; back when it was just us, two children trying to raise themselves in the city of thieves and cheats.

Damsel and devil. Liar and lure.

Mal remembered her role perfectly. "Oh, my goodness, look out!" she cried, throwing herself onto the nobleman as I whizzed past them, cutting her empty purse from her hip with a single slash of my dagger.

To his credit, the oaf was faster than he looked, latching onto the collar of my shirt with enough strength to tear the fabric. But I was faster, spinning out of his hold with a single twirl as Mal clung tighter to him with a shrill cry. Scooping the purse from the ground, I sprinted forward, knocking into a passerby as I went.

"My purse! No! That has everything in it–help!"

"Get him, boys!" the nobleman bellowed, his pack of friends scurrying behind me as their alpha sounded the alarm.

My route was careful–*familiar*. Over the crates of liquor outside the Cherry Blossom inn, then through Miss Sufu's tent of scarves, knocking as many of the silks off the hanger as I could. I'd have to pay her cleaning bill later, but if we pulled this off, I'd have the funds to spare. With another gust of my winds, the scarves flew into my pursuers' faces, the nobleman tripping as they entangled him.

I didn't slow as I hurtled over Mr. Tori's fence, weaving through market-goers like a fire-devil was nipping at my heels. In a way, there was, and had been since I'd turned ten.

Since I learned how to run. To flee.

The very motivated pack of scoundrels followed closer than I preferred. They knocked into people, toppling crates and merchandise, clay pots from Dunyas clattering to the ground, women screaming as they barreled through them, teeth bared.

Pricks. I shifted my movements, tearing hard left toward the less populated streets. The path before me opened up, the street widening and the wind howling as it filled the alleyway unobstructed.

Hiku City was mine. I wouldn't have some feral pups tearing it apart chasing me.

They could be wolves if they wanted. They could run as fast and hard as the Black River's currents, and they'd never catch me.

Not when I was a falcon. Not when I was built to *soar*.

Another left, then a right. Into the alley behind Madame Aheni's smoking den. There was no exit, but that didn't matter.

Focusing on the whirlwind in my chest, all it took was another sharp inhale, and my breezy accomplice swept upward, lifting me from the ground to the rooftops once more.

"Come back here, you bastard!" one barked from the street as my windy friend lowered me gently onto the high roof, just out of their reach.

I smirked down at them, even though the scarf wrapped around the lower half of my face obscured the action. This was my favorite part of the ruse; cat in a tree. Mal didn't need any more time, the little flame-fairy quick with her trickery, but I had a guilty pleasure of playing with my prey. "I'd rather not."

"Is this funny to you?" the nobleman growled as he caught up, face red and icy eyes frenzied with rage.

I cocked my head to the side. "Hysterical."

He pointed a manicured finger at me while he shouted, a little noble prick used to getting his way. "I will have you arrested!"

This time I laughed aloud, shaking my head at the poor bastard. Mal sure knew how to pick them. "Unfortunately, sir, you have to catch me first."

The man looked like he was about to scale the fifteen-foot wall himself just to wring my neck when we were interrupted by the back door to Madame Aheni's banging open, a smoke cloud filling the street.

The wind's song changed again, the final warning horn sounding retreat in my head. It was the perfect opportunity to escape, to dissolve into the smoke and let the wind carry me home.

I had a bad habit of staying past my welcome.

One last look. One final word. One stolen moment.

Madame Aheni looked like she was either thirty or ninety, her olive skin free of wrinkles but her eyes clouded with experience. The tyrant of a woman scowled at the lot of us, thin mouth frowning as she stuck her hands to her hips. "What is all this noise in my alley?"

The blond leader huffed over to her, the young wolf a giant compared to her frail form, his finger still trained on me. "This man is a thief!"

Hiku City was mine, but I had not built it. I'd only inherited it. The winds of change carved it from the rock and dust of Babylon, infusing every baby born to the eastern soil with the same misty mischief and cold cunning.

Madame Aheni had been steeped in it for years. She was not a wolf, but she did not need fangs or claws or a howl. She was a tempest trapped in flesh.

"And you aren't?" she sneered in the little wolf's face. "You and your friends left without paying last night. Or were you all too high to remember?"

I stood on my perch, interest piqued. I should've left already. I should have been halfway home to Mal and Aya and the boys.

One more minute.

"You're on his side?" Lord Loser jerked his head at me as his eyes narrowed at the woman. His pack chuckled behind him when he crossed his arms. An intimidation. A threat. "*Please.* Like I'd pay for that cheap crap in there. Piss off, lady."

One final jab.

"How much does he owe you, Jiya?" I sighed as I slid to the edge of the roof and plopped down, my legs dangling over the edge. A taunt. Territorial pride washed through my veins as the Nehir idiot noted the action, his gaze zeroed in on me like a dog toy held in front of an untrained pup's face.

Ms. Aheni picked the red poppy dust from beneath her fingernails, a wry smile twisting her features. "At least twelve gold marks."

I blew out a low whistle, the wind echoing the sound. Twelve gold marks. That could feed my little family for three months and cover half of Aya's medical bills. Disgust roiled in my stomach, the wickedness of men again stroking my appetite for justice.

I hoped Mal took them for everything they were worth.

I dangled her worthless purse on my pinky finger, letting the small pouch sway in the wind. Bait on a string. "Give the woman her money, and I'll give you this purse. Deal?"

The dog growled low, his pack closing in behind him as he took a menacing step toward me. The murky puddle of water on the ground next to him stirred to bubbling, despite being untouched.

So the pup was an *Enaisir* too. An aquamental, as typical of the northerners, but only a Qualifier. It was clear he couldn't fully control the element, just modify its properties–change its temperature, or shift its phase, but never influence its quantity or movement.

Good. We'd have a fairer fight that way.

With a leg up, he could probably snatch me from the roof at this angle. He knew it, too, his teeth bared as he stared at my hanging ankle like it was a bone. "How about you give us the purse anyway, and we don't rough both of you up for whatever con you're running."

No, the con is probably halfway to the Treehouse with four of your buttons, the sapphire broach you were wearing, the gold and rubied dagger you had, and your entire coin purse.

I slid off the roof on a cool wind, landing gracefully a step in front of him. I crossed my arms as I breathed him in. Like a bouquet of fresh flowers dipped in a sewer, I could smell his rage, his disgust, and the meager tinge of fear.

No remorse. No regret. Just his wickedness scenting the wind.

"Pay the woman and say you're sorry for the way you just spoke to her." My voice rumbled low in my chest. "Last time I say it nicely."

He was half a head taller than me, and built like he'd been trained in a grand estate his whole life by the best teachers money could buy, flanked by four other men in similar shape—but it mattered not. The streets had been my tutor, and I'd never failed one of their lessons. I didn't have the luxury.

His lips pulled back across his teeth in a snarl. "Fuck you, *Kurniv.*"

The Nehir insult slashed at my inflated ego, but barely made a dent. Such a poorly trained pup.

The wind blew dust straight into his eyes, blinding him, as my fist collided with the Lordling's nose. Hard.

"Ow! You bastard!" He doubled over, eyes squeezed shut, clutching his bloody nose as the red stained his pretty blue sleeves. He crumpled to the ground and did not get up again. But with a swipe of his hand, he splashed the hot water at me, burning the leg of my trousers.

A shame. I'd need Naveen to repair them.

For a beat, his startled pack assessed me as I did them. Two dumb and burly, twins by the looks of it, their cropped brown hair and wide-set blue eyes a match for each other; a shorter red-haired fellow, still cut beneath his expensive uniform, but less of a giant; and another blond that looked like he could be the leader's younger cousin, his entitled, boyish grin one of a man who'd never actually seen a real fight.

I was happy to give him his first instruction.

The twins lunged for me in unison, the muscle-heads' instinct faster than the others.

Another wind swept at their feet as I sidestepped and ducked. They crashed into each other, tripping the small redhead that had moved behind them. I jumped again as they scrambled to grab at me, stepping on the shorter man's back and leaping over their heaped bodies. It was clear none of them were *Enaisir*, Quantifiers or Qualifiers, otherwise they'd have used their magic by now; another advantage in my favor.

It was silly of them to go toe to toe with a full Controller.

"You son of a bitch!" the redhead groaned, holding his twisted ankle.

A snort escaped me. "Actually, my mother was lovely. You were right before about the bastard bit, though. How'd you know? Is it my nose?" My best feature, I was told, though they could barely see my face with my scarf and the hood of my cloak.

The young blond sneered at me as he stood next to his cousin, the bastard still clutching his bleeding nose. He drew a dagger from his sleeve. "Let's see how snarky you are when I cut your tongue out."

I rolled my eyes. "Well, that's not fair."

A wild grin as the boy aimed his knife for my heart.

His smile fell when I caught his wrist, twisting it until it cracked as I swiveled under his arm. It was only a fracture—not a full break—but enough to catch him off guard. He dropped the dagger with a cry, and I quickly snatched the full coin purse peeking from his back pocket. Using my momentum, I flipped him over my shoulder, the air rushing in a whoosh from his lungs adding to the wind's song.

I tucked the stolen purse into my own coat before turning back to the others, ready to give them a second lesson if needed.

One of the bulky twins finally found his footing, rushing to the Lordling's side as his brother crawled to the boy wheezing on the ground. The redhead shot me a glare that could melt steel, but his legs wobbled as he brushed off his fine pants, his fear scenting the air like the sweetest flower. "Let's get out of here. The little whore wasn't worth it."

"Yes, do tell her that if you find her again," I called after them as they hobbled away, half-dragging the bloodied noble behind them. I struggled to keep the smugness from my tone. "I'd love to see her face. Or yours, rather, when she rearranges it."

I had to admit, while I hated Nehir creeps skulking through my city, watching them run scared with their tails between their legs gave my wicked heart a thrill. The wind spoke the language of thieves and thugs, and I was fluent in its tongues.

I turned on my heel, ready to head back to the Treehouse, when Madame Aheni stepped into my path, an eyebrow raised. "Malina playing your games again?"

I shrugged, balking slightly under the weight of her ancient, knowing stare. "She invented them. Sorry for the trouble, Madame Aheni. Here's your money."

Lowering my scarf to flash her my most charming smile, I pulled the stolen coin bag from my pocket, tossing it to the woman. She snatched it from the air with ease, her hand snapping out like a lightning strike. I swallowed, my smile stumbling.

As a Controller, I wielded the wind, the breeze bowing to my whims a gift from my mother's people. It was the highest form of *Easinir*, giving me the power to influence the wind's properties, its movement, its quantity, and its very essence with just my mind. But Madame Aheni was *made* from it, a tornado trapped in tan skin and tawny eyes. She claimed to only be a Qualifier, which made her Opium Den the cleanest smoke on the continent, but I knew better than to test her limits or her patience.

Madame Aheni weighed the purse in her palm—weighed her choices. Weighed my *worth*, before tossing it back. "You keep it. You earned it today, boy."

I caught the coins, but kept my palm extended, unsure of this test. I was a thief, but I was not a charity case. I did not take from those who did not have too much. Madame Aheni's business was profitable, but it still relied on paying customers–not Nehir trash that took and tarnished everything they touched, thinking it belonged to them. "I can't–"

Aheni shook her head once, silencing all protests. Sharp eyes softened as she closed my fingers around the treasure. "For Aya. We miss that little face of hers around town. She's much better behaved than you."

My sister's name floated on the wind's back, my thoughts drifting to the Treehouse. To the most important, most worthy person in this Breath-forsaken city.

To the little girl dying before she even had a chance to live.

I lifted my chin so the tears budding in the corners of my eyes wouldn't fall. "You're a blessing from the Breath, Madame Aheni."

I stalked out of the alleyway before she could change her mind. But as I strode back toward my home, the wind's melancholy song followed, blaring the beat of trouble to come.

One last chance.

If only I'd heeded its warning.

Two

IRINA

lowers bloom even after the coldest winters. It was a lesson
the Maesters of Dunyas repeated daily, hoping the more they
watered me with the idea, the more it would take root and
blossom inside my soul.

But flowers never bloomed in glass vases. They were nothing more
than pretty ornaments to decorate a table, an afterimage of the glorious, living miracle they once were.

The silken dress my mother had shoved me into was one and the
same: an ostentatious attempt to try and capture nature's elegance. I
stared at myself in the floor-length mirror of my chamber, watching
the petal-blush fabric flutter in the early morning breeze that introduced itself through the open balcony doors. Corseted bodice
cinching my waist to a size Mother just barely approved of, the silhouette hid my hips as it fanned out like a spring rose, dusting the marble
floor with the same gentleness.

A beautiful vase for a flower snipped at the stem.

"This will have to do for the Masque. Irina, stop pouting," my
mother sighed heavily as she lounged across my emerald green duvet,

a servant fanning her face. Winter would be here soon, but the Summer Palace of Anastova was always hot, a result of my mother's Quantifier magic. The cold didn't fit her carefully crafted aesthetic, so she did away with it entirely, just as she did with anything that displeased her. So even in the dead of winter, we were forced to endure the sweltering, overbearing summer heat, Mama's fires burning through the rock channels she'd had the servants lay in the walls and floors.

My mother had a penchant for overbearing.

Gemma, the old servant weaving my earthen curls in braids, stopped her ministrations, sucking her lip in between her teeth. She knew Mother's tone just as well as I did. I stood straighter, wishing I could sprout roots through the marble floor—anything to steady me against the volcano that was my mother. My voice was softer than a butterfly wing as I painted on a smile. "I'm not pouting, Mama."

The Queen of Dunyas rose from my bed, lips pursed in displeasure as she waved the servant away. Gemma scurried off, head down as she ran for sturdier ground.

"Catirina." My full name was a curse as her molten gold eyes met mine in the mirror's reflection, hotter than the magma they stole their color from. Her slender fingers found my waist, pressing the soft flesh beneath the fabric, as if she was trying to smooth it away. Like I was made of wet clay to be sculpted by my mother's hands. "This Masquerade is everything this year."

The Masque used to be my favorite party of the year. The bubbly wine. The crystal chandeliers. The dancers shimmering with just as much enthusiasm as handsome strangers swept them off their feet, laughter and music glimmering through the air in succulent melodies...

Nothing sparkled anymore. Not without Nikolaj.

My throat constricted at the thought, the corset suddenly too tight. My lungs protested against the bindings as they begged to suck in more air, but I couldn't keep a breath down.

Just as I couldn't keep my brother alive.

The room spun as I panted in shallow gasps, grief closing in. My mother rolled her eyes, pinching my side again.

The flash of pain brought me back to my body, my corporeal cage. To my role as the quiet, compliant princess.

"We need an alliance." My mother's voice was tighter than my dress, a dark edge lacing her tone. *Fear.* "And you have quite the lot to choose from; more than your father and I had."

The words she didn't say screamed just as loud: we needed to keep our throne. Keep our crown. And a second-born princess without a backbone couldn't do that without a king to shape her.

I hated that this was what my life would be. Hated that my brother —my brilliant, charming leader of a brother—had abandoned me, his shoes too big to ever fit into. Hated that my mother saw me as no more than a pretty decoration to brighten some prince's throne room.

Hated that she was *right.*

"And which princeling have you already chosen for me?" My voice wavered like a loose petal in the wind, my fingers shaking as I thought of the prospects. The Sora Province heir was only fifteen, but his uncle was in his fifties. My stomach rolled at the thought of either, but Mother would go for someone more powerful. More impressive. More ambitious. More like *her.* My mind snagged on a name. "Avi from Jalta?"

The Jaltan king's nephew...a contender for the throne, if the rumors were true. King Odion's only proper heir left was his daughter Naria, and many of the nobility in that territory shared Mother's views. Women were not meant to lead. Mama might have been claimed by the Dunyasians, my grandfather's place as a nobleman securing her future here, but her mother had been Jaltan. Had been a lady–before the uprising. It would make sense that Mother would want to bring prosperity to both kingdoms and end that old feud.

Even if Avi looked like a hairy toe with bucked teeth.

At least he was my age.

But Mother shook her head, the action bringing me back to the moment. Back to the smoldering mischief in her gaze, a look that had only ever brought me misery. She sauntered back to the duvet, laying across it with a smirk still on her elegant face. "Drakkar of Nehir."

I whirled on my mother as my stomach bottomed out, the ground beneath me caving in like the hole in my chest. I wrapped my arms tight around my middle as if that would stop the unraveling. "*Nehir?*" I shuddered, the mere thought of the frozen wasteland of the northernmost kingdom and the horror stories that lived there sending a shiver down my spine. "Mama—"

"Drakkar is handsome. Refined." My mother silenced me with a vague wave of her slender hand, but the threat simmered beneath the casual gesture. Her eyes narrowed to slits. "And Nehir is full of resources. Money. *Medicine.*"

I sucked in a deep breath as I heard the words she didn't say.

Medicine that could've saved your brother.

Dunyas was the kingdom of natural abundance. We grew the best produce, our fertile soil tilled by expert farmers and Teramental *Enaisir*, the lush land blanketed with enough resources to feed all four kingdoms. And where there was good food and health, medicine always followed. Our medemental Qualifiers had perfected it to a scientific degree—which crops had the best healing properties, which herbs were best for poultices and potions. It was why we'd ruled above the other houses for so long—we were indispensable.

And yet, the best and brightest *Enaisir* in Dunyas could do nothing against the Blight. Nothing to keep my strong brother from crumbling to mere skin and bones, the sickness eating him from the inside out.

Nothing to save the future king.

Yet Nehir and Jalta both had somehow managed to stay relatively free of the Blight, Nehir most of all. Rumors from the medementals said it had something to do with the mountain hot springs—that their healing magic and their Qualifiers' purification techniques were the only thing strong enough to treat the infected.

A resource that had made Nehir considerably wealthy in recent years.

My mother's eyes met mine again, a rare softness in the molten amber. Like her heart was filled with the same grief and regret that snared mine. When my brother died, he'd ripped out whatever shriveled soul resided in my mother's chest and dragged it to the Ether with him.

"Flowers bloom even after the coldest winters, Catirina." She tucked one of my curls back into place, her fingers gentle for a moment. She'd always admired my silky, bouncy curls, so different from her coarse, straight black hair. The only mark of her Jaltan ancestry. But that's where the affection stopped. "Make nice with Drakkar tomorrow night."

I swallowed the lump of dread that choked me. "Yes, Your Highness."

"I'm your mother, Catirina," she gritted out, like the title didn't suit her at all anymore. Not without my brother. She spun me again to face the mirror, our reflections staring back at us. She rubbed my shoulders, but the action was far from soothing. "I only want what's best for you. Don't you want to be a happy Queen? To live happily in the palace for the rest of your life, without a care?"

I imagined it, as I had since girlhood. Tight dresses that crushed my ribs and uncomfortable jeweled tiaras that tangled in my curls. Stiff-backed thrones that bit at my ass and heeled slippers that pinched my toes.

Uppity nobles who preened and plotted for my attention. Ladies-in-waiting who gossiped and gallivanted as fake friends.

A prisoner in a palace. A flower in a vase.

"Yes, Mama," I lied with a smile, just as I had every day since Nikolaj's death.

Satisfied with the fib, she straightened out her own silken gown in the mirror, admiring the long lines of her figure. Then, her bony fingers pinched at my waist one more time, a final warning. "Don't let me catch you in Tasha's kitchen this week. This needs to be laced tighter."

"Yes, Mama." My smile fell as my hopes did. I'd never be small enough to fit Mama's expectations, just as I'd never be perfect enough to be a good queen.

I supposed Mama and I would both have to learn to live with the disappointment.

Sighing like she could read my mind, she held out an expectant palm. "Now give Mummy a boost, and I'll see you at supper."

Despite my resistance toward the rest of the castle's oppressive heat, the kitchens' warmth was never unwelcome. It was an embrace, and as I snuck through the servant's passages and into the bustling scullery, my shoulders relaxed.

"What can I do for you, deary?" Mrs. Tasha somehow knew I was there without turning around, her round frame facing the giant stewpot simmering over the open hearth. I salivated at the smell of whatever was in it, the herbaceous, savory contents divine even despite my preference for sweets. She was a Teramental Qualifier, as most of the servants who had *Easinir* were, but if I didn't know any better, I'd have sworn she had some kind of medemental training, because her food and gentle presence could heal all ills.

I needed a little of that healing today, the anxiety from the conversation with my mother still lingering in my gut like a stomach bug.

I plopped onto my favorite stool, more comfortable now that I'd changed out of the corset and put my wispy day dress on. The soft yellow fabric flowed with my curves, not in spite of them, ending just below my knees, making it easy for me to cross my legs and slump forward on the chair. I leaned my elbows against the wooden countertop without crushing my stomach like the corseted contraption would've.

Mrs. Tasha turned just as I painted on my loveliest smile, batting my eyelashes at her. "Do you have any more of those lemon cookies?"

Tasha's chuckle shook her round form as she tucked her hands into her stained apron, raising a thick brow at me. "Will your mother have my head if I give them to you?"

"Probably."

"Fine. I can't say no to you," she conceded with a grin, reaching into the top cupboard and bringing down the familiar, secret tin. Swift, able hands popped open the top, and the tangy-sweetness of lemon sugar instantly hit me. "But don't let them spoil your dinner."

I snagged one and bit into it, relishing the tartness on my tongue, wishing it could erase the sour pang sticking to my soul like dried syrup. "That's all I'm good for. Spoiling things."

At that, Tasha stopped her fussing, abandoning the cookies to cross her arms and level me with one of her famous, skin-peeling stares. "What on earth has gotten into your knickers and twisted them?"

I wiped the excess sugar from my lip. Tasha's kitchen had always been a safe place, somewhere to fill my belly and empty out the stress of my day, but this truth was harder to part with. Like saying it out loud would make it more real.

I swallowed my fear, spitting out the words I hated. "My mother wants me to marry Prince Drakkar of Nehir."

Tasha nodded, absorbing the words like a cleaning cloth disappearing a spill. "And what's his deal? Old? Ugly? *Both*?"

"No, he's around my age, and apparently handsome enough to garner my mother's praise...."

Tasha grabbed a cookie from the tin, biting into it with a smirk. "Then what's the risk of giving him a shot?"

I fisted my skirt, trying to find words to explain my dread, but Tasha had a point. What was so bad about following another one of Mother's rules? Especially if it came with a handsome, young prince and an easy future?

"It's just..." I stopped, and started again, tongue tying over thoughts I'd never imagined myself admitting out loud. "Nikolaj was supposed to be king. Supposed to rule. And I would've been there beside him, to help him...but I would've also married for love. Maybe one day."

Daydreams of a long-forgotten face floated to the surface of my mind, the reedy lullaby of violins and the gentle pass of a summer wind through dark hair...

"You've been reading too many romance books." Tasha broke my trance, her voice stern, but not unkind. A sad smile lifted her wrinkles. "Love is a privilege, girl. There are thousands of people in the town below and the farming fields beyond that would die for a chance to marry a handsome, well-off prince from Nehir. Girls who have truly difficult lives, who might one day dream of rising from the mud and muck long enough to come be servants at this very palace... but never anything more."

She placed a work-worn hand over mine, evidence of the hard life she'd lived—and the empathy she still managed to stoke like a gentle hearth fire.

"You're getting married for them. For your subjects. Stay strong."

I thought of my people—girls in light, soft dresses that got to taste the sun as they tended their gardens, girls who could sneak away with handsome farmers and tumble with them in haystacks, girls who could laugh and sing together and let their hands create and love and teach...

Wildflowers with roots instead of glass vases. With places to *grow* instead of shelves to decorate.

But someone had to play that part, too, so the kingdoms could go on living and loving. So peace could spread like seeds on the back of a summer breeze, could find nourishing soil in every part of the kingdom.

So the Blight could stop stealing brothers and breaking hearts.

"You're right, I'm sorry," I breathed out, wishing reality alone was enough to clear the selfish, stubborn weeds from my heart. I pushed back from the stool, the kitchen's warmth suddenly claustrophobic. "I'm headed to bed."

Tasha pushed the tin closer, that same tragic smile still hanging on her sweet face. "Take the cookies with you."

I lidded the tin and tucked it under my arm, grateful for the indulgent comfort, before fixing on a fake smile of my own. Tasha had always given me a place to unravel and repair, and now it would be my duty to lead people like her into fairer skies. "When will our guests arrive? Did the head butler tell you when to prep?"

"Few days. They're stopped in Hiku City now, but the day after they're headed to us, and they'll want a whole feast, so I'll be busy as all hell tomorrow."

I perked up, another daydream floating into my mind at the mention of Hiku City. The Capitol of Sora, a buzzing metropolis filled with art and music and laughter...

Or at least, it had been once. It'd been years since I had a glimpse.

Perhaps it was my chance for another.

I shoved traitorous thoughts down before their thorns could snag me and waved goodnight to Tasha. "Well, good luck. Thanks for the treat."

Nikolaj once had a knack for trouble that used to boil my mother's already-hot blood and turn my father's hair gray. His pranks had been legendary, all of the staff on guard should they ever fall prey to one of his mischiefs.

I'd never shared the same delight in disarray, the rules much easier to heed than facing my mother's wrath. But, whenever Nikolaj asked me to be involved, I'd shoved any lingering fear away and followed, desperate for my big brother's attention. To be loved by at least him, if not my parents.

I was ten and he was thirteen when he first showed me how to use fae-dust.

If our parents knew he had it at all, they'd have truly brought the hammer down; that magic had been outlawed in all four kingdoms ever since the peace treaties were signed decades ago, when the unification of Babylon was first ordered. The substance was too powerful for any one kingdom to wield, evidenced by the little information we had about the long-lost, volatile fae era, where it had been used to conjure portals and stage grand attacks between warring fae tribes.

While leftover relics from that ancient history were fairly common, where Nik had found such a rare, elicit material, I dared not ask; I'd been too enthralled by the idea of an easy escape. That first night, he took me to the Opera house in Hiku City to hear the music. We'd dressed in plain cloaks and stood at the back of the theater with the other peasants, bodies pressed tightly together and kept far from the nobility sitting up front. But it didn't matter that I couldn't see the stage.

I still heard it. It was the most glorious night of my life. The heady buzz of violins, the deep moan of the cellos, the bird-song of the sopranos, the warm velvet of the baritones...all echoing beneath the starlight of the open amphitheater in a glorious chorus.

I'd made a deal with my brother that I'd never tell my parents about his secret as long as he promised to bring me every year. And he did, three times, each one more spectacular than the last. Of course, that was before the start of the revolution, before the Jaltans attacked and burned the place down...

Before Nikolaj died.

I'd never used the fae-dust on my own, but if I was to be married off to Drakkar of Nehir, I had to learn how to do things for myself. Had to try.

Had to escape, even if it was just for a night. Had to hear the city's music, even if it wasn't the same, just to feel *something*.

I inhaled deeply as I grabbed the small velvet bag from its hiding spot in my chambers, beneath the floorboard under my tall dresser, so obscure not even my maids would find it. And just as my brother had instructed all those nights ago, I dipped my finger inside, letting the luminescent green dust coat my fingertip, dappling my skin in tiny stars. A buzz worked its way through my veins, a silent song calling to me just as it had so many years ago in that packed Opera House.

One last adventure.

Scrunching my eyes closed, I *wished.*

Hiku City.

I waited, holding my breath, bracing myself—

The sensation of being turned inside out hit first, my stomach climbing to my throat, and then—

Noise, everywhere, all at once. Hooves over cobblestone, dozens of footsteps shuffling about, vendors peddling their wares, loud laughter from a nearby gathering.

My eyes snapped open, the shadows of an alleyway greeting me, hanging paper lanterns beckoning from the street ahead.

Mother Earth, it *worked*. I'd done it.

Hiku City.

Everything I didn't have. Everything I craved.

I ran toward the street, drawn by the smell of something sweet and floral, grateful that I'd changed into comfortable trousers and a green cloak. It was an easy disguise, one no one would suspect a princess to wear.

As I stepped out of the alley, a woman knocked into me, dropping a handful of bright crimson flowers into a puddle on the ground. She shot a dark glare at me as she bent to collect them, the wind nearly blowing my cloak from my shoulders as she snarled, "Watch where you're going, girl."

"S-sorry, my mistake." I backed up, then fled as fast as my feet could carry me, deeper into the pulsing body of the crowded street. As much as I hated the impolite departure, I would not waste my limited time on pleasantries tonight.

The stream of bodies carried me naturally through the winding, stall-crowded streets, the warm red-and-orange glow of lanterns like strings of fireflies leading me to magic. My eyes could not drink it all in fast enough; the silken tents and scarves that flapped in the warm evening wind, the savory wisps of smoke that curled around us as a vendor handed out dripping skewers of charred deliciousness. The little kids huddled in a corner, their giggles shrill as they played a game of dice, the women humming merry tunes as they rearranged the sparkling trinkets on stands to draw in customers.

But my feet stopped when the wheezing drone of an accordion caught my ear. People bumped my shoulders as I wiggled my way out of the mass, until I was standing in front of a slim man in a bright green cap. A few others gathered around him, his dirt-caked face carved in a welcoming smile as he played his merry tune, a song I'd never heard but the other onlookers knew well, all of them humming along or murmuring lyrics beneath their breath.

My heart swelled, and though the accordion was not my favorite instrument, I still let it sway me, my hips dipping in time with the upbeat rhythm.

This was why I came, what I needed–the forbidden, wild merriment of Hiku City playing at my most hidden heartstrings.

Strings that snapped when I noticed the small girl sticking her hand into one of the other onlooker's pockets–snagging his coin purse.

My hands flew to my own pockets, relief flooding my veins when I found my fae-dust still housed within. But disappointment soured the music, the merry melody suddenly a dirge as I caught the man-in-the-cap's wink at the little girl.

This was a trap, a pretty spider luring bugs to its web. And while I knew even spiders and accordion players needed to eat, I couldn't help it as the back of my throat itched, tears on the near horizon.

I kept my mouth shut–calling them out would only bring trouble and too many eyes my way. But I turned and walked back into the crowd before I could become the girl's next mark.

Perhaps the adventure was still salvageable, the winding streets carrying me onward, that tug in my chest drawing taut as the buzz of life pulled me in again.

The streets widened–no longer crowded alleys with tightly packed stalls, but open roads with storefronts, the lights from within warming the shadowed cobblestone streets to gold. Multicolored roofs glimmered like a trove of gemstones, crimson and emerald and sapphire tiles sparkling under the starlit sky. I read the signs as I passed, committing them all to memory, knowing I'd need them to sustain me for quite some time.

Ms. Kusi's Fortunes, The Cherry Blossom Inn, Fox & Crow's Antiques and Curiosities...

"Lost, girl?" A voice startled me from behind, an old woman in a plain brown frock stepping in front of me so fast I nearly tripped.

"No, just wandering." My mouth formed a tight line, unease creeping beneath my skin as the woman's endlessly dark eyes stared at me. Wrinkles wove a crown of wisdom across her brow, her hair so white it practically glowed in the moonlight.

"Your hair is beautiful. Sell me a lock, and I'll tell you a fortune?" Her voice twinkled like wind chimes as she peered at me.

I swallowed hard, my tongue too lame to form a response. The fae thankfully no longer lived in our world, but Nikolaj used to tell me stories about them; the way the magic coated their very bones, the way they could see things beyond the natural eye.

I knew it was senseless, but a part of me recognized this woman as *other*, her gaze piercing my very soul.

She grinned wide. "No? Too bad. I see many paths that could unfold from your choices tonight alone."

She stepped closer, sniffing me, and I stumbled backward. I'd never been hunted before, but I supposed this is what it felt like, my heart stammering a furious beat to *run* in my chest.

My back hit a wall, and I looked up, a hanging wooden sign teetering over me.

The Crescent Inn & Brewery.

"Uh, I–um, have to go." I grinned and dipped inside without looking back, losing myself to the crowd within.

The worry in my chest only unknotted after a full minute when I realized she did not follow me inside. I exhaled, turning to scan the room I'd entered.

The small space was packed to the brim with bodies, all wearing fine clothes as they laughed and drank together. Many of them must have been travelers for the Masque. I pulled my cloak tighter around me, keeping my head down. I doubted they'd recognize me like this, without my mother's dresses and sparkling jewels, but still, it would probably be smart to keep a low profile.

I made my way to the bar, a heady high swirling in my mind. If this was my last night of true freedom, I was going to have my fill of it. First, a stiff drink, something stronger than the wine Mother let me sip at parties. Perhaps that would also let me forget the fear I'd felt in the strange old woman's presence, or my distaste for the accordion player's ruse. And then, maybe I'd find a kind stranger to help me find some better live music...

Maybe one to even dance with me.

I smiled widely at the barkeep, an old man with a gray beard on just his chin and a bald head. "One shot of whiskey, please."

With a grunt, he poured a knuckle's worth into a glass, the amber liquid sloshing as he pushed it toward me. "That'll be five coppers."

"Oh, I—" I stuttered, my cheeks flaming with sudden heat. What kind of idiot was I, not bringing any money? Of course, when I went out with my retinue, that was handled separately, but it's not like I was unaware. Instead, I plucked the ring off my left hand, an awful gold piece Mother had asked me to wear. "I'm so sorry, I forgot my purse—"

The old man turned his back, ignoring the ring and me entirely. "No money, no drink."

My jaw dropped as I decided which pieces of my mind I was about to give him, but the opportunity was lost in a flurry of movement.

"Get me more ice, you idiot." A man barked as he pushed his way closer to the bar, knocking me sideways. "Bastard broke my nose. My mother is going to have his head."

"Yes sir." The barkeep flitted away with a speed I'd not expected from someone his age, ready to follow this man's orders.

I swiveled on him, annoyance prickling along my spine. This was my night, and it was not going to plan. But I was not about to let some bossy brute stand in my way of a good time. "Hey, I was here—"

Blond hair sprawled across his head in indiscriminate directions, like he'd been hung upside down, a match for the dirt that sullied his finely made blue threads—

A uniform for Nehir nobility.

Mother Earth, this was a problem.

I lowered my head, panic surging to the surface. If I was caught, I'd be the one hung from my ankles as Mama flogged me with insults for hours.

"Sorry, milady, didn't mean to jump the line." The man pressed closer, his hand resting on my shoulder. *Crap.* He reached for the shot of whiskey the barkeep had left behind, ignoring that I hadn't paid for it. "Here, this is yours, yes? Don't mind the blood."

My gaze snagged on the crimson caking his fingers, and then upward, to his demolished, bloodied nose and swollen eyes.

Relief and pity twined together in my chest. He likely couldn't see very well with those injuries—Mother Earth's first blessing toward my escapades tonight—but it seemed like his evening had been even more disrupted than mine.

"Oh my word, are you all right?" I turned to him fully, examining the crooked line of his nose. He was likely handsome, but it was hard to tell with all the swelling. Poor thing would be permanently marked if a talented medemental didn't set it correctly. "I can–"

No, I couldn't say I'd heal it. My *Easinir* would attract too much attention, too much *fear*. I'd never forget the way they all looked at me all those years ago, eyes wide with terror and mouths set in disgusted frowns... even for an *Easinir*, I was *other*. I cleared my throat, catching myself. "I can fetch you some water, if you'd like."

The man smiled despite his injuries as two more bulky Nehir

nobles stalked next to him, brothers by the looks of it. But the blond still leaned casually against the bar, paying neither man any attention.

"Your company is comfort enough." He patted the stool next to him, an invitation. "Please, sit."

My rational parts warred with my desires. He couldn't see well, but I was testing my luck lingering here, when he'd likely attend the ball in a week. Would he recognize my voice? How on earth would I explain *that?*

But the thought of going home when I'd come so far, the thought of retreating to my room without at least one drink and a nice conversation...

I'd deal with the consequences later, just as Nikolaj would have. Tonight was mine.

"That's very kind of you." I scooted onto the seat, the three-legged beast not nearly as comfortable as I wanted it to be. But I took a quick sip of the whiskey, and the hot burn down my throat unknotted the apprehension in my spine. I turned to the man again, who was close enough that I could smell the mud and something both burnt and floral on him. "What happened to your face?"

"We got into it with some street rat. I let him get one shot on me, as a mercy. But you should see how busted he is." He waved his hands around like he was swatting away an invisible fly.

I tried to scooch back to avoid the gestures, but the other men had rooted themselves in the way, broad shoulders casting shadows over me. Something squirmed in my middle, a disquiet I had no name for.

"Oh, that's terrible." I kept my hands in my lap and my most polite smile on my face. I'd finish my drink, and then I'd find better company. The man seemed nice enough, but if he was brawling in the streets, perhaps he wasn't the sort I should be associating with anyway. I took another sip, the burn a welcome distraction.

But when a hand slid across my thigh, every muscle in my body tensed, fear souring the taste on my tongue. The blond's smile widened, dried blood staining his lips a deep, ominous red. "Don't worry, precious. I'm feeling better now that you're here."

Panic rattled through my uneven breaths, dozens of warning bells sounding in my head. This had been a mistake. I had no protection here, no friends.

No Nikolaj.

I had to get out, to get home, back to my gilded cage before I ended up in trouble's path. But I couldn't just use the fae-dust here, not without landing myself in an even bigger puddle.

"Well, I was just leaving, actually." I moved to slide off the stool, but his hand squeezed tighter, halting my escape.

He leaned further in, his hot breath on my neck. "Come on, precious. The night is young, and I could really use someone soft and sweet as you to help me lick my wounds."

My stomach threatened to reappear the two sips of whiskey, my hands shaking as I pushed against his arm. But he didn't budge, surprisingly strong in his hold. I tried to keep the quiver out of my voice, to no avail. "Please let go, it's getting late."

Where the hell was the barkeep? I looked over my shoulder, searching for any friendly face to aid me, but found none. I was so foolish, thinking I could just waltz into a foreign city with no guide, no protection...

I scanned my brain for any way out, any escape, but I couldn't think past the misty haze of fear that throbbed through my skull, my hands rattling and my breath short—

The hold on my thigh released as the man's already bloodied face smashed into the bartop, faster than I could register the cause.

I blinked, my heartbeat deafening in my ears.

"Did I accidentally smash that little walnut you use for a brain?"

A man in a dark cloak loomed over us, appearing out of thin air. I tried to swallow my scream as he ripped me from the stool, spinning me off of it.

The man sprawled onto the seat instead, crossing his legs. "The lady said let go, but I'd be happy to keep you entertained."

THREE

The path back to the Treehouse was one I could walk with my eyes closed and my ears plugged, and yet, my feet strayed as I wandered, the cobblestone streets twisting my trail back toward the center of town.

I should've gone straight home. Should've taken my spoils and settled with it.

But I was just a man with a wicked, heavy heart. And after my evening of hard work, the most feral parts of me demanded a stiff drink.

One more drink. One extra job.

Bars were the perfect place to pick up some extra coin, after all. I'd already earned enough today to keep the family fed for weeks, but the taverns teemed with easy pickings, all of Babylon traveling through Hiku City on the road to Dunyas for the King's Masque later in the week. Pickpocketing a few drunk foreigners while sipping a whiskey of my own would be the perfect way to round out a very lucrative day.

And delay the dread sloshing around in my gut like spoiled soup.

I shook off the thought of what waited at home as my traitorous feet carried me into The Crescent Brewery & Inn, the most famous haunt Hiku City had to offer. The second I crossed the threshold, the wind's whispers changed to revelrous cries, the ale-and-abandon scent washing over me. Bodies packed tightly into booths and around tables, a clamorous cacophony of laughter and swearing in harmony with the wind's new tune. The patrons all dressed well, nobles and wealthy merchants from Sora, Jalta, and Nehir traveling in large packs to the King's Masque, slumming it for a night of fun before they had to behave as their station demanded again. Silver buttons and jeweled cravats and fine leather boots didn't belong in the Crescent, but I certainly wouldn't complain.

A sea of potential marks.

I stumbled through the tables, not bothering to lower my dark hood, pretending to be another drunk partier headed for another round, making sure to snag as much loot as I could when I bumped into body after body. A full coin-purse from a tall merchant, a ruby-encrusted timekeeper from a rotund Sora noble...

I stopped in my tracks, nearly dropping my earnings as I spied three of the same bastards from Nehir lurking at the bar, all huddled around a single stool. The tall blond was waving his hands about, talking very animatedly for someone who had the daylight beat out of him just an hour ago. The burly twins both stood square on the other side, boxing in whoever he was talking to, their eyes scanning the room for threats. I didn't spot the younger blond or the redhead, both of them likely tending to the poor boy's broken wrist, but even so...

I should've turned on my heel and fled, letting the swiftest wind take me back to the Treehouse before I could make any further messes of my day. Before the Nehir idiots could spot me and call all the other nobles in the room to arms, their word law amongst the upper-crust, especially against a nobody like me. I'd known the owners of the Crescent, Mr. and Mrs. Tojiri, for years...and they liked me well enough, but not enough to step in and defend me at the detriment of their most profitable night in months.

I should've left. Would've, too.

Until my eyes snagged on who they huddled around like vultures, deep brown curls cascading over an ivy-green cloak.

A *girl*, large brown eyes blown wide with concern, full pink lips pulled in a rigid line that contrasted the softness of the rest of her. Her body curved generously; soft, plump thighs spilling over the edge of her barstool, stomach gently folding over the band of her high-waisted riding trousers. They looked expensively made, but unlike the other revelers here, they were not loudly so. She wore no jewelry or fine adornments, but her smooth amber complexion spoke of riches far beyond the ostentatious flaunts of the other travelers.

My pulse kicked up, blood heating, but not for the thought of what I might steal for once.

People in Hiku City were not made like this. Perhaps it was the mass starvation and deprivation, but the bodies in this town always looked fragile, even more so now that the Blight had reduced us further.

The woman at the bar looked like she sipped life straight from the source. And despite my better judgment, all I wanted was a taste of *her* on my tongue.

The Nehir wolves seemed to have a similar idea, all of them closing in on her like doe-eyed prey. I inched closer despite myself, just as the tall blond—his nose still bruised and swollen, his sleeves still bloodied —leaned in with that rakish grin, a filthy hand brushing one of her silken curls away. "Yeah, we got into it with some street rat. I let him get one shot on me, as a mercy. But you should see how busted he is."

Pompous, narcissistic liar. I couldn't help but grin, my unblemished face all the proof I'd ever need. But I paused, screwing my boots to where I stood before I could act too rashly.

"Oh, that's terrible." The girl smiled slightly, hands fiddling in her lap. Her body language screamed discomfort as she folded her shoulders in on herself, but I had to remember she was a stranger. Perhaps she was just nervous, a virgin having her first flirt with the exciting out-of-towners. And even if her taste in partners was ridiculous to me, who was I to ruin that for her?

The rational part of me agreed, keeping me fixed to my spot.

Another, less favorable part roiled with something green and sticky I hadn't felt in ages. Something I dared not name.

The wind shifted again, singing the chorus of conflict, as the Nehir wolf pressed a wide hand to her thigh, squeezing the supple flesh. Even over the din of the crowd, I could hear the huskiness in his voice. "Don't worry, precious. I'm feeling better now that you're here."

"Well, I was just leaving, actually." The girl moved to stand, but his wide hand kept her caged to the barstool. A breeze curled at my fingertips, urging me forward another step. I bumped into someone again, but I didn't care, my eyes fixed on the blond bastard's oppressive hold on her thigh.

"Come on, precious. The night is young, and I could really use someone soft and sweet as you to help me lick my wounds."

"Please let go, it's getting late." The girl squirmed again, and her bronze skin paled—the pretty blush rushing from her cheeks, a sick green stealing its place.

A similar ill rolled through my middle. I didn't know this woman, and I owed her no loyalty. She was a fool to be in this area alone— likely a rich, pampered priss having fun playing on the peasants' turf for a night, unaware of the danger the week of the Masque brought to our doors. But Hiku City was my home, filthy and wicked as it was, and I refused to let the men from Nehir spoil it any longer with their gilded shit.

At least, that's the excuse I told myself as I finally crossed the last few steps, nudging the back of the bastard's knee so he stumbled into the bartop.

"Did I accidentally smash that little walnut you use for a brain?" I sneered, and in a quick move, I spun the girl off her stool, earning a high-pitched, wide-eyed yelp from her before I quickly let her go. Before she could manage a word, I plopped onto her vacant seat, positioning myself between the Lordling, the twins, and her. I leaned back on the bar, the picture of nonchalance, crossing my legs for emphasis. "The lady said let go, but I'd be happy to keep you entertained."

The girl in question opened her mouth to respond—to demand answers or protest, I didn't know—but I silenced her with a dark look. The pretty idiot should've run already, but she stood trembling, frozen in her spot.

One last look.

Maybe the wind made women weak, too.

"You." The wolf straightened as he recovered, my hood and scarf easily recognizable.

He waved his hand, and the closer twin lashed out, grabbing the collar of my cloak, his hot, smelly breath steaming on my face as he growled, "Come to face us man on man this time, instead of hiding up on that stupid roof?"

His brother moved too, gripping my shoulder to keep me rooted to the stool. The wind's tune shifted again, those around us holding their breaths and listening in as the melody soured from revelrous to violent.

A part of me ached for it, another chance to spill some Nehir blood, to ruin the nobles' lives like they'd all ruined Babylon.

One strong punch. One stolen life.

But my face burned as wide, fearful eyes still stared at me, waiting for me to do something. To save her.

One more rescue.

I held the first twin's wrist, just like I had the younger boy's in the street. But this time, instead of snapping the bone beneath my fingers, I jerked him closer—close enough to bang his head against his brother's. "Something like that."

I ran before the wind could convince me to linger, grabbing the girl's arm and dragging her behind me. "Come on, milady, let's go."

Four

IRINA

"Come on, milady, let's go."

My legs had no choice but to follow, the numb things tripping over themselves as he pulled me through the crowd. We bumped into bodies left and right, and I finally had the sense to protest, words stuttering from my tied tongue. "I—I'm not going with you, I—"

"Come back, you *Kurniv!*" The blond's voice carried over the crowd, sending a fresh wave of fear rolling through my gut.

My legs pushed faster, ready to follow this stranger rather than stay with the danger I'd already met.

We shoved out the door, the night air stinging my cheeks as we toppled into it.

But before we could slow, before I could catch my breath, the cloaked man tugged me closer, and the wind howled a free bellow as it roared around my ankles and through my legs...

And then we were *flying*.

Soaring, the gust sweeping me off my feet so high my boots kissed the rooftops, a chill running down my back as the night air licked at my exposed neck. My hair whipped around me, blocking my view in strands of darkness until I managed to brush it out of my face.

Wrong choice.

My heart nearly leapt out of my chest. Over the rooftops, over the whole world, we rose higher and higher, Hiku City sprawling out before me like I was a bird circling its nest.

I tipped back, woozy with the sudden rush of it all, but a hand slid to the small of my back, steadying me in a gentle urge forward.

And though I knew I should be afraid, knew I should be screaming—

The song of freedom was the only beat singing in my heart.

Finally, the wind cradled us onto a small green rooftop, and the stranger guided us to the fire escape, winding us back down to the waiting street below.

My breath scraped through my lungs, my ribs struggling to widen enough to suck it all down, my neck coated with a sheen of sweat. But my feet beneath me felt strong, happy to be reunited with the ground.

"That was insane," I panted, turning toward the stranger as I mangled my hair back into shape.

Insane.

Horrifying. *Wonderful.*

He lowered the hood of his cloak, revealing a matted mess of cheek-length black hair. Despite the scarf still covering his mouth, I could tell he was young, closer to my age than I'd expected, his forehead wrinkle-free and his pale skin bright and lifted. Eyes the color of green tea-and-honey gleamed in the soft moonlight and distant lanterns, matching the thrill that threatened to burst from my veins. He took a step closer, and I sucked in a breath, waiting, *hoping.*

"Most polite ladies say 'thank you' after a gentleman rescues them."

Dread doused my excitement in bitter disappointment.

"Oh, so you deserve a pat on the back for basic decency?" I crossed my arms, holding myself tight to keep from unraveling. This was not how this night was supposed to go—not just one but *two* creeps ruining my fun. If this was the truth of the world, perhaps Mama was right—I wanted no part of it. I preferred the safety of my silver spoon and gilded cage.

But the stranger blinked like I'd slapped him, his brows flying higher than we'd been just moments before.

"Fair point." He rocked backward, eyes cast down toward the cobblestones. Shame softened his tone. "I'd offer to walk you home, but I've got to get going."

My concern vanished, but the dread did not. Somehow, him leaving me here *alone* sounded worse, as absolutely crazy as that was for me to even entertain. Not that I could let him see me safely home, but... "Some gentleman you are."

The stranger quirked a brow. His deep chuckle sparkled like the night sky hanging above, somehow bright and dark all at once. "You seem to have a type, then. You only pick 'gentlemen' with wicked streaks."

He had a point. This man had a dangerous side, as evidenced by his demonstration of easy violence, something that was clearly not born tonight, but honed over years.

Still, I found myself scrambling for anything to keep the conversation going. Anything to keep him here with me.

"So you *were* the one that gave him that broken nose?" I asked, and he nodded once. The side of my mouth lifted on its own whim. "Good work."

The Nehirite might not have earned that wound before I met him, but he certainly had after.

The stranger tugged down his mask, revealing a set of full, smirking lips. A dimple cratered the side of his face. "I am a man of many talents, breaking noses and disappointing pretty women chief among them."

Heat rushed my cheeks.

Pretty.

The noble's eyes had been so swollen, his declaration had meant nothing, clearly just a well-used line. But this man could see just fine, those interesting eyes open wide and drinking me in–at a polite distance.

Parts of me wanted a closer look.

"The flying part wasn't so disappointing." I wavered forward, intrigue warring against my instinct to flee. "You're an aermental Controller? That's pretty impressive."

His smile fell, expression hardening. His voice cooled. "It comes in handy."

"Oh." Awkwardness stretched between us as the air tightened, like the night itself was urging us back to our respective roles. Back to our separate worlds, mine a kingdom away, his...wherever masked strangers dwelled.

He obeyed first.

"Listen, I've got another little lady waiting for me, and I wouldn't want to disappoint her, too." Hands stuffed in his pockets with a nonchalant shrug, he jerked his head toward the street. "But if you follow the main road in front of this building, you should be safe. It's well lit. Just stay away from boasting nobles."

My chest deflated, my mind warring with that silly tug in my center that had craved adventure tonight. I should've been counting my lucky stars that I'd gotten away safely, that this stranger had decided he'd tired of me. All there was left was to find the nearest quiet corner to pull out my fae-dust and get myself home.

"I know where I'm going," I snipped, but even as I raised my chin at him, my eyes rolling, even as I turned around and walked away...

The last wild parts of me wished he'd ask me to stay.

"Sure you do," he laughed instead, baritone voice tickling the back of my neck like a summer wind.

Forgotten glimmers of a memory flashed, from a night warmer than this, from an era I desperately missed...but with a voice like the warm buzz of a violin, just a bit higher than his groaning cello...

"Thank you," I said as I turned around again, desperate for one last glimpse...

But the stranger was already gone, carried away on a breeze.

I fished the fae-dust from my pocket, dousing my finger in green powder and thinking of home. And when the warm clay walls and dusty pinks of my bedroom greeted me, I did my very best to forget the specific shade of tea-and-honey.

This was why I followed the rules, why I never developed Nikolaj's taste for mischief.

It was better to not know the taste of something sweet at all than to get a bite and have it taken away.

Freedom only led to disappointment.

FIVE

SHIN

The stained-glass domed roof of the Treehouse glittered in the starlight, the missing and cracked panes like the dark space between constellations. And despite the decay and disuse of the abandoned slums around it, ivy clinging to the stone sides and trash littering the front steps, it never failed to take my breath away.

Home.

My winds dropped me through a large hole, and I somersaulted into the main Den of the abandoned Opera House—what once had been a stage—landing on the soft bed of deep velvet curtains that now served as a rug.

"Look what the wind blew in," Naveen crowed from where he lounged across several of his favorite tattered velvet seats in the pit, the armrests torn out years ago to accommodate his ridiculously tall frame. The lanterns cast his dark skin in gold as he offered a wide grin. "Mal beat you again, by nearly forty minutes this time. You're losing your edge, brother."

I scanned the Den, but Malina was nowhere to be seen, probably already in her room hoarding over her treasure like the firedrake she was. It was just Naveen—my third in command after Mal, a title he earned by being the next eldest at twenty. But when we'd first found him at sixteen, he was just a Dunyas runaway who escaped the grueling farming industry and had a dream to never work hard again a day in his life.

I supposed I admired his consistency, because despite his high ranking in the family, he'd earned himself the award of the laziest thief in all of Babylon.

"I got distracted." I removed my cloak, hanging it on one of the free hooks in the backstage area that now served as our communal wardrobe, the once-dazzling costume stores replaced by our meager collection of rags and the few decent pieces we used for disguises. "Bastards started messing with Madame Aheni. Maybe if you had been making your rounds and stopping in to check on her like I told you, I would've beaten Mal back this time."

Naveen yawned and hopped from his seat, leaping the four-foot gap from the pit to the stage with ease. He shook out his dark brown curls to remove the evidence of his too-long nap. "I'll check on Madame Aheni tomorrow."

I clapped him on the shoulder. "See that you do. And that doesn't mean go and sample her merchandise, are we clear?"

"Fine." Naveen crossed his long, muscled arms. "What climbed up your butthole?"

I ignored his question, the rhetorical defense not worth either of our breaths. He knew any return to his old poppy-scented vices would mean exile, this time for good. The younger kids did not need to see him strung out, his mind addled and his choices blurred by the allure of the haze.

Nor did they need to see the cold sweats and shaking hands every time we locked him up to clean his system out, the begging and sobbing and bargaining that echoed through the Treehouse's acoustic halls.

I'd have kicked him out ages ago if he hadn't saved Aya twice, his Dunyasian knowledge of herbalism and Qualifier Teramental *Easinir* both skills I could never put a price on, and his gentleness with her a kindness I could never repay.

I pushed the memories from my mind, not wanting to dwell in dark pasts. None of us came to the Treehouse without our demons, and it was not my place to judge the way we all dealt with our own darkness. But I had too many people to protect now to let his shadows creep back into our shared home.

He followed after me as I climbed up the stairs to the balconies, into the other rooms waiting beyond, the faded frescos that watched us from the walls the only witnesses.

Still, he kept his voice low. "I smell the Crescent on you. Is that why you're late?"

I clenched my jaw, forgetting that I'd spilled that drunk Jaltan's ale on myself as I'd pushed him over.

"I made a stop at the watering hole." I kept moving, keeping my tone as nonchalant as possible. I trusted my family with my whole life, but as their leader, it was not my job to worry them.

At least, that was the excuse I conjured to convince myself that it had nothing to do with the flare of green envy that itched along my ribcage at the mere thought of Naveen learning about the woman—

My stomach sank to the pits. Breath above, I hadn't even learned her name. I'd just have to trust that the wind would blow her back in my path again one day.

I doubted it. Girls like her didn't stay in Hiku City, not if they knew what was good for them.

I tried to force a smile despite the sinking disappointment as I walked into the old corridor, the once-fine floorboards now creaky as the gaps between the planks separated.

"Sure thing, mate." Naveen nudged my shoulder as he brushed past me—sniffing out my bluff.

As suspected, a small face waited at the end of the hall, giant brown eyes brimming with excitement as they stopped on me.

"Shin! You're finally home!" Kas sprinted down the hall on gangly limbs before wrapping me in a tight hug.

I exhaled and ruffled his dark curls—identical to Malina's—his head only coming up to my chest. But he'd grow soon, the awkward angles of his thirteen-year-old frame adjusting for a spurt.

"Hey, kid," I grinned at him as he pulled away, noticing a lump in my pocket after—even though I hadn't felt his sleight of hand at all. I pulled out the object, a small metal tin. "What's this?"

I popped open the lid, the vague smell of pine and something earthy greeting me as my reflection peered back from the glassy surface inside.

Rosin.

"A present." Kas smirked, leaning against the peeling wallpaper. The kid was getting good, but he was as greedy as his older sister, his taste just as expensive.

That fact did nothing to diminish the warmth that spread through my chest, a fondness that settled deep into my bones at the thoughtful gesture.

I raised a brow as I reapplied the lid, careful not to drop the fragile gift. "And who paid for it?"

"Someone with enough money not to miss it."

Naveen flicked Kas's forehead as he beamed at him. "Hide it before Mal sees it."

"Before I see what?"

I spun on my heel as Malina appeared behind us like a specter, somehow not making a sound despite the usual groaning of the old building. Her full brows knit together. "What took so long?"

I painted on an unbothered smile. "You had your fun, I had to have mine."

Mal crossed her arms, but her expression eased, a teasing smirk lifting her mouth. "Let me guess—your fun included a trip to the Crescent."

I raised my hands in false surrender. At least she didn't know about the other trouble I'd gotten into. "Am I so predictable?"

"All men are." Mal rolled her eyes and squeezed her brother's shoulders. "Please Kas, when you grow up, let these idiots be an example of what *not* to do."

"You steal and cheat and prank as much as they do!" Kas whined, puffing out his chest in boyish solidarity. "Even more!"

Mal winked, pinching her brother's cheek. "Right, but *I* do it better."

Kas giggled, and Mal softened. She might have been made of

diamond-stuff, but even she had her tender spots, and all of them had Kas's name etched deep.

"Up for a debrief?" I asked, hoping to use her good mood to my advantage. As much as I wanted to keep some of the details from the others, Mal needed to know about the girl and the noble, just in case anyone came looking for trouble again.

"Aya is still awake." Malina jerked her head toward the Loft, Aya's private room. "Go kiss her goodnight, and we'll debrief after."

An arrogant, prideful part of me wanted to remind her exactly who gave the orders around here, but the wise parts of me knew better.

I might have been the head of this operation, but Malina was our backbone. I'd be dead a thousand times over if it weren't for her, but more importantly, the Treehouse would still be just an old, abandoned opera house, no more than a ghost of a once-melodic dream, the once-vibrant happiness just as faded as the peeling paint. Malina breathed life into this place, into all of us, knitting the seven of us together into a true family.

And if Malina was the thread, Aya was the needle—poking her way into every heart she encountered, carving a permanent space there.

A space that would forever remain as hollow and abandoned as the Treehouse after she...

No, that wasn't a road I would walk tonight.

I rubbed Malina's shoulder as I passed her, dutifully following her commands and the tug in my chest.

My sister waited. And I had no clue how many late nights she had left in her.

The Loft was breezy tonight, the threadbare curtains swaying as moonlight poured in, fighting the orange glow of the lanterns with swaths of night blue.

Aya sat at the windowsill, knees pulled to her chest and tucked beneath her oversized nightgown—a beautiful silk piece that had been left behind in the costume stores—as she stared from her tower over the world beyond.

My heart snagged on thorny thoughts. It was torture, to keep an

Aermental locked away like this. But the alternative was worse. Unthinkable.

Her head snapped to me as I knocked on the open doorframe, her short black hair—the same hue and texture as mine— fluttering like the curtains. Her smile knocked the breath out of me, brighter than the full moon, even though the dark circles under her eyes rivaled moonless nights.

I sauntered into the room, snagging the warm blankets from the cot that served as her bed before joining her on the seated windowsill, draping the blankets across both of our laps. "What are you doing up?"

Aya nestled into it, her skeletal frame drawing in the excess fabric.

"I always sleep better knowing you're safe and sound," she sighed, her round eyes pulled out the window again. "How was the game tonight?"

"Too easy." I smirked as I pulled her legs into my lap, rubbing the too-thin backs of her calves, hoping to help her sluggish blood flow. Her shoulders relaxed at the contact, relief spreading through her as she snuggled deeper into the blankets' cocoon. I continued my tale of the night's adventures, purposefully skipping over the parts where I picked fights and rescued pretty girls. "But we got a decent portion. Tomorrow, I'll take it down to Ms. Suliri's. I should be able to get enough to last a while this time."

Spring water from the Nehirite mountains, imported illegally, worth its weight in gold. But with what I captured alone tonight, I could buy enough to last a whole month, enough for Naveen and Riku to make their tinctures that helped inspire color back in my sister's face and reinvigorated her appetite.

Still, she gnawed her chapped bottom lip. "I don't like this."

My hands dropped in my lap so she couldn't feel them shake. "I don't either, but it'll be okay. They'll find a cure, and when they do...we'll find a way to get a hold of it."

Wide eyes snapped to me, their once-violet hue now a dull, muted gray. "No, Shin. I don't like putting you and the rest of the family at risk, I don't like the stealing..."

I scoffed. "It's not stealing when they make it so easy."

"Shin—"

"Don't you trust me?"

A resigned huff. "I do."

"Then let me do this. I have to do *something*." I grabbed her shoulders, hating how the bones poked sharply enough to bruise my palms. "Tomorrow, your medicine. Then maybe you'll even feel well enough to come to the Fool's Masque at the Crescent this year."

A spark lit in her eyes, fighting back against the dullness as she sat straighter. "Really?"

The Fool's Masque was the best party of the year, a free night where the lower class could roam and rave without the judgmental eyes of the nobility staring us down. It was a debaucherous scene, a stark contrast to the stiff, sparkling party the upper crust would have in Dunyas.

Aya had been asking for years, long before she got sick, and I'd always denied her petition. She was too young, too sweet, too *good*. But perhaps it was time to let her go...

Just in case it was her last chance.

My smile hid the ache that thrummed behind it. I brushed a strand of her limp hair out of her face. "Really. I'll even use some of the money to buy you a new dress to wear. But tonight, rest."

"Shin!" A panicked voice called just before Riku's lithe form dropped through the open window, his normally calm face grim. The icy knife he'd use to scale the outside melted immediately into a puddle as he lost control of the Qualifying magic. He panted as his eyes met mine, pure fear and something darker blowing his pupils wide. "Code red."

Code red.

Intruders in the Treehouse.

I leapt up, my stomach sinking down to the pits.

"What's going on?" Aya pulled the blankets closer, voice rising with concern, but I was already moving.

"Stay here, both of you." I ordered, plowing toward the door, a swift wind nipping at my heels.

Worry whirled in my head like a maelstrom. We'd been safe here for years, but now, on the same day I had not one, but *two* run-ins with Nehir nobles, someone decided to poke their head into the rundown part of town?

"You were followed. Five large men outside in uniforms, and a woman walking through the front door." Ren's warm voice had an uncharacteristic edge to it as he intercepted me in the hallway, his long strides matching mine. It was almost impossible to tell him and Riku apart, the identical twins both tall and willowy, their long, auburn hair even sticking up in the same places. But Riku was the moon to Ren's sun, cold calculation to warm embrace. And if they both were on high alert, we were in deep trouble.

Ren offered me my throwing knives—already anticipating my needs as I picked up my pace.

"Tell Riku to stay with Aya, and go alert Mal and Naveen," I ordered quietly, palming my knives. "Tell Naveen to hide the supplies, and you be ready to flood them out if I fail."

Ren nodded, opening the flask of water he'd need if all else failed, before shooting off in the other direction. As a Quantifier, he only needed a drop to make this place a lake in a matter of minutes, but it would cost him energy, and us our home.

I hoped it wouldn't come to that. I hadn't planned for a swim today.

I bounded up the stairs to the left—to the catwalk, where the lights were hung back when this was an operating theater. The perfect vantage point to watch any threats.

But something cold and wet snatched my ankle.

I lurched forward, slamming my hands against the stairs.

I turned too late as the ice crept up my legs and snared my wrists, wrenching me back into the hall. My winds blasted against it to no avail as numb pain flared up my spine.

My stomach dropped as my gaze snagged on Mal, Ren, and Naveen, held in similar icy snares, their mouths gagged with snow.

And to the woman standing between them, her white-blond hair woven into a crown atop her head, her Nehir-blue dress decorated with frost and snow, her stare laced with the same chilliness.

She grinned, white teeth gleaming like wolf's fangs. "If you value your lives, you'll stop moving immediately."

Six

SHIN

When I was sixteen and Aya was only seven, still just lost street urchins living in the dregs of Hiku City, a circus blew through town. Like the rest of the paupers and street rats, Aya, Mal, Kas, and I all flocked to the tents, pitched high just outside of the city proper, ready to catch even a glimpse of something that might make us believe in hope again, that might feed our hungry hearts with something new and magical.

But what we saw was the wickedness of man put on grand display, colorful horrors dressed as daydreams.

We could not enter the tents without money, so we snuck around the back, to where they kept the wagons. That's where we met Riku and Ren, the troublesome twins offering us a private tour when their master wasn't looking, leading us to where giant animals paced in too-small cages. Tigers, elephants...

And a giant, red-tailed Phoenix, its feathers dulled by captivity, its black eyes hollow and distant.

Aya's heart broke, and in her despair, I broke the lock to its cage, coaxing it out into the open. But the great bird did not fly away, did not take to the skies and soar toward greener pastures.

Its wings had been clipped, its cage not just the rusted bars it dwelled within, but the body that had become a trap of its own, a flightless bird that could never taste the skies again.

It'd been years since I thought about the poor creature, but now I had an inkling of how it felt to be caged, body and soul.

Ice bit at my skin as the woman dragged me, Mal, Ren, and Naveen down into the Den, the open skylights of the dome ceiling casting her pale form in pools of ghostly light.

But even if she was a ghost, I'd find a way to exorcize her and her goons, her very presence an affront to the Treehouse's sanctity.

Beginnings of plans unfurled in my head as I calculated our advantages. As of now, Aya and Riku were nowhere to be seen; hopefully the clever boy had gotten her to safety before they could be nabbed. And Kas had also managed to go undetected, but I knew he would be in the rafters soon. I ground my teeth together, hating that the youngest of us was the only one in a position to do anything right now. As the only other full Controller among us, he was our only hope. But luckily, the boy was more capable than most of the men I knew, the streets of Hiku City and our family of Lost Ones the only education he needed to learn the language of life.

Mal's eyes met mine from her cage next to me, two long blinks and a single-eyed wink communicating more than words could, our code clear.

Buy us time.

I needed no further urging.

Despite the cold clamping down on my limbs, I relaxed into the ice, a smirk tilting my mouth. "As cozy as this is, if you wanted to talk, you could've just asked. Who are you?"

With a deft flick of her hand, the woman conjured herself a throne of ice, brushing out her skirt as she took a seat. A display of power, but one that did little to impress. Still, her stare stung worse than the burn of her frost as it refused to waver from my face.

"I'll be the one asking questions." Her voice lilted as she fussed with her nails, relaxing back into her temporary throne. Another wave, and the others' gags vanished, a pool of water splashing around them. "I will let you all speak if you first tell me...where is my son's broach?"

The wind picked up around me, unheeded warnings blaring in my ear. So the Nehir pig sent his *mommy* to retrieve his trinkets? He was even more of a prat that I'd guessed. I thought of the sapphire broach Mal had definitely snatched and probably stowed away beneath the floorboards of her room.

Not that I'd let this sow know that.

The others stayed silent, too, the clever imps. I shot them each three blinks and two winks, the command to *let me do the talking*.

All I had to do was stall. Wait until Kas could get into a good position to burn the witch.

I sighed, leaning into the dramatics as I shook my head. "Unfortunately, I don't know who your son is, but I haven't seen any ugly fucks today, so I can't help you."

The purse of the woman's lips sent the thrill of triumph through me, even though I was still the one bound and trapped. But if I could worm beneath her skin, crawl through her veins...

Some fights were won with wicked words alone, one of the many dialects a good thief let the wind teach him.

"I know you have it," the woman spat, sharp nails rapping against the icy armrest. "It's made with fae-stone, you fool. I can track it from anywhere. And it was more expensive than your entire lives are worth, so I'll want it back."

My gut plummeted, my heart kicking into a furious beat.

All faerie magic had been scarce for centuries, and banned long before the Jaltan uprising, since it'd been corrupted and used for war and murder.

Sweat coated the back of my neck despite the ice. If this woman had access to fae-stones, we were not just dealing with some uppity noble. We were in shit deeper than the Black River, and it was my fault *again*.

"I'm sorry, so sorry," Mal piped in despite her orders to stay quiet, her voice draped in that sickening sweetness she saved for our marks. But still, it coated my nerves like syrup, blocking the fear with its viscous warmth. She continued with a soft smile. "Is this it? I just found it; I was going to put out a flier tomorrow to help find the proper owner."

Even with her wrists bound in front of her, she managed to produce the small, glowing broach from her pocket, the sapphire glinting in the dim stage lights. She lifted it at awkward angles, dangling it like a carrot.

The woman's eyes lit with a similar glimmer. With a burst of water, she floated the broach from Mal's hand to her own, long fingers gripping it with a too-intense grip that sent a shiver down my spine.

"Good girl," she crowed, smile souring sinister. But her gaze found me again, darkening to black. "But this doesn't excuse what you did to my son and nephew."

I rolled my eyes, a signal for my crew to keep quiet and stand down. Malina narrowed her eyes at me but didn't protest, while Ren's shoulders relaxed in quiet resignation. Even Naveen clamped his mouth shut, a blessing from the Breath that he was able to do so at all.

If all that was left was a beating, I could take it without Kas torching anyone. Roasting foreign dignitaries would likely only result in more trouble for us down the line, and I didn't want any other nobles sticking their shit-stained noses into my home.

But I had to make sure I took the brunt of it.

"Oh, *those* ugly fucks! I remember them now!" I laughed, the sound devoid of anything redeemable. I dragged my eyes over the woman, earning another grimace from her as I continued my taunt. "I see the resemblance, actually. You have the same nose that you clearly enjoy sticking in other people's business."

She shot from her seat, pale skin dappled in blotches of angry red as the blood rushed to her head. I braced, ready to take whatever fury she'd unleash on me—

But she was a wall of ice, unmoving except for the flash of her teeth as she cried out, "Sachir? Bring the girl!"

Every cell in my body went lethally, wholly still as a burly man with a thick black beard appeared on the balcony. Riku was flung over his left shoulder, the thin boy unconscious, a small bump visible on his forehead even from here.

But there was another still-kicking body tucked beneath his right arm.

Aya.

The tornado in my chest begged to be set free, to tear down the very walls and bring it all down on the woman's head. To bury her in rubble and ruin.

Aya thrashed against the man's hold, but he didn't relinquish an inch. Round, scared eyes met mine in the distance. "Shin, we're fine, don't—"

My voice rumbled low in my chest, thunder breaking over mountain peaks. "Touch her, and I stop playing nice."

The blonde snorted, sticking her hands to her hips. "You don't have any levera—"

With less than a thought, I stole the air from her lungs, tugging it with my mind. She doubled over, face purpling as she clutched at her throat, her ribcage. Eyes blew wide, bloodshot and swelling as they threatened to burst—

I was going to kill her.

And I was going to enjoy it.

"Shin, don't!" Aya screamed, banging against the cage of the broad man's arm. With a grunt, he squeezed tighter, my sister flinching in his hold. "Ow, stop—"

I was going to kill this woman.

But Aya and Riku would likely die too, their position on the balcony just out of my range.

Gritting my teeth, I let go of my grip on my power. The woman collapsed in a fit of hacking, struggling gasps, greedily sucking in the air meant for my sister, my family—

But she waved a hand, and Sachir set Aya and Riku down on the ground. My sister instantly flew to the boy's side, a gentle finger tracing over his injury. She nodded once, her shoulders relaxing in time with mine—he was breathing, but there was no escaping while he was knocked out.

"So you *are* an aermental Controller," the woman croaked between hoarse coughs, struggling to shaking feet. "Rare...and in a street rat like you? Excellent."

Heat pricked at the back of my neck, unease settling in my middle. Ren and Malina exchanged dark looks with me, both of them highly aware of what that information could do in the wrong hands.

Aermental Controllers *were* rare. Magic was passed down family lines, so those in power typically arranged marriages with other powerful *Easinir* to ensure more powerful babies. And much like one's eye and hair color, the type of magic one wielded often reflected a parent or grandparent's type, and some elements were less prominent than others.

Air was a recessive gene, and it rarely occurred in Controllers. There were only three noble families in Sora that had Controllers; even the Sora royal line, the most prominent aermental family in all of Babylon, were only Qualifiers, making them the weakest of the four kingdoms. They had no prospect of future Quantifiers or Controllers unless they married into them.

It made anomalies like me both rare and dangerous—two things the people of Sora frequently tried to stamp out or stick into slums like Hiku City.

I shoved down old memories that rose to the surface, focusing instead on the witch in front of me. I didn't care if she saw me as an oddity or a thief; I just needed to figure out her angle and twist it to my advantage.

Had to keep the Lost Ones and Aya *safe*.

"What do you want?"

She plopped back into her throne, panting while she grinned. "I'm here to offer a deal."

"Less posturing, more talking." Annoyance itched like flea-ridden rags across my skin. A bird whistle from the rafters let me know Kas was there—safe and ready to strike—but there was no way for him to free Aya *and* kill the blonde in front of me. Even if he did, we'd have noble blood staining our home, and more would likely come after us.

We were stuck in her icy clutches, birds with clipped wings and tight cages.

She knew it, too, as she leaned forward, ready to make her offer— one that would spell even more trouble.

"I did some digging on you." She grinned, and I froze, my ears ringing with numbness. My past was a phantom I'd long been trying to escape, and I would not let her haunt me with it. But the woman toyed with the broach, delight lighting her pale features. "You're quite a talented group of thieves, aren't you?"

The air swirled around me, the woman's hair standing on end as static crackled over her form. It was a parlor trick I'd learned from Madame Aheni, changing the air's property to increase electricity. But it was also a threat, a reminder of what I could do even with my hands tied behind my back. "We like to think so."

For the first time since she strode into the Treehouse, the woman had the right mind to look ever-so-slightly frightened, lips pursed thin and eyes stretched wide. But she cleared her throat, taking back the room. "Good. Because I'll need your skills sharp to kidnap someone for me."

"We don't mess with slave traders and traffickers," Ren seethed, eyes burning with smoky memories of his own haunted history. I nodded to him—a confirmation that I would never ask them to go back to the life they had before, not even if it cost me my own.

But if the woman knew what strings she was tugging, she didn't let on, sighing back into her seat. "You misunderstand. This is a *political* endeavor. The Princess of Dunyas will be at the Masquerade ball this year, and will be expected to choose an appropriate suitor. And I need her to choose my Drakkar."

Recognition sent a warning flare in my head, the name triggering old memories and distant knowledge...

Dread smacked me like a wall of solid rock, heavy and impenetrable.

Drakkar of Nehir.

Prince.

Not just in his prissy mannerisms, but in actual title. Not just a pampered lordling, but a royal in the flesh.

Which meant the woman in front of us was Queen Ecei, the Ice Witch of the North.

"The little shit you pummeled was the Prince of Nehir?" Naveen groaned as he figured it out at the same time, straining against his icy shackles. Broad shoulders slumped forward as he mumbled beneath his breath. "And you say *I'm* the screw up."

Water splashed in Naveen's face, tumbling him backward in a rollover most acrobats would be impressed by. Queen Ecei straightened in her seat. "You do not need your tongue to complete this mission, so I advise you to hold it."

"We didn't know who he was," Malina interjected, another attempt at winning her favor. "If we had, we never would have crossed him."

Ecei relaxed, ego sufficiently stroked, but it didn't change the fact we were still in deep crap.

I shifted, directing her attention away from my big-mouthed friends, stretching like a house cat on a windowsill. I had to play this right if I was going to get us out of it unscathed. "So you want us to abduct the competition?"

"Not quite." Ecei cocked her head to the side. "Your mark is Princess Catirina herself."

"What? *Why?*" Malina balked.

Before the Treehouse was my home, before Aya was the only person I cared about, before Sora Province and Hiku City could teach me the lessons of the wind's wicked tricks...

I'd been tutored in a different set of skills, carved into the fabric of my being from the day I was born, gilded across my bones. And though I'd left that life behind at ten with little Aya strapped to my back, the memories still clung to my heels like my shadow, something I could ignore but never truly separate myself from. Something I couldn't forget.

But as I strained against the Nehir woman's icy hold, two lessons from the life before drifted through my mind on a covert breeze, reminding me of the wickedness of mankind.

One: that greed was the root of all ills, a sickness more potent than any Blight. Every heart and head was touched by it—and the real trick was figuring out what fed each person's individual vice.

And two: that cunning was more valuable than any riches, what you could *do* for a person always more advantageous than what you could give them.

"Why us?" I rocked forward, letting the wind tug whatever greedy heartstring had brought this woman to our doorstep. I jerked my chin to Sachir in the balcony. "You clearly have competent people already."

Ecei shrugged, expression neutral. "Nehir can't be held responsible. I need someone with no traceable ties to my kingdom."

"Where do you want us to take her?"

I watched both Malina and Ren stiffen out of the corner of my eye, neither happy that I was entertaining this plot at all; I ignored them, focused on the bob in Ecei's throat.

Whatever it was she wanted with the Princess, she wanted it badly. *Desperately.* The scent of her desire wafted through the open room, a rotten floral stench that had already begun to eat at her from the inside. Her smile was a thin veil of misdirection. "Back here, to Sora. Neutral grounds. Then my people will come to collect her from you."

"Why?" Ren pressed, his voice barely above a whisper. He and his twin had a particular dislike for anything resembling slave trade.

"I promise, my intent is not to hurt the Princess in any way. It's simply political assurance. My son needs a reputation boost, and this is an easy way to handle it."

I mulled it over, trying to fit the pieces together. Though the four kingdoms of Babylon were supposed to be treated equally according to all of the unification agreements, Dunyas was the most influential kingdom by far. Their produce and access to the rivers and roads made them necessary to keep all four kingdoms fed. But they also only had one heir now—after the Crown Prince died of the Blight—and from rumors, she was just a Qualifier that was half-decent with sprucing up house plants. Which meant as far as power went, Nehir and Jalta were the only two royal houses with full Controllers in their ranks—Ecei in the North, and Lord Avi and Princess Naria in the West.

And Drakkar was a poor excuse for a Qualifier, as evidenced by our fight this afternoon. Which meant that Jalta could make a play for Catirina's affection–Avi, the nephew of the Jaltan King, was a prominent Controller.

But if Ecei could claim that Drakkar rescued the Princess after some lowlife thieves captured her...

It would secure Nehir's favor, even if it meant weakening the royal line in the long term. And it would keep the Jaltans out of Dunyas, a sentiment many who misunderstood the uprising could get behind. It had been fourteen years since the Jaltans had threatened the unification of Babylon, invading Sora and Dunyas without provocation, claiming they'd killed King Odion's heir. Dunyas's superior numbers shut it down quickly, and without proof of foul play, the Jaltans had to accept full responsibility, making them the villains of Babylon overnight. And even though it'd been over a decade, many people still treated them as such, prejudice hard to overcome.

Ecei wanted to keep it that way.

I sighed, shoving any last morals and convictions to the side, letting my wicked heart out of its cage, hoping it might restore my wings. "What's the payout?"

Ecei waved a passive hand. "I will let you live."

"Not good enough."

Ecei snorted. "So should I kill you now instead?"

"Sure, but the Masque is only a week away, and I know the other thieves in Hiku City." I yawned, feigning boredom. "None of them can pull it off."

Ecei stared at me a long moment, that festering desperation pulling just beneath her transparently pale skin, her jaw clenching and unclenching as she chewed on her next words before spitting them out. "Fine. Name your price. I can afford to sweeten the deal."

I smiled, victory stirring up the dust in my chest. I might be a bird with clipped wings, but Ecei was caged by her own vices, her greed creating steel bars around her. "You heal my sister from the Blight, you pay us enough to start over if we need to, and my whole crew walks free."

"Shin, no—" Ren hissed.

"That can be arranged." Ecei cut him off as she sat back in her throne, a hand placed across her chest in a mockery of the royal oath. "I swear I will cure your sister's illness and give you all the chance at a new life. You just have to deliver Princess Catirina to me by the end of week. Do we have a deal?"

I held my breath, weighing my choices. This would be difficult. *Dangerous.* Not just logistically–a kidnapping was hard to pull off, especially in the palace of Anastova during the most guarded event of the year. And even if it wasn't, to put myself in a room with that many nobles was beyond risky, even for a wicked fool like me.

But all doubts drifted away on a dark wind when I made eye contact with Aya in the balcony, still hovering over Riku's head.

I could save her. Both of them.

All of them.

And even if it meant tearing off my own wings, even if it meant I could never taste the skies again...

The choice was easy.

"Yes."

A flick of her fingers, and our icy prisons melted in an instant, splashing us all in cold water. I twisted my numb wrists, desperately trying to coax life back into them as Ecei stood over us, that same avarice brimming in her crystal stare. "Good boy. Now, I will drop off some proper attire for you by tomorrow. You'll all need it for the Masque."

And as she turned to go, the wind whispered one final warning in my ear, the song of change a war cry in her wake.

Nothing would ever be the same.

SEVEN

IRINA

Forks scraping across fine porcelain plates filled the empty space that conversation should've occupied as I sat with my family around our too-large dinner table, picking through the roast quail Tasha had prepared for us. My appetite had been scarce these last few days, my thoughts hungry for something else.

Green tea and honey, a laugh like nightshade.

Breezy dizziness, rooftops like sparkling treasure.

It'd been a whole week, and I'd yet to clear his silhouette from my mind, or the remnants of the caked green fae-dust from beneath my fingernails.

But the real imprint had been marked across my heart like a postage stamp on a raven-sent letter, the experience unerasable even though I'd left it behind. The night, the danger...*him*...it'd all been a brief flash, faster than a lightning strike, far too quick to ever catch. But the scorched earth of my soul would be forever scarred by it.

"Ri-Ri? Darling, did you hear me?" My father's bass voice pulled me from the trance, his tilled-soil stare piercing through the misty haze of my daydreams.

"Hmm?" I cleared my throat, nearly dropping my fork as I looked up at him. "Sorry, Father, I was lost in thought."

A warm smile stretched across his face, his broad frame softening. Father was both a king and scholar, a master of many things, but he'd never managed to learn the art of staying cross with me. Thick brows lifted. "Imagining your future prince?"

The quail turned to ash on my tongue, the burnt aftertaste of my actual wishes coating my mouth in a film of sadness. Still, I did my best to return his smile, a falsehood I'd gotten good at over the years. "Something like that."

Father, as always, did not notice the change in my demeanor, instead forking himself another generous mouthful and shoving it into his fleshy cheeks. He chewed as he spoke, earning an eye-twitch from my straight-backed mother at his right. "I received a message from Lord Hizan today, mentioning that his son Avi was rather excited to make your acquaintance. Make sure you say hello tomorrow."

My stomach clenched, the meager bites of dinner I'd managed threatening to make a second appearance. I hoped the lowlight of the candelabras masked my discomfort.

"Avi?" Mother set her silverware down, the usual twitch turning to a full-blown grimace. "Dear, I thought we agreed Prince Drakkar would be an excellent—"

"Yes, well, Lord Hizan's letter also included details of the new mines they are opening in the Helsin mountains." Father waved his silver butterknife like a conductor's wand, painting the picture of the mountain range in the air, his eyes alight. He winked at me. "Very profitable. Worth a hello, right, Ri-Ri?"

"Of course, Father."

My mother's face went a shade of scarlet to rival the slim-fitting burgundy dress she wore, but I paid it little attention for once in my life.

Drakkar, Avi...no matter which noble I made merry with tomorrow, nothing could ever fill the void that a single moonlit night in the windy, winding streets of Hiku City had carved from my flesh.

My father licked the backside of the knife, his dark curls bouncing as he nodded emphatically. "Good girl."

The pet name stung harsher than if he'd hollered at me.

Good girl. Pretty flower. Voiceless doll.

Was that all I'd ever be? Did I have a *choice*?

Perhaps I'd never taste the night air on the back of a phantom wind again, never feel a cool touch on the small of my back that set the world ablaze, but...

But Nikolaj would want more than *this* for me. Would encourage me to stake my small rebellions behind soft smiles and pretty pretenses.

And part of me could finally admit that I wanted more, too.

"Perhaps you and I should discuss our first impressions after the ball, Father." I cleared my throat, wringing the cloth napkin in my lap to settle my trembling hands. "I'd love to be a part of the decision making, to really weigh the options together—"

My father's chuckle silenced me, specks of food debris flying from his mouth and sticking in his cropped beard. "Oh, don't fret, dear. I know that would be a bore for you. Say hello to everyone tomorrow, dance, and *enjoy*. Your mother and I promise to pick the best match."

The obedient, practiced part of me recoiled at the gentle-but-firm admonishment, ready to crawl back into my glass vase and shrivel away. But another foreign thing inside me—something that had perhaps wormed its way beneath my skin in Hiku City—squirmed with disquiet, new roots grounding my feet beneath me and strengthening my stance. "But if I'm meant to rule, shouldn't I at least *learn* how to make those choices? You always invited Nikolaj into meetings with you—"

As soon as his name left my mouth, I knew my mistake.

"Catirina, that's *enough*." My mother's fist rattled the table, her whole form quaking as she struggled to compose her upset. My father placed a hand over hers—rubbing soft circles with his thumb—but his dark gaze flashed to me, hurt brimming in it.

Any strength I'd mustered snapped back at me like a rubber band, stinging against my skin.

No, I was no Nikolaj. I never would be. My parents had lost their favorite child and were doing what they could with the spare.

They didn't want me to rule. They didn't think I could.

Perhaps they were right.

"Yes, Mother." I hung my head, fighting back the burning tears prickling at the back of my eyes. In Dunyas, rebellions were squashed. The farmer's union, the Jaltan uprising...mine was no different.

"Eat your dinner." My mother delivered the killing blow, picking up her knife and fork and carving into her quail like she was imagining it was all the parts of me she wished she could simply cut away. "I don't want to see you sneaking sweets later. Your skin has to be clear tomorrow, and you know how terribly you bloat."

Her insult simply bounced off of me, the ringing in my ears too loud to process anything else. For the first time in my life, the thought of anything sweet made my stomach roll. Even Tasha's cookies couldn't satiate the appetite for purpose that left me hollow and aching, that made my chest want to cave in on itself.

But flowers in vases no longer tasted the water from the soil, no longer drank the sunshine and turned it into life itself.

No longer dreamt of flying through the star-ridden night on the back of a warm breeze. No longer dreamed at *all*.

"I'm not hungry." I pushed my plate away, the savory aroma suddenly stinging my already wet eyes. My chair made a horrible scraping noise against the marble floor as I shoved back, my head still low. "May I be excused?"

"Of course. Sleep well." My father's pitying smile sucked the last drops of power from my veins, leaving me with just the void again. "Tomorrow is a celebration. Get some rest."

To both his dismay and mine, I did not.

❧

Fanfare echoed through the courtyard all the next morning as dignitaries and nobles from the furthest reaches of Babylon arrived at our front door, ready to enjoy the ball. Many would be staying the night in guest suites, perhaps even longer if their business went well and new alliances were forged.

But as I waited in my own rooms, fiddling with the wildflowers in the box outside of my balcony, I couldn't help the sense of dread that filled my heart. My sleep had been a fitful toss-about of half-formed nightmares, and Mama would be livid at the dark bags that decorated my under-eyes as a result.

None of it mattered.

I couldn't do this.

I couldn't dance and laugh and smile with these men, all of which just wanted me for my crown, my title. Couldn't pretend to love them in return, when I'd already had a taste of what real chemistry could feel like, what excitement really meant.

A small part of me knew I wasn't giving them a fair chance. Perhaps Drakkar was not like that—maybe he could be kind and thoughtful too, and I wouldn't know any better without meeting him.

But as Gemma wriggled me into the petal-pink gown that afternoon, my hair styled in a long wall of ringlets at my back, the laces and pins felt more and more like shackles, trapping me for eternity.

At least I could hide behind the pearl-and-opal encrusted mask resting across the bridge of my nose. It sat just above my apple-round cheeks, creating a shadow that slimmed my circular face.

Maybe Mother would be pleased, after all.

That would make one of us.

"Catirina, are you ready?" The devil herself appeared like a phantom in my doorway, an emerald-green mermaid style gown hugging her frame in a way that would be scandalous if the sparkling jewels embedded into the fabric didn't hide the finer lines. Her gaze raked over me in an appraising sweep, my hands shaking under her scrutiny. Her lips pursed, but she blew out a breath, sinking into her hip. "Pretty. It's time to go."

My stomach plummeted, reality weighing it to my toes as sweat coated the back of my neck in cold moisture. "I'm actually not feeling well, it's—"

My mother's look could flatten mountains into dinner plates.

"Oh, *enough*. You know what we have riding on this," she hissed, that lava-hot rage steaming just beneath the surface of her finely crafted facade. But she was right—we all had parts to play tonight. Hers, the doting, loving, enigmatic queen; mine, the obedient idiot to be auctioned off to whichever noble-born man had the deepest pockets. She lifted her chin, looking down her slim, straight nose at me. "Let's go."

I shut my eyes and let myself take one last grounding breath, imagining the air I sucked in was the same Hiku City wind that had given me courage last week. Then, on a resigned exhale, I followed my mother out the door.

Music floated from the hallway as I followed her through the east wing and toward the grand ballroom. The orchestra was the only part of the evening I was determined to enjoy, but the undertones of guests murmuring amongst themselves and my own furiously beating pulse throbbed out of time with the tempo.

"You look so lovely, Ri-Ri!" my father exclaimed from where he waited at the top of the stairs, the buttons of his gold suit jacket and turmeric-colored vest straining against the push of his tall and round frame. He challenged the tailor's shoulder stitching as raised his arms to welcome me into a hug. "How precious!"

I stopped short of his grasp, panic rising. My knees wobbled, the pointed heels I stood in suddenly too tight, too shaky...

Don't worry, precious. I'm feeling better now that you're here.

Precious, like the Nehir noble had called me last week. *Precious*, he'd said, as his hand invaded my thigh, as he smiled down at me with wolfish intent...

And there was no dark stranger here tonight to save me from *these* wolves, from the men that would vie for my crown with that same predatory intent tonight. From my own parents who would hand me over to them with a bejeweled grin.

I stepped back, out of my father's reach. "I'm sorry, I can't..."

But my words were drowned out by the trumpet's blaring alarms, the fanfare beginning as the announcer cleared his throat and bellowed, "Now announcing King Boris and Queen Vera of Dunyas, and their beloved daughter, Princess Catirina, Heir Apparent to the throne of Dunyas."

"Smile, Irina." My mother's sharp pinch on my arm propelled my leadened feet forward toward the staircase. She linked arms with my father as they cascaded down the stairs, her smile brighter than the thousands of jewels she wore tonight as her free hand trailed over the gold railing.

And against my will, against every instinct in my body, I followed. My hand grasped the railing in a white-knuckled embrace, the metal the only thing keeping me upright as I descended.

Into the pit of vipers and wolves, all of them beaming up at us, teeth bared and dressed in their finest as they all fought for even a moment of our attention. But I knew the truth now. They'd all clamor for my favor tonight, but most of them would not spare a second look at a scared girl in a bar, content to turn a blind eye as one of their own devoured her.

I wished I could run back to Tasha's kitchen, to the warm calm of the only place in this palace that felt safe. Or better yet, that another friendly wind would sweep me far away, a kind stranger in a hood more inviting than the masked monsters waiting below.

But there was no escape.

Stair after stair.

Breath after rattling breath.

I miraculously reached the bottom, my face already red and hot, my chest tight as the laces of the corset dug into my supple sides. But there was no space to relax, no unwinding the core of worry as the crowd pressed closer, all eager to greet us. A blonde woman in a regal, ice-blue gown flitted first to my parents, a deep curtsy ballooning her expansive skirts.

"Your Majesties." Her cool voice carried as she rose. "Your Highness."

I swallowed, a strange familiarity twinkling through me. I'd never met this woman—never met most of the nobles, really, a second daughter hardly invited to dignitary dinners before. My parents preferred to keep me in my tower—on my pretty pedestal where I served them better as an *idea* rather than a reality. And yet even behind her midnight blue mask, there was something I recognized in the tilt of this woman's chin.

Mother opened her arms wide to embrace her, planting a kiss on each cheek. "Queen Ecei, it is lovely to see you!"

I inhaled sharply, greedy for fresh air.

Queen Ecei of Nehir. The Ice Witch of the North.

My future mother-in-law, if Mama had a say.

She smirked as she stepped back from my mother's hold, looking her up and down with a gaze that was almost as reproachful as the ones my mother typically saved for me. "You as well, Vera. I swear, you look younger every time I see you."

I tried not to let the flare of rage that ran through me show, something resentful coating my palms in sweat.

But Mother did not balk, fanning herself with her hand. "It's the heat, it's *great* for the skin. You should visit more often!"

"Oh, but the hot springs at home are just as restorative. I can't be away for too long." Ecei tilted her head, and for a brief moment, I was impressed, her sugary sarcasm a talent I'd love to mimic one day. But when she waved someone over from the crowd, all other thoughts and feelings ran from my head, replaced with a searing, heavy panic that throbbed like a headache. "I'd like for you to meet my son, Prince Drakkar. Drako, dear, come say hello."

A dark blue mask covered the last hints of a faint purple bruise across his tall nose, but his blond hair hung in soft, loose waves around his face, nearly hitting his chin.

And the smile he wore—wolfish, *familiar*—made me want to fold in on myself and run screaming.

"Your Majesties." He bowed low enough to wrinkle his light gray suit as he took my shaking hand, pressing a kiss to my knuckles. "Princess Catirina."

I could barely breathe, everything swirling around me, the ground beneath my feet shuddering and pitching like a rocking ship.

No no no no no. This could not be real.

Did he recognize me? If he did, would he tell my parents?

No, none of that mattered, not when he was out of place that night, too.

But the bloodied, terrible man at the bar, the wolf that had wanted to swallow me whole...was a prince? Not just any prince...

The one my mother had chosen just for me.

My future husband.

"You—" I stuttered, my tongue a useless, limp muscle as I fought the blinding fear that choked me. "I—"

"Don't mind her, she's nervous," my mother laughed, the shrill sound piercing my heart as she nudged me *closer* to him, so close I could smell the champagne already on his breath tonight. She placed a hand on his bicep, tossing her head back in another forced guffaw. "Who wouldn't be with a charmer like this?"

"You look beautiful, Princess, though it's clearly inherited," he crooned at us both, giving my hand a squeeze that was meant to reassure, but instead sent a jolt of terror up my arm. "It's a pleasure to meet you. I do hope we can get to know each other tonight."

I swallowed, inhaling air desperately through my nose.

He didn't recognize me, it seemed; perhaps the only boon I'd be afforded tonight.

But my head still thrummed with vicious fear, consuming me from the inside out like rot.

I couldn't do this.

"Yes, of course." I pulled away, finally commanding my tongue into action. If only I could get my feet to follow, one brave step back at a time... "Um, if you'll all excuse me, actually, I have to—"

My words died beneath the swell of the orchestra, my father's resounding clap a death knell. "Oh good, the music has started! Let's dance!"

Drakkar leaned closer, reaching for my hand again. "Care to dance, Princess?"

"Go on!" Ecei beamed at her son, their smiles twin in appearance as she shooed us on, my mother nodding at her side, "What a grand idea!"

My protests had no power left as I let him lead me to the dance floor, my feet following out of numb obedience. We passed bodies as we went, but I couldn't make out any faces, the ballroom a smudge of color and scents that slammed against my mind.

His hand wound around my back and lifted my other arm, and I did my best not to faint, the room spinning before we even began our dance.

But then *we* were spinning with it, my stomach churning in time with the orchestra. The music accosted my ears, just senseless, screeching noise as I fought to stay present in my body.

I couldn't do this.

But I *was*, against my will and despite myself, as Drakkar held me tightly.

"A lovely evening, is it not?" he drawled in his Northern accent as he twirled me around, his own doll to animate. The lights of the ballroom blurred together, my eyes unfocused as my head continued to twist in a dizzying spiral.

"Yes, beautiful." My response was automatic, impersonal, a line I'd been given only to regurgitate. But my soul was miles away, my mind disappearing to the warm streets of a city of smoke and starlight.

Broad hands gripped me closer, chaining me back to *this* body, *this* night. "You know, you seem familiar, but I'm sure I wouldn't have forgotten someone as lovely as you. Have we danced before at one of these?"

My legs shook, anxiety trembling through me. I turned my head, hiding my face. "You must be thinking of someone else. I don't normally dance."

A slow smile split his face.

"First time, then? Don't be nervous, precious, I promise to be a gentleman tonight," he breathed against my cheek. "We're betrothed, after all."

That tiny, undying spark of rebellion reared its head again, my jaw grinding over my words. "Not officially."

"Semantics." He dipped me low in time with the music, my head rushing at the sudden shift in gravity. He tugged me back up, a chuckle in his chest reverberating up my spine. "But I promise to treat you well. I've been told I'm an excellent dance partner."

He winked, the innuendo raising all the hairs on my body.

I couldn't do this.

Finally, *blissfully*, the music came to a stop, and so did the spinning.

My legs were as malleable as flower petals beneath me, too boneless to stand on their own. But Drakkar did not let go, his hand still sprawled on my back, his fingers still clutching mine.

"The song is over." My voice was a whimpering half-plea, but I didn't care. I needed to get out, to get away....

I could. Not. Do. This.

"Another will start in a minute."

I pushed against his chest slightly—not hard enough to draw attention, but enough to put some much-needed space between us, so I could breathe and *think*. A half-cocked idea finally floated to the surface, and I stumbled over myself to get it out. "H-how about some refreshments first?"

He smirked, brushing a curl back over my shoulder, his fingers leaving a chill in their wake. "I'm already refreshed by your beauty."

My heart fell to the floor, tired of beating too hard.

There was no escape. No choice, no—

"May I cut in?" A dark voice spoke behind me, and my spirit soared before I even turned around.

Dark hair was slicked back to match the pitch-black suit he wore, his mask just a simple ebony silk scrap across his face.

But even in the lowlight of the chandeliers, even behind a new mask, there was no mistaking those eyes anywhere.

Green tea and honey, a laugh like nightshade.

Breezy dizziness, rooftops like sparkling treasure.

For the first time all night, I took a deep breath, my lungs hungry for clear air. For *his* air, warm and bright and real.

"You're *here*."

EIGHT

SHIN

The russet clay steps of Anastova loomed high above us, the Palace-on-the-Hill an indomitable presence. Baskets of lush, exotic plants hung from every light-post, their shadows across the steps like fingers reaching, ready to snare us.

I tugged at the itchy collar of my dress shirt as Mal and I made the slow ascent up and up, the air too humid in these parts, the wind a slow, sluggish thing coiling around me like a cobra ready to squeeze. But there was no turning back, even if the air whispered warnings in time with the merry music wafting from the grand ballroom.

"Remember the plan?" Mal murmured through red-painted lips, her wild curls tamed in a bun at the nape of her neck. A fox mask sat atop her button nose, matching the flowing, burnt-orange dress she wore. She was a vision—a living flame, a fire-fox tail swishing in the breeze. It was bold, but that was the point.

Lure and liar. Damsel and devil.

One last ruse. One final job.

If we could just make it through tonight, we'd be free, our lives no longer chained to the dregs of Hiku City. *Aya's* life no longer dangling on a single, worn thread.

"I find the princess, you distract the suitors," I repeated as I offered Mal my arm, escorting her up the last few steps. Jade-and-pearl encrusted doors opened wide to invite us in, a beast's yawning maw ready to swallow us up.

"Naveen and the twins will be waiting for us at the stables near the conservatory. We have three hours." Mal let go, halting just outside the door. Even behind her mask, her glare bore holes into my forehead, the air warming to a blistering hot around us as Malina's rage simmered. "Don't screw it up again."

My fingernails carved crescents into my palms. "Are you implying I messed up last time?"

She sucked her teeth. "We wouldn't be in this shit if you hadn't stayed too long."

"This isn't shit, it's a job. A very *profitable* one, at that," I hissed under my breath, just loud enough for her to hear. Other partygoers passed by, paying us no mind as the enchanting scene inside lured them in. Still, I dared not raise my voice a decibel. "You ask me, I say I fixed our problems."

Mal held her breath, the pixie of a girl usually content to stay angry when she was in one of her moods. But ever the professional, she shoved it down, exhaling a warm breath as her jaw unclenched. "No surprises, Shin."

I smirked, glad to have my friend back. I needed her support just as intensely as I needed the wind at my side. I flicked her nose, a familiar tease. "No promises, Mal."

I ducked just out of reach before she could swing back at me, her irritated laugh nipping at my heels as I dove into the crowd of nobles, ready to disappear into their ranks.

The ballroom sparkled brighter than a star, half-a-dozen crystal chandeliers radiating a kaleidoscope of fragmented color across the enormous room. But the people shone just as brightly, a fresco of jewels and silks and masques of every hue decorating the patrons.

Dressed in all black, I faded into the background like a shadow, but that was perfect. I needed to be forgettable, intangible as the wind that carried me.

I danced my way through the murmuring crowd, not a single self-absorbed noble looking my way. *Good.* The less that noticed me, the better. I simply had to find an easy vantage point to watch from, and wait for my opening. And as soon as there was a lull in the festivity, as soon as I could get the princess alone for a moment, I'd strike. I snagged a glass of champagne off a passing silver tray and downed it in a gulp, letting the fizzing, bubbly liquid give me wings.

If only it'd given me sense, too.

An old man in silver servant's livery stood at the bottom of a grand marble staircase as horns blared, the royal family manifesting at the top.

The crowd went still, sucking in a breath of anticipation in unison.

"Now announcing King Boris and Queen Vera of Dunyas, and their beloved daughter, Princes Catirina, Heir Apparent to the throne of Dunyas!"

Applause broke across the room, and my chest dropped.

Queen Vera glided down the stairs in a gaudy emerald contraption, weighed down in jewels that probably took two-dozen miners in the Jaltan mountains a year of dawn-to-dusk work to dig up. Next to her, the bumbling King Boris beamed, his white teeth stark against his dark skin—his smile probably designed from the same porcelain farmed and forged by work-worn, southern Dunyasian hands.

But for once in my life, it was not the greed that made my stomach stir.

The Princess walked behind them, her steps wobbly and unsure, each one matching the tempo of my slow-beating pulse. Her hand reliantly clutched the gilded rail, and fingers around my own heart squeezed. The soft pink dress swished around her form, a light wind tossing the southernmost strands of her hickory hair.

And even with the pearl-mask covering half of her face, even though pink flushed her bronze skin in a way soft green did not...

I'd recognize her anywhere.

I'd seen her in every dream I'd had for a week.

The girl from the bar.

Princess Catirina.

My *mark.*

In a single breath of a moment, the crowd swarmed the royals, and I lost her again. Talk buzzed around me in different keys, like an orchestra of mismatched players tuning before the overture began. My ears strained against the chorus, trying to pick out the single instrument of her voice.

But then the real music started, swelling as an upbeat waltz breathed life into the grand room. The crowd moved with it, nobles lining up to dance, bows and curtsies the first choreographed steps of the night. It was a routine I'd learned long ago, one where partners swapped in and out, meeting each other again, old and new—

And in the middle of the dance floor, ignoring the structured flow of the dance, the princess swayed in the arms of a tall blond man in a gray suit.

Drakkar.

The wolf that'd already tried to sink his teeth into her once.

A wolf that clearly hadn't learned his fucking lesson.

Forgetting my mission, forgetting exactly whose *mother* employed this endeavor, I moved, too.

But a mousy brown head of ringlets blocked my path, a pale girl in a violet dress curtseying before me, a jeweled tiara nestled in her complicated up-do.

Wide brown eyes blinked up at me, the young noblewoman flushed with embarrassment. "May I have this dance?"

I raised my head, watching that swath of alluring pink float further away, but unease settled in my stomach.

I couldn't just storm up to her, couldn't rip her from Drakkar's arms—

And I couldn't flat out reject the poor girl in front of me. That kind of disrespect for decorum would turn too many heads, would betray my position as *other…*

And put me farther from my target.

I nodded, offering her a hand. With shaking fingers, she took it, and we both were moving in tempo.

My feet took a moment to remember the steps, stumbling at first, but my muscles could not quite forget the *three-two-one* that had been hammered into me as a boy.

The dance brought the girl close, but I kept my arms stiff as I led, allowing a breath of space between us. I looked over her short head again, to where the Princess still danced out of time with Drakkar. But the girl smiled up at me, brown eyes crinkling with the action.

"My name is Hana of Sora," a flute-like voice chirped, matching her tiny stature perfectly. "What's yours?"

I blinked at her, panic fluttering in my chest from a moment as I scraped for an answer.

Princess Hana, if I remembered correctly.

I was not supposed to be here. To be dancing with a princess, with *anyone* that could potentially remember seeing me here at all.

But I had to give her an alias before I stuck both of my feet in my mouth.

"I, uh...Vo-ix. Vox, I mean," I picked the first Dunyasian name I could think of. "Of Dunyas."

Lashes batted in a frenzy. "Vox. What an interesting name. I don't think I've seen you before—"

The music paused and shifted, the signal to the dancers that a partner switch was in order.

Relief flooded my veins as I spun her away, "Have a nice night."

Her face fell, but a man in a green suit and a bird mask quickly recovered it for her, offering his hand with a genuine grin.

I took the pause to scan the room again, looking for the Princess—

She was only halfway across the room now, just a few bodies between us, but the Nehir bastard hadn't let her out of his hold, his hand pressing into her back in a far more intimate way than the dance called for.

I darted around two more noble girls, cutting in front of a round older man in a red cravat who was closing in on a girl half his age. I didn't care about the woman he danced with, but it put me closer to my goal, one more rotation before I could get to the Princess.

"Hey, that's—" he protested as I stepped up to his dance partner, offering her my hand with a bow, but he didn't finish the sentence as she graciously took the bait I offered, spinning in time with the music.

Luckily for me, she was quiet for the first movement of the routine, barely looking my way. Perhaps she was just grateful to have avoided the other man's attention, which suited my needs just fine.

The choreography brought her as close as her overstuffed, cream-colored dress allowed, the rich fabric carving ample space between our frames.

But the swan mask that covered her face was familiar in a way I hadn't expected. Her dark, straight hair had streaks of rebellious scarlet in it, and it was tucked tight to her head in a design that sparked recognition in my most hidden parts.

The Jaltan pursed her lips as she asked a question that set my heartbeat to double-time. "Do I–do I *know* you from somewhere?"

I turned my face away too fast, fear thrashing against my ribcage.

"Unlikely," I coughed, faking the heavy, vowel-stretching Dunyasian accent as best as I could. "New around here."

"It's just—" she started, then stopped. "Nevermind."

She stayed blissfully silent for the last of the partnership, twirling away when the music demanded without a look back, onto the next partner.

Relief blew away the sweat from the back of my neck as I set my sights on my final destination.

One last dance.

The music stopped as the song reached its conclusion, and the players readied their next symphony.

Drakkar still held her, but her small hand pushed at his chest, and it was the only invitation I needed, interrupting just as I had a week ago at the Crescent.

"May I cut in?" I cleared my throat, eyes locked on Drakkar's face. Bruises peeked from beneath his mask, and a sick sense of triumph rattled through me.

But it was the Princess who responded, a small breath blowing from her round lips as she swiveled to face me. "You're *here.*"

Something in my chest leapt at the words, a bird learning to fly for the first time on the back of a new breeze.

Why *was* I here? By the Breath, what was I doing?

Why couldn't I *stop*?

One dance. One look. One night.

Drakkar's smile darkened to a grimace as he tucked Catirina under his possessive arm. "Don't worry, friend, we're fine here."

He didn't recognize me from the bar; otherwise, he would've already pitched a tantrum like Kas used to when we didn't let him eat candy before bed. And Ecei had instructed us to keep quiet with her son about her dealings, so he surely didn't know my ultimate goal.

But I couldn't help myself as I took another step, breathing him in, my smile made of daggers. "This dance calls to swap partners."

"Oh, my, I wouldn't want to be impolite," Princess Catirina jumped in, long eyelashes fluttering as she worked her con on him well enough to impress Malina. She squeezed the Prince's arm before taking a careful step toward me—only her shaking hand betraying her actual discomfort. "Drakkar, how about we dance the next one?"

The Prince's eyes flicked between us as he ground his teeth, but he tucked his metaphorically tied hands behind his back. The lovely scene around us was a prison of decorum that even a prick like him couldn't break free of. "I'll go get us those refreshments."

He stalked off without another glance back, and Catirina loosed a breath as she watched him go, full lips curling upward.

"I feel refreshed already," I scoffed; something roared with victory in my chest as the orchestra began their next tune, the first velvety violin notes of a slow waltz singing through the air. With a deep breath, I extended a hand. "Princess Catirina?"

This time, when she placed her warm palm in mine, a jolt of electricity ran up my arm.

And then, we were dancing.

Flying.

My feet followed the steps by muscle memory; but this time, there was a lightness, my mind captivated not by the routine, but by the opal-and-pearl mask in front of me, by the silk between her shoulder blades that brushed my fingertips, by the glorious warmth of her hand in mine...

"Lord..." she started, and then giggled, the sound brighter than the flute's distant trilling. "I don't even know your name."

"Shi—" I started, and then stopped, remembering the lie I was supposed to tell tonight, the ruse I was supposed to be keeping as tight as the mask on my face. Guilt surged in my stomach, and I missed a step, tripping over my own two feet and almost toppling us both. "Shit, sorry."

The princess tossed her head back in a laugh that sent her satin curls cascading over her bare shoulder. "Your name is Shit Sorry? You must not be from around here."

Delight stirred again in my middle, chasing away the lingering taste of dread from the back of my tongue. Renewed and revived, I carried her along to the music again, spinning and twirling in time with the orchestra's swells and dips.

"My name is Vox Koishi." I offered a lie and a truth together, some strange part of me desperate to be seen, to be *known*. "You're radiant."

That stare flicked up to me, and only then did I realize I'd said the last bit aloud. Heat flushed the back of my neck as I searched for a cover up, but found my tongue lame and useless.

"Thank you." She beamed, sheepishly hanging her head, an action that brought her unconsciously a step closer, barely a breath between us. She looked up again, the corners of her mouth downturned. "But it's the dress."

A flurry of emotions slammed together in my chest, so fast it was hard to differentiate them, like trying to pick out specific snowflakes in a blizzard. I was in too deep already, wandering too far off into the unknown. I had to get back to my base, had to remember the mission that brought me here, and what—no, *who*— was at stake if I failed.

The Princess was lovely, but she had everything. She didn't deserve Drakkar pawing at her, but if anyone had the resources and access to stop his advances, it was her. She lived in this splendor and extravagance, breathed it in and ate it for breakfast, whereas my sister—my poor, innocent sister—sat waiting for me in the Treehouse, cold and sick and *dying*. She was the one who really needed me.

But there was a riotous, blaring part of me that wanted to dance in the chaos, that wanted to bathe in this woman's warmth and light for just a moment more, that wanted to see her glowing smile one last time before I had to be the one to kidnap it from her.

Despite my better judgment, despite the very reason I was here tonight, despite everything at stake...

One last secret. One last smile.

I leaned in, whispering against the exposed shell of her ear, "This dress *is* pretty, but not everyone can make a green riding cloak look like a ballgown."

My words were unassuming, but the message hidden beneath was a call into the night, louder than the music surging around us.

See me. Remember me.

"It *is* you," she gasped, clutching my hand tighter, her smile brighter than the chandeliers dangling above us. She stumbled to a stop, halting us both as she looked up at me; expectant, *wanting*. "What are you—?"

"May I cut in?" A wobbling voice dragged me from the trance of her stare, a round face with a neck beard peeking over Catirina's shoulder. The man was a head shorter than her, the burgundy fabric of his suit hugging his slim, boyish frame, but he kept his chin high as he looked up at Catirina, the Jaltan national emblem carved into the side of his silver mask.

Lord Avi. Nephew to King Odion. Another suitor.

Something itched beneath my skin, green and contagious as it spread through me.

"Oh, I–" Irina spun to face him, her hand still clasping mine. She offered a polite smile, fumbling as he waited expectantly—

"Excuse me, sir, may I have this next one?" another interruption, this time from a voice I could pick out from a crowd of thousands.

Malina's smile was warm, but her gaze was hot enough to burn the sun itself to cinders, contempt and reproach radiating from her tiny frame in waves of rolling heat.

I swallowed hard, shame washing over me like a kid caught with his hand in the candy jar. But there was no escaping her wrath, not now, not without a public display of violence that would rattle the very foundations of Anastova.

"Save the next dance for me." It was a plea, not a request, as I gave

Catirina's hand a squeeze before turning her toward the neck-bearded oaf. The disappointment swimming in her eyes cut deeper than a knife to the ribs, but she nodded, taking the Jaltan's hand.

I bowed to Malina in the customary fashion before sweeping her up in the dance.

"We can't be seen together," I said through a tight smile, avoiding her gaze entirely as I scanned the crowd around us. Many people ignored us entirely, swept up in their own dances, while others were distracted by Lord Avi and Catirina bumbling around the floor together. I exhaled, a small kernel of relief rooting itself within me. "But make this quick."

"What the hell was that, Shin?" Malina hissed as we glided across the floor, puncturing and bleeding out any comfort I'd felt in the moment before. "Dancing with her so publicly? Interrupting others?"

Part of me knew she was right, and I hated it. This was not the plan. My role was supposed to be a shadow, a phantom that no one could place at all, but I'd soiled that on a whim and a wish that could never come true.

But the wind was a shifting, ever changing thing, never stuck in one shape, always expanding to fit its container. And my wickedness would be just as malleable, my arsenal of tricks not yet bled dry.

I could save this. Save us. Save Aya.

And maybe save a lost princess in a gilded cage from some half-baked suitors that didn't deserve to walk across the same ground as her.

One last game. One final chance.

I shrugged as I dipped Mal. "I gained her trust."

"You drew attention to yourself."

"It's easier if she willingly comes to me rather than us try and force her out," I snapped back, my voice tight as a violin string. "I know what I'm doing."

Or at least, I'd figure it out.

Ecei paid me to get the Princess to the Treehouse. She did not pay me to make her fall in love with Drakkar, or to make sure their union went well. That part of the plan was entirely hers to fuck up on her own, and once I had what I needed for Aya and the Lost Ones...

Well, perhaps it was time to start dreaming about *after*.

Golden eyes leveled on me, Malina's knowing stare scraping beneath the bluff. "Do you?"

She twirled away again, leaving me in the ash of her fiery wake with a stone in my stomach that could keep even the wind from flying.

But the last spark of hope I had lit like a dry wick as she sauntered over to Lord Avi and Catirina, tapping the former on the shoulder with her most winning smile.

A gift...or perhaps a chance to prove myself.

Liar and lure. Damsel and devil.

She winked at me so fast no one else would catch it, but I understood the meaning clear as day.

One more shot.

When the young, toe-faced lord accepted her hand, leaving Catirina behind, I moved.

"I'll take it from here," I said before the man in the green suit and ridiculous bird mask could get his turn.

He frowned like a spoiled child. "But—"

I didn't hear the last of his words as I wound my arm around Catirina's waist and took her free hand, propelling us back in time with the music.

But this time, I did not abide the choreography, instead letting my feet tread a path of their own, fueled by the music: the light twinkling of the piano, the deep lullaby of the cellos, the broad declarations of the woodwinds. Something thrummed deep in my chest, a call and answer I hadn't heard in years, the wind's song a foreign language as it sang something *new* in my veins.

Catirina's gaze did not leave mine, her hand firmly planted on my shoulder in a white-hot touch. Nor did she miss a beat, trusting me to lead the dance, moving with me in strange synchronization. Even as her cheeks flushed pink and her breath drew short, our tempo fervent and free, she kept pace.

"That's not how this dance is supposed to go," she whispered, but she did not pull back, breathing me in, following my steps.

"I don't care." A lie, to her and myself. Then, "I couldn't help myself." A truth, more dangerous than any other.

I dropped her hand, planting both of my palms on either side of her waist. Then, as the music drove toward its last crescendo, I dipped low before lifting her above my head, the rustle of pink skirts in harmony with the sway of the retarding melody. A surprised giggle tore from softly parted lips as I lowered her gently again, her arms wound around my neck.

"I'm glad." A breathless sigh rattled through her, her fingertips against the sensitive patch of skin at my hairline sending shivers down my spine.

I didn't realize when the music stopped. Didn't realize we'd stopped, too, both of us just standing there, our eyes locked.

Our breaths mingling. Our hearts beating in time.

Until the King of Dunyas cleared his throat behind me, shattering the quiet with the force of a rockslide. "Catirina, come say a proper hello to Avi, will you?"

His arms crossed over his massive chest as he stared at his daughter, his mouth a terse line.

Catirina blinked at him, then me, like she too had been swept away in the daydream of our dance. "I..."

"Go." I planted a kiss on her knuckles, murmuring low against her soft skin, the wind carrying my message so only she could hear. "Meet me in the conservatory when you can get away."

Catirina frowned, but nodded once before following the King, the pair of them walking toward the foot-faced boy and the middle-aged man from earlier that had been ogling younger girls—assumedly Lord Avi's father.

"Who was that boy?" The wind swept the King's suspicious inquiry toward me as they fled, Catirina glancing back over her shoulder once.

"No one, Papa."

If only she meant it.

If only I wanted her to.

NINE

Vox.

Vox.

Vox.

Like a heartbeat, his name beat against my ribs over and over, drowning out the droning conversations that dragged during the formal dinner. Mama's whining gossip as she chattered with Queen Ecei, Hana's shrill laugh and Naria's polite chuckles, Avi's stuttered questions about the most absurd topics, Drakkar's vile innuendos and my father's half-chewed opinions... they all faded into the background, the percussive reminder of *him* the only thing pulsing in my mind.

Of course, Vox was absent throughout, only Mother and Father's closest allies getting to sit at the King's private feast. Ecei and Drakkar sat next to my mother, placing Drakkar in my direct eyesight, whereas Lord Avi sat to my left, his father, Lord Hizan, and Princess Naria of Jalta completing our side of the table. Across from them, Hana of Sora, her younger brother, Haro, and King Lin represented the air territory, all major kingdoms accounted for. The rest of the partygoers would wait outside, Vox included, eating from the generous buffet the servants had set up in the main ballroom.

But even with all of the most 'important' people in Babylon sat around my table, I barely paid any of them attention. Even Hana, who'd once been like a sister, her and my brother's relationship a constant through the years. I used to follow her around at the Masques, hanging on her every word as she taught me the ways of the world with her soft smile and snuck me champagne with a shimmering smirk.

But tonight, I couldn't be bothered, my mind fully occupied, too excited about the future for once to linger in the past.

I'd sit through a thousand stuffy dinners for just another dance with *him*. For another moonlit moment of freedom, for another chance to feel his hands on my waist, the world shrinking as he lifted me into the air like I was no heavier than a feather...

"Catirina, you hardly touched your food." My father stabbed a piece of the steak from my plate, forking it into his own mouth. "It's getting cold."

I blinked, coming back to the dining room, back to the normally empty table now filled with my should-be friends. I cleared my throat, setting down the fork I'd been absentmindedly twirling in my hand. "I'm really not feeling my best."

It was not a lie. I felt like I was floating, untethered to the world, a planet in orbit around a new and glorious sun.

"Then perhaps the Princess should get some rest?" Drakkar leaned forward, the picture of false concern painted across his drawn brows. We'd all taken off our masks to eat, the bruising around his nose now on full display. I stifled a smirk as he placed his hand over his heart, turning to my father. "I wouldn't want her to stay on our account. Her health is my first priority."

My mother swooned, but my father nodded, looking at me again like I was just a little girl up past her bedtime. "Perhaps it *is* time for you to retire, Irina. We need you well."

But I wasn't a little girl anymore. In just a week, something had changed and grown within me, a butterfly cracking through the confines of its cocoon.

Still, I would not forfeit the opportunity to escape this cage, the conservatory calling my name like a siren's distant song. I stood, bowing to our guests. "Please excuse me, and thank you all for coming."

Ecei wiped her mouth with her cloth napkin, nudging her son in the ribs. "Drakkar, why don't you escort the Princess to her quarters?"

Drakkar choked on the piece of chicken he was swallowing, pushing up from the table awkwardly. "Yes, of course."

I shook my head—too fast, too eagerly—feigning a smile to cover my panic. "No, please, I wouldn't want you to miss out on dessert! Our cook Tasha makes the best sweets. I'm happy to go by myself."

Drakkar stepped forward. "But—"

"Oh, I'll walk with you, 'Rina!" Hana burst from her seat down the table, her ringlets bouncing with the action. A bright smile captivated her small face.

Dread knotted my stomach, but I fought to keep my own polite grin in place. "Oh, Hana—"

"I really insist." She skipped around the table, violet skirts swishing. She was two years older than me at twenty-three, yet it seemed her girlish demeanor would never change. "It's been ages since we've had us-time!"

At that, Papa clapped his hands, the first budding tears lining the corners of his eyes. "Excellent idea! Your excitement makes me happy to see." He stroked his beard, an old habit when his heart wore heavy. But he kept his voice bright, head high. "Hana, you know we still see you as family."

The room went silent, all life sucked out of it, the hole in my chest collapsing into a black pit.

No one said what we all were thinking: if Nikolaj was still here, Hana might have been the next queen.

Another lonely girl my brother abandoned. No; a girl the Blight had made a widow before she'd even gotten the chance to be a wife.

She linked her arm through mine and hugged me close to her side. "I'll see my little sister out, then."

Drakkar dropped back in his seat with a resigned huff, but no one looked up from their plates, suddenly intrigued by the porcelain. Not even Ecei dared protest, her thin lips welded tight together.

Hana turned her too-bright smile on me, and even though she was half a head shorter, I felt smaller than a babe. With surprising strength, she pulled me from the room, calling over her shoulder, "Goodnight, everyone!"

Grateful as I was to be in the hallway again, away from Avi's incessant chatter and Drakkar's possessive stare, the tug in my center pulled taut; the conservatory was half a castle away and in the opposite direction. The chatter and clinking glasses from the ballroom downstairs floated like music toward us, but it was a chorus I would not be joining again, a different song humming inside.

Vox.

Vox.

Vox.

I had to lose my chaperone, nice as it was for her to rescue me. As painful as it was to leave her alone again.

"You really didn't have to—"

Hana spun, round eyes narrowing as she stepped in front of me, blocking my path. "Oh, please, I saw the way you were dancing with *him* before." She smirked, sticking her hands to her hips. My stomach dropped, fear prickling at the back of my neck, but she giggled, covering her mouth. "His name was Vox, right? Are you meeting him now?"

Heat flushed my cheeks, my breath short and sharp in my chest. "That's—I don't—"

She pressed her finger to my lips with a wink.

"Hush. Your secret is safe with me. I remember what that was like, with Niki." Her gaze softened, a wistfulness dragging her away for a moment. My ribs ached, the thought of my brother stabbing through me twice in as many minutes; but I couldn't imagine how hard it must have been for Hana, his would-be-queen and should-have-been wife. Her throat worked as she swallowed. "Go to him. If anyone comes looking for you and can't find you in your rooms, I'll be your cover. We'll say we had a sleepover like old times."

Something kindred bloomed in my chest, a flower that had never gotten its chance to take root, but still managed to blossom anyway. Hana was not my sister by law, but she was in action, a kindness I would not soon forget.

I grabbed her hand, squeezing it once. "I owe you."

"Yes, you do." She squeezed back, "And I will take my payment in all of the details about that handsome new beau of yours."

A sigh of relief blew from my lips, not just for her kindness, but in the knowledge that I still had a *friend* in this prison. That I was not alone...not if I didn't want to be. If I let myself live, and let someone else *in*. "Breakfast tomorrow, then? I'll have Tasha make the blueberry scones."

"It's a deal. Don't do anything Nikolaj wouldn't do—actually, scratch that," she laughed, the sound full of both joy and unending sorrow. "Don't do anything he *would*."

I pressed a quick kiss to her cheek, nodding once before turning on my heel to go.

Nikolaj would be proud of the girl I was tonight, taking risks and letting myself follow my own drumbeat for once, not dancing to Mama's rules or rhythm.

But I couldn't think of him, couldn't linger in that sadness.

A beat pulsed on, calling *his* name.

Vox.

Vox.

Vox.

"Vox?" I whispered as I walked through the conservatory doors, the gentle haze of gold and green enveloping me, plants of every shape and size hanging and growing in metallic planters. It was a display of the Teramentals' mastery, that such *life* could grow amidst the gold and glass, but for once; I was not here to get lost in the cultivated wilderness.

I was on a hunt.

The room was too humid, the air so thick sweat clung to the small of my back in an instant. But the fragrant plants scented the air sweeter than Tasha's baking, and the night sky glittered above through the glass ceiling, giving the space a false openness. The trickling of the grand fountain in the center was the only music present, not even the sound of another breath reaching my ears.

My stomach fell, disappointment crawling over my too-warm skin. Did he not come? Had he left already?

I wandered deeper, the plants closing in on me, branches arching like the bars of my cage...

"Hi." Vox grinned as he popped out from behind a bush of Mama's favorite tiger-lilies, misting in front of me faster than a ghost.

"Oh!" I stumbled back, my shock quickly fleeing to make way for relief.

He was *here*.

I blew out a grateful breath. "There you are. You spooked me."

Still in his black suit, he stepped out from his strange hiding spot, brushing off the errant dirt from his trousers. But he'd abandoned his black mask, those honeyed-tea eyes on full display.

My breath caught as he stared at me, his chest rising and falling as he took me in. His grin expanded to a full smile. "Sorry for hiding, I didn't know if you'd show, and I didn't want to get caught by anyone else." He tucked his hands behind his back, rocking on his heels. A deep dimple appeared on his cheek. "Walk with me?"

I mangled out a nod, and he laced his hand through mine, tugging us forward.

My heart danced a brisk jig as I followed him further into the conservatory, jasmine blossoms and peonies and rare orchids reaching toward us, curious spectators to our rendezvous. But my thoughts centered solely on his hand in mine, his palm a cool counter to my clammy one. And for once in my life, I was too nervous to be self-conscious, my head spinning at the contact.

I cleared my throat, grasping for any conversation to break the awkward quiet that'd settled between my lips. "If it's not too forward to ask...what you were doing at that bar in *Hiku City*, of all places?"

Vox slowed, twisting to face me. "I could ask you the same thing, *Princess.*"

I shrugged, masking the way my chest squeezed tight. "Can't a girl want a night of freedom before her future is signed away to the highest bidder?"

His eyes narrowed, like he was trying to unknot some tangled thing in his head at that comment. But that mesmerizing, elicit dimple remerged, chasing away any disquiet. "Can't a man need a breath of fresh air?"

"I could use some, too," I admitted, my sweaty palm trembling in his. I jerked my head toward the garden doors, the sprawling lawns beyond beckoning. Maybe out there, I could catch my breath, could slow my hammering heart. "Walk outside with me? My mother keeps this place too hot."

Vox snorted in agreement before leading the way again, unlatching the door with swift fingers and twirling me out into the welcoming night. My giggle floated into the suddenly open air, dancing away on the breeze that ruffled my skirts.

A glassy, star-studded black sky greeted us, the air outside of a friendlier sort, and I inhaled deeply, tasting the fresh-cut grass and sleeping roses of the towering garden hedges.

"Much better," Vox murmured, but his gaze did not leave my face, calling forth a new blush that had nothing to do with the heat. I hoped the glow of the golden lamps softened the shade of red.

Despite my embarrassment, I took a brave step toward him, the evening shadows emboldening parts of me I didn't know I possessed. "So, my cloaked rescuer, what were you running from that night?" I quirked a brow, but it quickly fell, a new pit opening up inside me as clearer memories rushed in. I tugged my hand back, realizing he'd never dropped it, a sickness souring the air. "Wait, didn't you say you had a—a *girl*—?"

This time, it was Vox who laughed, the sound just as wicked and wonderful as I'd remembered. "You misunderstand. She's my little sister."

"Oh." The single syllable blurted from me, a victory cry blaring through my heart.

It shouldn't have mattered–I barely knew this man. Yet it did, more than I cared to admit.

Vox's laugh fled, the corners of his mouth dipping. His gaze tore from me, his profile cast in creeping shadows as he stared out into the gardens. "She's...sick. I guess I needed a break from the responsibility."

I didn't need to ask to know he meant the Blight, the grim set of his jaw one I could pinpoint on any face, old or new. Something in my chest pulled taut, the weight that drooped his shoulders one I knew well—though he carried his *for* his sibling, whereas mine had saddled me with it, along with the dark grief of his absence in my world and a crown.

"What's her name?" I whispered, winding my hand through his again, relishing the cool touch.

He swallowed, turning back to me, a new mask of something dark veiling his features. "Aya."

"Pretty."

"You are."

I blinked, disarmed again.

I gulped down words I was not yet courageous enough to spout, instead pivoting faster than the dancers in the ballroom beyond. I walked along the lit path, our hands still linked and swinging between us, the tall hedges surrounding us fully, though part of me wished they'd swallow me whole. My heels echoing along the stone walk, I reached for a new topic that would lead me to safer ground...or that would at least distract me again from the calloused skin beneath my fingertips.

"Your name is strange, though. Vox is Dunyasian, but Koishi is what, Soran?"

Surprise lifted his brows. "You're quite the linguist."

"My brother had a knack for languages. It rubbed off." I didn't try to hide the sadness in my tone, nor the pride, Vox's soothing presence somehow giving me the strength to summon both. Everything good I knew came from Nikolaj, his wisdom and mischief both keeping me company even now that he was gone. And for the first time in a long time, I wanted to share those bits with someone else, not just keep them tucked close to my chest where no one could take them from me. "You would've liked him. He had a rebel streak, too."

"I heard about what happened to him, and I'm sure you've had your fill of *sorries.*" He slowed us both and gave my hand a squeeze.

"But from what I've heard, he was the closest thing to a decent noble that exists in our world."

Tears burned at the back of my eyes, but I blinked them away.

"Not a fan of your own kind, then?" I snorted in surprise, but not a disagreement in the slightest. Nikolaj was the best of us all, noble or not. Then again, reaching for something more palatable, "Koishi—I feel like I've heard of them before. As in the Koishi silk traders, from Sora?"

He looked away again, lips thinning to a line as he let go of my hand. "One and the same, though I'm not much involved in the family business."

The darkness that colored his tone was a warning flag, a sign not to press. But though I desperately missed his hand in mine, I did my best to weather the sudden storm, shrugging to dispel my own anxiety. "Wish I could say the same."

"You don't like being the Princess?" He squinted at me, the corner of his mouth twitching to a grin.

I sighed, trudging up to a nearby bench, plopping onto the stone seat. "No."

"Why not?" His long legs carried him gracefully, and he lowered himself next to me. His shoulder brushed against mine, sending a new wave of goosebumps across my flesh. But there was something that edged his tone and scraped beneath my skin, guilt prickling across my arms and back as he spoke, "You have *everything* here."

"All of this?" I waved vaguely at the hedges and the looming palace behind us. "It's meaningless. It's not happiness."

No, happiness was a moonlit dance and a jaunt through Hiku City. Or the glorious surge of an opera house, with my brother humming along next to me.

"But you're the Princess. One day, the Queen. If you don't like the way things are, change them," Vox scoffed.

I snapped to face him, fisting my silken skirts, wishing I could tear them to shreds with my bare hands. "I can't even change *clothes* without stoking my mother's contempt. I've never been offered a single choice for myself, and it's—" I quelled the hot rage that burned my throat, swallowing it back. My grip on the fabric went white as I wrangled my emotions under control. "I'm sorry, I've said way too much."

His hand covered mine, and my clutch slackened beneath it. His eyes flicked up, stoking something else in my chest. "No, I get it. I wish I had other choices, too." His thumb rubbed a soft circle across my skin, and a shudder ran down my spine. Then, "If you could choose, what would you do?"

I paused, breath catching in my chest. "No one has ever asked me that before."

"Well, think about it." Vox's gaze bore into mine, an urgency burning in it. He turned, leaning close, clasping my hand tighter. "Say I *could* sweep you away right now and take you exactly where you wanted to go, and I could give you the life you wanted...what would you ask for? Where would we go?"

I stopped breathing, a single word tingling through my skull.
We.

A truth unlocked, a desperate wish for that *we* blossoming in my core.

"Hiku City Opera House." I straightened my shoulders, the command a dangerous declaration of desire.

"What?" His brow knotted, almost puncturing my ballooning hope. "That place burnt down years ago—"

But I shook my head. I would not be deterred, his earlier words singing in my soul.

If you don't like the way things are, change them.

It was something Nikolaj might have said.

"So?" I lifted my chin in mock authority, the first decree of a would-be Queen tumbling from my lips. "You asked what I wanted. Well, I'd want to be a singer at the Hiku City Opera. So you'll just have to restore it for me, Vox Koishi. Your princess demands it."

His eyes glittered brighter than the stars, his dimple a wide valley I wanted to explore.

"Spoiled much?" He swallowed, his throat working hard as his gaze dipped to my mouth.

Under his scrutiny, my tongue darted out to run over my bottom lip, my torso moving forward on its own volition, like a magnet pulling my very soul. "Always the gentleman."

"Well, if my princess demands it," Vox leaned in close, one loadstone calling another. My heart thudded so loudly in my chest, I almost missed his next words. "Let's go. Right now."

The tether snapped, and I sat back. "*What?*"

"Hiku City Opera." His mindless fingers toyed with the end of a curl that'd fallen forward; there was nothing but pure, primal intention in his eyes, a promise swimming in their mossy pools. "I'll fly us there right now."

There was no doubt in my mind that he meant it, too.

But a swarm of worry buzzed through my head, the glass of my vase pressing in around me. "But the party, my *parents*..."

"You'll come back in no time, and they'll all be waiting to scold you then." He blew out a laugh, but his gaze scanned my face, searching for something I didn't know that I could offer. But he pressed on, a gentle determination lacing his baritone, "Or, you could stay, and they'll scold you for something else anyway. I'm offering you a *choice*."

I stilled, the world coming in and out of focus.

A *choice*.

An adventure.

One last night in Hiku City Opera. A night with a man whose every word set something new on fire in my soul. Whose every movement made my heart skip two beats.

But the 'yes' that parted my lips did not get a chance to escape as a form lunged from the hedges, thick arms wrapping around me like vines of steel.

A scream tore from my throat instead, and a man's hard body yanked me upright like I weighed nothing, caging my arms at my sides.

"Got her!" he grunted in my ear.

"Naveen, no!" Vox cried as he vaulted from the bench, but my captor took a step back, and Vox halted.

Dread rumbled through me like a rockslide.

He knew my captor's name?

"Let me go!" I wriggled against the man's hold to no avail, all other thoughts rushing from me as the panic rose to boiling in my blood. "That is a command from your princess!"

"Hold still, milady." He squeezed tighter, restricting my movements. Hefting me up, he pushed forward, moving fast despite my weight. Helplessness sank to my toes, my heart racing.

Another flash, and two more bodies flew from the hedges on near silent feet. Two boys, black cloaks wrapped around their shoulders, their matching faces half-covered by scraps of cloth.

One splashed water at my wrists and ankles, the other snapping his fingers...

And they bound me in ice.

I thrashed again, but the ice bit at my skin so hard it drew blood.

"Help me, please!" I whipped my head around to Vox, desperate, begging—

He moved fast as the wind, my rescuer finally springing into motion—

And fell into step *next* to my assailant.

A sobering calm froze its way through my veins, every muscle in my body going rigid as reality crashed against my mind.

"This isn't necessary, you idiots," Vox growled at the man—no, *Naveen*, he knew his *name.* I glared at him, hurt tremoring through me, but Vox kept his eyes forward, avoiding my gaze.

"Dammit, Shin, you were supposed to be here an hour ago, we're losing precious time." Another voice— a woman's—hissed, as a small girl in an orange gown materializing from the hedges as well.

Recognition sang through me. She'd been at the party, she'd been dancing with Vox....

No, not Vox.

Shin.

His name was Shin.

And this was all a trap of his sick design.

"You manipulative *shit!*" I bellowed, a rare, visceral rage steaming out of me, my voice an earthquake shaking my whole frame.

"Shh, quiet, sorry." Naveen clamped his broad hand around my mouth, moving faster. "We can't alert the guards."

Shin's eyes finally flicked to me, but there was no familiarity in them, just a hard adamant wall of purpose.

Real, genuine terror finally gripped me by the throat, silencing all protests.

The guards were all in the palace tonight, or lining the front steps. No one was supposed to be 'trampling around' in the gardens—Mama's orders.

They wouldn't hear me from here, no matter how loud I screamed.

No one was coming for me.

I was being *kidnapped.*

"You, there!" A gruff voice ordered as we wove through the hedges, and my heart leapt, new hope flying through me. A man—no, a *guard*—stepped from around the corner, buttoning up his trousers beneath his armor.

A guard, taking a pee break. In the wrong place, but at the Mother-Blessedly right time.

He grunted. "What's this ruckus?"

Naveen dropped me onto my own feet, but his hand still clamped around my arm, holding me to him as he whispered to Shin, "I thought there weren't guards on this patrol."

But this was my chance. I tugged free of his grip in a quick jolt of strength, my voice hoarse as I screamed, "Help! It's me, Catirina—help!"

The guard went still, his hand flying to the sword as his hip. "Princess?"

"Yes!" A sob tore from my lips as I hopped toward him despite my bound ankles, dizzy and desperate. "Help, please, I'm being kidnapped!"

"Oh yes, please, help us!" The other girl knocked me over as she nudged past me, my knees slamming painfully as I hit the ground. *Lying witch.* I groaned, agony shooting up my legs as she flung herself into the guard's arms, crocodile tears suddenly streaming down her cheeks. "These thugs found us, they're taking us—"

I pushed back up on my hands, panic rattling my heart again. "Not her, she's one of them!"

"Everyone, halt," the guard growled, eyes darting between the girl and me as he unsheathed his sword, dropping into a defensive position. The others went still, Shin and Naveen and the boys all throwing their hands up in surrender. Relief washed over me as he pointed his blade at the girl, the sharp end coming right below her chin. "What in Mother Earth's—?"

In a movement so fast I almost missed it, the girl twirled beneath his blade, and held up something white to his face–

She clamped the cloth over his mouth.

His eyes rolled back in his head, and his sword clattered to the ground.

Then he did.

Every bone in my body shook with fear as I eyed the girl, small as she was, as she stood over him, the victor in this duel.

This was not a game, and she was certainly not playing.

The girl stuffed the cloth back into the folds of her dress, her head on a swivel as she scanned the hedges. "Keep moving, before we attract others."

"We said no killing, Malina," Shin whisper-yelled as he shot to the guard's side, fingers flying to his neck for a pulse. But even from here, I could see the guard's chest rising and falling, slow, steady breaths snoring from him.

"Don't worry, Shin, he's just unconscious. It's a mild dose," Naveen cautioned as he lifted me and tucked me over his shoulder again; this time, I didn't protest, horror numbing me body and soul. He picked up his pace, jostling me without letting up his iron hold as we turned the corner out of the gardens and toward the south stables, a dark carriage already horsed and ready. The twins darted ahead, one opening the carriage door, and Naveen hurled me into it.

The other twin followed me inside, shards of ice like blades in either hand, his expression unreadable as he clipped out cool words. "Sorry, milady, but you have to stay put, or we'll have to dose you, too."

I marked the ice, fear leadening my limbs into submission. There was no way I'd make it past him without being skewered. And though I knew that if this was a mission to kill me, I'd already be dead, the cold glare of the boy and Malina's calculated cruelty were enough to caution me from attempting anything foolish.

But a small, rebellious spark found the courage to look past him, to where Shin stood just outside the door, firing fast hand signals at the girl.

"You—" My voice quaked with a vicious blend of hurt and rage, my eyes prickling with tears. "You *tricked* me."

His jaw clenched as his eyes snapped to me, a crack splintering in the wall of darkness behind them. "I can explain everything, I promise."

But without anything else, he looked down as he stepped into the carriage, ducking his head before slumping onto the bench across from me. The girl quickly followed, shutting the door behind her, while Naveen and the other twin circled around to the coach's seat.

A stone settled in me as the carriage started rolling, defeat and panic battling in my tossing gut.

I'd *trusted* him.

I'd been a fool.

"*You tricked me,*" I repeated, each word a cut this time, my anger at both him and myself a dagger in my hand. "But I swear, whatever you all are plotting, whatever you *think* you're getting away with, when *my mother* finds out, you will all be hunted like the pigs you are, and I will personally see to it that you rot in prison for the rest of your—"

Without warning, the boy next to me moved, slashing out and smacking me in the face with another flash of white—

A cloth.

Blackness dragged me under.

TEN

SHIN

Men were wicked, vile creatures, and I was no different—a fact I'd proven to the world and myself tonight.

Catirina was still fast asleep when the carriage pulled into the airfield just outside of Anabrevi Forest, the second leg of our trip home carefully plotted and funded by Ecei. Naveen's deep *whoa* slowed the horses, and Catirina's chest rose and fell in even, full breaths, her mouth slightly open, her head lolled against the window.

It wasn't supposed to go like this.

She was supposed to come willingly, swept away into a bright promise of the next adventure. I was supposed to be her *savior*, not her captor.

It hadn't been the original plan, but it was the only one that felt right. The only option that kept Aya healthy and Catirina happy. But this...

I'd seen wickedness firsthand, had fought it tooth and nail, desperate to keep its odious stain away from my city and my people.

And despite my code and my crest, I'd just *invited* it in, tainting this poor girl's whole life in a single night of villainy.

The carriage door swung open, Ren dropping in to grab the unconscious Princess. Riku flicked his hand, dissolving the ice around her wrists, before brandishing a short length of rope to replace it.

My stomach knotted at the sight of her wrists bound, but I shoved it down, focusing on the mission ahead.

"Gentle with her head," I still chided, sliding out of the carriage first.

The canvas husk of the deflated balloon sprawled across the cropped field, the basket—just large enough to fit us all—prepped and ready. Between my Control and Malina's Qualifying heat, we'd be flying in no time, home before dawn.

Hopefully, the sunrise would usher in a brighter outcome to this situation, though doubt snared my chest in angry, pricked vines.

"Riku, give me a hand, she's heavy," Ren grumbled from behind me, and I spun on my heel, the twins both struggling to lift Catirina out of the carriage like she was a sack of dirty laundry, not the Princess of Dunyas. Not a *person*, deserving more respect than we'd given her. Malina leaned against the carriage, picking her nails as Naveen led the horses to the stable, neither of them coming to the twins' aid.

"Or you're weak." I knocked Riku out of the way, tucking my arms beneath her back and her legs to cradle her. Her head dipped, resting naturally in the crook of my neck.

It wasn't supposed to go like this.

Adjusting my hold, I huffed out a breath, walking up the hill to the basket. "Let's move out."

The balloon ride to the Treehouse was near silent, the huffing wind the only background noise. Though we were miles above the ground, my whole crew tucked tightly in the small basket, sharing the weight of what we'd done tonight. What we had yet to do.

This was bigger than knocking jewels off nobles too rich to notice, or cheating at cards to beat out a proud bluffer who needed humbling.

No, this wickedness was a haunting sort, something we'd never outrun or outplay.

I focused my mind wholly on my task, the air a steady stream from my fingertips as I commanded the balloon higher, faster, Malina's consistent heat the only aid I needed.

When Hiku City finally glittered beneath us, the rooftops like lightning bugs arranged in neat rows, I let my wind siphon away, slowly and surely. The city grew to meet us, Malina and I working in silent synchronicity to carefully drop us on top of the Treehouse's secondary roof—a nice, flat expanse of stone tucked behind the main building, just out of sight until we could get rid of the evidence.

The Lost Ones worked quickly—Riku and Ren rolling up the giant deflated balloon tarp as Naveen carried Catirina inside, Malina and I on his heels. Carefully, he set her onto the soft audience chairs, his favorite haunt—another kindness I'd have to remember to thank him for—before exiting up the stairs to his room. Malina and I hurried toward the backstage area of the Den, shedding our disguises for less recognizable attire.

When we both were wearing our normal trousers and tunics, mine all black and hers muted grays, I finally found my voice.

"This would have been smoother if you followed my lead." I crossed my arms, leveling her with a dark stare. "It wasn't supposed to be like this."

Saying it out loud made it even more inescapably true.

No, I was supposed to carry a *conscious* Catirina here on a breeze and a laugh, supposed to show her the palace I'd made out of my will and determination alone. Supposed to let her hold fond memories in her fingertips, a moment of escape until Ecei came to collect her and take her home...

But my best friend could call my bluff better than anyone, her eyes narrowed in sharp contempt. "You were chickening out." She poked my chest hard enough to bruise my skin and my ego. "I made the necessary calls."

I brushed past her, stalking into the main area of the Den, my rage rising like a gale-storm in my gut as I crafted half-truths. "I had her eating out of the palm of my hand, Malina. Begging me to fly her to Hiku City Opera! *Here*!" I gestured broadly to the Treehouse, now a taunt to its former glorious title.

"And then what, Shin?" Mal's gruff tone softened, my name a piteous thing on her tongue. "You betray her in the morning when Drakkar and Ecei come to rescue her?"

My jaw snapped shut, wired closed by the uncomfortable truth. "That's not–"

"We were hired to play the villain, Shin. Devil and lure," she huffed. "Not prince and rescuer. We can't afford to screw this up."

My ears rang as each word pinged against them like raindrop on a roof.

It wasn't supposed to be this way.

"Where am I?" a voice croaked, and I spun on my heel.

Catirina groaned as she sat up, huddling into the side of the tattered velvet seats. Her eyes darted around the room until they settled on me, a fresh wave of hurt bringing tears to their corners. Guilt stabbed at me as she hugged her legs to her chest, awkwardly resting her bound wrists on her knees.

"You're awake." I approached tentatively, reaching for the flask of water at my hip. I crouched at the edge of the stage, extending the peace offering toward her. "Here, drink this, it will help the headache."

She sank further into her seat, throat bobbing. "What, so you can knock me out again? *Poison* me? I don't think so."

I winced. "I wouldn't—"

"Wouldn't *what*?" She held up her bound hands, jaw clenching and unclenching. "Untie me, then."

Fear and regret wrestled in my chest as I set the flask down, but I was denied a chance to speak first as Malina sneered, "You'll run, and that isn't safe for anyone."

For a Pyromental Qualifier, Malina's tone was cold enough to freeze hell.

I shot her a scalding look over my shoulder. "Malina, go tell the others she's awake. We should all have a proper conversation."

Her mouth pressed into a tight line, her hand sticking to her hip. "And leave you alone to make goo-goo eyes at her again?"

Rancid, rage-fueled thoughts burned the tip of my tongue, ready to spew hotter than Kas's fire, but I swallowed them down. Malina's insubordination cleaved at every fiber of my carefully woven craft, of this *family*; her attitude as of late threatened far more than just this mission. It threatened the very foundation of what we were to each other.

But I did not have the time to process that now, to have it out with her in the way we desperately needed to. So I'd have to simply use this to my advantage, her aggression an easy counter to my clear-headed countenance.

Liar and lure. Captor and negotiator.

"Enough," I ground out, praying to the Breath she'd take my lead for once. "*Go.*"

Malina swallowed, scrutiny darkening her gaze; but thanks to whatever generous stars stared down at us, she walked away without another word, off to rally the others.

And giving me my one opening.

Catirina watched her go, shoulders at her ears with tension. When Mal was out of earshot, she murmured, "She's charming. Is she always that *friendly*?"

I ran my hands through my hair hard enough to rip a few strands from their roots. "I'm sorry about her. I didn't want things to go down this way."

Catirina still just glared, repeating her earlier question: "Where are we?"

I plopped onto the lip of the stage, my feet dangling over the short gap to the pit. If I was going to make this right, this was my only opportunity.

"Hiku City Opera." I flung my arms open with a shoddy attempt at a smile, gesturing to the ruins of the once grand hall that I'd converted to my own personal sanctuary, dingy and decayed as it was. "Don't you recognize it?"

For a moment, round eyes dragged over the room, memories swimming in their depths as she rationalized the past with the cold present.

A chill ran up my spine as her gaze fell on me, the warm springtime that I'd gotten to know and *like* replaced with a solid wall of rocky indifference.

"What is it that you want from me, hmm?" she clipped out, back straight as an arrow. "Ransom? A political favor? Get it over with so I can go home."

I gnawed at the inside of my cheek, the tangled web I'd snared myself in tonight tied tightly enough that even my strongest winds couldn't free me. "It's not that simple."

"I might have been a fool to trust you, but do I really look *that* stupid?" The Princess scoffed, tears budding against her long lashes. "I can handle an explanation, and I deserve to know why I'm here."

Hurt slashed at my softest parts, the truth a blade through my ribs.

She deserved an explanation. Deserved the world, really. A *choice.*

And I'd taken that from her tonight, my own greed and desperation blackening my heart. Even though I'd promised her more. Even though I still wished I could give it to her. Which made me worse than Drakkar, Ecei, and her parents combined.

I sighed, my guilt a noose around my neck. Hopping from the stage, I gently placed the flask next to her, stepping back to give her some space. "Drink something first. Then we'll find you something more comfortable, and we can—"

"Comfortable?" A mirthless, hysterical laugh bubbled from her as she snapped forward, sitting at the very edge of the velvet cushion. "I'm in a burned-down hideaway with strangers who have kidnapped me, knocked me out, and tied me up, and *now* you're worried about my comfort?"

The blade in my chest twisted. This was not how it was supposed to go. I held my hands up, grasping for stability. "Please, Catirina, if you'd just calm down—"

"I will not stay calm for my own demise!" She thrust to her feet, her voice bounding through the acoustic hall. "I have been calm and quiet and malleable my whole life, and it has gotten me *nothing.* And the one time I tried to put myself out there, this is what I get. So no, I will *not calm down.*"

I clenched my hands, fighting for control over my own anger as it shuddered through me. "I understand, but I'm trying to—"

"You understand nothing!" she shrieked, survival instincts and adrenaline finally giving way to a tidal wave of rage. Rage I deserved. Rage that made my own blood boil. She pointed a finger at my chest, a wobbling declaration of war. "You are a vile, lowlife liar, worse than any of the pricks you claim to hate!"

Despite the words echoing my own thoughts, they sliced through the last tattered strands of my reservation, guilt and hurt and fear all blending into my own dagger of vicious fury.

I stepped closer, my voice a thunderstorm. "Fine! Throw a tantrum, then, see if I care if you spend the night cold and hungry because you want to be a stubborn wi—"

"Shin?"

My name—a quiet, sobering condemnation—pulled me back to center, my anger crashing and retreating just as quickly as it came.

I spun, and my heart sank, the air fleeing from the room.

"Aya," I breathed; she stood preternaturally still, her mouth parted in disbelief and denial as she took in the scene before her. "You're supposed to be with Madame Ahen—"

"Shin, *what are you doing?*" She propelled into action, her steps staggered and weak, but full of purpose as she closed in on Catirina. "What is this?"

"You weren't lying about your sister." The Princess's voice was so low, I barely heard it, a stark contrast from her booming vitriol.

But my focus was still locked on my little sister, who stared at me now with more venom and hurt than I ever thought possible.

"It's not what it looks like," I lied—the feeblest, most piss-poor excuse I'd ever given in my whole life.

"I don't care what it looks like, Shin, untie her!" Aya stepped in front of Catirina, shielding her with her rail-thin frame, like *I* was the monster. Her accusations hurtled at me with the force of a hurricane. "She's the Princess, and she's scared! Is this what you've become?"

My world shattered and crumbled, all thoughts just as broken and fragmented in my head. "I—I just—" I stuttered to find a single coherent word, a thought, *a way out*, but none manifested from the wreckage.

"Thank you." Catirina rescued me from my fumbling with a quick look I didn't understand. She stepped from behind my sister, turning to face her with a warm, disarming smile. "Aya, was it?"

My brain swirled as it tried to catch up, to recalibrate, but I was still just a disjointed mess of conflicting guilt and horror.

"You must be Catirina." Aya's shaking fingers struggled with the knots of rope around Irina's wrists, her returning smile gentle as the moonlight seeping in from the domed ceiling.

The Princess nodded, extending her hands so Aya had easier access. "Irina, actually."

"Irina." Aya beamed as she finally freed the knot, the rope falling away to reveal raw, chapped skin. "I'm so sorry, my brother is an idiot, but I promise he's not a bad guy, he just makes *terrible* choices."

I winced, another strike right to my most wounded bits.

"I can hear you." I finally found my voice, but it sounded far away and foreign, a stranger's, not my own.

No, perhaps I just didn't recognize myself. Not anymore.

"Good, then maybe you'll listen," Aya snapped, disrupting my pity-party-for-one; then she collapsed onto the chairs, her energy zapped. Her face paled as she peered up at me, the circles beneath her eyes as dark and hollow as her voice. "This is wrong, Shin. I don't care what that terrible frost woman said she'd give you, but this is so, *so wrong.*"

"Frost woman?" Catirina chimed in, and to my surprise, sat next to Aya instead of running off immediately, her hands carefully folded in her lap. "You mean Queen Ecei?"

I nodded, a small bud of hope blooming from beneath the debris. "That's why I wanted to explain—"

"You're working for Ecei?" Irina whispered, and that was somehow worse than her shouting. Those caustic tears wet her lashes again, full streams running rivers down her face. "Was everything a trap? You and Drakkar playing some strange good-guy bad-guy thing from the bar—"

"No. By the Breath, *no.*" I sprang forward, catching myself just before I could wipe the tear tracks from her cheeks. I dropped my hand, clenching it at my side instead. "Ecei cornered me *after* the bar. And she made us an offer I couldn't refuse."

Irina blinked, and I knew my quick glance at Aya spoke volumes more than any words could. But, despite the way they sat heavy on my tongue, I forced the words past my lips—dangerous truths I hated to speak. "I didn't have a choice. I'm sorry I took yours."

Irina opened her mouth, but our conversation crashed to an

abrupt end as Riku hurtled over the balcony, Naveen, Kas, Mal, and Ren all hovering near the railing at the same time.

"Shin, we have visitors," Riku hissed as he landed gracefully on the stage, the former acrobat making it look far easier than it should. But the sharp set of his slim jaw revealed his panic, eliciting mine in response.

"Who?" I gripped his shoulder, speaking low enough so only he could hear. "Ecei said her people wouldn't be here until the morning..."

A curt nod, as he jerked his head to the balcony. "Not Ecei. Come look."

My feet and my winds took me up the stairs to the balcony two at a time. Aya and Irina clamored up behind me, but I was in too much of a hurry to tell them to wait behind.

The others huddled around the window from the back of the balcony that overlooked the dingy old front steps, but they parted as I stalked to it, clearing my view.

Despite the hazy dark of nighttime, the full moon hung bright enough to illuminate the forms gathered on the steps below.

An ivory dress, stark against the blackness. Violent red streaking her hair.

All sensible thoughts eddied from my head, replaced with a vicious, beating fear that lashed me from the inside out.

"Princess Naria?" Malina whipped around to face me, brow raised. "What is *she* doing here?"

"Shin!" the princess called from the steps, her voice echoing through the quiet streets. "Shin, I know it was you!"

I know it was you.

Your fault, boy.

They found me.

I froze, my heart seizing, the blood running to my toes, begging me to escape, to flee...

A violet flash of light, another dress appearing next to Naria, disheveled brown curls framing a panicked expression.

"Rina, if you're with him, please come out! This isn't funny anymore!"

"Hana?" Irina's voice hollowed out as she appeared at the windowsill, fingers clutching the frayed curtains for support. But relief sagged her shoulders, and my stomach dropped. "Mother Earth..."

"How'd they get here this fast?" Naveen shuddered, stepping away from the window, hiding Aya behind his broad back.

I shook my head, horror leadening my tongue.

They'd found me. *Us.*

"Please, Irina," Hana called up from the steps, somehow *knowing* her friend was inside. *They knew, they knew, they knew.* "I have Niki's stash, we can go home right now and be done with this mess before it gets ugly!"

The color rushed from Irina's cheeks as she stumbled back. Her eyes went wide. "Fae-dust."

No, this wasn't happening. I wouldn't let them catch me. Catch *Aya.*

The wind was a wicked thing, but it was mine. And I'd never stop running, the wind at my back all I needed to survive.

I spun on my family, the ones I'd chosen, the ones I trusted. "Everyone, last stand protocol. We have to go, *now.*"

Malina's brow crinkled. "But Ecei—"

"We'll have to find a new rendezvous point," I cut her off, grabbing Irina by the hand and tugging her toward the rooms, ready to grab what we needed and go. Footsteps behind me signaled the others' pursuit. "If Naria and Hana are both here, the Soran and Jaltan guard aren't far behind. They know my real name somehow, and they know Irina is here. We do not need anyone getting a stronger whiff of what we've been up to, or who we've been dealing with. It would be war."

"You want us to leave the Treehouse?" Aya's voice broke, and something cracked inside of me, too.

This place was home, run down and ruined as it was. The only thing any of us had ever called ours.

I stopped just short of the Loft, scanning the faces of my people. Riku and Ren looked at each other, skepticism written across their faces as they communicated in their silent twin language. Aya stared at Naveen, her bottom lip trembling, as he kicked the ground, his jaw clenched tightly. Malina tucked Kas beneath her arm, the boy's face gaunt, hers brimming with rage.

I wanted to give them more than this. It wasn't supposed to be this way.

But home wasn't a place, it was a people. *These* people.

And they would all survive this. No matter what it cost me.

I huffed out a determined breath. "We don't have a choice."

A hand ripped from mine, Irina planting her feet. "I'm not going with you."

Right; she wasn't part of this, one of us. She was a *princess*, a girl I'd ripped from her home, her people tonight. They waited on the steps outside for her, ready to risk their own lives and use outlawed magic to rescue her from my fiendish clutches.

And yet, she was the key to my salvation. To my family's. To Aya's.

"Irina, please," I begged, sacrificing all pride, all honor. None of it mattered now, not when my wickedness was finally catching up to me, calling all bluffs. "If they think we took you, their guards will hunt us down. They'll shoot first, ask questions second."

Arms folded across her middle. "Why should I care?"

I swallowed, my heart a thunderstorm against my ribs.

One last chance. One more favor.

"Because you want to be the kind of noble that does." I met her eyes, taking in all the anger and hurt that waited there, offering my own sincerity for the first time since the gardens. "The choice is yours."

And for the first time all night, I meant it.

This was not how it was supposed to go, but this was all I could offer to make it right.

Something unlocked in her soil stare, like earth revived after rain, and I let loose a breath.

Malina surged forward, terror choking her voice. "Shin, no, we've—"

I reached for her hand, a peace offering long overdue. "We're not kidnappers, Mal. We'll keep them safe another way." Malina gaped at me, rare tears lining her eyes, but I turned back to the Princess, my decision secure. "Irina, go to your friends, if that's what's best for you.

The kids and I still have a head start on Ecei and the guards, and we'll manage a way around her."

I turned without hesitation, into the Loft to collect mine and Aya's go-bags, my steps somehow lighter despite the dread still running like ice down my spine.

It wasn't supposed to be like this.

The wind and I were two wicked creatures, born to outrun trouble. Born to *soar*. I didn't know how, but with the breeze beneath me, I'd figure out a different way to save my sister and my family.

One last adventure.

"Fine. What's the plan?"

It took me longer than I'd care to admit to process her words, to even rationalize that they came out of *her* mouth...

But Irina stared at me expectantly, waiting. *Choosing.*

When I didn't respond, my mouth hanging open, she snapped her fingers impatiently. "Mother Earth to Shin! How are we getting out of here without hurting the princesses, hmm?"

"I don't—"

Irina threw her hands in the air, letting loose a groan. "If you let their guards catch you, or if you don't take me to Ecei, you're all good as dead, right? And I'll be safe either way, whether I go with them tonight or Ecei tomorrow." She spelled out the grim fate that awaited us, her head held high like a princess. No, like a *Queen*. "But I'm a better person than you, so I don't want your blood on my hands."

Gratitude welled so thick in my throat, it was hard to swallow, to speak. "Thank you."

She shook her head, her arms tight at her sides. "This isn't for you. This is for *me*. Now what. Is. The. Plan?"

I nodded, that small flower of hope the only thing giving my heart wings, the fog finally abating from my murky head.

One last escape.

"Follow my lead." I grabbed the two bags we stored beneath Aya's cot for emergencies only and hoisted them across my back. "Lost Ones, time to build the campfire."

The Lost Ones inhaled a collective breath as the puzzle pieces clicked into place, Naveen running a hand over his broad face. "Oh, Mother Earth, we are *so screwed*."

I nailed my courage to the last wicked parts I owned, letting it gild my bones.

It was time to see how well an opera house could burn down *twice*.

FIRE

Eleven

Hana had the fae-dust. She was *right outside*, Naria at her disposal, ready to rescue me from this nightmare, from the hurt and anger that pierced my flesh from the inside out...

But one question kept me from running into her arms. One tiny, defiant spark of something other. A rebellion that had been planted in me the first time I stood in this building ten years ago, the swell of an orchestra and the thrill of my brother's mischief settling deep in my soul and taking root.

What would Nikolaj do?

Nikolaj wouldn't let a little girl die. Wouldn't let any of these teenagers die, not for his own pride.

And Nikolaj wouldn't run back home to marry the man whose mother put the ransom on her head in the first place.

I didn't know the exact parameters of Shin's deal with Ecei, but if I had to gander a guess, she wanted Drakkar to be the one to save me tomorrow in exchange for medicine for Aya. Wanted to take all the credit for my rescue, which would surely put my parents in her silken pockets.

But I would never marry Drakkar, even if I had to run away to prevent it. Even if I had to turn my back on Hana tonight.

What would Nikolaj do?

Nikolaj would follow Shin further, would collect the evidence he needed to end Ecei's schemes. Nikolaj would also find a way to stick it to Shin, too, to turn his own con against him. But most importantly, Nikolaj would make sure he found the medicine for Aya first, no matter what bargaining that took. Not for Shin, not for his own merit, but because it was *right.*

Nikolaj would act like a king.

So I would, too.

I pinched crescents into my palms, grounding myself to my brother's memory. "Fine, what's the plan?"

Shin gaped at me, upswept eyes wide in disbelief. The moment lingered too long, an unwanted guest at this soiree. I snapped my fingers, impatience and excitement lighting fires beneath my flesh. "Mother Earth to Shin! How are we getting out of here without hurting the princesses, hmm?"

The others' eyes burned into me, my brother's legacy a thing to behold, asynchronous with the frightened, crying girl they'd bound and kidnapped mere hours earlier. But only a few stuttered syllables worked their way out of Shin, his tea-and-honey gaze distant, like I was a stranger he was seeing for the first time. "I don't—"

Of course, he hadn't really seen me, not like I'd thought. I tried to ignore the sting of that sentiment, throwing my hands up in sheer frustration. I didn't have time for his inner realizations or conflicts. Neither did his little band of thieves, if Naria had any say. The girl had always been a force of nature, an inextinguishable flame burning bright despite all the ways her family tried to squash her. And Hana, bubbly and kind as she was, had a streak of determination that I'd seen strip grown men bare of their armor, her airy disposition a weapon that molded to whatever shape she willed it.

What would Nikolaj do?

"If you let their guards catch you, or if you don't take me to Ecei, you're all good as dead, right? And I'll be safe either way, whether I go with them tonight or Ecei tomorrow." I lifted my chin, letting my brother's ghost embolden me into the kind of leader he might have been if given the chance. "But I'm a better person than you, so I don't want your blood on my hands."

Shin finally snapped, and the faraway look dissolved into something soft and so *much more dangerous.* "Thank you."

I shook my head, his *gratitude* a dirty word that crawled over my flesh. But I didn't need to forgive to do the right thing. To prove that *I could.* "This isn't for you. This is for *me.* Now what. Is. The. Plan?"

Whatever hesitation plagued Shin the moment before blew away with the cool breeze that flitted through the room. Springing into action, he grabbed two bags from the cluttered, tattered bench, his steps sure and quick. "Follow my lead. Lost Ones, time to build a campfire."

Whatever that meant sent a flurry of anxious energy through the others, Naveen even echoing a deep groan. "Oh, Mother Earth, we are *so screwed.*"

The parts of me that were crafted by my mother thought—distantly—that fear might be appropriate, a prickling of it crawling up the back of my neck. But Nikolaj did not know fear, not even in his last days. Not even when the Blight devoured him, bit by bit, the darkness creeping further into his gold eyes.

So I would not be afraid, either.

Not that Shin left room for it. Riding whatever adrenaline had spiked in his veins, he dictated and pointed like a seasoned leader, barking orders at the Lost Ones as he brushed out of the room. "Two minutes to pack. Malina, to the back, prep the balloon. It'll be the lure. Naveen, Twins, take Aya and Irina down to the river, give us an escape route."

Malina launched into action without a word, beelining up a set of stairs, stealing some of the tension with her. Naveen and the twins darted out a moment later, the clatter and crashing from the room beyond indicating their frantic packing.

Unsure and out of the loop, with limited options and even less information, I followed Shin.

Stomping over creaking floorboards past the afterimages of faded tapestries hanging in tatters against the walls, I hustled to match his pace. Aya fell into step next to me again, like we were old friends in a familiar pattern. Violet eyes crinkled with a soft smile. "Don't worry, Princess Irina. We'll make this right."

Nikolaj would've liked her, this butterfly whose clipped wings kept her stuck under a rock with beetles and bugs like Shin and Malina.

I liked her, too, little though I knew about her. It wasn't *her* fault she'd been cursed with such a shit brother when mine had been so wonderful.

I wouldn't let her die the same gruesome death he did. If Shin was this desperate to throw his lot in with Ecei, she had to have something potent enough to beat back death.

We wound around the corner, and the tapestries gave way to old curtains and a maze of ropes, lit only by a few scattered oil lamps as we entered the upper level of what had to be a backstage area. But instead of climbing up into the rafters, Shin led us down a flight of spiral stairs, the metal clanging with each dizzying step we took. It fed to a plain, tightly latched door, and Shin quickly threw back the locking mechanism, opening to the where the back of the Opera House butted up against the thinnest channel of the Black River.

"All packed! What's my assignment?" The boy I hadn't properly met yet screeched to a halt at the top of the stairs, hanging over the metal banister. He couldn't have been more than thirteen, if that, even with his long, awkward limbs. His hair had the same wired, curly texture as Malina's, the resemblance apparent even to a stranger like me. But in direct contrast to his sister's stoicism, he bounced on the balls of his feet, round face alight with wonder as he tracked Shin's movements, awaiting an answer.

Shin twirled, a smirk twisting the left side of his mouth, that deceitful dimple popping out. "You're with me, Kas."

A fervent nod, and the boy hurtled down the stairs. With a quick hand signal to Aya, Shin swiveled left, and the young boy chased him down the hall. Neither of them looked back, their mission clear as they disappeared behind a heavy curtain, and a part of me hoped I'd never have to see Shin again...even as I stared too long at his back.

Aya ushered me out the door, the cool night air kissing my skin and washing away any errant feeling that lingered past its welcome. I wrapped my arms tightly around myself, the Hiku City breeze an unfriendly guest as it hustled through my skirts.

My teeth chattered while I hid against the Opera House, the black river lapping against the stone wall that separated it from the street. I'd never been this close to it before, and the dark moan of the churning current scraped at my ears.

It wasn't too late to turn back. I could run out front, get Hana's attention, and fly back to my too-warm room in the palace, where I'd never have to feel the sting of a chilly night again. Where I'd never have to listen to the eerie music of the river's song.

"What am I doing?" I whispered, half to myself.

"Not getting your friends or any of us killed," Naveen answered as he burst through the door, two giant packs strapped tight to his back. An admittedly charming side-smile crossed his face, his dark skin blending into the gentle night around us. Brown eyes softened in a way that reminded me too much of my brother. "Sorry about before, Princess. I promise that's not how I usually approach a lady."

My chest seized, the gentle nudge from Nikolaj in the afterlife all I needed.

I didn't want cozy bedrooms—not anymore. I wanted to keep myself safe, I wanted to find a solution for a sick girl, but I also wanted a good adventure to stick it to Ecei and my parents.

I smiled up at Naveen, shoving down any grudges I'd crafted from our first encounter earlier. It wasn't his fault, either, that Shin was a liar. At least Naveen had been an honest thief. Hadn't tried to woo me first or play with my heartstrings. "Apology accepted."

"Let's move," one of the twins—I couldn't quite tell which— commanded as he shoved through the door, the other brother hot on his heels. I shut out all thoughts of Shin as they set a trotting pace further down the road, away from the sanctuary of the Opera House's warmth.

With a nod from Naveen, we stumbled after them, my heeled shoes regretfully biting at my poor, blistered feet. It'd been a long night, and I was not dressed for shadow-veiled escapes. But I was not the worst off, Aya's breaths coming in short pants as we wove through the burnt ruins of this neck of the city, the serpentine river winding alongside us.

"Slow down," Aya pleaded, watery drops lining her eyes as her breath scraped through her throat in hoarse drags.

"C'mere." Naveen held out a hand, and she took it, the large man effortlessly hoisting her into his arms despite the massive packs on his back, not missing a step. "I've got you."

I've got you.

My gut lurched, but not from the exercise, a misplaced envy wrapping itself around me in tight, green vines. "You all are really close."

Criminals with a code of honor. Thieves and kidnappers with bleeding hearts.

Meanwhile, my parents had no qualms about auctioning me off to the son of a woman who'd enlist struggling people—teenagers, mostly —to do her dirty work.

"Of course we are. We're family," one of the twins called over his shoulder before somersaulting to my side. A sunny grin squinted his light eyes, his copper hair dancing with the breeze. "I'm Ren, by the way, the handsome twin. I'm sorry as well, but I'll tell you all the dirt on Shin on the way if it makes up for it."

Ren extended his hand to shake mine. I took it, just like my brother would've wanted. Like I—secretly—wanted to, also. "Deal."

The other twin—Riku, by process of elimination—held up a hand and halted our party as we turned into what looked like it used to be a town square before the city expanded further west. Now, it was an empty, dirty space, rotting wood and murky puddles the only decorations. After the Opera House Tragedy, this entire neighborhood had gone to ruins, the Blight only decimating it further.

An abandoned square for the Lost Ones.

With sharp nods to each other, both twins lifted their arms, and the water in the puddles gathered together. Another synchronized twist of their wrists, and the water grew and shaped itself, hardening into ice.

I inhaled, awe soaking through my cold limbs. Were they

Controllers? Or just a Quantifier and Qualifier, two halves of a whole that complemented each other?

Without dropping Aya, Naveen flicked two fingers, some of the moss-covered wood scraps fusing with ice to create a sculpture. My eyes widened at the mastery, watching the artistry...

No, not just a pretty art piece...something far more functional.

A sled.

Two sharp, slick rails of translucent ice lined the bottom of the curved sleigh, the wood forming three rows of neat benches on top.

All we needed were some horses to drag the vehicle, and the image would be right out of the Nehirite picture-books my maid Gemma used to read to me as a little girl.

"Pretty impressive for some lowlife thieves, ey?" Ren hopped up and straddled the middle bench, tucking both hands to his hips as a triumphant smile stretched across his face.

I nodded, admiring the craftsmanship, running a finger across the cold structure. "Pretty impressive for a bunch of kids with no formal schooling. Where do you learn to use your *Easinir* like this?"

Ren beamed, like I'd just told him he'd won a million gold pieces. A reminder that he was still young, maybe eighteen at the oldest, desperate for praise. For a *place.* "Shin taught us a lot, and sometimes the prostitutes at Madame Tsojo's brothel helped."

My head snapped up faster than I wanted it to.

"Oh." My face heated scarlet, the mention of such an establishment sending a flurry of worries through my head as I again noted their ages.

I supposed that also meant that I wasn't the only girl Shin toyed with. *Figures.* He'd learned his tricks from the best liars and flirts in all of Babylon.

"Ignore him, he's bluffing. The girls at Tsojo's don't give him the time of day." Riku crossed his arms, a long eyeroll the first sign of any emotion from him. Strange, how different two people wearing the same face could be. If Ren was all smiles and bids for affection, Riku was his antithesis, cold and sharp and reserved.

"He likes attention," Aya giggled as she slowly climbed onto the front bench.

"Only because my sweet Aya never gives me any." Ren tickled her side, sparking a fresh wave of breathless laughter from the slight girl.

Despite myself, I bit back a chuckle, too.

Naveen jumped in next and patted the seat next to him and Aya. "Princess, you can sit here. We'll wait for the others' signal."

Reality slammed back into me, the sweet excursion in my mind coming to an abrupt end.

This was not the first day of school, not a place to make new friends, even if they were just a bunch of charming, lost children who needed a home.

No, I was on the run, in a city that ate naive girls like me for breakfast, the weight of two powerful kingdoms' forces at our backs.

And I was choosing to go with these young miscreants, to dive deeper into the unknown. To refute the safety of people I trusted for a chance at something else. Something *more*.

What would Nikolaj do?

"The princesses will be okay?" I gnawed my lip as I stared at Naveen, desperate for confirmation. For some kind of sign that I wasn't making the biggest mistake of my life.

Instead, a different signal boomed, and any words that he might have placated me with drowned in the blast.

The ground shook, toppling me into the sleigh. I caught myself on the ice, palms stinging as they cut open. But I hissed and ignored it, turning toward the thunderous crackling—

The balloon floated high in the sky, silhouetted in a strange gold glow...

Fire.

Even from blocks away, I watched as it consumed everything, the whole domed structure trapped in the riotous flames' hungry jaws...

For the second time in my life, I watched as Hiku City Opera *burned.*

"Naria! Hana!" I cried, stumbling back toward the crumbling building, the fire casting the world in jealous, consuming orange and red.

My breath snagged in my lungs.

The princesses were over there. *Hana* was over there, possibly hurt—

Pale skin, blistered and charred to black.

Light; blinding, searing.

Eyes wide with terror, mouths set in disgusted frowns.

I screamed again, dizzy as I imagined them trapped in the smoke, in the debris...

"Shh, it's okay." Strong arms wrapped around my middle, tugging me back toward the sleigh, away from the radiating heat. A voice like night murmured against my hair, "They're fine, Irina, they're fine."

I twisted, pushing away, but green-tea-and-honey eyes settled me as his stare locked on mine.

"He's okay!" Gasps of relief.

A voice like a bright violin. "Thank you. Are you a fairy?"

"Irina, *breathe*." Shin's grip loosened, but he did not let go, his fingers at my waist anchoring me to my body. "Naria's a Pyromental, yes? A full Controller. She can't get hurt there. And Hana will likely chase that balloon. I promise, they are *okay*."

My breath returned to my chest, heavy and fast and all at once. "You should have *warned me*," I panted between shaking heaves.

But the air blew away my panic with every inhale I devoured, my heart slowing again to a steady rhythm. Shin's gaze didn't leave mine.

"Add it to the list of things I need to apologize for." His cheek dimpled and he let go of me. "We needed distractions to keep them busy."

"That was fun." Kas bounded up next to us, soot and ash darkening his features, but his smile was all sunshine.

Shin ruffled his hair, "You did good, kid."

"You could've been killed in that fire!" I stammered, imagining Kas's tiny face devoured by the incessant flames...

Someone help!

He's just a boy!

"But we weren't." Shin shrugged, that same annoying grin unshakable from his face.

I opened my mouth to rebuttal, but he climbed onto the back of the sleigh, Kas scurrying to the front. Shin turned to add over his shoulder, "Come on, Princess, before our chariot melts."

My body and mind warred, danger still licking waves of fear over my spine.

These were not ordinary people. Not even ordinary thieves. No, these daredevils were kidnappers and *arsonists,* no sensibility or rationale among them.

But perhaps I had no sense, either. Because only one thought still remained, the others dusting to ash like the Opera House at my back.

What would Nikolaj do?

I plopped next to Shin without another word, tucking my arms tight around my center.

Aya smiled from the front row, a knowing twinkling in her stare, and Ren exhaled a quiet *yes!*

"Let's go, before they catch on." Malina's voice sobered everyone as she catapulted from a nearby rooftop, gingerly landing on two feet. She slipped gracefully onto the front of the sleigh, her curls a tangle of whatever madness she'd gotten into.

Perhaps Naveen had been right before.

I was so *screwed.*

Shin's grin widened as he lifted his arms. "Everyone, hang on!"

And then, for the second time since I'd met Shin, we *flew* into the night.

Twelve

SHIN

A far tamer fire crackled in the hearth at Madame Tsojo's brothel as my crew gathered at the front desk, the painted face of the matron herself narrowed at us in an accusatory glare.

I brushed on my sincerest smile—one Tsojo loved, even if she refused to admit it out loud. "Thanks for taking us in for the night, Madame Tsojo."

She leaned over the counter, her corseted breasts nearly spilling from the deep 'v' of her crimson dress, but the way the fire glowed in her pitch-colored eyes stayed any naughty thoughts with searing fear. "I swear by the Breath, if this gets me or my girls in trouble, I'll hang you myself."

She meant it.

But I was out of options. Madame Aheni's den was a no-go, since the Nehirite princeling had spotted me there before and knew of my connection with the old tornado of a woman.

Which meant I had to endure the oppressive heat of the brothel's shadowy walls, the symphony of moans hardly decent for my crew of teenagers, never mind the Princess of Dunyas. But the girls here were kind, always looking after me, and Tsojo had clothed Aya and I back when we were truly living on the streets; often with things patrons had left behind, or scraps the girls had grown out of or...*stained*...beyond use. Either way, it was a kindness I'd never forget.

And that I always repaid with interest.

Shin Koishi did not like unpaid debts.

"Good thing everyone here is known for discretion, yeah?" I flipped a gold mark from my pocket and tossed it onto the table. It was the last of Ecei's upfront payment—something I'd hoped to save for an inn or better transportation to our next stop. But if the wind had taught me anything, it was that silence was priceless.

Tsojo tucked the shimmering coin into her ample cleavage, but her rouged lips still pursed. "Don't push your luck just because I like you, boy."

If this was what *liking* me looked like, I dared not tempt her fury.

"You know you're my favorite, too, right?" I propped an elbow on the counter and leaned my face into my hand, waggling my brows at her. "Just don't tell Madame Aheni, she gets jealous."

"Sweet talker." She cracked a small grin, and I took it as a sign of victory. "You've learned too much from the girls here."

She was right, again.

This city had taught me everything I knew, the girls that worked for her not excluded. They'd mastered the art of flattery and deception, the fine dance between truth and temptation, and I'd reaped as much as I could from watching them work.

Wicked or willful, I knew I could do this, too.

I sucked in a breath, letting it soothe the tangle of nerves that still wrenched in my gut. My crew needed this to go right, but so did Tsojo and her girls. Everyone that touched this ticking bomb risked it blowing up in their faces, and I had a duty to ensure that it was Ecei that received the brunt of the blast.

I slipped the letter from my pocket—the scrap small, but a key to my victory—and pushed it toward Tsojo. "By the way, if some high-paying customers come looking around these parts tomorrow, give them this."

Tsojo's eyes flicked to the unassuming parchment—adorned with my chicken scrawl handwriting simply detailing a location with little context—then back up to me. Her voice hedged on a razor's edge. "No trouble?"

I couldn't lie to the woman who'd written the rulebook on it, so instead, I offered a separate truth. "None I haven't risked for your girls." I fiddled with my soot-covered clothes, but kept my expression cool as I pressed my leverage. "Is Via feeling better?"

I hated to use my friend to my benefit, but I didn't have a choice. I hadn't helped Via last year so I could get something out of it. When she'd shown up at Madame Aheni's one night, her body bruised and broken in ways that'd shattered things in me, too, trembling in pure fear and a primal rage, I swore I'd help her no matter what. No one deserved to be taken advantage of like she had; and though I'd never caught the Nehirite prick that'd defiled her, when she'd needed a place to lay low for a bit—a place to wait for the baby to come—all of us Lost Ones had happily opened the Treehouse to her.

Tsojo had been able to keep her business's reputation intact because of that, too. None of the other girls had to be afraid with Naveen acting as a bouncer three nights a week, and Via had a safe place to heal—body and soul—with Tsojo's clientele none-the-wiser.

Tsojo's expression softened, flames fading to embers. "She's doing real well." Her throat bobbed—Tsojo's love for her girls was her one humbling trait. She sighed, grabbing a key off the wall and tossing it to me. "Upstairs, room all the way in the back. But only one, and you'll have to share."

Ren sauntered closer, smoothing out his shoulder-length hair, overhearing our exchange, "I could always stay in Kalla's room…"

Tsojo erupted, a finger pointed at his most valuable bits. "I'll have your itsy-bitsy pecker sliced off and hung from the rafters like mistletoe by morning if I see you creeping near her again."

"Fine," Ren grumbled, but I smacked him over the head anyway for good measure.

I stuffed the key in my pocket before Tsojo could rescind her generous offer, flashing my brightest smile again. "We'll be no trouble."

I pushed Ren up the stairs, the rest of the Lost Ones following on my heels. It was a Breath-blessing that Riku preferred male company, because it would've been impossible to keep an eye on both of the slippery idiots in a place like this. I tried to keep my expression neutral as the chorus of fleshy slapping sounds and wet grunts echoed through the long hall. Mal covered Kas's ears, and a bright red blush chased the gray from Aya's skin-color.

It was the longest hallway I'd ever been down in my life, especially with the Princess's gaze burning holes through the back of my already-ashen shirt.

"Here we go," I said as I quickly fit the key through the slot in the door, turning it open. The scent of must and regret smacked me as the hinges creaked open, and a room just larger than a closet greeted me. In the center, a single bed wore threadbare white sheets, dark curtains blotting out the light from the single window. Holding my breath, I walked in and flung them open—to reveal the dazzling horizon of a brick wall facing us.

Silence was priceless, but this was a punishment, not a favor.

I painted on a smile. "Nice and cozy."

The others filed in, the air even more claustrophobic as our body heat radiated through the small space. Irina folded her arms around her middle, swallowing hard. "We're all staying in this room? *Together*?"

"Not the luxury accommodations you're used to?" Malina scoffed, but even she wore a frown as she took in the space.

Something prickled along my spine as Irina winced, her eyes downcast.

"Malina, you can always sleep outside." I cleared my throat—knowing that I'd likely do just that, the bitter air of the chilled night a welcomed friend after even just moments in this coffin. I ran my hand through my hair, shame sloshing in my gut. This was not how this was supposed to go. "Sorry, Princess, but we did just burn down our own home, so we're a bit put out, too."

The Lost Ones all shifted on their feet, the uncomfortable truth finally catching up with us. Even after we finished this mission, we'd have to use Ecei's money to find a new Treehouse. A new place to belong.

Aya's gaze found mine, watery and bright.

It'd been a while since we were truly lost.

But we'd start again, somehow. We always did.

"It's like a slumber party?" Kas offered sheepishly, one leg twitching with renewed anxiety. But he smiled at the Princess, and her shoulders loosened.

"You can stay next to me, Irina." Aya linked arms with her.

"And far away from Ren, if you know what's good for you," Naveen snickered, tossing Ren's hair, auburn strands sticking up at distressing angles.

The boy just shrugged. "What can I say? I'm a cuddler."

"I've been trying to escape since the womb." His twin rolled his eyes, plopping onto the dusty bed with a heavy sigh.

"Did Riku just crack a joke?" Kas chuckled, wide-eyed as he joined our normally icy friend on the edge of the bed.

The very corner of Riku's mouth tilted up. "It's been a long night. I'm in a mood."

Something in my chest shattered, then reforged, warmed and welded together by my family's love.

We would start again. We always did, always would.

Together.

And that made me the richest, luckiest man in the four kingdoms.

I did not have to fake my smile this time as I leaned back against the windowsill. "Anyone else hungry?"

Naveen stretched, long limbs brushing against the low ceiling. "I could eat."

"You just want to ogle the ladies downstairs." Malina whacked his arm, and my giant friend cringed away. But she didn't manage to knock his grin from his face.

He raised a brow, a challenge to the fire-pixie. "They ogle me right back. It's mutual ogle-ry."

Aya blushed again, and I couldn't help the chuckle that wound up from my chest, light and sweet as a summer wind. We were in shit deeper than the Black River was long. We had not one, not two, but *three* separate kingdoms on our tail, and only one tenuous alliance in our pocket. We were homeless. Penniless. Plan-less.

But we'd endure. We'd start again.

I rubbed my eyes with the heels of my hands, then hopped up, ready to lead us into whatever chapter came next. "Let's go get some food, but we stay in the kitchens. No *mingling* with patrons."

The others were already shuffling out the door, Ren and Naveen leading the charge despite my warning, when a small voice stole the air from my inflated chest.

"I think I'll stay." Irina withdrew, facing the cobwebbed corner. Her back was to me, hiding her expression, but the hitch to her voice was all the information I needed to know that if I could see more, I'd find tears. "I'm not hungry."

The others went quiet, exchanging looks and passing the baton, a silent war of 'not my problem' raging between them.

Aya glared at me, and I lost the game before I'd even started playing.

"Why don't you stay with her then, Shin?" There was a bite of poison behind her flower-sweet voice. "I'll bring you both something back."

I opened my mouth to protest, but she bounced out the door and shut it firmly behind her, leaving Irina and I alone in the room.

Her message was clear, no code needed to decipher.

Fix your mess.

I sighed, but the air was stale and tight in my chest, an anxiety I thought I'd eradicated from my life in boyhood. Even with fewer bodies in the space, I'd never felt more cramped.

Slim slivers of moonlight managed to work their way through the dingy window, casting Irina's dark skin in a sheen of silver. The plain gray cloak we'd given her wrapped tightly around her shoulders—like if she removed it, she'd unravel too. But the hem of her pink dress— torn and dirty as it was—peeked from beneath, dusting against the wood floor.

A faint reminder.

She didn't belong here. I'd taken her from the finery she'd known and shoved her into this hovel for my own gain.

I stared to the floorboards, my guilt a blindfold I couldn't look past, as a long, awkward silence stretched between us. But I had no idea what to say—what to *do* to make it right.

Fix your mess.

"Ecei has a treatment for the Blight, doesn't she?" Irina spoke first, voice hollow.

My head snapped up as she creaked across the floorboards, sitting on the edge of the bed. I swallowed down my guilt and my pride, offering her something far more valuable instead.

The truth.

"No, a *cure*," I managed, hesitant at first; but then I couldn't stay my tongue, the words tumbling from me like a hurricane blasting against a shoreline. "She caught me after our scrape in the bar, and when she found out about Aya...well, she made me an offer. It was better than letting us all get arrested for assaulting a noble, and it gives Aya a chance."

Irina didn't react, her gaze distant out the window, somehow looking far beyond the discolored brick wall.

"A cure for the Blight," she whispered on a shallow breath, shaking her head. Then she turned to me, like she'd remembered I was in the room, too. That it was *my fault* in the first place. Eyes narrowed, she pulled her cloak tighter. "Why does Ecei want me kidnapped?"

I shrugged as her stare burned me worse than a sunburn after falling asleep on Madame Aheni's tar roof in the summer. I had nothing left to offer her other than assumptions and educated guesses. "So Drakkar can come and rescue you, make himself look good?"

"My mother will filet her like a steak when she finds out." Her eyes rolled, and the action unlocked something in me. I expelled a breath, my stiff back relaxing against the wall.

"I think we're meant to take the fall for that, actually. Which is why we'll be gone as soon as Ecei comes to collect you at the border in three days." I'd put the coordinates in the letter Tsojo was meant to pass on, and I only hoped it would be enough to not have Ecei shoot me point-blank. I groaned, a headache beating between my brows.

It wasn't supposed to go like this.

Irina shot me a sharp look, an unspoken '*What do* you *have to groan about?*' carved in the soil of her stare. I bristled beneath it.

"Don't fret, Princess. You'll likely be home by week's end, and Prince Drakkar will be right there to remind you this was all a bad dream."

I couldn't help the venom in my tone—not toward her, but toward Drakkar. Would she let him sweep her away? Would his sins be erased by mine?

I shook out my hair. That line of thinking would get me nowhere fast.

It didn't matter anymore, anyway. What did I care which prince she got stuck with?

She shifted toward the edge of her seat, eyes lining with fresh tears and something I dared not address. Something I'd seen a glimpse of in a world far away, in a warm garden embrace that I could never return to...

It had only been a few hours since our time at the ball, but it might as well have been a different universe entirely.

Her voice was not the scalding criticism I'd imagined, but instead soft as a flower petal as it caressed my skin. "If you had just told me about everything, about Aya, I would've—"

I winced at my sister's name, my protective parts surging to the surface in a gale storm before I could manage them back.

"You would've what?" I huffed, crossing my arms against my chest like that'd somehow protect me. "You would've saved her yourself, would've come with me, or confronted Ecei?"

Irina threw her hands up, that little bit of fire rising to greet me. "I don't know, something!"

I pushed off the wall, my own misplaced fury beating through my veins as I stepped toward her. I knew Irina was all good intentions and hope, but those were things I'd lost years ago, far before the Blight had made me even more jaded. Things that'd burned down into rubble-and-ash piles like my home tonight.

"All of those roads would've ended with me dead or in prison, and my sister still sick." I stabbed through her ballooning hope and naivety, hating myself for it. But if I didn't, life would teach her those lessons in a far harsher way. Naivety was dangerous. It got pretty girls kidnapped...or worse. "I don't have the luxury of parents who would level kingdoms to protect her."

"Yes, *I've* been kidnapped, but I should feel bad for *you*." She stood, a hand on her hip, her sass on par with Malina's now that she'd decided I was just another prick. Finally, the criticism I'd been waiting for—and deserved—came pouring out. "Did you ever think that maybe it's your own fault you're in this mess? You act all high and mighty, but if you're really concerned with Aya, why not just get a decent job and try to make something of yourself, hm?"

The expression I made must have warned her she'd stepped over the line, because she went quiet.

My voice was a low, vicious thing, meant to slash and disarm. To protect me from my own shame. "Spoken like a princess who has had *everything* handed to her."

She grimaced, but did not falter, soil stare fixed and sturdy. "Spoken like a criminal who likes to convince himself he's somehow morally superior."

Her words stung.

The truth often did.

I stared down at her, our breaths mingling in the dusty, claustrophobic room. I hadn't noticed how we'd gotten this close again, hadn't paid attention if it was her feet or mine that'd brought us here.

But just like it'd been in the bar, and in the ballroom...

I couldn't resist the pull of her, a string reeling a kite back to earth.

I sighed, running a hand over my face. My sister always said I was a stubborn ass, and all I'd done tonight was prove her and every soul in Babylon she was right.

Wicked, fickle men.

"I'm not superior...trust me, I know that." I fell back, despite how desperately my legs hated to pull away, conceding ground to the Princess. Ground she deserved. I continued, my voice stumbling over the true explanation rather than my usual string of excuses, "I'm desperate. My sister is more important to me than any of your world's shiny morals and ideals. Those are real luxuries. My life is about survival. I do whatever it takes."

Irina sucked in a deep breath. Held it, as she watched me. Appraised me.

My skin scrawled, and I hated every part of me desperate for her approval.

"I don't agree, but I do understand," she finally blew out, and my shoulders unknotted, the traitors. She sat again, slumped over, like the adrenaline of the day had finally been punched out of her with this last round of low-blows. But the strength in her dark gaze was unshakeable, solid as the Helsin Mountains in the west. "That's why I came with you. Because Aya deserves to survive, and my parents need a wakeup call."

Oh, what a call that'd be. The wind whispered gleeful spoilers in my ears, thrilled at the mere thought of wickedness being challenged on such a grand scale.

I had no doubt that this time, Princess Catirina would make herself heard by all of Babylon.

Still, I shifted on my feet, unsure how to proceed in this tenuous alliance. What was my role now? I couldn't be the masked savior with no name or agenda who could sit and banter in dark alleys. And I certainly wasn't *Vox* anymore, the dashing escape artist who promised her the moon and stars under a garden canopy.

Which left my least favorite role of all.

Myself.

I clenched my fists at my sides to stop them shaking. Shin Koishi didn't do well with unpaid debts. "Thank you, by the way."

"I don't want your thanks." She waved me off, another crucial strike. Tears watered the warm brown of her eyes, and she looked to the floor as they fell, each tiny, splattered droplet an anvil of guilt pounding through me. "You did what you had to, I get it. But everything tonight...it still hurt. One truth does not erase the other. Your intentions weigh less than the impact you make."

I sucked in a breath. A reality I knew far too intimately.

I watched her for another long moment, counting each tear. Each sin I'd committed against her, each injury I'd have to compensate for one day, if she gave me the chance.

Tomorrow, I'd make a start.

"I told Ecei to meet us at the border in three days. That way, nothing bad happens to any of my contacts here in Hiku City, but also so you can perhaps provide tangible proof to your parents that she was involved." Her gaze snapped up to me again, but I turned around, facing the bricks and the cold night outside. I unlatched the window, needing more air than this tiny room could offer. Needing space from the weight of this Princess's stone stare. "Three days is enough time to get a letter out via raven. Madame Tsojo has one downstairs, and I've already paid the fee."

I hopped onto the ledge before she could respond, leaving her with a choice of her own.

"Where are you going?"

I looked back over my shoulder, finally able to draw out an impression of my signature smirk. "I'll sleep on the roof tonight. Keep watch."

I climbed the fire escape without another word, again realizing just how priceless silence was to a coward like me.

I stayed on the roof for hours, long after I heard the others stumble back into the room, their giggles and whispers—Irina's included—wafting upward from the still-open window.

Irina must not have closed it; whether to give herself some much-needed air, or to leave it open for me, I didn't speculate.

Either way, I didn't return to them, even after the chatter had quieted down and sleep found them all.

The fading night sky was the only company I needed. I stretched out on the tiled roof, stars twinkling above as they watched on, a comfort I'd always loved as a boy.

But even tonight, the stars' watchful stares did little to soothe the anxiety swirling in my head as it all caught up with me. Despite the exhaustion of the day that settled deep in my bones—aching, blistered feet, sore, tired arms, and a headache that felt more like a small man with a giant hammer had taken up residence just behind my brow—sleep evaded me like air filtering through a wide net.

What was I *doing?* I'd never had trouble coming up with plans on the fly, always living by the seat of my pants.

But there was too much at stake now for me to play games.

I'd lost everything tonight. My home, my security, every mark we'd had scrimped and stolen and saved…

And yet, I'd never had more to lose.

I was so wrapped up in my own piteous thoughts, I hadn't heard the roof hatch open hours later; when a sultry voice called my name, I snapped up to my feet, the dagger I'd tucked into my sleeve unsheathed in the same breath.

"Shin?" Via's deep crimson curls swayed in the wind, a smirk on her full mouth as she climbed through the hatch and settled on the ledge. Her eyes flicked to my knife, but her grin only widened. "Whoa there, hot stuff, calm down."

I tucked my weapon away as embarrassment heated my cheeks, falling back to a comfortable crouch as I offered my friend an apology shrug. "Reflex."

Via took a deep breath, wrapping the silken fuchsia robe tighter around her curvy frame. She must have just finished with a client, not bothering to fully dress. It was certainly not the kind of attire a sensible person wore on a chilly night, but Via had always been that way for as long as I'd known her—she'd rather be senseless and dead than unfashionable.

She'd come close a few too many times for my liking.

Still, silken and silly as she was, her presence had a way of warming the very air around me. Madame Tsojo's place had been the safest bet for us—but I'd be lying if I said there wasn't a part of me that'd craved the simplicity of my friend's kindness tonight. Rouged lips pulled into a real smile—not just one of the half smirks she dazzled her clients with. "How's the Forgotten Prince of Hiku City today?"

Normally, I'd bat the title down with a quick quip, but tonight I shot her a wink and leaned in. "Better now that you're here."

Via raised a brow as she swung her bare, toned legs onto the roof, stretching out.

"*Flirting* with me?" she challenged, not out of shyness—no, Via Hashin didn't possess a single shy cell in her body—but out of a knowing that came from reading people's desires for a living. And though this dance was not new for us—we'd both found escape in each other's presence more than a few times—the look she scalded me with said that she knew when I was running from something I should be fighting for. "It must be bad."

I huffed, the con up, as I flopped back onto the roof, staring up at the stars again. They were duller now, the deep blue of the sky already lightening into more of a soft gray as the sun crept closer to waking. Still, I wondered if the stars could see through my bullshit as keenly as Via could. I ran a hand over my face, not looking at her as I heard her shift closer. "I made some mistakes. Or *choices,* really, that I'm not proud of."

That was one way to say *'I kidnapped the Princess of Dunyas after dancing with her all night and burned down my home hours later at the whim of a psychopath regent who'll be stalking me come morning,'* but I couldn't quite manage fitting my mouth around that mess of a sentence.

A soft hand whacked my shoulder. "So make better ones."

I moved my arm, fixing her with a dark look. Normally, my friend's antics were all I needed to lift my spirits, but I'd been weighed down by ironclad chains today. "Oh? Is that all it takes?"

"Mhmm." She nodded, red curls bouncing against her warm skin. She picked at her fingernails—an old habit that lingered no matter how hard Madame Tsojo tried to scare it out of her. "Men walk in here every day and think I am less than them because of what I do. That somehow, I must've made some dire mistakes along the way to end up here."

I opened my mouth, ready to fend for her honor, but she held up a finger to my lips—Via had never really needed my rescuing, not in that way.

She pulled her bronze knees close to her chest. "But living this life, even after all the bad that's happened? It's a choice. It gives me back power. Purpose. So their perceptions of me don't matter when their coins line my pockets. And one day, it'll be *their* money that lets me move on to something bigger and better."

I sighed, imagining the coins and more I'd take from Ecei when this was over. I didn't agree with her methods or her politics, and it rubbed me all kinds of wrong that her and her prick son would always be seen as *better* than me because of their status. Why terrible, awful people like them got to have *everything* when good folk like my Lost Ones had nothing was an unfairness that would gnaw away at my gut like an ulcer for my entire existence.

But her coin could give me something far more important than what anyone thought of me: my sister's life.

And now that Irina was tentatively on board with the plan, it didn't have to rob anyone else of their agency.

Still, there were quiet, traitorous parts of me that sat uncomfortably in my too-tight chest, wishing I didn't have to be disliked for the way I chose to survive.

Your intentions weigh less than the impact you make.

It'd hurt when Irina said it, but it didn't make it any less true.

I patted Via's knee—a polite touch, but affectionate all the same. "Perhaps I should've considered your line of work. At least it's honest."

Fire lit behind her eyes, the gold warm as sunshine despite the night air. "While you're handsome enough for it, that's not what I mean. Just don't forget that sometimes, it doesn't matter how we get there, but only that we *do*."

My stomach coiled as it worked over her words. Intentions and impact...maybe those were concepts only the wealthy had the time to ponder. But in my world—mine and Via's—we didn't always have the choice between more than one path to success. Sometimes, we just had to walk the path we were given, and find a way to make it bend toward where we actually wanted to go.

And riding the wind's back, I had a knack for carving my own path.

I sat up, against the protest of my sore muscles. I needed sleep, but I'd survived worse on less. Offering my friend the same comfort she'd given me was higher on my priority list. I nudged her shoulder as I shimmied closer. "Tsojo said you're feeling better?"

Her eyes crinkled as her cheeks lifted into the brightest smile I'd seen from her since the incident nearly a year and a half ago. "Much. I even got to see Vox today. He's getting big, and the tailors are nice folks. He'll grow up well." Her voice shook ever so slightly as buds of moisture touched her mascaraed lashes. "Thanks to you, Shin. Thanks to *your* choices."

I didn't know if she'd feel the same way if I told her I'd used her infant son's name to lie to *several* royals tonight, but I choked up over the ball of emotion that rose to my throat all the same. I hadn't helped Via for anything in return, but she'd given me more back tonight than I could ever repay.

I'd lost everything.

But with friends like her and the Lost Ones, I knew somehow—perhaps after a decent clip of sleep—I'd find a way to make things right again.

Fix your mess.

I would.

I shut my eyes and laid my head back on my arms before she could call me out for the droplets lining my eyes.

The hatch screeched as it opened again, followed by a familiar snort. "Are you two clothed?"

My stomach twisted into knots. I kept my eyes shut. Maybe if I pretended to be asleep, Mal wouldn't scold me as harshly.

"Why, Malina dear, are you *finally* interested in seeing me naked?" Via cooed, a blissful distraction, but I could hear the genuine intrigue undercutting her tone. It'd been years of trying, to no avail, an uncommon phenomenon in a woman like Via's line of work.

Too bad Mal was only interested in things that were shiny and could buy her more shiny things.

As predicted, Mal countered with a sharp, "I'm running out of ways to say 'No thanks.'"

"Fine, then." The pout was evident in Via's voice. "I'll take that as my leave."

She planted a quick, sweet kiss on my cheek, and I opened one eye just as she sauntered back toward the roof hatch. "Nighty night, Prince Shin."

She disappeared, the opening swallowing her back down, until another form blocked my view, towering over me at this angle.

I squeezed my eyes shut again.

Rustling sounded next to me as Mal's breath tickled my cheek. "You don't have to pretend to be asleep."

My nose wrinkled on its own, betraying my disguise. I sighed, sitting up to scratch the itch and leveling Mal with a warning look. "You didn't have to join me."

She plopped down next to me, eyes narrowed as she chewed down the lecture she'd prepared. Then, with a stretch, "It beats sleeping with Naveen's knee up my ass."

I heard the joke for what it was—a truce between best friends who couldn't afford to be at each other's throats. I stared at my hands, too nervous to meet her diamond-hard gaze. "Are you mad at me for burning our house down?"

"Yes," she said simply. "Are you mad at me for not following your lead and accidentally pissing off Soran and Jaltan royalty?"

I smiled; a small, forgiving thing. "Yes."

She blew out a breath, exhaustion devouring her tiny frame, her shoulders hunched and her head falling forward. A hand wrapped around mine—forgiveness radiating through her warm touch. "We're still in this together, though, right?"

I flopped back down onto the roof, tugging her with me. She groaned under her breath, but settled closer the next moment, her heat warming us both.

Mal and Aya and Kas and I were family–these roofs and streets our nursery and playground. No matter what scrapes and setbacks came our way, that history and loyalty were the only things the world couldn't take from us.

That made me a richer man than any noble in all of Babylon. Prince of the Lost and Found, favored by the ever-watching stars above.

"Always, Mal." I kissed the top of her head before tactlessly blowing an errant curl out of my mouth.

She laughed, smacking my arm. "Always."

THIRTEEN

IRINA

I dreamt of Nikolaj.

Nothing concrete, just the echoes of him. His hearty laugh, his sparkling smile. The way he'd smelled, like earth and patchouli, herbal and sharp just like he was.

Of his warm hands in mine, of the way he tucked me in some nights when I was afraid...

The way his voice sounded, low and rich...

"Shh, be quiet."

No, that wasn't his voice, was it? It was similar, but this one had an edge I didn't recognize, even in the liminal space between sleep and wake.

"You're going to wake her up!" a different voice chided—younger and cold. Definitely not Nikolaj, then.

Something jolted the bed, and a woman's voice cut through the whispered bickering. "So? It's time anyway; we're losing daylight."

My eyes fluttered open, the last grains of the dream slipping through my subconscious fingers like ashes, my brother vanishing again into the Ether. I sat up, tugging the blankets with me as reality rained down. "Where...?"

Dust floated in sunlit streams and my eyes adjusted, the bare walls of the decrepit room coming back into focus as the small gathering of expectant faces watched me.

My stomach sank as I remembered where I was. Who I was with.

To my relief—and regret—Shin was not waiting with the others. Only Naveen, Aya, Malina, and one of the twins...Riku, I guessed, based on his flat expression. Malina waited arms-crossed in the doorway, her scowl ever-present, but the others seemed far more relaxed, Riku lounging next to the window while Naveen and Aya stood side by side, twin expressions of mischief and excitement on their faces.

Naveen smiled brightly, his voice the one that was only a few shades darker than my late brother's, and my gut clenched again as he spoke. "Good morning, Princess. While we apologize for our terrible behavior last evening, when we, you know, kidnapped you, today, we are at your service!"

Naveen bowed low, and Aya followed his lead, a giggle in her throat. I couldn't tell if Naveen was teasing me, but if Aya trusted him, I supposed I did, too. Despite sharing a gene pool with Shin, the girl had no talent for deception, her expression readable even to naïve princesses like me.

"What time is it?" I rubbed my eyes, clearing the lingering tears that'd sprung while I was asleep.

"Just after dawn," Riku declared as he opened the window—when had it closed? I'd left it open last night, just in case—and another wave of dust kicked up as the morning breeze flitted through the space, breathing life back into it. "We know it's early, and we hope you'll sleep well at the next stop, but we thought breakfast was more important."

My stomach grumbled like he'd summoned it. When had I last eaten?

A different anxiety chased away my appetite as more of the last twenty-four hours surged to the surface of my memory.

"What about Ecei?" I flung the blanket back, wrapping my arms around the middle of my filthy dress as I padded out of the bed, the coarse wood floor biting my bare toes. Not that it mattered. I had worse problems to deal with than a few splinters. "She'll catch up."

The others grimaced at the reminder of the devil on our heels, Aya huddling closer to Naveen, but to my surprise, it was Malina who let out a sigh.

"We can spare breakfast." She pushed off the door, her scowl softening into something less aggressive, something closer to an exhausted frown. "We all need our strength."

She walked out without another word, but despite her generally chilly demeanor, the knots in my stomach loosened slightly, undone by her clipped reassurance.

Aya's shoulders relaxed too as she held out a hand, her graceful smile returning. "Come with me. I'll take you to the bathhouse and we can get ready while the others finish up downstairs."

Blush lit my cheeks at the very idea of bathing in an establishment like this, but I held my tongue, the sweat stains on my back and beneath my pits a greater horror than facing a few service girls in the bathroom.

Though as I followed Aya down the hall, early morning groans echoing from some of the rooms, I was tempted to just withstand my own stench and hold my pee in for the rest of my life if it meant I could get out of this place sooner.

Aya turned a corner and pushed into double doors, and I followed, my feet sluggish, but I'd come too far to turn back now. Luckily, we found the giant bath empty, warm water from a pretty bronze faucet already filling a square tub large enough to fit six people.

"Thank you, Aya," I sighed, tension easing out of me like the water trickling into the tub. I was glad I'd never have to see it filled to capacity.

I dipped into one of the nearby bamboo-doored stalls—relieving myself quickly in the small chamberpot—before padding toward the bath, ready to shuck off my ruined dress and scrub myself clean of everything that'd transpired since leaving Anastova.

But another woman bursting through the doors stayed me, my heart jumping to my throat with a little embarrassing squeak.

"Hiya, Aya." The woman nodded to the girl, a smirk on her full lips. She stuck her hands to the hips of a bright pink robe that barely concealed her impressive curves, revealing long legs fully exposed to the top of her thigh. Her gaze swept over me as I tried to keep mine on anything *but* her, my face redder than her hair. "You must be Irina."

"Yes, I—" I stammered, arms wrapping around myself again in an old, protective habit. "I—I didn't catch your name."

The woman's smile softened, and she sauntered over to me, squeezing my arms. "I'm Via. Don't worry, Princess, I'm a friend of Shin's." She said it like that made it better, but instead, something wicked squirmed in my middle, a twisting thing I couldn't quite name. But she thankfully turned away before the feeling could show on my tell-all face, beelining toward Aya. "So, what's the plan?"

Aya dipped a hand into the bath, testing to see if it was warm, but she gnawed at her bottom lip, an unease returning. "I'm sorry, Princess, but...well, we're going to try and keep a low profile, but it might be best to disguise you while we move, at least until we reach Ecei at the border. So Via is here to help me. She's a whiz with cosmetics and costumes."

Her words were all careful, like she was trying not to offend me, but she needn't be. I nodded, the weight in my chest lighter already. When I'd first met Shin, my disguise had been a boon, another form of escape. And I wanted nothing more than to crawl out of my own skin right now and remove myself from all the trouble I'd already caused, to let the last day be a bad memory I never looked at again.

I cleared my throat. "Let's do it."

Via's brows rose, like she hadn't expected my compliance, but she rolled with it, nodding toward the tub. "Bathe first, and then I'll work my magic. Don't worry, the others know this room is off-limits for our special guest's privacy."

Not ready to back down, I let that twisting thing fuel my courage as I stripped—self-conscious with Via's eyes on me, but I didn't let it show—and lowered myself into the warm bath.

Both Aya and Via scurried around, and I noticed that they both were already cleaner than I was, potentially having bathed before I'd even woke up—so I took the opportunity to scrub at my skin until it practically sparkled again, the floral scented soaps along the ledge of the tub surprisingly high-quality; though I supposed it was a necessary investment in this kind of business.

I kept all of my subconscious biases at bay, not about to look down on those who'd offered me such kindness.

After I'd washed every crevice at least three times, I leaned back into the now cool water, savoring the bite of the chill. Mama always kept things in the palace scalding hot—so hot, I could barely breathe as the humidity licked through my lungs.

Who knew a brothel in Hiku City would be this close to paradise?

"We'll have to tie this up…" Hands ran through my long hair, and I jolted as Via laughed, twisting my curls around her fingers before she stepped back, assessing me again. "You have lovely hair, by the way. But dry off first. I brought you clothes. Tara had things that should fit."

I took the towel Aya offered, wrapping it around myself as I shuffled out of the tub, draping my soaking wet wall of hair over my shoulder. The curls were just as heavy and oppressive as the heat of home, the back of my neck always just a little sweatier than the rest of me. By the time I'd finished dressing, there was a huge wet splotch on the soft green tunic Via had fetched for me, my hair bleeding moisture everywhere with no sign of drying properly without a Qualifier's heat.

I'd learned from the best gardeners in Dunyas that one could preserve cut flowers from wilting by trimming the stems once a week. It sliced away the deadest bits, prolonging life just a moment longer each time.

Perhaps I needed a similar trim, to preserve the last parts of rebellion that existed inside me.

What would Nikolaj do?

"What if we cut my hair?" I blurted out, looking into the tall mirror over the wash bin, as Via came up next to me, ready to braid the long, tangled locks.

Her perfectly sculpted brows shot to her hairline. "What?"

I sucked in a breath; no turning back. I'd come too far. "It's my most recognized feature. My mother is obsessed with it—" I cut myself off. I wanted to teach my mother a lesson, to show both of my parents what I could do when tested...but protective parts of me still felt uncomfortable dragging their names into the mud with me. I cleared my throat, meeting Via's eyes in the mirror. "We should cut it. *Short.* To be safe."

My stomach jumped when Via's expression stretched into a feline smile. "I like it."

Aya bounced happily behind us, the most energy I'd seen from the girl since meeting her. Perhaps she'd trimmed some dead ends from her life, too. "I'll go get you the scissors."

She was back faster than the wind, and with each snip, each cut and giggle as the two of them worked, my fear and loneliness abated.

Each cut was a choice. No, a *declaration*.

I wouldn't be bogged down by long, cumbersome vines any longer. I would be as free as a petal in the wind.

And anyone who got in my way—Drakkar, Ecei, my own parents—

Well, I'd snip them away just as easily if I had to.

By the time they finished, leaving a pile of dark, half-dried curls on the bathroom floor that Via assured me someone would clean up for us, I felt light as a feather.

Free.

So free, I didn't even care how silly I must have looked, my curls tight to my head, the longest strands barely brushing across my brows, just long enough to tuck behind my ear.

It was a freedom short-lived as we entered the bustling, tightly packed kitchens on the first floor. The claustrophobic space was narrow but long, a broad bamboo table laid out with stools surrounding it, and on the far end, an impressively large stone oven and stovetop radiated heat. Smells wafted to greet me—bacon and something sweet, setting my stomach grumbling—and every set of eyes swiveled to me as I crossed the threshold. My skin crawled as they stared, all of them frozen in their tasks—Kas, Ren, and Riku setting plates, Ms. Tosjo pouring juice into cups, Naveen and Malina crouched over a strange contraption, and Shin...

Shin, wiping sweat from his brow with a towel, smudges of flour and grease on the apron wrapped around his waist.

I gulped, fighting the urge to cover my hair with my hands and run for the hills.

"There she is!" Ren said first, and I'd never been more grateful in my entire life. The plate he held clattered onto the table as he waved me over, beaming.

"Princess, you look wonderful." Naveen sat back in his chair, and another knot unwound in my chest, the compliment such a far fetch from my mother's scathing criticism.

"Oh, thank you," I murmured, taking the closest seat to the door —the farthest from Shin.

There had been something in the room last night, a moment again where he wasn't the liar or the thief, but the boy who'd saved me from Drakkar in a bar. The man who'd danced with me and made me laugh until my sides ached at the ball.

I couldn't let him be both. Couldn't let *myself.*

But that didn't mean I was about to abandon my newfound cause. So rigid boundaries between us would have to do.

Via plopped down next to me, flinging her arm around my shoulder like we'd been friends for a decade, not less than an hour. "She's a real beauty. And while she's got great hair, the short look brings out those amazing cheekbones."

"And your eyes," Shin added so softly, it took me a minute to realize he'd said it. But he just continued on, taking the seat on Malina's left, like maybe he didn't realize he'd said it out loud, either. Or maybe it was another taunt, another trap to lure me back in, to get me to say something in return that would damn me.

Rigid boundaries, Catirina.

Malina raised a brow at him—okay, so he definitely said it—but Shin ignored the look, grabbing a few slabs of bacon from the platter and topping his plate with a generous helping of fluffy, scrambled eggs.

My cheeks heated more than the oven, hot enough to burn, but no one commented as they filtered around the table—Aya sitting on my other side, Ren and Riku next to her, and Kas next to Naveen, filling out the space.

"Food is getting cold, eat up!" Madame Tsojo said as she placed the last plate—a steaming tray of berry-filled pastries—right in front of me, and I could've kissed her for it.

The others didn't hesitate to load their plates—Mal shoving a double serving for herself and onto Aya's plate, and Naveen with enough to feed three men—so I ignored the automatic prickle of shame that scraped beneath my skin as I helped myself to two of the pastries and a scoop of eggs.

"We have to get moving soon," Malina spoke while chewing a strip of bacon, not bothering to look up from the contraption she was tinkering with. I squinted, looking closer—there were gears and scraps of metal I had no name for, but in the center, a bright sapphire the size of my thumb knuckle *glowed.*

Curiosity tumbled through me, but I would not tempt Malina's fury further. If there was anyone I had to watch out for, it was her.

So I shut my mouth around the berry pastry, nearly moaning as the sweetness coated my tongue. The juicy berry compote dribbled out the corner of my mouth as I struggled not to make crumbs with the light, flaky breading, but I didn't care enough.

"Wow," I said aloud, unable to contain my sheer joy. I looked at the brothel owner with newfound reverence. Tasha was an incredible cook, but this had to be made with magic. "Madame Tsojo, this is *amazing.*"

"I didn't cook, I just put the table together." Tsojo shrugged, taking a bite of her own berry delight. "Shin's the chef. It's why I let him take over my kitchens at the ass crack of day."

My eyes widened to the size of Naveen's plate as I glanced at Shin, shock smacking into me.

"Oh, well." I set the pastry down, wiping the corner of my mouth. "Thanks."

Shin smirked as he forked another mouthful of eggs into his wicked mouth. "Even thieves have to eat."

There it was, that dimple. The one that belonged to my rescuer, my dance partner.

Not today. *Never again.*

Embarrassment lit my face in flames again as my hands shook. I was tired of his teasing, of his games. I blew out an exasperated breath, pushing my plate away like a sullen child. "Is the recipe stolen too, then?"

His smirk fell, and the table went quiet, everyone pausing mid-chew as reality soured the food to bitter.

My stomach twisted as I cursed myself. Yes, they were thieves, but most of them were teenagers, likely orphans…though I hadn't exactly asked, too consumed with my own plight to bother. But it was clear that they'd all had a rough time of things, and because of me, they'd had to burn down their own home last night. And aside from the kidnapping bit, they'd all tried very hard so far to make things up to me, treating me with kindness and consideration despite the limited options. They'd let me sleep alone in the only bed while they all shared the tiny floor, and they'd woken me up, clothed me, and now fed me without asking anything in return aside from my presence.

But that didn't make Shin any less of an adult, or any less of a liar. I understood his conundrum better now, but it didn't erase the hurts. He'd stolen something I couldn't get back. My trust.

I looked down at my hands, my appetite fleeing. This was a *mess*, one a haircut and some pastries couldn't fix.

"Anyway, Irina," Ren broke the silence, a false brightness to his voice, like he was trying to chase away the storm clouds I'd allowed in by swatting them away; a futile effort, but a generous one nonetheless. "What's it like being a princess?"

"I don't know, good? I guess?" I pushed my eggs aimlessly around with my fork. I needed the fuel, but my gut was uncooperative as shame wriggled through it. "I'm definitely very fortunate."

"Must be nice," Kas blurted over a too-full mouth, bits of eggs flying from his lips. I fought a laugh. "How big is your bathroom?"

Malina tore her eyes from her work for a brief second to glare at her brother. "That's a rude question, Kas."

He shrunk back in his seat like a kicked puppy, and my chest ached, so I cleared my throat, slapping a smile on my face. "Bigger than the room we shared last night. I'd rather have slept in my tub than that bed, if I'm being honest."

It might have been a spoiled, selfish thing to say. It might have proved Shin right—that I was just a privileged, naive princess with no concept of real struggle.

But the smile Kas gave me in return made it worth it. Malina's frown relaxed with it, like seeing her brother smile was a rare enough magic to untangle the knots from her scowl.

And the look Shin offered me—one of curious surprise, not contempt—made my heart do things I wasn't even willing to admit to myself.

"That makes two of us," Naveen chuckled, and more of the tension in the room dissipated. "Sorry you had to deal with Kas's snoring."

"I wouldn't snore as loudly if I didn't have your elbow in my back all night," he grumbled in return, pointing his fork at Naveen's face with a frown that he'd borrowed from his sister.

Naveen held his hands up in surrender, and I laughed despite myself. "My brother used to snore, too...it was actually comforting."

Again, I managed to suck all the air from the room. Not that their hearts snared with the same grief mine did, but they all looked at their plates, none daring to even look across into the realm of the dead.

Perhaps that was a commonality among all classes and creeds. Whether you were a richer-than-the-Mother noble or a poor thief, none felt comfortable speaking of the departed.

A significant problem, when so many had been stolen indiscriminately by the Blight.

The Blight that Ecei had a cure for.

A cure that could've saved my brother.

My fingers tightened to a white-knuckled vise around my fork.

"Prince Nikolaj, right?" Aya hedged, her knee nudging mine beneath the table in a gentle show of support. Despite being sixteen, the girl had more empathy than the entire population of Anastova combined.

"Yes." My grip relaxed as I swallowed the lump in my throat.

Nikolaj would've liked her best.

He'd been that way too, at the end. The only one unafraid to speak the truth.

Maybe the only people that knew how to talk of the *after* were the ones staring it in the face.

I sucked in a breath and offered Aya a real smile. I couldn't bring Nikolaj back, my only connection remaining to my brother in my dreams. But I could save Aya. And then, the rest of the continent, if I had my way.

"What do you normally eat in the palace?" Riku, to my surprise, chimed in quietly, stabbing himself another pastry; he'd eaten three already, and I couldn't help but admire another sugar fiend when I found one.

My brother would've been impressed, too.

I took a bite of my own pastry again, my appetite renewed. It would be a shame to waste the food, after all, even if Shin made it.

I swallowed the mouthful before responding, "The cook, Tasha, is amazing with savory, inventive dishes, but I have a major sweet tooth, so usually I steal desserts from her when my mother doesn't notice."

"So you're a thief, too," Kas noted, his head cocked to the side. My skin instinctively crawled with his words, but it wasn't an insult or accusation; just an observation. A black-and-white assessment from a young boy who still could see the world in simple truths.

"I suppose." I took another bite of my pastry. Life was not that simple, not really. But the lying hands that made this decadence didn't taint its sweetness. Perhaps the circumstances that created this group didn't have to get in the way of us helping each other meet our goals, either. I wiped the berry bliss from my lips again and sucked the excess off my thumb before nodding to Kas. "Maybe we're not that different, after all."

Green-tea-and-honey softened as Shin stared at me from across the table. As he tracked the motion of my thumb in my mouth.

This time, I didn't shelter myself against his gaze. I soaked in it, letting it soften my jagged edges.

Finally, he cleared his throat, pushing back from his seat. "Everyone finish up. We have a long journey today, and we've been in Tsojo's hair too long."

No one waited, all jumping to his command. Liar and leader, then. Somehow both, just as I'd been princess and pawn for so long.

The others cleaned up in a frenzied whirlwind, pots scrubbed and dishes cleared in a scarily efficient pace. I helped where I could; stuffing a few of the extra croissants in the loose pockets of my loaned pants and wiping down the table with a cloth after it'd been emptied. It was unfamiliar work, but I relished the opportunity to be useful for once.

The sun shone gold, climbing just above the rooftops by the time we were ready to depart—our meager packs on our backs and our hoods pulled over our heads as we said our goodbyes to the brothel.

"Come back safe, Prince Shin." Via stood in the threshold and stroked his face, and I bristled.

"Why does she call him that?" I whispered to Aya, crossing my arms around my chest.

Aya pursed her lips. "It's a nickname. He...helped her out of a bad situation last year, and they got very close."

Close.

By the way Shin leaned ever so slightly into her touch, I had a pretty decent idea of what *close* meant.

Shameless flirt.

I might have accidentally said that bit out loud, because Via's soft-as-satin curls whipped around as she trained her stare on me.

"I say it because I've never met a man who acts more like a prince than he does," Via declared loudly enough that two of the sleepy merchants in a stall across the street grumbled at her to keep quiet.

"You're embarrassing me, Vi." Shin gritted his teeth as he waved to the merchants—a casual apology—but his face tinted a shade that matched Via's hair.

Absentmindedly, I ran my hand through my own short curls. A reminder of the choices I was making, of the focus I needed. I smiled at Via, grateful for the lesson she'd given me today, even if our very different lives meant we would never truly see eye-to-eye. "You must know a different Shin than the one I've met."

"Maybe, or maybe you just haven't had the chance to see much, yet." Aya shrugged, seeing through me like I was made of glass. "Like you said. Maybe we're not all that different."

For the first time since I'd been taken from Anastova, a small, hopeful part of me wished she was right.

A glossy black carriage pulled by two beautiful chestnut horses clattered over the cobblestone, redirecting my focus.

"Well, Princess, get in," Shin sighed as he lurched the door open, dropping into a ridiculously low bow. "Your chariot awaits."

I stuck a hand to my hip, a brow raised. "Where did you get this? *Whose* is it?"

Shin gnawed his lower lip, fighting a smirk. "We're just borrowing it from a friend of Via's."

My eyes rolled, but I got into the carriage, murmuring under my breath as I slid across the fine leather seats, "Petty thief."

Shin leaned against the door, his smile reaching his eyes. "And now, you're my accomplice."

FOURTEEN

SHIN

The wind changed as we clambered on the road out of Hiku City, northward bound toward Nehir. It was no longer friendly, not the accomplice I'd come to know like the back of my own hand; instead, it was a wild, skittish thing, whispering threats of danger down my back in icy gusts. The horses' hoofbeats echoed the breeze's quiet warnings as cobblestone shifted to dirt roads, homes and buildings replaced by wandering airships above and houseboats along the river. While Hiku City and the eastern coast of Sora were both hubs of transportation and commerce, the more rural Soran communities that dared dwell between the frosty caps of the giant Kawayama Mountains and the widest, deepest stretches of the Black River had always been sparsely populated. But since the Blight's conquest, these small towns had suffered the gravest losses, entire communities wiped out in weeks, or forced to relocate when business ran dry as a result.

By noon, we were a few dozen miles out of the city, and we hadn't seen another soul.

There was comfort in the quiet, despite the fiendish wind; it gave me a chance to think, to *plan*, without interference. Of course, I could hear the others chatting merrily in the carriage, but I didn't mind, the pitch of their voices a white noise in my head that helped me focus.

I had two goals, now, and neither of them seemed to want to work with the other. First and foremost, Aya needed a cure. She'd been smiling all morning, as energetic as I'd seen her in years as she got to play dress up with Irina, and my heart twisted as I realized how sorely she'd needed a friend. But as good as it was to see my sister up and about, I knew better than anyone that this would cost her. The crash was coming, and when it hit, it'd be big.

A small, terrified part of me wondered if she'd survive it this time.

But on the other hand, there was the issue of the Princess's safety. Irina had started out as just another job, but I couldn't forgive myself if she got hurt by Ecei in this process. She deserved a safe, happy life with whatever over-fluffed noble she chose, just as much as my sister deserved to live. I was many terrible things—a thief, a liar, a runner. But I wasn't a human-trafficker, and if I couldn't guarantee Irina a decent end to this journey, I wouldn't hand her off, no matter the cost.

It was on my shoulders to find a way to satisfy both needs.

"Are we there yet?" a whine pulled me from my thoughts as Malina climbed up to the driver's box, plopping onto the cushioned bench next to me.

"Funny." I rolled my eyes, but scooted over to accommodate her better. I'd be lying to say I didn't appreciate her company—even when we were at odds, Malina was the only person I could truly unwind around. I jerked my head toward the hand-drawn map perched in front of me, courtesy of Madame Tsojo. "We'll hit Kisari by evening. It'll be our best bet to find somewhere to stay and get some food in us."

Malina nodded, but stuck a thumb toward the stagecoach. "They won't recognize our *baggage?*"

By baggage, she meant Irina.

The comment shouldn't have rattled me, but it did, my feathers ruffled as I swallowed back the rebuttal that flew to the front of my lips. It was not my responsibility to protect the girl, gentle as she was. She had more than I could ever have, and had done nothing with it. It wasn't my job to placate someone who had the whole of Dunyas at her fingertips, yet insisted on painting *me* as the lazy, greedy one.

So I shoved down the silly, self-righteous instinct and instead focused on Malina's question. We *did* have to lay low, and my partner-in-crime knew how to hide and redirect just as well as I did. "Did you recognize her this morning?"

She shrugged, crossing her feet on the front of the footboard. "I don't bother looking much. I just don't want her to bring trouble."

I pursed my lips at her; her contempt toward the Princess was warranted, but no longer helpful. I understood Mal's commitment to the role of villain, but Irina had been compliant enough once we got her out of the Treehouse; she hadn't tried to harm or screw us yet, despite having every right to. Without her help with Ecei, we'd be so eternally lost.

I sighed, Aya's words from earlier floating around me like smoke that wouldn't clear no matter how much I waved it off.

Maybe you just can't see each other clearly yet.

But I had seen Irina. Not as the Princess or my mark, but the layers beneath those masks, her true form revealed in the gentle moonlit night.

I cleared my throat, offering my friend a long overdue explanation. "The night Ecei nailed us, Irina was in the Crescent."

"What?" Malina jolted forward, nearly toppling off her seat. She ran a manic hand through her mess of curls, twisting to face me head-on as hurt dripped from her acid tone. "And you didn't *tell me*?"

"I'm telling you now." I flashed a smile, one that said '*Please don't kill me, I'm sorry*' before nudging her with my arm. This was as smart as poking a feral tiger, but I'd learned how to handle Malina years ago. She'd never bite me, no matter how I pushed her. But her narrowed, boiling hot gaze demanded more information, and required it *now*. I stared ahead, trying to slow my heartbeat to match the horses' steady gait. "That's why I was late. She was talking with Prince Drakkar himself in a tavern full of nobles all on their way to *her* ball, and none of them noticed. Ecei could've trapped her herself that night if she'd known, and this all could've been avoided. But not one of the bastards recognized her."

It was mind-boggling, still, that they hadn't figured her out that night. But I supposed it just reaffirmed something every beggar on the street knew, something anyone who didn't fit among the upper crust had learned the hard way.

Most nobles couldn't see shit past their upturned noses.

"But you recognized her, at the ball. Which is why you changed the plan." Malina flopped against the seat, head lolling back as she took a deep breath, the tiger sedated. I watched her, a pit opening in my gut; she looked so tired, the bags beneath her round eyes deeper than I'd seen them in years, the frizz of her curls even more pronounced than usual.

I patted her knee, wishing the small touch could siphon some of that heaviness from her back. She was my partner and best friend, but she was still my charge; my responsibility. Even if she was only two years younger than me.

I sucked in a breath, letting it rejuvenate me. I needed to be strong for all of them, Malina included. "Either way, I don't think a bunch of bumpkins from Kisari will recognize a princess they've never seen when so few of her own kind can place her."

Malina nodded, running a hand over her face. "Well, that's good enough for now. How much money do we have?"

I grinned, thanking the Breath for the first small moment of good luck we'd had in weeks. "The gentleman we're *borrowing* this carriage from left some silvers in the bench, so enough for food and to rent more than one room tonight."

"Maybe not two rooms, that's a bit steep," she cautioned, but the familiar twinkle returned to the pixie's dark gaze. "But we could spring for a few drinks?"

I handed her the reins for a moment as I stretched my arms, relieving the built-up tension from my back. My spine crackled and popped in several spots, evidence of a night on a roof and a life on the run. Breath above, did I need a stiff drink and a bed almost as much as I needed air in my lungs. "Why not? We've earned it."

Malina snorted, cracking her own neck. But something still wrestled in those eyes that I knew too well, embers of a fire that wouldn't be stamped out entirely. Her grip tightened on the reins. "I like you better when you tell me things, Shin. I've had enough of the secondary agenda."

Guilt and logic tangled together in my head. She was right; we'd always been on the same page, a necessary strategy if we were going to survive. I hated leaving her out of the narrative. But that required a trust that neither of us had been willing to offer as of late; a cycle of missed steps that had us dancing to entirely different beats.

"I like you better when you actually listen to me, Mal," I retorted, my jaw tight. "We could've worked together sooner if you weren't so stubborn."

The fire surged for a moment, but then her face split in a wide grin. "I'll stop being stubborn when you stop being stupid."

A real, honest chuckle made its way up from my throat, the comfort of our normal bickering unknotting more tangles from my too-tight chest. This is what it was supposed to be like, between Malina and I. These were the roles we knew best.

Liar and lure, damsel and devil.

Stubborn and stupid.

I beamed. "Deal."

"And because I want you to not be stupid…" she hedged, lower lip sucked between her teeth as she wrangled her words into submission. "Don't let a pair of big eyes and a soft smile make you lose your head. You know how this ends for all of us—Aya included—if we don't play it smart."

Her tone was not unkind, but it was sharp, just as pointed as the breeze against the back of my neck.

I watched the dirt road for a long moment, the soil turning beneath the horses' hooves, the surrounding trees abandoned by all but the ghostly wind that rustled the branches. Malina was right. If I wanted to save my sister, if I wanted to get back to Hiku City and start again, we had to be clever. But leaving Irina in the dust wasn't an option, either. "I'm focused, Mal, I know what's at stake. But I also don't need to be cruel. She's had a rough time."

Malina huffed, resigned. "We all have."

That was the understatement of the century. The last week had been one of the worst I'd had in a decade, and even then, the time away from my last escape had softened the edges of those particularly harrowing memories. We needed the wind to shift in our favor, for it to sing the song of luck and victory for once instead of the echoes of war to come.

"Have you gotten your device to work yet?" I eyed my friend, hoping the fire-sprite had a win up her sleeve for me. I'd had my reservations when Malina had stolen the broach again; double-crossing Ecei was not on my to-do list in this lifetime or the next.

But when a smile chased away the lingering smoke from her expression, relief flooded my veins.

"Naveen and I finished it this morning." Deft fingers tugged the metal contraption from her pocket in a swift motion, the sapphire center gleaming in the midday sun. She pointed to the odd gears and shining antennas as she explained, her voice pitching higher as excitement and pride made her soar. "I had Naveen Qualify the stone to reverse the magnetic pull, and then I added a heat sensor...but now, the fae-stone will warn me when Ecei is near, so we can prepare, but she can't track us directly. Our last location would have been Tsojo's."

Right where we wanted Ecei to go, my letter waiting for her. Now we just had to hope and pray to the Breath above she'd take the bait and not kill us for it.

I stroked my friend's curls, pressing a quick kiss to the top of her head. "You're the best."

"I know," Malina snorted as she leaned into the embrace, and for the first time since that night at the Crescent, things felt right again. Whole. *Hopeful.*

I should've listened to the changing wind.

A burnt-coral sky chased the setting sun as we reached the small city of Kisari, the only relatively large establishment left on this side of the Kawayama Mountains. But even from the outskirts, it was easy to tell that this place was barely a shell of its former self, the buildings crumbling beneath tangled walls of ivy and signs coated in thick layers of dust as the carriage rolled deeper into the streets.

By nightfall, we managed to reach the inner city, luckily finding a few lit streetlamps and people in rags hurrying about the town square as they settled for the night. But as we passed, they fixed us with dirty, *hungry* looks, assumptions and accusations written in their sunken stares.

I hated how the fancy stagecoach painted a target on our backs, but we had no other alternative if we were going to reach Nehir in time. So I stayed alert, scanning every face as we passed, searching for fellow thieves among the small crowds, or worse—people desperate enough to become one tonight.

Finally, the rickety creak of a nearby sign drew my attention, light pouring from the wide windows of a large wood-front building. The ivy had been beaten back here, only a few defiant tendrils reaching up toward the patched roof, and the front door stood sturdy on its hinges.

"The Frog Hollow Inn." I squinted to read the uneven sign, the wood decaying in spots. It definitely seemed like a place toads would rest their slimy heads for the night. "Sounds cozy."

"I don't care, I just need to stretch." Naveen popped his upper half out of the coach's window, eyeing The Frog Hollow wearily.

"And eat." Riku appeared next to me in a swift motion, too quiet for his own good.

"And *sleep*," Kas whined loudly from within the stagecoach, his voice cracking over the word.

I sucked my teeth, contemplating. Something about the spot nibbled at the back of my mind, a warning I couldn't quite make out despite my fluency in the language of danger. But it was unlikely that we were going to find a better option any time soon, and my back had knots on top of knots. The other Lost Ones were fighters, but they were still young. Still growing. We needed a break.

"Fine. The Frog Hollow it is." I tugged the reins, directing the horses around the corner to a small stable behind the building.

By the time we had them boarded and the carriage emptied, my stomach rumbled like thunder, demanding immediate attention and erasing any doubts I'd had about stopping. I'd gone hungry before, but after years of comfort in the Treehouse, my gut seemed to have forgotten what it could handle.

"Do you think we can get more than one room tonight?" Irina asked me quietly as she stepped out of the carriage, her gray cloak wrapped tightly around her despite the relatively warm evening.

I opened my mouth to respond, parts of me roaring with victory that she decided to talk to me directly, not just through sideways comments or reactive jabs.

"No," Malina interrupted before I could speak, hefting her small pack over her shoulder before marching toward the front door. "Too expensive."

Irina frowned as she followed, eyes narrowing as they flicked between Malina and I. "I know you all slept on the floor, so I'm not complaining, it's just—"

"Don't worry, Princess, we don't need sleep when your lovely face is around to awaken our spirits." Ren threw an arm around her shoulder, tucking her into his side, the action both casual and confident. Irina stiffened for a moment, but didn't pull away.

A different animal squirmed in my gut, a beast I thought I'd buried in a ballroom in Anastova.

"Ignore him," Aya quipped, rolled her eyes as she trudged after them with slow, shaky steps.

I moved to catch up with her, ready to support her weight, but Irina nudged Ren's side and slipped out from his embrace, instead looping her arm through Aya's.

"I know, I know, or it'll go to his head," Irina snickered, a smile breaking across her face like a wave against the shore.

Warmth spread through my aching chest, unwinding thorny brambles that'd been there for so long, I'd grown familiar with their weight.

I cleared the lump from my throat with a cough, my winds propelling me forward in a quick jolt to meet Malina at the front door before she could barge in without a plan. I splayed my hand across the splintering wood, glaring at my companions from beneath it in a singular warning.

"Everyone stays quiet. Let Malina and I do the talking. These folk aren't typically as welcoming as the city dwellers," I reminded them, relying on the information that I'd gotten from Tsojo and Aheni to get us through this long con. None of the Lost Ones—myself included—had been out of the city aside from our trip to Dunyas in ages. We were not on our own turf, and it put us at a disadvantage I didn't like, especially considering the sensitivity of our mission. My winds drew tighter around us, blocking out the noise from the street—and silencing our conversation to any eavesdroppers that might be prowling about. "Remember, we don't need to draw unnecessary attention. It's already strange that we're traveling in such a big group, and protecting the Princess is our primary goal."

Irina's gaze darted up at me from beneath thick lashes, surprise transcribed in their deep brown, but I shifted toward the others, my mission too important for my flippant heart to get in my way.

Nodding heads signaled my crew's understanding. As feral as they all were, they understood the code of survival, its blood-red brush-strokes written into every scar and scrape among them.

Satisfied with their compliance, I swung the door open, stepping over the threshold and into the part I had to play tonight.

The inside was just as dusty and disordered as the exterior, the wooden bartop cracked in spots, the surrounding stools standing on uneven, untrustworthy legs. A few other bodies—five, by a quick count—huddled around one of the small tables, nursing mugs of something that smelled worse than piss, flies buzzing around the lanternlight that highlighted more gaunt cheeks and broken stares.

Frog's Hollow, indeed.

I kept my distaste from my face, confidently strolling up to the barkeep with a warm, too-trusting smile swiped over my face.

"Good evening, sir!" I pitched my voice high—like I'd seen far too many annoying tourists do in the Crescent's embrace. "Is there any availability left for the night?"

The bald man turned, wiping out one of the glass mugs as he scrutinized me. I did the same, noting his stature casually. He was almost as tall as Naveen, his bloated, pale skin wrinkled around the corners of a mouth set in what seemed to be a permanent frown. His thick chin wobbled as he croaked, "For how many?"

"There are eight of us total, but we can share if need be." I gestured to my group behind me, beaming with pride that would surely grate on any man's nerves. I leaned against the bar, letting my shoulders sink in feigned submission, my voice still too loud for the quiet, half-dead bog. "You see, we're all headed to a family reunion back in Yoroko, but we've been riding in the carriage all day, and we could use a few hours' sleep—"

The barkeep grunted, cutting me off from giving him my entire falsified life's story. But he pursed his lips, looking at the rest of us too closely for my liking.

"Family reunion, ey?" His gruff voice scratched like wood chips against bare feet as he set the mug down, hands gripping the side of the bar like he could snap the thick boards in half. "You don't look much like family."

My stomach lurched beneath his heavy stare, but I kept my ignorant smile intact, clapping like an idiot at the fool's parade.

"It's technically two families, really." I waved my hands emphatically, nodding to where Irina stood in the middle of the group. I was overselling it, but if I annoyed him enough, perhaps he'd move on without a deeper look.

On cue, the barkeep sighed and looked to where Irina and Naveen stood out from the rest, their deep skin marking their southern heritage.

"See my wife there, with the short hair? The tall one is her brother," I explained the difference away, Irina's face blooming pure red. I winked once at her before tugging Malina closer and ruffling her curls. "My sister here and the rest of my siblings are all meeting their parents for the first time since the wedding. It's really an overdue reception."

"Yes, it's very exciting." Malina pinched my side, but fell right into her role without hesitation, batting her long lashes at the barkeep, her voice sweet as honey. "We all wanted to make the trip, but with the Blight, it's been difficult. I'm only a single seamstress, and his wife is unfortunately a bit slow...so she washes clothes for me, but the pay isn't what it used to be."

I shot Malina a glare for the underhanded quip at Irina, but the man's broad hands released their death grip from the ledge, his frame softening under her candied coaxing. His tongue darted quickly across his bottom lip, like it was about to strike out and swallow Malina at a moment's notice. "Money is tight around here too, with all the blasted taxes and the Blight. Do you have coin?"

"Yes, a few silvers." I slipped him two, more than enough for what this toad-stooled shithole could offer. Still, I'd rather overpay and have fewer questions asked than have to haggle in unfriendly waters.

The man grunted again, snagging the silvers with swollen fingers and tucking them into his apron. "We only have one room."

Disappointment twisted through my ribs, but I didn't let it translate across my face, my dimpled cheeks unwavering from their posted grin. I snuck another copper onto the wood. "And perhaps something to eat, if the kitchen is still open?"

The man flinched, hands clenching at his side, sending a trickle of apprehension running like sweat down my back.

"It's closed. My wife cooks, but she's been ill," he snapped out each clipped word, a pain I knew too well hidden beneath his layers of gruffness. "I've got some jerky and bread you can take."

I should've just nodded, should've taken my crew and the jerky to the room and let us get some Breath-damned sleep. But the wind tickled the back of my neck, urging me on.

One more favor. One last kindness to erase my recent sins.

"Perhaps I can help out for the evening?" I rolled back my sleeves, peering behind him toward the kitchen entrance. From the size of this place, it couldn't have been too small, even if it was a mess. I wrapped my truths in a careful lie as I smiled again. "I'm a cook myself, back at a small hole in the wall in Hiku City. It's got nothing on this place, but I could whip something up, offer your other guests a hot meal."

The barkeep swallowed tightly, his bullfrog chin trembling with the action.

"There's nothing to whip up," he rasped, as he shook his clenched fist. Not at me, but at a larger, looming, unseen adversary we all were running from.

Hunger. Sickness.

Death.

Vicious blame poured from him. "The Breath-damned

Dunyasians haven't sent produce up this way in weeks. We're getting by on scraps ourselves, but with my wife sick, we haven't been able to travel into the city to restock on supplies."

Some of the other heads in the bar lifted, grunting in famished agreement.

The Frog's Hollow might have once been a place of rest and respite, a warm inn where hot stew with fresh frog legs from the river were served by the bucketful. But now, it was exactly what it'd named itself: hollow.

Much like the rest of Babylon since the Blight had carved out our insides.

I nodded to the barkeep, the pangs of hunger and loss still too fresh in my gut to ignore his. "I hear you, sir. The room and the jerky are more than enough."

"But that can't be right," a voice nagged behind me, and my stomach clenched with a different pain—fear knotting my intestines as Irina stepped forward, her brow furrowed. "The trade agreements all say that Dunyas sends deliveries all the way up the Black River once a week."

"Pssh, you were right about this one," the barkeep snorted at Malina, twirling his finger by his temple in an unkind gesture typically saved for the total wackjobs. But the darkness that crept over his expression chased away any humor of the moment, his nose twitching as he glowered at Irina. "The agreements don't mean shit to those southern cocksuckers. It's *always* this way after their Breath-fucked party. They're all too drunk and high to get back to work. Not that they do much of that anyway."

"You could say that again." Malina stroked his ego with a smile, but it didn't quite read as sincerely this time.

The wind's song turned sinister, and I stepped closer to the Princess, gripping her arm before she could walk herself into thicker mud. But she jerked herself from my grasp, her own anger deepening the red of her cheeks. She trembled as she spoke. "The people of Dunyas work very hard, and the Masque is a celebration that they earn as a reward."

"The nobles of Anastova haven't sweat in years, girlie, and the farmers are all too opium-whipped to give a shit," the bald man growled, nostrils flaring as his voice carried through the bar. "By the Breath, what pipe are you smoking?"

Irina blinked, tears lining her lashes, and my facade slipped away, protective parts rallying through my muscles as I tensed.

One last jab.

"Hey, watch how you talk to my wife," I warned through a tight smile as I tucked Irina beneath my arm, my eyes never leaving the old frog. But I didn't need to hear the wind's alerts to know this would turn messy fast if we didn't find a way to sweep it under the rug. "Dear, you must be tired. Why don't we head to the room and get some rest? All of us?"

The others nodded—Ren and Kas shuffling Aya closer to the staircase while Naveen and Riku pulled closer to me; reinforcements, just in case.

The owner eyed our little group—noticing how young we were, most likely—and pulled a key from his pocket with a scoff and a glare.

Victory bells rang in my head until Irina opened her mouth again.

"Fine," she pouted with a sniffle and a dismissive wave—and folded herself closer to my side. "I don't need to argue politics with someone who clearly doesn't know very much anyway."

At that, the other patrons' heads swiveled again—the insult a declaration of war to desperate hearts already looking for a fight— and the barkeep's expression went purely animalistic.

"If you want the room," the man dangled the room key in front of me with a sneer, exposing the full maw of half-rotted teeth, "you'll teach that whore wife of yours to shut her stupid mouth."

Two distinct things happened at once, neither of them things I could've predicted.

Irina gasped like she'd been smacked across the face.

Then, something in me *snapped.*

I barely recognized my own voice, low and taunting as it was. "If you'd like, I can teach *your* wife a little something, too."

Wrong thing to say.

Faster than I imagined for someone his age, the man leapt halfway onto the bar top, his fist skimming just below my jaw as I spun Irina and me out of the way. The Princess yelped in my arms before I shoved her behind me, positioning myself between her and the barkeep.

"Well, shit," Naveen huffed as the other patrons hopped up, shouts erupting. But he dropped into a grappler's stance, long limbs strong and ready. Here—and in Hiku City—the poor and desolate stuck together, having nothing but each other.

The owner huffed as he slid over the bar, face beet red and bloated with pressured rage.

So much for a good night's sleep.

Two things happened in tandem again, reality splitting into cross breezes.

Like clockwork, Malina scrambled on swift feet to the door, directing the kids out, giving me the freedom I needed to unleash.

And then the toad of a man attacked, his hands reaching not for me, but just past me—locking around Irina's throat.

One choked sob escaped her mouth, fingers clawing at his hands for purchase, but she didn't get a chance to latch on.

Instinct took over, and I *became* the wind, a gale force of rage that blew the man so fiercely he flew across the room. He slammed into the far wall with a sick crack, rotted wood splintering under his weight as he crashed into a table.

The bar descended into madness.

The five other men sprinted to us, slurs spitting past their lips as they attacked.

"City-dwelling pricks!"

"Just a rat with a Dunyasian whore."

"I resent that remark," Naveen grunted as he tripped one, smashing him into the next. They both groaned as they hit the floor, Naveen standing over them with a frown. "Very impolite."

Shoving Irina back—hoping she'd have enough sense to flee for the door after Malina—I lurched forward. In a singular, practiced motion, I snatched one man's cloak and wrapped it around his neck, yanking back until he choked and fell, the wind leaving his lungs.

Mentally, I latched onto his air, his lungs squeezing until his eyes floated to the back of his head, unconsciousness dragging him under. I released him, sending him off to dreamland for a bit.

With a snarl, another made a break for me, dipping low to snag me around the middle. A good trick, but too slow. I used his own momentum, pressing against his shoulders to leapfrog over him, sending him stumbling toward Naveen. "Catch!"

Naveen did—wrapping his long limbs around the man and lifting him three feet off the ground before slamming him against the wall. The man slumped to the floor, and Naveen tossed me a smile. "Good throw."

I laughed, the adrenaline pumping through me the only fuel I had left. It would be another long night after a series of them, and maybe that was the reason I was so distracted. So foolish.

Two things happened at the same time.

Irina stood in the doorway, eyes wide with abject horror as she shouted, "Watch out!"

Exactly as the fifth man—the one mark I'd forgotten to keep my eye on—sent a silver blade whirling through the air.

For the first time in my life, the wind said nothing at all as the knife embedded itself into Naveen's side, and my friend fell.

Fifteen

IRINA

Silver flashed, and then all I saw was red. On Naveen's hands, spreading across his white shirt like wildfire.

Fire.

Naveen burned, the fire consuming him as he crumpled to the ground—

No, not burning. *Bleeding.*

And it was my fault.

The man who threw the knife made a horrid choking sound, and fell to the floor in a lifeless heap, silenced.

I didn't have it in me to be afraid or concerned for the stranger as I watched Shin drop his hand, shadows clearing from his dark gaze. Then he was at Naveen's side in a breath, a hand on his neck, feeling for a pulse. His voice broke and shattered into a thousand tiny pieces as he called his friend's name. "Naveen?"

Someone help!

He's just a boy!

Shakes rattled my frame as I stumbled forward, knees crashing into the wood as tears blurred my vision. Shin cradled Naveen in his arms like he was no bigger than a child, careful of the knife still sticking out of his side, hefting his mass to a sitting position. Naveen's head lolled into his friend's chest, and I never thought a giant could look so *small.*

The fire spread, soaking the floor and Shin's hands in crimson.

My fault. All my fault.

"I'm so sorry," I sobbed, a small burst of hope pinging my lips into motion as Naveen's eyes fluttered open and closed, his breathing shallow. "This is all my fault, I'm so sorry."

I reached out a shaking hand, but green-tea-and-honey eyes cut to me in a vicious slash, their hue a poisonous green.

"Not now, Irina," Shin clipped out, my name dripping with that same venom; he stroked his friend's brow, his dimpled smile returning so forcefully it had to ache. Petal-soft words floated from his lips, and a gentle breeze tossed his friend's curls. "Hey, Naveen, stay with me, bud."

Naveen groaned as he doubled over, a semiconscious hand gripping his bleeding middle. Shin quickly covered his hand, adding pressure to the spot around the knife. As if together, with willpower and grit alone, they could stop the fire from spreading. "We have to keep this here until I can fix you, bud."

I must have repeated my *sorry* out loud, because Naveen's warm gaze flicked to me, fog clearing as he blinked to focus.

"It's not that bad, Princess." He smiled through a wince. "I've had worse."

Guilt stole the breath from my lungs, choking me on my own sins.

Don't worry, Ri-Ri. I'll be fine.

But it wasn't fine. Not then, and not now.

I'd been helpless to save my brother, and I was helpless now. But this time, it was *my fault.* If I hadn't opened my mouth, if I hadn't riled the barkeep with my silly notions of loyalty, there would have been no match to light this flame. No spark to set Shin and Naveen's world on fire.

My fault.

This is what happens when you speak, girl.

Stay in your room, Irina!

The door crashed open again behind us, but for once in my life, I didn't startle, my body numb as I watched Shin hold Naveen's life in his palms, both of them grinning at each other to mask their pain.

"What's the hold–?" Malina started, and then stopped. Then, a single syllable that held the weight of the whole world. "*No.*"

Shin's throat bobbed as his gaze flicked to her, bloodshot and broken. "Malina, get the kids out."

"What?" Malina's voice cracked and fissured, as did parts of my soul. She skidded to his side, a hand on Naveen's knee. "I'm not leaving you."

"Go, before they wake up." Shin jerked his head to the barkeep and the others, all of them knocked out, but breathing. They'd recover, and soon. All but one, the knife-thrower's body an abandoned, breathless lump where he last stood.

His death was my fault, too. A desperate man trying to find a meal, dead because of a fight I started. Over a problem I had no business to speak on. In a world where I didn't belong.

"I'm so sorry," I repeated again, but the words were shallow, not enough to convey the pit of despair and regret that yawned wide in my chest.

Malina's tear-soaked lashes fluttered as she whipped to face me, top lip quivering in a snarl. "You useless bitch."

Useless.

Yes, that was the word for it. For the failure that I was. For the space I took up despite everyone else's wishes.

Useless as a flower in a vase, a decoration that always got in the way.

"*Malina,*" Shin warned as Naveen shuddered, urgency chasing away that smile of his. Gingerly, Shin laid his friend back on the ground, yanking up his ruined tunic to examine the wound—

The fire had become a molten, flowing pool on the floor, warm as it hit my knees and turned my gray trousers to deep rose.

Shin's face went white.

I knew only what I'd been able to read from stolen medemental books, but the angle of the knife as it protruded from Naveen's side told the whole story without a word. There were no herbs or tinctures that could fix this.

"I'm going to get help." Malina stood, a determination setting her spine straight while the rest of the world bowed beneath the weight of this grim reality. "We have some of Madame Aheni's stock in the carriage. I'll get it for the pain, and we can stitch you up."

"No, no drugs." Naveen's hand clawed out in desperation as he snagged Malina's calf as she turned to go, rooting her in place with the last of his strength. "I won't do it again."

"Naveen, we have to stop the bleeding," Shin removed his friend's hand from Malina, nodding at her to hurry. With one last boiling hot glare at me, she sprinted through the door, swifter than a lightning strike.

"I said *no*, Shin," Naveen grunted, his eyes trailing after Malina with a sunken stare, followed by a humorless chuckle. "You're not always the boss, mate."

I'd seen that stare before.

Saw it every time I closed my eyes, the image of it burned into the back of my eyelids, haunting my every rest.

Saw it in every lingering dream, where Nikolaj still dwelled with me, a constant reminder of my failures.

"We have to move you." Shin's head swiveled on an axis, like he was looking for any answer hiding somewhere in this rundown tomb, hoping a solution would jump out from the cracks in the floorboards.

There would be none.

There never was.

Live for both of us, Ri-Ri.

Shin tried to lift Naveen, but the wounded man cried out and slumped deeper into the ground, like he'd dissolve into it along with the blood stains.

"No going on that." Naveen's voice took on the same hollow, floating quality Nikolaj's had. Like it was already half to the Ether. His body shook, but his words were steady as he gripped his friend's hand. "Hey, listen, get the kids out, okay? Help Aya, she needs you. I'm okay, I promise."

Don't worry, I'll be fine.

Eyes shut.

His breath hitched.

My heart cracked.

My fault.

"No, no, no!" Shin's panic sliced me open as he grabbed Naveen's cheek. His brow furrowed as he forced air into his lungs, a half-choked plea strangling him. "Stay with me, man, please."

Naveen's eyes didn't open.

They wouldn't.

My fault.

Shin's tears watered his friend's face like rain trying to reanimate the dead soil after a drought. "Come on, Naveen, *please.*"

And that *please*—that single hopeful, ruptured word—cracked open a lock inside of me.

Stay in your room, Irina!

Don't you dare do that ever again!

I moved before I could think, before all of the rules I'd lived under my whole life could leash me.

Pale skin, blistered and charred to black.

Light; blinding, searing.

I reached toward Naveen, his skin already cold as I skimmed my fingertips over the wound—

"You've done enough!" Shin pushed my hand away, his shoulders shaking with silent sobs, his eyes brimming with a thousand cruel words he wanted to hurtle at me, until I was just as cut up and broken as Naveen.

"Please," I breathed his own word back to him as I wiped a tear from his cheek, and he flinched beneath my touch. I winced, but I deserved that, and so much more, for what I'd done to these people. For what I had to do to make *right.* "Please let me help, we don't have time."

His expression did not change, hatred pouring out with his tears. But when I moved again, he didn't stop me.

My eyes closed as my hands pressed into the wound.

And my eyelids burned red with fire as light erupted.

"Don't touch him!" Malina cried from behind me, but her voice was a million miles away. My only focus was the heat in my palm as it tugged from the deepest parts of me, the force within surging to the surface in blinding agony.

"Oof, that tickles, Princess," Naveen coughed, and I pressed deeper, gritting my teeth around the pain that shook my limbs. "You should buy a man dinner—*agh!*"

I yanked the knife out without warning, clearing the obstruction, and Naveen's cries echoed my own torment, my bones threatening to break beneath the pull of a vortex that siphoned from my very soul.

"I'm sorry, it's the only way." I squinted an eye open and groaned through my clenched jaw, my body tremoring. "It has to be quick."

Quick, or I'd fall over the edge and burn out, fizzling into nothing. Quick, or the skin and muscle I was stitching and Qualifying with life would tear again.

But the blood stopped, fire halted and extinguished, as Naveen's flesh reunited with itself beneath my touch. As cells and sinew were made whole again.

As I revealed the one thing I swore I never would. The one thing that kingdoms would kill for if they knew about it.

When it was done, I slumped back, head spinning as the world blurred in and out of focus.

And for the second time in my life, I lifted my weary head to face the truth.

Eyes wide with terror, mouths set in disgusted frowns.

"What did you just do?" Malina whispered, but she was staring at Naveen, not me, in disbelief.

At *Naveen,* who sat perfectly upright, fingers frantically searching his abdomen for a wound that no longer existed. "*How?*"

Only one pair of eyes settled on me. Green-tea-and-honey, wide with shock and something more familiar. Something *horrifying.*

Recognition.

His mouth parted on quiet words I didn't understand. "The fairy from the fire."

He might have said something else, something that I wanted to hear, but it didn't register as exhaustion stole my consciousness.

Sixteen

SHIN

Fragmented memories assaulted my mind from every angle.

The buzz of violins. The screams of onlookers.

The scent of burning flesh—my flesh.

Pain. Everywhere. All at once.

Then a girl, so small, she had to be a fairy. Magic, warm and soft as it cleared my pain. A voice, sweet as stardust she whispered to me. "One more breath. You can do it."

I thought it had been a dream.

But as I caught her before she could fall face-first into the pool of my friend's blood, as I cradled her in my arms...there was no denying that she was real. And *alive*, by the thrum of her heartbeat beneath my crimson-soaked fingertips.

I'd wanted her dead five minutes ago.

Now, I didn't know what I wanted. But holding her and never letting go felt like a good start.

Hold on, don't let go.

"We need to go now." Malina's whip-crack tone startled me as I blinked back into the present, foggy memories of my past clearing away.

I nodded, urgency reanimating my limbs. Fuck, this was not the way it was supposed to go. The patrons would wake, and when they found one of their own dead—by my hand, a horror I couldn't dwell on—they'd be out for blood. *My* blood. We had to get the kids to safety fast, before this mess came to hunt us down.

I looked to Naveen—*Naveen,* who was alive and whole, shock still splayed clearly across his face. "Can you walk?"

"I—I think so, yeah." He wrenched himself up to stand on wobbly legs, leaning on Malina for support. But he stayed erect, a grin breaking through the stone. "Good as new."

Not a dream. Something far more powerful.

A *belief.*

Irina didn't stir as I lifted her, carrying her through the threshold toward the others, leaving the nightmare of The Frog Hollow behind.

"What happened?" Aya paled to match the moonlight as she noted Irina's unconscious form and the blood still drenching all four of us in vicious maroon.

Kas shook as he ran to Malina. "Whose blood—?"

Naveen pulled the small boy to his chest, wrapping him in a tight hug. His throat bobbed. "Don't worry, firecracker, I'm fine."

I swallowed the lump that threatened to choke me. We'd been so close to losing him. If I was the head, and Malina was the backbone, Naveen was the heart. Beating and thriving and pushing us all on, even when we wanted to tuck tail and run.

I held Irina closer to my chest like a lifeline as I tried to command my too-fast pulse and scattered mind into submission. The Lost Ones needed me clear-headed. We'd come too close tonight, and I had to fix this mess before anyone else got hurt. I sighed as the first whispers of a plan echoed through me.

One last escape.

"We'll have to forgo the carriage. It's too obvious, and they'll come looking for us."

The others groaned, but there was no time for protest. No time for anything but fleeing, all of us burnt out and shaken. Without their normal eyerolls, Kas and Malina hopped into the carriage, grabbing as much as they could hold to bring with us.

"Sled?" Riku rolled up his sleeves and shut his eyes, readying what was left of his power.

"Sled," Ren echoed, scraping from the bottom of the barrel for the energy necessary. We needed sleep and food, our bodies all at the limit, but we were survivors. We'd made more from less before.

At least, that's what I told myself as I watched the twins' heads bead with sweat, their ice craft smaller than the one they'd made last night, the structure not as solid as any of us wanted it. But it was all we had, and we'd make do.

"I've got her." Aya tucked an arm around Irina as I lowered her onto the seat, violet eyes bloodshot with tears that wouldn't fall. "Help the boys."

It took all my effort to remove myself from the Princess, from her warm presence. Like somehow, by just keeping my hands on her, she might heal me of the memory of tonight, might turn it all into a bad dream like she had over a decade ago...

But by some unseen strength, I wrenched my hands away, instead bracing them on the already melting rail of the sled. We wouldn't get far if I didn't move us fast.

"Hold on," I told the others, and a still-bleeding part of myself. "Don't let go."

I didn't wait for a reply as I commanded the wind to carry us to safety.

Irina slept curled against the damp cave wall, my cloak propped behind her head for comfort...not that there was much of that to spare in this small, makeshift hideaway at the base of the Kawayama Mountains. It was a far cry from a soft bed and hot meal, the moldy scent an affront to every sense, but it was the farthest we could get without all burning out after the last few nights. There was no rest for the wicked, but even thieves needed sleep. Still, despite the rocky bedding, the others managed to nod off once we arrived, their bodies crashing in heaps of limbs as they cuddled together—Aya, wedged between the sprawled-out twins, Malina and Kas cocooned in a shared blanket—all of them snuggled around the small fire Kas had lit with some kindling.

Only Naveen and I were awake—Naveen, too energized with whatever magic flowed through him, claiming he felt like he'd slept for a month straight; and me, too anxious to even close my heavy eyes for a second, knowing the nightmares that waited behind them when I finally did.

So both of us sat and watched the others breathe, tracking the ins-and-outs of their chests, like at any moment they might stop. Naveen found a small branch to whittle, crafting a flower into its face with a jagged rock he Qualified, while I hummed a lullaby, half to the sleeping ones, half to soothe my own knotted gut.

I didn't know exactly when, but at some point, Irina shifted closer, replacing the cloak with my lap as a pillow. I stiffened at first, the contact abrupt and unfamiliar...but not unwelcome. Another breath, and my hand stroked her hair aimlessly, the melody of my lullaby finally settling into my bones.

For two people who'd brought each other nothing but trouble, it was strange how soothing it was just to be in each other's presence.

Hold on, don't let go.

The morning rays had just begun to caress the edge of the cavern's opening when Irina spoke, her voice hoarse with sleep and a deeper exhaustion I knew too well. "What happened?"

Easinir burnout.

So even fairies had limits, then.

Still half-asleep, she shuffled up from my lap, rubbing her eyes, and my hands missed the *realness* of her in my palms. But before I could reach out again—to do what, I had no idea—Naveen crawled to her on awkward limbs and grabbed her still-sleepy face, pressing a quick kiss to the top of her disheveled curls. "I don't know what you did back there, Princess, but thank you."

Sitting back on his heels, with a flick of his wrist, he produced the small, hand-carved flower, presenting it to her like a fresh bloom.

Irina blinked away the last of her grogginess, tears lining her eyes instead as she took it, holding it to her chest. "No, I'm so *sorry.*"

There it was, that word, so ugly and uncomfortable and *real*.

Real, that the only reason that he was breathing right now was her.

Also real, that her uproar was the reason he'd been hurt in the first place.

I didn't know where that put me. Put *us*.

So I shoved my canteen in her face, the water sloshing like the unease in my gut. "Drink this."

She sat back as she brought the water to her cracked lips, sipping it slowly like it might bite her. Like *I* might bite her, if given the chance. I kept my expression neutral—so unsure of the wild, aching thing in my chest.

"Thank you." Her head dipped, eyes downcast like she couldn't bear to look at me. "I—"

"Naveen, go rally the kids." I cut her off before we both got caught in the never-ending flurry of apologies we owed each other, jerking my head to the horde sleeping on the other side of the cave. "We have a long day ahead of us."

Naveen raised a brow at me, eyes flicking between Irina and I; but for once in his blessed life, he said nothing before trudging over to the others, beginning the harsh routine of waking them up.

Irina and I sat in an uncomfortable silence for a long moment, both of us looking at the floor, saved only by the din of the Lost Ones grumbling to waking.

After several too-long seconds, I gave in.

"We're even," I blurted out, and instantly, relief sagged my exhausted shoulders, the words themselves salvation.

There was no finding logic in this madness. No tallying the score between the two of us, with all of the ways we'd intentionally and inadvertently hurt and saved each other. So it was time to let the wind carry it all away, erasing the history and heartache between us.

"What?" Irina's head snapped up, the dying firelight casting her soil-brown stare a warm caramel I tried not to get stuck in.

"We kidnapped you. We're handing you over to a spoiled prat and his mother." I smirked, but it felt forced, like my mouth had other things on its mind. "You burned my house down and got my friend stabbed. So, we're even. Clean slate."

Irina's brow furrowed, the creases between them etched with worry. But whatever she wrestled with ended in the same conclusion I had, a small, hesitant curl of her lips signaling her concession. "In my defense, I did *heal* your friend, and technically you burned your *own* home down...but even sounds good."

My fists clenched on their own accord, the memories fresh and old battling for attention.

The scent of burning flesh—my flesh.

Pain. Everywhere. All at once.

Magic, warm and soft as it cleared my pain.

Naveen's blood already cold beneath my fingers.

Light—endless, limitless—as it warmed the world back to life.

It felt like a dream. But it was a *miracle.* I kept my face neutral, my question dispassionate. "Speaking of that little parlor trick you pulled...how does it work?"

Soil hardened into diamond, her fists balling in her lap. "I don't know."

"Don't lie to a liar, Irina," I chuckled, letting my head fall back onto the cave wall and my eyes shut. I couldn't remember the last time I'd been this exhausted—too exhausted to even *bicker*, my favorite pastime. "But I suppose you don't have to tell me."

Her hand gripped mine tightly, and I stilled, breath catching in my chest. "You can't tell Ecei. This information could be very dangerous in the wrong hands. It's why my family has kept it a secret."

I peeked at our entwined hands, then at the determination and dread resting on her high cheekbones, before turning to face her fully. If she could lead with vulnerability, so could I. "I won't tell a soul, Princess. Neither will the others."

She had no reason to believe me. I'd lied to her and manipulated her from the moment we met. But perhaps those sins had been forgiven, washed away in the blood and sweat of the last few nights. Because despite all I'd done to push her away, Irina leaned closer, unburdening herself of her secrets.

"I really don't know why I have this gift. Some of the medementals believe it's a super recessive combination of Teramentalism and Pyromentalism. Others say it's a rare genetic mutation leftover from the fae era." Her voice was barely above a whisper as she dropped my hand, but there was a heaviness to it that settled like a stone in my middle. "But it works similarly to most Qualifying *Easinir*. I can manipulate the Quality of the element, but not the Quantity—I can't regrow limbs or anything like that. So Naveen will probably still be dizzy until his body can replenish the blood loss."

She looked over to my friend, hunched over the twins—the heaviest sleepers—like she was waiting for him to pass out or keel over at any moment. But perhaps she didn't know the full extent of her power, because I'd never seen Naveen look more *alive* in our time together. Like she hadn't just healed his body, but had somehow erased the years of malnutrition and addiction from his narrative, his skin clear and smooth, his eyes bright and dewy.

I framed my question carefully—not wanting to push her too far and risk her clamming up again. I much preferred when she let me in. "So you're a blood *Easinir*, then?"

There had been rumors of them before—Aquamentals so talented, that they could manipulate the moisture in blood to their will. Though it was rare for such a talent to pop up at all—never mind in a Dunyasian bloodline.

She shook her head. "Not quite. My element is life."

I did my best to quell the shock that burst through me like a firework cracking on a clear night.

She must have been a dream, because never in the history of Babylon had that been real. At least, not to public knowledge. Not even full Controllers could manipulate living beings—it went against everything anyone knew about our gifts. It sounded more like a leftover relic of the fae era, a legend long-dead.

No wonder the Dunyasians had hid her away. Hers was the gift of life—and many would want her dead for it.

I blew out a humorless laugh, puzzle pieces falling into place. "I'd heard you were a Teramental...good with plants."

Irina shrugged as she stroked the browning, wilted leaves of a single weed that'd managed to sprout along the cave wall. "It was an easy excuse. Most Teramentals are good with plants because they manipulate the quality of the soil." At her touch, the small weed slowly melted from a dying brown to a verdant green. "I can change the fiber of the plants themselves—their very lives. And it works on humans too—but the bigger the organism, the harder it is."

Which was why she'd collapsed after healing Naveen. A big guy like him probably took all of her juice.

A tug at my center set my sights on the others, all stretching and shifting as they roused from sleep. On *Aya*, whose skeletal form was more pronounced in the early morning gray, her thinning hair sticking up in clumps, the bags beneath her eyes endless and heavy.

A wilting flower, desperate for some life.

Tears pricked the back of my eyes as I dared the question, afraid of the answer. "What about the Bli—?"

Irina silenced me with a wince. "I can't. What the Blight does to the body...I can't fix it once it's started." Her words were quiet, but they punched holes through my chest all the same, stealing my breath. But despite the choke in her own throat, she pressed on, the explanation beating against my numb senses. "Trust me, I've tried, and all the tutors and physicians in Dunyas have tried to teach me what I need to know to help me figure it out. But once the cells start reproducing on their own, start forming masses in the organs and tissues...I can't change the Quantity. Can't reverse the growths. So even if I do change the quality of the healthy cells, once the cancer starts, I can't do anything unless the physicians cut it out, but that's hard. It always comes back, because we don't know the cause."

I pinched my thigh to keep alert, despair threatening to crush me into the hard rock behind my head. Of course I hadn't been the first to ask. "You tried with Nikolaj."

Her frame softened at her brother's name. "Every single day. There were days that it did...*help*. Gave him more energy, minimized the side effects..."

My throat bobbed as I looked at Aya again. "But it wasn't a cure."

"No, it wasn't."

No, the only cure that anyone had ever heard of was up north, safely hidden in Nehir, the least affected kingdom. Somehow, they'd cracked the code and found a way to fix what even the power of pure life couldn't heal.

And as much as I didn't want to let go of Irina, as much as I wanted to huddle her close and keep her for myself, as much as I wanted to pretend our slates were finally clean and we could start again...

I needed her. Not in the way I wanted her.

Hold on. Don't let go.

I'd have to learn how to.

I pushed off the wall to stand, my legs sore and stiff beneath me. But I still offered Irina a hand, not willing to let go just yet. "Ready to get walking?"

The others—finally up and ready—groaned, echoing my own displeasure. I'd gone soft in the Treehouse, my body not conditioned for lack of sleep and cave crouching. But the wicked world would not wait for me to be in my best shape—it would beat me while I was down if I let it, and I didn't have the time for a kick in the pants today.

We had a long road ahead.

"We're walking?" Irina frowned as she let me heft her to standing, her warm hand buzzing in mine with energy. I raised a brow as my aches faded ever so slightly—curious if this was her *Easinir* at work—but she stared back blankly, simply awaiting the answer to her question.

"We don't have a choice. We have to stay hidden until the next city."

"What about the sled?" Irina asked again, but her gaze was trained on Aya—on the slouch to her stance, on the shallow breaths that barely expanded through her protruding rib cage.

I gritted my teeth—not at Irina, but at the mess we were in. At myself, for not being able to fix it.

"*Easinir* zaps energy, even for the best of us." Riku saved me from the answers I didn't want to breathe life into, rubbing the back of his neck as shame and disappointment crept up it. "None of us have had a proper sleep or full meal in too long to manage."

Irina's frown stretched upward into a soft smile as she grabbed his hand, giving it a light squeeze—my chest seizing in tandem. "I'll do my best to help where I can."

Riku's expression melted, the Ice King a puddle in the princess's hand. Not that I blamed him; her warmth could even thaw the ice caps from the Nehir mountains into slush.

Maybe Irina and I weren't the only ones with clean slates. Perhaps her power did more than heal wounds, but also mended broken bonds. Repaired mangled first impressions.

I didn't want to think about what that would mean for us all when it came time to part ways.

Without much more fanfare, we packed up and bid farewell to the cave, pointing our sights north. Malina and Kas took the lead, venturing further ahead to scout the terrain for any bandits or other travelers we didn't want to run into. But for the rest of us, it was a slow crawl through the forest. The chilly wind bit our cheeks to light pink and misted our breaths to vapor plumes, our inhales shallow and sharp. At this pace, we'd be late to the border; but hopefully in the next town, we'd manage to find a place to rest and a faster form of transportation to borrow again.

We were barely an hour into our trek when Irina and Aya fell behind, their breathing labored and their feet sluggish.

"What, all those steps in Anastova didn't prepare you for some hiking?" Ren teased as he circled back, but even his brows drew tighter together as he paced alongside them, his focus on my sister's wavering form.

Aya looked down, fingers wringing together. She hated feeling like the dead weight—even if she was the lifeblood of this crew.

"I don't actually get out much back home." Irina shrugged, diverting some of the attention away from Aya. Whether she truly was struggling with the hike, or was just there to make Aya feel less alone, I'd never know, her expression too guarded to reveal much. Either way, it reanimated my sister, her head perking up as the Princess spilled her truths. "My family likes to keep me safe in the palace."

"Huh, sounds like someone I know," Aya quipped, tossing me a look that spelled trouble. For a moment, I almost mustered up a laugh, her sly comments typically contingent on her feeling well enough to think them up. But when she stumbled—just an inch, catching herself on a protruding branch—my heart fell to my toes.

"Don't push yourself," I chided as I offered her what wind I had left— a lumbering, tired breeze to ease some of her weight—but there was not much more I could give, and too much that needed carrying. My gut twisted, panic writhing through me like a knife to the gut. Perhaps this was what it felt like for Naveen—my magic bleeding out as exhaustion fought my limbs, my life suddenly outside of my own veins where I least preferred it.

But much like she had with Naveen, Irina splayed her hand over my sister's shoulder, a brief, brilliant flash of light sparking through the woods so fast, I almost thought it a trick of the hovering sunshine.

"Is he always such a mother hen?" Irina snickered, linking arms with my sister with a smirk. A thousand retorts flew to the tip of my tongue, ready to defend and disarm her like she had me.

But when Aya stood straighter—color returning to her pallid skin, Breath above, a shine even omitting from her silken hair—all of my witty responses died at the back of my throat, caught in the trap of a thick, sticky emotion.

"So much for even," I grumbled, tongue lame around that ball of gooey gratitude. "Now I owe you one, Princess."

Brown eyes met mine, something stirring in their tilled irises. And then a wink, lightning-quick as she tucked a curl behind her blush-reddened ear. "That one was for the haircut."

And when she and Aya both blew past me—arm in arm, matching smiles on their features—I supposed this was all a dream, after all.

It could not last. In two days, I'd wake up, and she'd be gone.

The sun began its descent below the treeline while we were still an hour away from the nearest town, stealing the heat and zapping the last of our already waning energy.

We needed to keep moving, but if I pushed the kids any further, we'd need Irina's power to revive all of them. So, with a huff and a pit in my stomach, I sounded the command for everyone to take a few minutes to rest. Qara would wait a few moments longer.

No one protested. Naveen leaned against a tree trunk while both twins opted to crash onto the mossy forest floor. Kas, young and sprightly as always, stayed standing, but took the time to stretch out, gangly limbs tugging in every direction as his joints popped in sick bursts. Irina excused herself behind a nearby tree, a blush painting her face to match the red streaks of dying sunlight.

With her new friend gone, Aya slumped onto a small tree stump, her grimace deepening as she rubbed at her sore ankles.

"Here, Aya." Mal whipped out two smooth stones from her pants pocket–both Qualified to a warm glow–and pressed them gently against Aya's calves. "These will help."

"Thanks, Mally." My sister let out a satisfied groan, taking the stones from Mal and pressing them against her lower back instead, leaning forward as the warmth unknotted her sore muscles, and Mal broke out into a smile.

But it didn't reach her eyes, her gaze unfocused as she stared into space again. She stood, brushing the dirt from her trousers, looking more lost than I'd seen her since I found her in the sewers.

I swooped next to her, tugging once on an errant curl. Mal swatted at me, but I dodged, instead looping my arm around her shoulders. "You alright?"

She nodded, voice low enough that only I would hear. "It was just scary."

I tucked her closer. "I know."

She sighed into me. "We could have lost him."

My eyes darted to Naveen leaning against the tree, holding his canteen high out of Kas's reach, the smaller boy jumping and laughing trying to snatch it from the giant.

This would have been a very different trip if Naveen...if Irina hadn't...

I swallowed the lump in my throat, my arm falling away from Mal so I could wrap it around my own middle. Like my muscles remembered the feeling of stanching Naveen's wound better than Naveen's own body did. "I know."

Mal shook next to me, a chill running down her spine. "And if it had been Kas..."

My mind went blank at that, the thought too dark to entertain.

If it had been Kas, I would've followed him into the Ether and pulled him back myself.

This was a dangerous game, one I'd been playing for far longer than I wanted to admit. I'd always lived on the razor's edge, need and wickedness keeping me sharp. But it was my risk to wager, not my crew's.

I looked at Aya, the stones fading as her body borrowed their heat. As her lungs borrowed each shaking breath.

"We can turn back," I blurted out, not sure if I was asking Mal to stay or leave. To play accomplice to my sins or absolve me of them. "If I'm asking too much of you all…"

"No. Aya needs us," Mal cut me off, that gemstone-hard certainty lining her voice. Lining my backbone in diamond-plated rigidity. "We see it through, no matter what."

If only I'd known then what *'no matter what'* would cost.

SEVENTEEN

IRINA

I'd never been one for much exercise—a quality my mother hated and often warned would do me no good—but by the time we finally reached the outskirts of Qara, I was inclined to agree about its uses.

Muscles I didn't know I had ached, my feet and knees throbbing as my bones considered breaking. My skin itched with layers of dried sweat, red splotches discoloring my normally smooth arms and face to an angry rust. It'd been bearable at first—walking alongside Aya, who kept a comfortable pace, chatting and bantering with the twins and Naveen to pass the time. Even when Malina and Kas would circle back to us with updates, I didn't mind Malina's presence, her clear orders and mapping skills making the journey less arduous and Kas's cheerful grin propelling my feet further.

But after the sun had fled beneath the treetops, a chill settling into the air, we all felt the sting a little sharper, moods souring and hopes dying with the approaching dusk.

So when we stumbled into Qara—a much smaller town than Kisari, right where the river practically bumped up against the mountains—I almost cried with relief as we approached The Breeze Haven Inn & Tavern. It was less spacious than The Frog Hollow, but the lights and laughter pouring from inside spoke of fortune and food to be had, and when Shin nodded his agreement, I almost smacked a kiss on his cheek.

Almost.

He and Malina walked into the inn without a word, just throwing one of those signals to the others that meant *stay put until I say so.*

"Not to rub salt in a wound, Princess, but do us all a favor—please try not to pick any fights at this one." Naveen slumped over as he trudged toward the door, whatever energy my magic had given him zapped with the dying sunlight. He leaned against the frame, letting the structure steady him as we waited. "I need sleep and a bath."

"I'm not much of a fighter," I retorted; shame licked my chapped skin, creeping hot across the back of my neck.

I'd shut out my guilt—locked it away in the small, crowded box where I kept all of my other unsavory feelings—but there was no denying what I'd done. Last night, my actions had gotten a friend hurt, and a man *killed.*

None of Shin's pretty notions of clean slates could erase that.

This is what happens when you speak, girl.

Stay in your room, Irina!

A snort pulled me out of the box again, a blue eye winking at me from beneath messy copper bangs. "You should consider it, if the whole Princess thing doesn't work out. You have a natural talent."

"What do you know about talent?" I huffed at Ren, brushing past him with false confidence despite the pit threatening to drag me back.

"See? Fighting already." Naveen quirked a smile.

Tears bit the backs of my eyes, that guilt roaring up without a leash, but a hand on my arm chained it before it could escape.

Riku's normally icy expression warmed to an understanding I hadn't expected. "Ren and I grew up in the circus. We know how to tell the difference between someone with an act and someone with a *gift.* You've got the latter, Princess."

Something sparked in my chest, spreading through me like wildfire. My throat tightened, a surprising relief I didn't know I needed unwinding inside me.

I'd never been seen as gifted. A tool, yes. A toy, even. A *spare*.

But a gift?

No, a gift was what these strangers had given me when they'd sprung me from my cage. When they'd given me the chance to fly for myself.

"Can everyone start calling me Irina?" I croaked around the ball in my throat. I couldn't shed my title like a molting bird, no matter how much I'd outgrown the previous version of myself. But perhaps for a night, I could pretend to be someone else. Maybe even myself, for a change.

Aya smiled first. "Sure thing. Let's get some grub, Irina."

With another signal from Shin and a bit of bustling, we managed our way inside and to a table this time, the inn packed with customers laughing and cheering over warm food and friendship.

My stiff muscles eased, the scent of deep herbs and sharp spices reminding me of Tasha's kitchen, of the warmth and love I always felt there. But as much as I missed that small sanctuary, this place beckoned me further. From the rafters hung small glass orbs, tiny fires burning inside them—definitely the work of a talented *Easinir*—that lit the place in dancing light. None of the tables or chairs matched—some of them high-backed and regal, others merely cushioned stools, the tables both round and square and lacquered in every stain of wood imaginable. But even without cohesion, it somehow gave the place a whimsical charm that made me want to sit and stay a while.

And at the front of the room, across from the bar, a small stage jutted up three feet higher than the rest of the tiled floor, an upright piano waiting open for a player. It was a dingy instrument—the keys yellowed by age, the wooden bench rickety—but it still spoke of a luxury I hadn't expected from the Breeze Haven.

Entertainment.

Whatever lack had carved through The Frog Hollow seemingly hadn't touched this place, more of a reason for me to believe the barkeep had just been a surly man with a bad attitude, his complaints projections for his own failings.

At least, that was the story I let myself believe as we devoured our rations—roasted chicken and some heartily cut potatoes basted in a butter and curry sauce that almost had me moaning over each giant forkful I allowed myself, for once not worrying about how much I ate in front of others. If this place—only a day's walk north—could be touched by such plenty, then perhaps Babylon was not doomed after all.

After we'd stuffed ourselves—the conversation limited as we each attended to the beasts roaring in our bellies—Shin, Malina, and the twins excused themselves from the table without a word, headed toward the barkeep at the back of the room.

"What are they doing?" I murmured to the others, munching on a cinnamon cookie despite how tightly the waist of my pants bit into my protruding middle.

Kas shoved two of the small sweets into each of his cheeks, crumbs tumbling from his lips as mischief lit his eyes. "Bargaining."

I set my own treat down on the plate, unease chasing away my appetite. I hadn't even thought about what it would cost us for such a respite, and I had no idea how Shin had been managing money as we traveled. We'd fled The Frog Hollow without the silvers he'd given the owner, and without the carriage, I doubted we had anything valuable to offer.

My tastebuds turned to ash, the food bittered by reality. Was this what it was like for them in Hiku City? Had each meal laid such a grave toll on their shoulders?

I swallowed despite my dry, guilty tongue, asking though I feared the answer, "With *what?*"

But Kas was immune to the discontent that plagued me, bouncing in his seat as he bit his cheek to hide a smirk. "They—"

Aya held up a hand, silencing him with a stern look that I'd seen on her brother's face too many times already. "Don't spoil it. She'll see for herself."

On cue, the barmaid clinked a knife against a glass, silencing the gentle rumble of voices in the tavern. Flour and spilled drink stained her salt-and-pepper hair and worn apron, but she held her chin high, commanding respect like a queen as she scanned her castle. After a moment, she cleared her throat, a beaming smile captivating her laugh-wrinkled face.

"Ladies and gentlemen of the Breeze Haven, please welcome some very special guests!" The owner raised her glass, gesturing to Shin and the others. "Tonight, all the way from Hiku City, the most amazing traveling troupe of players to grace all of Babylon, The Misted Muses!"

Cheers and hoots erupted, and Shin and the twins bowed, Malina dropping into a deep curtsy. My gut fell and rose with them, and I had to scrape my chin from the floor as I whipped to Aya. "What? *They* are the Misty Muses?"

Of course, I'd heard of them, even in Dunyas. For the last five years, they'd been the most popular touring group in all of Babylon, earning accolades even in noble circles. Though I'd never seen them before, Nikolaj had raved about the acrobats and players, promising me that he'd one day take me to see them perform.

It was another promise he broke.

But one I'd make good on for myself, tonight, having unwittingly traveled with them for days.

"No, they are the Mist-*ed* Muses, not Misty," Aya corrected with a wink, and the promise shattered again. "Close enough, though."

I stared incredulously at Shin, impressed again by his ability to lie in half-truths.

"Con artist," I grumbled beneath my breath, but my words died as Shin took the small stage and sat on the rickety piano bench, the wood creaking beneath him.

He inhaled once—green-tea-and-honey eyes surveying the crowd—while the other three got into position, taking grandiose poses in front of him.

And with an exhale, his fingers touched the old keys, and the entire tavern was transformed.

This was no longer just an inn and a rundown piano—it was the grandest stage I'd ever seen, the music soaring through the room with expert precision and artistry, the crowd instantly under his spell. It was not the stiff waltz we'd danced to at the ball, but instead a dynamic, fluid thing, his fingers making magic with each brush against the keys, despite their slightly discordant pings.

As he played, the twins and Malina began their performance—slow at first, their movements finding the tempo, but soon they were diving and flipping over one another, twirling and spinning with expertise. As they went, the twins made small orbs of ice, juggling them in their deft hands while Shin's fingers never stopped playing, his melody moving and swaying in time with them. The twins tossed the orbs between each other, rainbows of water streaming from their palms as they dazzled the gasping, grinning onlookers.

And amidst it all, Malina *danced*. Hips swayed and dipped, lithe and unrelenting, and her feet carved intentional paths across the stage, sparks dancing in her wake. As she moved, mist rose from her skin when she heated the twins' water, creating a shadowed effect that dazzled the audience. Her curls floated and flipped behind her, every last inch of her a rhythmic, melodic creature, the perfect counterbalance to Shin's soaring melody.

I didn't know why it twisted through my ribcage like it did.

Against every instinct, I tore my eyes from her, instead watching Shin. Watching his hands, stroking every key with masterful intent. His chest, each even-tempoed breath rising and falling in synchronicity with the music. His eyes, staring at everything and nothing at all, like he was both fully in the moment and trapped in some long-ago daydream.

Before I knew it, I was under his spell, too. All of the twins' tricks and Malina's motions faded away. The 'oohs' and 'ahhs' and ferocious claps from the crowd drifted into oblivion.

All that was left was him and I. And this song, filling every inch of the liminal space between us. Mending cracks in my soul that I'd forgotten long ago.

The heady buzz of violins. The deep moan of cellos.

Eyes like a warm spring breeze, like leaves falling from a tree.

I didn't even realize I was crying until a hand reached out and swiped a tear from my cheek, breaking the enchantment and lassoing me back to the tavern's walls.

"Dance with me Prin—Irina?" Naveen dried the tear from his finger with the hem of his shirt before jerking his head to the center of the room, where a small gathering of patrons had shoved the tables out of the way to join the dance, their clumsy feet far less graceful than Malina's, but their smiles bright enough to warm the room even without her Qualifying heat. Naveen's expression matched theirs as he offered me his hand. "I feel like a million marks."

I took his hand before I could convince myself not to, letting him drag me to the makeshift dance floor.

My body didn't possess Malina's captivating grace, especially with stiff muscles and numb joints from a day of walking. But I let myself dance anyway, ignoring the aches, my feet keeping time with my racing heart as Naveen led me around the floor, spinning me like a flower petal in a gust of wind.

This wasn't the slow, calculated waltz I was used to. Not a structured, polite thing. No, this dancing was uninhibited. Lawless.

"Slow down!" I laughed, my breath a sharp, scraping thing in my lungs, but I didn't care. Not even as I stumbled, Naveen catching me by my arms before I could smack my face into a chair.

This was chaos. Directionless, whirling madness.

Freedom.

I *loved* it.

"Can I cut in?" Aya asked behind me as I righted myself, stepping back from Naveen. As my dizziness abated, I noticed the stars in her light eyes as she looked at my dance partner, expectation and excitement swimming in their depths.

Naveen grinned at her, his straight teeth flashing. "You're up for a dance, little butterfly?"

A pang thrummed my heartstrings as Aya's face flushed crimson. Is that what Hana had seen on my face during the ball? That same nervous joy—one part foolish, three parts brave?

My gaze drifted to Shin again, still playing as people danced, even though Malina and the twins had taken breaks. Sweat beaded on his forehead, his whole body one with the piano as he performed, but his focus didn't waver, lost to the music.

I blinked before I could lose myself, too.

"Be my guest; I need a drink anyway." I smiled at Aya, squeezing her hand. Carefully, I let just a kernel of my power slip through my littlest finger and into hers, so small that the flash barely registered in the bright room. But still, she stood straighter, inhaling sharply as more color siphoned into her cheeks.

She kissed my hand before letting it go. "You're a good friend, you know that?"

The weight of the word hit me with an unexpected force, stealing my breath from my already-abused lungs.

Friend.

I didn't know if I'd ever had one of those before. At least, not one that hadn't been my brother's or my parents' first. But somehow in the last few days, despite all of the horror and turmoil we'd faced, I'd made one on my own.

Friend.

I tucked the word into a formerly empty corner of my heart before turning to the bar, my sore limbs suddenly less heavy.

My relief was short-lived as I slipped into the empty barstool next to Malina, who sipped a drink while listening to the owner speak, their conversation pricking beneath my skin.

"It's a real shame, what's happening around these parts," the owner sighed as she stuffed her hands into her apron pockets, the corners of her lips pulling down and emphasizing the slight wrinkles. Up close, there was a tiredness about her I hadn't noticed before, a heaviness that sagged her mouth to frowning. "If my boy Driss didn't happen to own a small barge, we'd be in the same place. The greed is getting out of hand."

The usual harshness I'd grown accustomed to fled from Malina's tone, replaced with a strange softness as she nodded. "You all do the best you can, Sayeda. None of us have the power to change it."

Flashbacks to The Frog's Hollow threatened to consume my mind, but I shoved them away. I'd been such an ignorant brat, whether or not they were right. It hadn't been my place to pick that fight, and now a man was dead because of it.

I couldn't scrub clean that blemish on my soul. But I wouldn't make the same mistakes again. Despite my unease, I wrestled my courage to find my voice. "What are you two talking about?"

Malina shot me a look that might have sent me running for the hills a day ago, hoarding her drink closer like *I* was the thief. Like I had taken something vital from her. "Don't worry about it. It's not your kind of conversation, trust me."

The dismissal stung, but I didn't let it deter me.

Malina didn't like me—not that she had any reason to. I'd brought trouble to their world with every step, and had been next to useless in carrying the burden.

I wanted to hate her back. Wanted to turn my envy into something bitter and caustic, to let it make me feel powerful for once in my life.

But even so, I admired her.

Because she was everything I was *not*. Strong, capable. Clever and commanding, even with nothing to her name and no title to lean on. She crafted luck out of misfortune, and did so with a clear head and the skillset to see it through.

Nikolaj would've been impressed, too.

And perhaps it was the adrenaline or exhaustion, but I wanted to make her like me back. Wanted to be her *friend*.

And I wanted to know the people of Babylon better, too. Hear their stories, see their lives. If I was going to be in charge one day, they deserved that much. They deserved a version of me that maybe even Malina could respect.

With my bravest, brashest parts, I grabbed her arm, an unspoken plea for her to show me how. "I want to understand."

Malina stared at me, unblinking, as she assessed my utter *lack*. But when she didn't respond—didn't tell me where I could promptly fuck off to—I took it as a victory anyway.

I turned to the barmaid with a smile, ready to be let in.

Her gaze darted between Malina and I for a moment, but when Malina didn't protest, the woman—Sayeda, Malina had called her— spoke, a crack in her voice that ran soul-deep. "I was telling your friend that things have been bad around here, ma'am. Everywhere, really." She shrugged, but as she leaned against the bar, her eyes glazed over, sadness frightening away the merriment of the scene around us. "The coast folks and the city dwellers have it slightly better, just because the stuffy royals need them around to keep their Poppy Dust moving and their whores pretty...not that it's all that much nicer. But the rest of us get left to rot."

I inhaled deeply, chewing on her words like the vegetables Tasha used to make me eat as a kid. All I wanted was to spit them back at her —to run toward something sweet and sugar-coated instead. But much like the bland, harsh broccoli stalks I'd been forced to swallow, these truths were necessary for my growth.

Parts of Babylon were suffering. And whether or not my parents knew about it, whether or not they'd tried to help, even, didn't matter. Didn't erase the pain that was written clear as day on this woman's face, or the anger the other barkeep had blurted out at us, however misplaced.

One truth didn't erase the other, and the impact weighed more than the intent.

I'd told Shin as much a few days ago, yet somehow, I hadn't taken my own advice.

I nodded, acceptance and something hotter surging through my veins. Something that almost felt like *purpose*. "How would you fix it?"

At that, both Malina and Sayeda looked at me like I had seven heads, blinking back their surprise in unison. When I didn't hop up and exclaim I was only teasing, Sayeda scoffed, "Psshh, I dunno. It doesn't matter."

But I saw just a glimmer of it, hiding behind her eyeroll, that same thing that had let me spill my secrets to Shin that night in the garden, and again this morning in the cave.

It doesn't matter. I have no choice.

If you don't like it, change it.

Hope. Belief.

And I only needed a small seed to make it grow.

"If you *could* change it, though," I pushed, desperate to water that belief into something more; into a change, tangible and real and useful. "What would you do?"

Sayeda's eyes narrowed, and Malina's grip on her drink tightened —like they both knew how frightful it was to plant that wish. How dangerous, even.

But Sayeda must have been made of metal, because her eyes swept over the tavern, a queen reclaiming her precious throne, no matter how small the kingdom. "First of all, I'd make sure Poppy Dust was only used for medicine. That shit is a Blight in itself."

At that, even Malina's stony facade chipped, a twitch in the corner of her mouth revealing much as she made a quick glance at Naveen. "Do you know anyone who has had to deal with the addiction?"

Guilt again unleashed its fangs upon my already-bleeding heart as I remembered Naveen's fear from the night before when Malina had mentioned the opium, the way horror had taken over his bloodless expression. If I hadn't saved him, would he have bled out? Or would they have stitched him up, only to throw him back into the vicious maw of the poppy-haze's ravenous appetite?

I didn't want to think about which fate was worse.

There was a hitch in Sayeda's voice again as she continued, "My boy, Driss, before he got clean. Messed him up real good for years."

I cleared my throat, trying to dispel my own discomfort. This was not about me—not anymore. "He must be strong, to have overcome it."

"That he is." A muscle clenched in the woman's jaw, the only indication of the horrors she might have endured alongside him. "But so are the people who still fight with it. Lots of them use it to manage the misery of not having a *purpose*, if you ask me."

I shifted on the stool, knowing that feeling all too well.

"How would you help them?" I asked, keeping myself steady, trying to emulate her easy strength. "Hypothetically."

Her and Malina exchanged another long glance, like this didn't quite make sense to either of them; I didn't push, simply waiting for them to decide this wasn't a trick or a trap. Finally, Sayeda turned around, pouring ale into a mug from the tap before setting it in front of me—a truce, then—with a smile. I took a sip—acceptance—even though the bitter foam made me wince.

She stifled a laugh and she started, "I dunno why you want to know, girlie, but I'll tell ya. Me, I'd put more dedicated barges on the Black River, like the one my son runs, and set to finding ways to build more roads through to Jalta. It would make transportation easier, and it would give people good, honest jobs."

A different bitterness coated my tastebuds. "But Jalta—"

She waved me off before I could finish the thought, a single raised eyebrow dispelling any of my criticisms before they could even take shape. "Ya know, my son's wife is Jaltan. She's a sweetheart—and an *Easinir*. She made me the lights." She gestured to the pretty hanging orbs that filled the space with warmth, like they symbolized their maker's same affability. A deep pride straightened her back, that same regality etched into her features. "And they're hurting there, too, since so few merchants will trade with them. Many of them think the uprising was a stunt to keep power centered in Dunyas, but you didn't hear it from me."

I set my drink down and inhaled sharply, Malina freezing in her seat next to me.

That was no longer just an empty wish, but a revolution—a treasonous, treacherous thought that could spell threats to her and hers if heard by the wrong people.

But if I was going to rule, I needed to hear it—the whispers of rebellion—before they were shouts echoing for war across all of Babylon. "How do you mean?"

The owner's gaze darkened—secrets withheld in their embers—like she'd meant to cross that line. Like it had been a test, and I may have failed. She opened her mouth—to condemn me or to challenge me, I'd never know, because an arm draped across my shoulder stunted our conversation to a startling halt.

I hadn't realized the music had stopped.

"Everything good over here?" Shin lilted as he wrapped himself around me, his words a music of their own against my cheek. Chills ran down my spine at the contact, my stomach doing backflips to rival Ren and Riku's. "My wife troubling you?"

At that, my stomach practically packed up and walked out, all thoughts abandoning my brain except for one.

Wife.

I knew it was a part of the con, a disguise to keep me hidden, but it sent fireworks bursting through my chest anyway.

"Oh, you're married?" The darkness cleared like smoke from Sayeda's expression as it broke into a wide smile. She wiggled her finger between the two of us in a taunt. "Why didn't you say so? Breath above, I'll put you up in the honeymoon suite, give you some privacy from the rest of your troupe!"

I did my best to hide the embarrassment that lit my cheeks to crimson, nudging Shin off me as I waved my hands. "Oh, please, don't trouble yourself—"

"I insist," Sayeda declared, shutting down my protests as she slid Shin another key, this one with a heart crafted into the silver bow. "Love needs to be celebrated when it can be. Your wife is a great listener. Lifted my spirits a bit."

She winked at me, and something settled between us. Perhaps I'd passed her test after all.

But before either of us could challenge her rule, another patron called to her from the other end of the bar, and she swept away to serve him, a queen that bowed *to* her people's will.

I stared at the key, still waiting on the bar, like it might bite my finger clean off if I dared touch it.

"Another room?" Naveen noted as he approached, hovering on Shin's other side, a brow raised as he appraised the heart-shaped key.

Shin cleared his throat—like he'd been transfixed by the small silver trap, too—before he straightened, the musician and conman gone, replaced by the leader of this troupe instead. "Irina, you and Aya should share—"

"That'll look suspicious," Malina grumbled as she shoved off her stool, taking her mug of ale with her. With a swift strike, she stole the key from its perch before slamming it into Shin's chest with a shove that was a stride too far from friendly. "You've dug your hole, you get to lie in it, Shin."

She stalked off without another word toward the table Ren and Riku occupied with Aya and Kas, leaving Shin holding the key against his sternum with his mouth pressed in a tight line, his brow furrowed.

Rejection tickled at the back of my mind, a sharp sting I didn't want to name. Of course, Shin could say silly things to random barkeepers, could play the part of doting husband for a ruse while eyes were on him. He was a performer, after all, if tonight's entertainment was any indication. But why would he want to share a room with me, when Malina was his perfect counterpart? When she matched his every note with a step of hers, strong and confident and capable?

I was just a wedge between them, a Blight on their lives. And no matter how desperately I wanted to fit in, wanted to make *friends*, it didn't change the fact that when this was all over, I'd be sent back to my pristine cage, and they'd be better off for it.

"I don't mind sharing, and I'll stay out of your way. We were in the cave last night, I'm sure we can make do." My smile was a thin veil to the well of insecurity that opened wide within me, but I snatched the key from Shin, careful not to let my fingers brush his. I had my limits to what I could endure right now, and I had a feeling that would carve something from me I couldn't grow back. His gaze wrenched away from Malina to fix itself on me, a wistfulness in their depths that almost sent me over the edge. So I shrugged, tucking the key into my pocket, sheathing my heart all the same. "But I'm pretty exhausted, so I'll head up, if that's alright."

I'd never been one for exercise, and I'd had enough of it today to last me a year; but I ran from the bar and up the stairs faster than I'd ever moved in my life, before I could lose myself to Shin Koishi entirely.

Eighteen

SHIN

Nighttime in the Breeze Haven offered a different version of the wind's song, one I'd been craving for days, my skin itching for just a note of it:

Rest.

Sitting at the piano bench, the wind wrapped itself around me in a gentle embrace as I stroked the first key. And with every note, more of me unknotted, tense muscles relaxing as I exhaled fully for the first time in days.

It felt good to play, to let my music tell the story of the last week. To pour it all out, a siphoning of every ache and hurt, an outlet for the storm pent up in my chest. I chose my favorites; rearrangements of nostalgic lullabies from my childhood, impressive, expressive pieces from my days at the Opera House, and even my own rendition of one of the songs from the Masque, one that'd been nibbling at my inner ear since I'd heard it.

I played for the Opera House, burnt to cinders again, my home likely irreparable. My safe haven destroyed.

I played for the men at The Frog's Hollow, for their lives forfeit to a stupid bar fight. Their cruelty a symptom of Babylon's plight.

I played for Naveen, who'd come so close to meeting the same fate. Who had all but said his goodbyes as his blood permanently marked my hands and heart.

I played for Aya, who'd be next if I didn't see this all through. Who'd been grinning through the pain, as she always did, despite the cloak of exhaustion that hung around her tiny frame.

And I played for Irina, whose eyes blew wide with wonder as she watched. Who danced until she was breathless, a flower petal swaying to the wind's music, letting it sweep her away.

Who *smiled*, like she'd never been happier in her entire life.

Like always, the Lost Ones met me for every note, their performance the perfect counterbalance to mine. But even when they'd stopped flipping and dancing, even when the patrons—Irina included—found their seats again, sweat and exhaustion hanging from their bright smiles...

I played. Until my out-of-practice fingers hurt, and the wind demanded a new song of me: the percussive snores of sleep.

But even though my body begged for that deeper rest, I couldn't drag myself up to the 'honeymoon suit' Sayeda had offered us, knowing Irina was there, waiting. I didn't want to face that conversation yet—to tempt myself further into dangerous territory I was already standing at the border of.

So, like the coward I was, I sipped a whiskey, waiting for the patrons of The Breeze Haven to clamber out to the night beyond or up to their rooms, cheeks ruddy and spirits high. Waiting for the moon to creep higher and higher outside the window, its bluish glow a welcome softness. Waiting for night to quiet the wind's song as the laughter and voices outside hushed, replaced by the melodic chirps of crickets and the haunted coos of owls.

Waited until it was just me, Sayeda, and four of the Lost Ones left behind. Aya and Kas had climbed up the stairs to the other guest room hours ago, not long after Irina—both of them exhausted, Kas's head heavy despite how he whined that he was fine.

So Naveen, the twins, and I sat tucked into the mismatched chairs around a table while Mal and Sayeda chatted at the bar, the fire-pixie helping to wipe down the counter—and hopefully securing us some transportation for tomorrow. Part of me wanted to help, but my dead-tired legs couldn't find the will to move themselves. So instead, I drank, and let the reality of the last week numb away as my family sipped from their final cups, too.

Ren polished off the last of his drink—a light honeyed mead that Sayeda allowed the younger patrons to have as long as they ate with it —and nudged Naveen. "You look good for a guy that was almost dead yesterday."

The misplaced joke was a punch to my gut, my whiskey threatening to return itself, but Naveen whacked Ren's shoulder, swatting the taunt away like a fly.

"I *always* look good." Naveen winked, but his smirk didn't quite stretch as wide as it usually did, an exhaustion still present in his gaze that no song or rest could purge.

Riku—sober and sharp as ever—narrowed his eyes, not missing the bluff, either. "Are you all right, though? You're still on the pale side."

My knuckles whitened as I appraised my friend—his normally deep skin ashy, a gray tinge still lingering alongside the bronze.

I'm okay, I promise.

But Naveen patted himself down, his shoulders finally unknotting. "I swear, I've never felt better," he said, then jerked his head to the cleared space in front of the stage. "Did you see me busting a move out there? I was tearing up that dance floor."

My grip eased; he *had* been dancing for most of the night, twirling Aya and himself in uncoordinated, laugh-veiled steps.

Ren leaned in, brows drawn in a put-on-worry. "I mean, I saw you flailing around...but I assumed you were having some sort of fit. You call that *dancing*?"

Naveen stilled. Grinned. "You know, I think I feel well enough to start hitting."

Then *swung*.

He clipped Ren on the ear, earning a string of swears I was pretty sure he taught the younger boy himself. But Ren was fast and lithe, countering with a jab right to the kidneys—right above where his wound would have been.

"Enough, both of you." I shot forward in my seat, fear kicking up my throat and chasing away all of rest's hard work.

Blood, red and thick, staining my hands.

Get the kids out, okay?

Ren and Naveen both stilled, flopping back into their respective chairs. My heart roared like thunder in my chest, too panicked for the storm to roll out again.

"He started it," Naveen grumbled, forgetting that he was three years older than Ren and supposed to be wiser for it.

"I'm finishing it." I cleared my throat, the lump dispelling, as I counted my friend's breaths. In and out. I fell back into my seat, exhaustion claiming me once more. "Seriously, Nav, are you all right *here?*" I pointed to his temple, and then mine—begging the fragmented memories to stay back, just for tonight.

Naveen swallowed thickly, humor fleeing for a flicker of a breath. "I will be."

The wind changed its tune again, rest faltering in favor of something deeper, something harder to look at but just as necessary. Something we couldn't run from.

His answer didn't offer the reassurance I craved. I dragged my hands across my face, hoping to wipe away the last traces of fear as I offered the boys a truth. "Breath above, we are in over our heads with this."

"Yes, yes, we are," Nav chuckled, taking the last deep gulp of his own drink, likely trying to drown the discomfort in liquor.

"But we're all strong swimmers, Shin," Riku cut in, curling deeper into his chair. "We can handle our own."

They could, and they always had. Ren and Riku had been survivors long before they found their way into my life, performers that were barely ten years old by the time they were dazzling crowds—and withstanding their brutal master's lash. Naveen had been through worse, his time on the farm a story written in blood and sweat, his struggles with the Poppy Dust after just as harrowing. Mal and Kas were both forged in fire, escaping the slavers that had stolen them from their homes in the Jaltan revolution, managing on their own for weeks before I found them.

And Aya...

I had been raised by Hiku City, but Aya had been born to it. She'd only been an infant when Mama passed, and she still managed to grow up well despite my lack of experience as a caretaker. And now she fought to survive every day, battling back the Blight with the strength of a thousand men, somehow all contained in her fragile, frail form.

The Lost Ones knew how to *live,* despite a world that preferred us all dead.

But I didn't know how many more close scrapes and *almosts* we could afford.

Blood, red and thick, staining my hands.

I'm okay, I promise.

"Aya had a good time tonight," Naveen mused quietly, like he could read my thoughts. I suppose after the years we'd spent together, he probably could by now. He sat forward in his chair, conviction straightening his spine, unencumbered by the weight of his fatigue. "We all want to see her have a million more nights like this. It's worth the risk."

Riku nodded, icy eyes clear and determined. Ren smirked, tickling Nav's healed side. "And now we have an Irina to patch us up when we get boo-boos."

Naveen flicked him again, but I ignored their squabbling as one word clanged through my skull, just as incessant as that ear-worm melody from the Masque.

Irina.

My heartbeat stuttered at her name.

Irina, who could influence life itself. Who had a power thrumming through her veins that all of Babylon would likely kill for. Power that *saved.*

Irina, who'd healed flesh and spared us from tragedy, at least for tonight.

Irina, who made my sister smile more than she had in months.

Irina, who was likely fast asleep upstairs, alone in a strange room, far away from the life she knew.

I shut her name out of my mind, focusing again on my family in front of me. On the people I was charged to protect; the people I *chose* to call my own, no matter what my foolish heart wanted instead.

"We have to be careful going forward." I pointed at the boys, one by one, making eye contact with each of them to ensure they understood. This was not a request, but an expectation. An *order*. "No more *almosts*."

Nav and Riku nodded, both of them shrinking at the authority in my tone. They were my family, but I was still their leader, our hierarchy necessary to keep us safe.

Ren rolled his eyes. "Such a mother hen."

But he didn't protest further—knowing the limits of our boundaries. Knowing that our true strength was not our *Easinir*, but our bonds, the streets-tested, survival-born synchronization that had helped us through this far.

And that would carry us all home at the end of this.

"You'll get wrinkles if you keep frowning," Mal sighed from behind me, sneaking up quieter than a silent breeze. I jumped, earning a snicker from her and Sayeda both.

The boys all laughed at my expense, but silenced themselves as I flattened them with a glare, choking back any taunts they had brewing in their thick skulls.

"What are you still doing down here, boy, when that pretty wife of yours is upstairs?" Sayeda raised a brow, crossing her arms. She snorted, nudging Mal's side like they'd known each other for ages. "Men these days don't know when they've got it good."

Mal's grin fell, replaced by a grimace.

I kicked her boot before she could blow our cover, painting on a smile to snag Sayeda's attention before she could notice. "She's out of my league, isn't she?"

It was a ruse, a quick redirect to keep our cover.

And it was entirely true.

Sayeda, sharp as she was, smirked like she somehow knew both. She waggled her finger toward the stairs. "Go start groveling now, and you might be forgiven by daybreak."

The wind's music changed again, no longer avoidant, but demanding. Alluring, like it too called from the rooms above, a song for the girl who waited there.

Irina, who danced tonight like there would be no tomorrow. Who let my sister dance, too, just in case there wasn't.

"On it." I winked at Sayeda, before doling out *one last demand* to my charges. "The rest of you, to bed."

Groans erupted from the table, Naveen slouching in his seat, Ren's eyes rolling so hard, they nearly popped out. "Yes, Mummy dearest."

I showed him a glimpse of my favorite finger before stalking toward the stairs, the wind propelling my footsteps.

Rest—*and Irina*—beckoned.

"Someone carry me," Naveen whined from behind me, but I didn't turn back. If I kept glancing over my shoulder to check on their every move, we'd never find the end of this road.

"You're too big," Ren grumbled in retort—loud enough for me to hear even as I took the steps two-at-a-time—their brotherly banter uninterrupted despite the *almosts* that still tainted the air around us with odorous worry.

"You're too scrawny. Come on, please?" Naveen retorted, before his last words floating up to follow me—*one last reminder*. "I almost died today, remember?"

I winced as I hit the landing.

I wouldn't forget anytime soon.

"I could light a fire under your ass if that motivated you, Veenie." Mal's stern warning countered my thoughts, heating the ground beneath my feet, too.

I couldn't let the fear slow me down. Couldn't let it shackle me in indecision. We had to keep running, like we always did. Outpacing anything that sought to snare us. Soaring *above* the wolves that hunted our steps.

Flying.

With the wind at my back, I worked my way down the hall, the heart-shaped sign on the door clearly indicating which suite would be mine for the night. The suite where Irina waited, a princess-turned-healer, her very presence soothing an ache I'd had for far longer than I cared to admit.

One last ruse.

If only it was all pretend.

I opened the door, ready to find a soft patch of floor and let the Breath drag me under for the night...

When Irina sat up.

Nineteen

IRINA

With all that had gone on in the last seventy-two hours, I had entered a new level of exhaustion that I hadn't known existed. I was used to the quiet, chronic kind of tired—the one that made everything sparkle a little less, the one born of boredom and idleness. But this kind of fatigue felt like trying to stand straight during an earthquake, like the world would give out beneath me any minute and my mind and body would be devoured by the weariness within.

Yet despite how desperately I yearned for sleep, despite how comfortable the bed was—a large mattress that could easily accommodate three people with pillows stuffed full of real feathers—I could not find rest.

Hours ticked by, and my mind raced. Tracing over every detail of my adventure thus far, reliving every moment of shame and triumph, creating alternate narratives to what I could or should have done differently, or what might come next.

I had been a fool in so many ways. Despite all the books I read and the lessons I sat through day in and day out with my tutors, I knew nothing of the world. Of the reality that my people suffered through. My parents couldn't have known either, otherwise they would have done something already...

Either way, it was up to me to make it right. One person had already died for my ignorance. And even if his death was a result of his own violence—he'd been the first to draw a weapon, after all—I would not let the cycle repeat. I had to listen and learn, and I had to do it fast. So whoever my parents chose for me to marry would either have to come on that journey with me, or learn to stay out of my way.

But whenever I wandered down that particular path—thoughts of marriage and partnership and ruling alongside someone...

My mind always came back to thoughts of a honey-stained hazel stare, snagging on his presence like the thorns of a hedge maze I couldn't see myself out of.

Where was Shin now? Singing and dancing with Malina downstairs? What would he do when I left? Would I ever see him again?

Did I *want* to?

Yesterday morning, the answer had been a clear *no*. Sure, he'd fooled me into liking him the first time, and we'd since reached a level of civility that made our journey tolerable, but that didn't make me want to linger in the hurt any longer.

But something had shifted in the cave, and again tonight when he played. Like something in his song had reminded my heart of a piece it'd been missing for so long, a piece it'd gotten accustomed to beating without, but now it could not imagine being separated from again. A lullaby that my soul remembered, even if my head could not—

The door creaked open, and I sat up with a start, pulling the blankets tighter to my chest. I was fully clothed aside from my boots and cloak—both of which sat in a neat pile next to the door—and yet I felt exposed as Shin's form appeared in the doorway, his silhouette doused in the soft blue of the witching hour's moon.

The air in the room changed, tinged now with an energy that zapped away all of my spiraling thoughts, captivating my head instead with his essence, his sheer *presence*—and made me self-conscious of my own.

"Oh sorry, I didn't realize you were still awake." He shut the door quietly, his expression drawing tight with unease; born of disappointment or regret, I couldn't tell in the lowlight. "Did I wake you?"

I slunk back down, pulling the blanket up to my chin as I turned onto my side—a less vulnerable position than meeting his gaze. "It's not your fault. I just have a lot on my mind."

There was quiet as he shucked his boots off, both of them thudding to the ground the only sound. Then, a breath, as a weight pressed into the far corner of the mattress.

"Do you—I mean, clean slate, right?" he asked softly, an uncertainty in his tone that I'd never heard from him. "Do you want to talk about it?"

The question ripped open my shoddy stitches, the ones I'd used to stanch wounds he'd dealt to me. I sat up again, this time hugging my pillow like a shield—a barrier between Shin Koishi and my confused, careless heart. "Does a clean slate automatically make us people who tell each other their worries?"

Shin sat on the edge of the bed, one foot tucked beneath him as the other dangled off the side, his hands clasped in his lap. In the moonlight, he looked young—his hair a tousled mess, his expression unsure and open.

I wondered which mask of his this was, which role he was performing with no one but me as an audience.

Whichever it was, it was effective, his moon-kissed gaze full of a sincerity I hadn't seen since the garden. "We were friends before we were anything else, you know."

Friends.

I didn't know if I loved or hated that word. If I wanted no part in it, or if I wanted more than I dared say.

"Were we?" I pulled my knees tighter, another wall of defense between me and that too-raw stare. "I recall you saving me once and then trying to kidnap me, but I don't quite remember friendship…"

A dimple flickered in his cheek. "You're deflecting."

My head fell between my knees, too weighty for my neck to manage on its own, my defenses waning when named. "Can't a girl need a break from all the heaviness?"

"Can't a man try help you carry it?"

I peeked over my knees, his smile glinting in the blue haze. Somehow, the half-dark made all of this so much easier, so much less real... and all the more vulnerable at the same time.

He could hurt me again. He could take my words and use them as knives, could riddle me with wounds I'd never truly recover from.

But the alternative was never knowing, never having this moment, and that felt somehow more wrong. And even if it hurt, when I went back to my role as the dutiful princess, I'd need memories to keep me company, even if they were barbed.

So I sat up, letting the blanket and pillow fall away, letting myself dwell in the discomfort of being, metaphorically, stripped bare. Freeing myself to the misty moonlight and the truths it sought.

"I was never meant to rule. It was supposed to be Nikolaj. And after he died, I wanted it even less. How could I, when he was so much better at all of it, and I was...so much less experienced?"

Out loud, it made even more sense. What good was a queen who not only didn't *want* her crown, but didn't have a strong enough head to wear it?

But Shin didn't jump to call me a spoiled princess this time, didn't agree with my laid-bare flaws or point out ones I'd missed. Instead, he tilted his head, like he was looking at me from a new angle. Like he could *see*. "You've always had to hide because of your gift. That's not your fault."

I blinked back my surprise, warring with myself not to cover up and flee from his assessment again.

Not my fault.

At the thought, a weight I hadn't noticed I'd been holding rolled from my shoulders, unknotting aches that had become semi-permanent between them.

It wasn't my fault. Not entirely.

But it was my responsibility now. And I was not ready.

"My fault or not, it doesn't mean I'm equipped to handle this," I admitted, thoughts swirling again like kicked-up dust as I spoke them aloud. "And hearing about what has been going on outside of Anastova...the people of this continent deserve *better*."

I thought back to Sayeda and Malina downstairs, to Via and Madame Tsojo and the other women I'd met in the last week. Compared to them, I had everything; yet I lacked the one quality they all possessed that made them *better* suited to queendom than I'd ever be.

Purpose. Something to fight for.

Shin shifted, both feet crossed beneath him now, his shoulders straighter. He stared at me for a long time, that same soul-scraping look that made me wriggle in my seat, heat burrowing in my middle. Then, "If you don't like the way things are, change them."

I stilled, the words from our night in the garden registering deep within me. This time, it wasn't a dig, but a challenge. A *goal*. When he'd said it the first time, I'd met him with excuses—with all the things in my way, and all the things I was too afraid to confront.

But I didn't have any excuses tonight. No more walls to hide behind or protect myself with.

"I'm going to try," I said instead, believing it for the first time in my life—though doubt still lurked around dark corners, waiting to snatch me when I turned away. "But I don't know where to start. And I highly doubt whichever idiot my parents marry me off to will understand it."

Shin's frame tensed, and I didn't know what bruise I'd accidentally poked as he turned away, his face cast in shadows. I waited, anxiety clamming up my palms, not wanting to push him further. Wishing to sit in this liminal peace a little longer, like I had while he'd played; not as Princess Catirina and Shin Koishi, but as two strangers on a moonlit night, swept away by a waltz and a whispered truth.

Shadows cleared as Shin decided to stay, too. But his voice was further away somehow, like he was already drifting back to the reality we both wanted to avoid, tethered to it by a purpose I didn't have. "Whoever you...end up with...I'm sure you'll convince them. You're a fighter."

As it had when Naveen had said it, the word elicited shame that rolled through my gut, hot and bitter as bile. Not because being a fighter was bad or wrong; but because it simply wasn't true. I'd never fought for anything. And people got hurt through my inaction, not my conviction.

"No, I'm a hider." The words wobbled as tears rushed to my lashes, bursting with salt and self-pity. "I always listen and follow orders and hide away. People are safer that way."

This is what happens when you speak, girl.

Stay in your room, Irina!

It didn't feel so true, not anymore. People suffered more when I turned away. When nobles like my parents and I refused to see or speak on their behalf.

Shin shifted again—just an inch closer—but the air in the room warmed, suddenly shallow and stuffy. Too close, too *real* for even the moonlight to soften and shield.

His eyes were just as hot on my skin.

"You know, not everything was a lie that night. At the ball." He stopped, like he couldn't quite catch his breath. I waited, hanging on every inhale. "I—my life wasn't always like this. I had prospects—some impressive family business. With the Koishis, actually. That *is* my real name–or at least, my mother's maiden name that I adopted. But I ran away from it all when I was young."

More truths wrapped in lies, more secrets hidden by wearing them on his sleeve. My heart hammered against my ribs, a repeated call for him to keep going, a perilous want to know more. "Why?"

His eyes didn't leave mine, and for the first time since I'd met him, there were no masks. Not the performer or the conman, not the leader or the thief.

Just Shin Koishi. Just a boy who—telling by the wide-eyed stare he gave me—was just as scared and lonely as I was.

"Because when things get rough, I fly away. I always have. My mother used to say I was built to soar." He looked down at his tightly clasped hands, shutting some of the vulnerability away, but he didn't stop talking. Didn't stop telling the truth for once...or at least, more of it than I'd expected him to share. "And when she passed, and it was just me and Aya against a lot of bad things...I took her, and I flew."

I imagined it for a moment, vivid as a painting in front of me.

Shin, young and afraid, with an even tinier Aya to look after. His mother gone, the world chasing him...

I didn't know the full context of his past. But I knew one thing more certainly than my own name.

It wasn't his fault.

"No, Shin." I reached across the vast expanse of the bed, my hand resting on his knee. "That means you *stayed*."

His throat bobbed, words I'd never hear stuck in it. Then, the vulnerability in his eyes shuttered; he withdrew, my hand falling away as he swung his legs off the bed—flying away again, his words distant and clipped. "You should get some rest. It's late."

I battled the broken, insecure part of me that wanted to duck under the covers and hide, clenching my fists in my lap.

"You're deflecting." I served his words back to him, but just like that, the make-believe space was gone, reality seeping back into the room. He stood, gathering one of the feathered pillows to his chest, and I sighed, disappointment squeezing my middle. "What are you doing?"

When he faced me again, it was his favorite mask—Shin, the irreverent fool, the cocky thief with a heart of gold—that chuckled, "Can't a man get some sleep?"

He tossed the pillow on the floor next to the bed, swiping the spare blanket with a flourish.

I raised a brow at him, unamused by his performance this time. "On the floor?"

He made a show of looking around the room. "Do you see another option?"

I shot him an exacerbated look, and the corner of his mouth tilted upward. Still just a boy, this time needing a playmate. Needing someone to laugh away the hurt with. Still running...but this time, asking me to chase.

I hurled a spare pillow at his face with a snicker. Maybe I needed someone to run after, too.

"Don't be a prude. Via would mock you for it," I taunted, and when his brows flew upwards, victory blared in my chest. I patted the bed. "There is plenty of space here, dummy."

I was grateful for the dark, knowing how red my cheeks must have burned, but I wouldn't turn back. Whatever this was now—friendship, a truce, a clean slate—I wasn't ready to let go. Not yet.

Not until tomorrow's sunlight tore it from my grasp.

His head tilted, but he scooped both his pillow and the one I'd thrown off the floor, placing them as a divider between us as he climbed onto the mattress and laid down. "I thought I was being a gentleman."

"*Pssh*, now you're really talking crazy," I snorted, turning my back to him and pulling my thick comforter around me. I'd played this hand myself, but I wasn't brave enough to stare it in the face; not yet. "Just get some sleep."

"All right. Goodnight, then." There was an awkward quiet as he settled, adjusting until comfortable, while my heart pounded so loudly it was a wonder he didn't hear it from his side. Though I'd woken up on his lap in a cave this morning, this was somehow more intimate, more vulnerable.

More exciting.

More *real*.

Even so, it didn't take long for our breaths to steady, and my heartbeat eventually slowed, the never-ending exhaustion creeping back into sore limbs. Eyelids fluttered shut, the drag of drowsiness pulling them down, my body losing its senses as the bed enveloped me in weightlessness.

Still, I heard the half-whisper that escaped his lips, whether he meant it to or not. "You're going to make a great queen someday, Princess."

But by the time I worked up the courage to open my eyes again, he was already asleep.

Twenty

SHIN

Morning brought with it a dread that sat in my stomach like an anvil, weighing me down into the soft bed. The sun's first prying rays nudged me from sleep, my eyes cracking open long before they wanted to, to find Irina sprawled across her side of the bed, her mouth parted slightly and her short hair poking in every direction. Laying on her stomach, her arm tucked beneath the pillow, the curves of her form peeked from the half-discarded comforter as her one knee hitched up; like in her sleep, she was trying to crawl deeper into the mattress. Deeper into my mind.

Though the wind was mine to command, the sight stole my breath.

I was used to flying. To soaring.

But all I wanted to do now was stay, just a few minutes longer. Last night, too, when I'd told her the short version of what my life had been. When she'd looked at me, not at my masks, like she *saw*. Like she understood.

No, Shin. That means you stayed.

I couldn't stay. Our time was up. Breath above, it had never even begun, not really. There was no time or place where Catirina and I had a future. No life where that made sense. The only one that did had been abandoned long ago, burned away with the Opera House, killed in a fire like the rest of my past.

So I wrenched my heavy body from the mattress as quietly as I could, slipping my boots on and slinking out the door like a disrespectful prick, putting as much room between Irina and I as I could.

Not that any distance would ever be enough to snap the tether that she'd leashed me with.

I stepped into the hall, closing the door behind me as quietly as I could, to find Malina already dressed in travel clothes and waiting, her arms crossed. "Sleep well?"

"Like a baby."

Pleasantries out of the way, she huffed down the hall, knowing I'd follow. "I spoke with Sayeda this morning. Her son and his wife are willing to take us up to the border on his barge."

That same stone in my gut shifted, the wind murmuring hesitations in my ear. Malina had done her job well, befriending the woman and her family, and a boat ride on the river sounded like a much better alternative to another day of walking. And the faster we got to Nehir, the faster we could trade Irina off, and we both could move on. Could *heal*.

But the barges typically operated under strict time schedules—a power play by the four kingdoms to control and regulate trade. And while I was not an expert on the Black River's operating orders, I knew well enough from living next to it for as long as I had that ships never sailed on Soulsdays—a weekly day of rest granted to us by the oh-so-generous nobility—especially not the first one after the Masque, when most people were still nursing their hangovers and finding their way back home.

I slowed my steps, catching Malina by the elbow and keeping my voice low. "It's a rest day. There shouldn't be any boat traffic."

Malina's jaw clenched, the embers in her stare a fever-blaze. "Which means we can move faster, drop the Princess off, and maybe be back by supper."

She slipped out of my grip and stalked off back toward the rooms, likely to rouse the others. I watched her go, the mass in my middle growing.

I wasn't the only one struggling, and I needed to keep my eyes on my crew. My *family*. Ecei had brought the winds of change to our door, both good and bad; but if any of us were going to get back to our lives, this needed to end.

I needed to let go. To hell with boating rules and regulations. If Driss and his wife were willing to take the risk, I'd never been afraid of breaking a few rules.

And no doubt Ecei would appreciate a timely arrival after the mess we'd made.

The Lost Ones and I were packed and ready within the hour. Sayeda was generous enough to pack us food for the way, our picnic and precious cargo in tow as we all boarded.

The barge floated behind the small, chipped-paint tugboat, the engine already gurgling next to the flat dock. Driss and his wife had already prepped the space for human cargo, crates serving as benches on the shallow deck, blankets laid over them for comfort.

"Welcome aboard the Current Chaser, folks," Driss greeted us with a bright smile as we boarded, offering both Aya and Irina a hand onto the floating surface. "Davke and I are happy to be of service today."

He wasn't much older than I, maybe just past thirty judging by the few lonely strands of gray that hid in his brown hair, but his skin was tanned and tight to his face, the result of long days worked in the sun. His wife, Davke, waved from the tugboat, her loose-fitting clothes and long dark hair billowing with the wind's gentle caresses; but she didn't sway an inch, even as the river and wind rocked us.

Hopefully their experience would be enough to make this journey easier.

We stayed out of the seasoned sailors' way as the barge shoved off from the dock and began its wobble up the wide river. The Lost Ones and I all firmly planted in our seats, none of us willing to challenge our untested legs on the ever-moving surface; instead, we enjoyed the view as the sun rose higher and higher, warming the air to a balmy spring-like temperature despite autumn's reign.

Light glittered off the river's dark face like starlight, more brilliant and lovely than the chandeliers in Anastova. Fitting, that our journey would start and end with such radiance.

Perhaps these memories would sparkle more than they'd wound, one day.

It was a perfect morning.

And I'd never been more unsatisfied.

Irina leaned across one of the crates, propped up on her elbows as she tilted her face to the sun, her bronze skin cast in gold as it kissed her cheeks. When she stretched, her back arched, the curves of her hips and stomach folding in on themselves in a way that twisted my lowest parts with desire.

I ripped my stare from her, my wayward spirit needing an escape yet again. I couldn't let my wickedness be my weakness, or we'd all be consumed by it.

The wind carried me as I hopped the gap between the barge to the tugboat, where Driss and Davke manned the gears and levers that controlled the machinery. I cleared my throat, gently begging their attention. "Thank you for your generosity. You sure we won't get you in trouble?"

Driss fiddled with a few of the controls before stepping away, plopping onto the captain's stool. Reaching into a small crate next to him, he produced two bottles, a fizzy amber liquid swirling in each. With a quick flick of his thumb, he removed the metal tops before handing one to me. "No one patrols these parts anyway. 'Sides, it's the least we can do for *the* Misty Muses. My mother's place is going to be packed for weeks just so they can listen to her *describe* your performance."

"The performance was really something special, wasn't it?" a voice said behind us, sweet as honey, and I startled, nearly dropping the bottle. Irina smirked at me as she leaned against the side of the boat, curls dancing in the breeze, but I looked away before I could get sucked back into her. How she'd managed the gap between the tug and barge without making noise surprised me, but as I turned to look —and noticed Aya conveniently pretending to sleep on her crate—I deduced she had help from my traitorous sister. Irina pressed on, making herself comfortable, "But the real talent is you, Davke. Sayeda told me you made her lights?"

The woman blushed as she dipped her head, brushing away the compliment. "Oh, you're so sweet."

But Irina didn't let her run from it—much like she hadn't let me flee, either. "Where did you learn that?"

Davke's large eyes rounded with wonder at the Princess, hands balling in her skirt, like no one had bothered to ask her that in a long time. A tentative smile stretching across her face, the woman spoke, her accent more pronounced than it had been before. "I—well, I worked in a glass factory back home. You need fire to make glass, so a lot of the Pyromental *Easinir* in Jalta who aren't strong enough to work in the mines go to the craft factories—glass, textiles, jewelry. Many of the others hated the work, but I didn't mind it."

"Well, you must be one of the best," Irina said, and though Davke didn't respond, she stood straighter, her hands unwinding—the Princess working her magic and breathing life back into a person without even a touch, this time.

I took a swig of the fizzy drink—a sweet, fruity flavor that complimented the bubbled texture—hoping it might soothe the ache in my chest.

"That's my wife, all right." Driss squeezed Davke's hand, beaming. She leaned into his touch, the two of them sharing a silent moment before Driss broke it, pointing his bottleneck between Irina and I like it was a conductor's wand. "So, when did the two of you get married?"

I coughed, fizzy liquid searing down the back of my throat and up again, spouting through my nose. It took several seconds of pounding at my chest to clear my lungs, my nostrils burning. Irina snorted, but turned away when our gazes clashed across the small deck.

I'd forgotten—stupidly—about our little ruse. About the roles we were still meant to play, at least until sunset called her home.

Husband and wife.

Maybe in the next life.

"Driss!" Davke smacked her partner's shoulder with a light *thwack.* "Please excuse my husband, he likes to meddle."

"It's why you fell for me." He winked at her, fighting a grin that wrenched open my still healing wounds. But he pressed on, a softness to his gruff voice. "Listen, I get it. Looks like you two are in the middle of a scuffle, but sometimes the best thing is to remember why you got together in the first place."

I couldn't help but steal a glance at Irina, small, riotous parts of me thrilled to see her watching, too.

One last look.

In this life, we were princess and pauper, born of divided worlds that could never unite. But there had been a night—albeit, a lie— where we'd been something else. A brave girl at a bar and a foolish man looking for a reason to stay. Strangers who stumbled into each other's worlds and made them better for a moment.

And even if we could never go back, even if our paths were meant to fracture tonight, I wanted her to remember that version of me best.

One last dance.

"We met in a bar," I said aloud, feeding both Driss's curiosity and my own masochistic need for her to *see* me one last time. "Some *ugly* Nehir prick was making her uncomfortable, so I took some creative liberties with the shape of his nose, and my wife here was head over heels."

Irina blinked those long lashes, surprise registering across her face for only a moment before she crossed her arms, sinking into her hip.

"Oh, *that's* how it happened?" she challenged. "If I recall correctly, after you made a big show of being the tough guy, you dragged me away from my drink, and asked me to *thank you* for being a 'gentleman.'"

And there it was—the fire that'd captivated me that night, burning in her expression. No, not fire...light. Warmth, pure and bright enough to expose all my bullshit. Enough to reduce all the shadows that chased me to bad dreams.

She stared at me with it now, and I met her gaze, soaking it in like sunlight on my skin, not caring if I got burned anymore.

Driss chuckled and Davke rolled her eyes, teasing, "What is it with men, hmm? Driss made a move on me by telling my boss to start looking for my replacement, because he was going to marry me one day."

"I knew the moment I saw you," the sailor said unashamedly, stealing the words I'd wanted to say right from my mouth. He kissed his wife's knuckles, earning another sheepish smile. "And even though it took us years to save up enough to make it happen, I wasn't wrong."

Irina's arms flexed, still crossed, her chest rising and falling in heavy breaths as we sat there, eyes locked, holding the moment before it disappeared beneath the horizon and night stole her from me. Then, so soft I wasn't sure if Driss and Davke even heard her, "Love has a way of bringing people back."

One last hope.

Whether it was to them or for me alone, it sounded too much like a wish for me to handle. Wishes didn't come true in Babylon, not for thieves and runaways like me.

Tearing my gaze away, I took another deep pull of the fizzy juice before pushing off the opposite rail, nodding to the Captain. "Thanks for the drink and the company. I'll go check on the others."

And like I always did, I fled, leaving Irina behind with the Captain and his wife, retreating back to the Lost Ones.

But as I swept over the rail and onto the barge, my sister sat up, looking not *at* me, but past me, violet eyes wide with concern.

"Do you need another boost?" she called, a feeble hand raised. Around me, the wind stirred, my sister's shaky breeze turning my head—

To where Irina was already climbing over the rail, stretching her legs to jump back onto the barge. She stumbled, arms flailing as she caught her balance, but righted herself quickly despite the unsteady surface.

"I just don't have my river legs." She grinned at my sister as she stood next to me, shoulder to shoulder. She didn't look at me, still focused on Aya, but she didn't need to. The message was clear, cracking wide my defenses and spurring life from organs I thought long dead:

You run, and I'll follow.

One last chase.

But the wind changed abruptly, and Irina brushed past me, hopping onto the crate with Aya and Naveen, inspecting my sister like a doctor, eyes narrowed as she pressed a hand to her forehead. "Do *you* need a boost?"

Worry replaced all wistfulness as I bounded to her side. Crouching next to the crate I grabbed my sister's calf and massaged, kicking myself that I hadn't paid closer attention, my head snagged up on sentiments I couldn't afford or change. "You're not feeling well? What's wrong?"

"I'm fine, you worrywarts." Aya swatted both Irina and I away, scooting back further on the crate toward Naveen. But even as she said it, her face paled further, and she swayed into Naveen's side for support. "I just don't have my river *stomach.*"

Irina's mouth flattened into a forced smile. She took Aya's wrist—like she was feeling for a pulse—and a small spark of light flickered where they touched. "Well, we'll have a cure for you by nightfall. And maybe Ecei can throw in something for seasickness."

Color flooded Aya's cheeks again as she smiled, easing closer to Naveen as relief unknotted her shoulders. But the crease between Irina's brow remained, and my gut twisted over itself as I read the truth in that thin line.

There was no running from this. No more lingering in moments past or wishing for more. Aya was living on borrowed time, and our line of credit was about to expire, even with Irina's help.

So Irina needed to leave if my sister was going to survive.

And I'd have to lose one part of my heart to protect another.

Before I could stop myself, I grabbed Irina's hand and squeezed it —a silent show of gratitude and regret.

A *thank-you* and a *goodbye.*

Irina's eyes misted as they met mine, and she squeezed back.

Hold on, don't let go.

My fingers slipped from hers even so.

Twenty-One

Sun reflected off the Black River's face in twinkling flashes, so small and erratic it was easy for my mind to get lost in the daydream. I pretended each tiny orb of light was a fairy, ready to sprinkle fae-dust over the Current Chaser and transport us all away to a place where dreams came true.

Where it could stay like *this*.

Like Riku and Ren, bickering as they huddled over a pair of dice, the highest roller betting the other to do increasingly risky and outright ridiculous dares that varied from holding their breath in a handstand to licking Naveen's dirty socks—much to Naveen's dismay.

Like Naveen and Aya, huddled together on the crate, Naveen telling stories about his—likely exaggerated—escapades as a bouncer for Madame Tsojo's, while Aya's face still burned pink; from the magic I gave her, or from warm cadence of Naveen's voice, I'd never know.

Like Davke teaching Kas small tricks, her Quantifying magic and his Control blending seamlessly, his eyes wide as fire danced across their fingertips in wonderful, impressive shapes: a horse, a tugboat, even a pair of small figures that looked suspiciously like the twins flipping over each other in perfect, blazing synchronicity.

Like Malina, *humming* to herself as she examined the dials and gadgets at the front of the tugboat, Driss happily naming each part she crouched over; the pressure gage, the thermometer, the throttle, and other words that sounded like gargled nonsense to me, but made Malina's lips twitch upward toward her freckled cheeks.

Like Shin, sitting next to me again with one foot tucked beneath him, the bottle of fizzy liquid dangling dangerously between his fingertips as he watched over all of them. His shoulder brushed against mine as he relaxed, an ease about him that stabbed at my ribcage in repeated, brutal bursts.

But as the sun sank deeper and deeper, hanging low enough to brush against the horizon, the sparkles on the water faded, the fairies passing through the twilight gate again, back to the fae-realm, leaving me and the others behind.

"All right folks, hang tight!" Driss called from the helm, shifting the tugboat into a lower gear, slowing our chug up the river ever so slightly as we entered a shallower pass. "We're almost to the border."

The border. From there, it would only be a short walk in from the river to where Shin had set the rendezvous point.

I wished we could come to a halt, wished I could turn around and live instead in the embrace of the Breeze Haven, watching the Mist*ed* Muses perform each night, lounging around on a sun-bathed barge all day.

Sitting next to Shin for as long as he'd let me.

"What will you do when you get home?" Naveen asked, amber eyes turning a mahogany red in the setting sunlight as they trained on me.

I pulled my knees to my chest, the sunset stealing the warmth that'd caressed the day, the autumn chill setting in its absence—much like the hope that slowly cooled in my chest, light fading and flickering. I had a lot to do when I returned, my time for daydreaming gone. "Well, first, I need to tell my parents about Ecei and Drakkar's involvement in all of this. I sent my parents a raven back in Hiku City telling them I was okay, and I used my royal seal so they'll know it's real, but whether or not Drakkar's intentions were to try and woo me, there will have to be political recourse."

Tonight, when I met with them, I'd play Ecei's game. I'd make sure Aya got her cure, and then I'd thank her and Drakkar for negotiating for my safe return. Then I'd take them to Dunyas with me to 'celebrate.'

Little did they realize, I'd be celebrating their fall from grace.

If only Nikolaj could be there to see the look on her face.

A voiceless part of me wished Shin and the others could see it, too.

"Are you really going to marry Drakkar after all of this?" Aya pried, gnawing at her bottom lip. She was the one who was breathing borrowed air, the one who didn't have a proper home to go back to when this was all done, but she still offered me another kindness after all the trouble I'd brought her.

My first *friend*.

Shin peeked up at me again, but quickly looked away. Even so, he sat straighter, like he was still hanging onto the conversation—waiting for my answer.

"No," I answered easily, confident for the first time in a long time, emboldened by my friend's comfort and concern. I would play the role my parents wanted of me—I'd marry and strengthen my kingdom and ensure our domain. But I would not do so with Drakkar, even if my life depended on it. I continued, trying to ease the divot between Aya's brows, "I promise, anyone but him. My father had wanted me to speak with Avi of Jalta, and he seems like a fair enough person to be around."

Fair, indeed. Gentle even. Placid. *Plain.*

Boring.

My eyes grazed over Shin, secret wishes yet again skimming to the surface—

To find him looking back, again. Not fleeing; instead, something demanding and defiant burning in his blown-wide pupils.

Naveen cleared his throat and patted my knee, snapping me from the moment. I turned to him, blush heating my neck, but the sincerity in his waiting stare sobered it, dispelling the ache from my chest. "Whoever you end up choosing...well, if they ever give you trouble, you can call us."

My spine straightened, even as my throat constricted around the many emotions fighting their way to my tongue.

In Anastova, I didn't have people that acted *with* me instead of on my behalf. Sure, there were people who cared—Tasha, Hana whenever she visited...my parents, even, in their own protective way.

But since Nikolaj died, no one ever fought for me. No one ever stood by my side, ready to take on the world.

This band of thieves had done more for me in a week than all of the nobles in the palace had in my whole life.

I didn't want to let go. *Couldn't.*

And I didn't need fairies to carry us off to a perfect world.

If you want things to be different, change them.

I'd somehow make *this* world the one I wanted it to be.

I swallowed down the fear and insecurity that stayed my words too many times before. "About that...well, I know you have busy lives, and you can say no...but how would you all feel about staying in Anastova for a while?"

I looked to Aya—the easiest reaction to gauge—my heart soaring as she perked up immediately. Naveen raised a brow, but didn't shut me down, propelling my plan further, excitement stirring in my chest at the prospect.

My palms sweated, but I let that flurry of hope spiral, let it spread roots and take a firm stance in my gut. "At least while you figure out a new place to live! It would be good for you, Aya, while you recover, and I'm sure the medementals would be willing to help you learn new tricks, Naveen. And Shin, you could work in Tasha's kitchen—"

"Thanks, Princess, but we'll have to decline." Shin's grin was warm, but his cool tone snipped the stalk of the flower before it could fully bloom. His gaze trailed toward the falling sun, his pale face kissed by its fading orange glow. "Hiku City is home."

Home.

Without me.

Tearbuds watered the corners of my lashes, but I blinked them away, ignoring the hole left behind from where the hope had been weeded out, leaving me empty and seedless.

"Of course." I pitched my voice higher, hoping it masked the hoarse lump that made swallowing difficult. "Well, if you ever want to visit, you know where to find me."

He opened his mouth to respond—to decline again, or to offer pity-filled *maybes*, I would never know—because he was silenced as Malina dropped next to him, her shoulders tense and her expression that hyper-vigilant *blank* that only she possessed. Her arrow-sharp gaze squinted at the horizon, directing Shin's attention to follow. "Do you see that?"

Shin and Naveen both went rigid, Shin leaning into a crouch to try and better make out the image. I squinted against the sunlight, craning my head to try and see what she did, too.

When I finally saw it, all silly notions like hope and home fled from my gut, ran out by a spine-tingling dread.

Shadowy figures waded along the shallow edges of the riverbank not too far ahead, like sirens that'd slunk from the river's depths, silhouettes blurring against the dusk. As my eyes adjusted to the bright, details sharpened their images from monstrous imaginations to something far more horrifying.

Men. Soldiers, judging by the blue Nehir uniforms they wore and the rifles strapped across their backs. But sense evaded the picture still, as the men's heads were covered not by the standard bowled helmets, but by full-faced *masks,* adorned with circular disks that looked like breathing apparatuses...

My hands shook as I held my breath, fear halting my lungs.

Something was very, very *wrong.*

"What are they doing?" Naveen hissed, but Shin hushed him with a flash of one of his hand signals. Shin crawled off the crate with an unnatural quiet, his winds muting his footsteps as he inched closer, firing off more signals to the others, bringing the rest of the group to a full, easy silence without a word.

Without the din of chatter, we could hear the soldiers bark orders to each other, their voices carrying across the valley, even with the chug of the tugboat. They hadn't seen us yet, consumed in their heavy task.

"What is that shit?" Malina dared ask aloud, against Shin's command.

She didn't wait long for an answer.

Carried between two of them at a time, giant metallic jugs splashed against the surface of the water, spilling black ooze into the river. As the current churned the substance, it hissed and dissolved, all evidence of its existence erased except for the strange, chemical odor that wafted down on the changing wind.

Several truths clicked together at once, panic blaring against my skull in violent waves that rattled my whole frame.

I fell back, my legs numb, held breath expelling on the deadly realization. "They're *poisoning* the water."

The water that flowed *downstream* from Nehir, into every territory south of it. Into Hiku City, built around it. Into its aqueducts and faucets and reservoirs—into every home of the overcrowded metropolis. Into the Jaltan mountains, where it pooled in caverns that ran alongside the mines that thousands of people worked and breathed in, day in and day out. Into the waterpicks they used to drill through thick rock.

Into Dunyas.

Into the farmlands where we grew our food.

Into the soil that gave birth to nearly every herb and crop harvested and transported across Babylon.

Into our medicine.

Our *bodies*.

Clarity broke free of the pollution, my mind racing.

Nehir had a cure for the Blight because they'd *created* it.

"Everyone down, now," Driss growled as he killed the engine, his genial countenance evaporating as his brows pulled together. As he must have realized what we'd stumbled across, too. "Davke, hide them."

But it was too late.

We'd been spotted.

"Oi!" A soldier hollered, the unmistakable sound of his rifle cocking reverberating through my body. "*Chaser*, what the fuck are you doing here on a Soulsday?"

"Stay quiet," Driss warned before stepping forward, raising his hands above his head in surrender. "Sorry to trouble you, but I have special cargo I was told to deliver to the border!"

The soldier waded closer, his voice still booming through his mask as he aimed his gun at Driss. "What fucking cargo?"

"Get rid of them, Jet," another soldier called, and bile sloshed up my gullet.

Driss raised his hands higher even as his voice dipped, "We mean no harm. Please, feel free to board and I'll show you."

I didn't have to be familiar with a con to smell his bluff, and neither did the Lost Ones. They all tensed as the smell of trouble doused us all in primal fear. Whether or not they understood the gravity of what we'd just witnessed, they were all survivors, sensing real danger when it chased them.

But despite his previous claims, Shin Koishi didn't fly away. Shin Koishi always stayed for the ones he cared about.

His hand twitched—another order to stay quiet, to stand down—as he hopped up next to Driss, his hands raised to match.

"We have special clearance from Queen Ecei. It's a high-level transport." He puffed out his chest, his voice claiming the natural authority of a prince. No, a *king*, strong and sure of his command. With another quick sleight of hand, he produced something from his pocket—something that glittered and sparkled in the dying sunlight. "She gave us this as a sigil, to ensure our safe passage."

It took me a moment to recognize Malina's trinket from Tsojo's brothel.

For the second time that day, a small seed of cautious optimism burrowed in my chest. They'd have to let us pass with that, let us *live*, or risk Ecei's rage. And then we could figure out exactly who'd been behind this nefarious plot, how deep it ran. We'd deal with it, my parents would have to take action—

The gunshot blew a wide hole into any hope I had left.

I jerked forward as Shin flinched, panic animating my limbs into a stumbling crawl as a scream tore through me. "No!"

But when *Driss's* body fell back onto the boat—blood staining the wooden deck from where it poured from the wound between his lifeless eyes—simultaneous relief and terror flooded me.

Shin was all right. But Driss was *dead.*

Stunned quiet stole time for a stretched-wide moment.

Then hell broke loose.

Davke crumpled to her knees next to her husband, her inhuman wails ricocheting through my bones as sorrow leapt up my gut.

"Get down!" Shin cried at the same time he dove for cover behind the rail, the chorus of rifles being cocked offering us only seconds to respond.

Instinct taking over, I slid behind the nearest crate, dragging Aya and Naveen with me. Out of the corner of my eye, I watched Malina snag Kas, panic written across her face, and the twins crouched out of sight in unison.

Just as the soldiers opened fire, a tornado of bullets hurtling toward us. They thunked as they banged against the metal hull of the tugboat and splintered through wooden crates, a cacophony of angry war drums beating for our deaths.

"Get the rest!" soldiers screamed over the whizzing, head-splitting booms.

"No witnesses!" another replied, a glee coating his gruff voice, splashing signaling their pursuit. "Don't let anyo—"

He cut off in a strangled whimper before a louder splash tore through the world—the uncanny sound of a body dropping.

Despite my racing heart blurring my vision, I dared a peek over the crate, straining my neck to make sure it wasn't one of *ours*...

To where Shin stood at the helm, hands raised, stealing the air from the soldiers that drifted close enough, sweat clinging his shirt to the contours of his sturdy back. Unafraid of the guns.

Not flying. *Staying.*

"They have an air Controller!" someone cried, and the water bubbled around us as a Qualifier mounted a counterattack, the river shaking the boat. I ducked again to cover my head as crates toppled over one another, wood splitting when the heavy cargo pitched and fell.

A strong arm belted around my waist, yanking me out of the way —Naveen. He shoved Aya and I against a crate, his hand bracing against the wood as it hardened beneath us—petrified by his Qualifying touch.

"Thank—" I started, but stopped as a sick *crackling* filled my ears, the sound of wood snapping like bone. I flinched, preparing for something to collapse—

When the smell of smoke assaulted my nostrils, burning the hairs in my nose and choking my lungs.

Fire.

Always fire.

But instead of crippling me, fear shot me to kneeling so I could see over the chaos.

My eyes snagged on Davke. On the lighter in her hand, the remnants of a crate already burning at her feet. Shin crouched just a few steps in front of her, one hand still raised as he clung to the pitching rail with the other, still fighting, still trying...

No.

No, no, no, no.

I reached for Davke, my limbs wobbling as the boat did, the rest of the noise fading away. That same siren screamed again in my head, a warning of danger that shook my very soul, and I yelled as loudly as I could. "Davke no, no *fire*—"

She raised her bloodstained arms, a vicious smile carving her face. "For Driss."

The fire tore forward, blazing toward the soldiers—

And the black river *exploded,* blowing Shin Koishi into the water.

EARTH

Twenty-Two

SHIN

A flash of light, of *pain*, and I fell through time.

The buzz of violins and the groan of cellos sang their dissonant song as the other musicians warmed their fingers, the bumble of the audience a percussive rhythm that kept time with my heartbeat.

I was going to play today. Going to make Mama proud—in her hometown, no less. The nice blonde lady had promised me Mama would be here, listening. And maybe afterward, I could visit the baby, too. She was getting big—almost two now—and knew how to say my name finally. Though I'd need to be sneaky, or my father's men would catch me again.

Maestro Benjin raised his brow at me when I first arrived. "Your father is all right with this?"

"Yes!" I lied, already too talented at it for my own good. I smacked on a smile that even charmed all of my father's men-the same ones I conned into driving the carriage tonight. "He says he paid you instead of a Jaltan tutor for all of my lessons because you're the best, but I need to get better at being in front of a crowd if I'm going to fulfill my duty."

Benjin's eyes softened, and I knew I'd won.

So I sat amongst the other players, the grand glass ceiling painting the stage in a melody of starlight as the house lights dimmed and the audience hushed, breathing in the magic that was about to happen.

Like the others, I tucked my violin beneath my chin, the familiar grooved wood resting against my shoulder as my calloused, aching fingers kissed the strings at the instrument's neck—waiting.

There was a small burst of applause as Maestro took the stage and bowed, but the hush settled again as he turned to us, his baton raised.

And then, with the first swish of his hands through the air, we played.

Music filled the quiet, a bird stretching its great wings and flying through the crowd as we all performed as one. It had been a while since I'd played, my fingers clumsy at first as they danced out the notes, but soon memory consumed my muscles, and I got to fly with the others. Got to soar.

Until a scream shattered the harmony, an out of tune note that set the song out of tempo.

"Fire!" the first panicked voice called from the audience— in the pit, where commoners watched—then joined by another as chaos replaced harmony. Some of the other musicians dropped their instruments, stopped their playing—but I kept going, my violin and I not ready to stop, not yet. Nobles in the boxes above peered over their rails, clutching hands to their mouths and chests—

Maestro stopped conducting, and turned to see what was happening—

And then the world was on fire.

"Riku, freeze it, or it will explode again! The substance is combustible!" a voice cried from a million miles away, the panic in her tone clear, though the words made no sense.

But pain ripped through me, my lungs searing, my *skin*....

I fell again, too tired, too heavy to stay here.

• • •

Hiku City Opera House burned, a great wall of orange flame and black smoke rising up to blot out the starry night.

Another mass of red toward the back of the room–soldiers, dressed in crimson on black. Why were they here? Had they attacked? *No, that couldn't be–*

"Run!" Maestro screamed above the noise, and I did, tripping as my legs went numb beneath me. Dropping my violin as a body crashed into me, smoke blurring my vision.

No, not my violin!

Mama had given it to me. Had taught me to play.

Where was she?

"Where is he? Where is *Shin*?"

The voice said *my* name, this time, like it cared. Like it was as desperate for me as I was for it. My eyes blinked open, but all I saw was red–in deep blotches across my chest, my legs.

As my vision blurred, the pain tore through me again, like fire was eating its way through my bones, my veins, my everything.

My eyes shut. I couldn't stay. Not this time.

"Shin!" someone screamed—to warn me—but I ignored them. I scrambled, dropping to my hands and knees to crawl for my violin. Feet stomped around me, bodies running from the stage.

Between the forest of legs, there it was, the red wood a beacon. I reached for it—

A flash of light.

The scent of burning flesh—my flesh filled my nose, a rotted, ashy smell that brought bile up my throat.

Then pain. Everywhere. All at once.

My vision went white, then black, as the pain devoured my face, my stomach, my legs.

Another sensation tugged at my middle, something like being hoisted through the air...

Floating, like ash on a breeze.

My consciousness dimmed in and out of focus as the pain ate more of me.

Then.

"Wake up!"

"Come on, Shin, please," the voice begged, *pleaded*, but it was still far away, beyond a veil I could not pierce.

"I've got him, Irina." Another voice—deeper—more familiar—and the faint feeling of flying again. The pulse of a heartbeat against my ear, stinging against my legs and arms where hands grasped me. "Just save him."

"Someone save him, he's just a boy!"

"Ri-Ri, no, we have to go—"

Pain faded, and my eyes cracked open.

A girl, so small she had to be a fairy, floating in and out of my bleary eyes. Magic, warm and soft as it cleared my pain. A voice, sweet as stardust she whispered to me. "One more breath. You can do it."

"Stay with me," sobs shook her voice. Shook my frame, too. "Come back to me, Shin. Hold on."

"Hold on, don't let go."

My eyes opened fully against the blinding light, and as it faded, I could see the fairy's cheeks spattered with starry freckles. Tears dragged down them, and I wanted to reach out—I lifted my hand, and a destroyed, charred sleeve fell back. But there was no mar on my skin. Not a single burn. Just a thin layer of ash that smeared against the pale.

"Are you a fairy?" I sat up too fast, the world spinning. "You saved me.*"*

The girl blinked wide eyes, a smile breaking across her face. "You're safe now."

"He's okay!" someone shouted as the light dimmed. I blinked, taking in my surroundings. We were outside now—smoke clouding the sky—

The Opera House stood in front of us, but the roof had half collapsed, giant puddles of water from the Easinir's intervention drowning the steps. Horror lanced through my gut. Was Mama safe? Was she even here?

But despite the panic that surged, murmurs crowded as bodies pressed closer to us, blocking out my view of the structure, faces contorted as they watched the fairy with narrowed eyes and deep-set frowns.

"What is she?"

"Who did this?"

"Jaltans? The fire—"

"Come back, Shin," the voice said again, stronger this time. A command, not a sobbed plea. A princess giving her subject an order.

I groaned, a distant ache throbbing in my head, my skin tight and strange as red stained the insides of my eyelids...

Fire.

No, *light.*

I opened my eyes, and my vision flooded with Irina. Tears again smeared down her star-freckled face, but there was a determination in her gaze, burning like the world around us. Her hands pressed to my chest, that light pouring from her even though there was nothing left to heal. No wound left to stitch together, the red disappeared.

I clasped my palm over hers—my sleeve somehow both burnt and soaked—as I sat up, my thumb tracking circles against her skin. "Hey, shh. I'm okay. I'm safe."

Irina blinked, registering my resurrection. Dragging in deep, steadying breaths, her lip wobbled. Then she pressed her forehead to mine. My other hand clasped around the back of her neck, and hers balled into a fist against my chest, as her breath heated my face. "You can't die on me. You *can't.*"

Jagged breaths passed between our lungs, uniting us as we sat there, foreheads and noses brushing, hands clasped between our fast-beating hearts.

She saved me.

Again.

Body and soul.

My hand dragged down the side of her neck, relishing the softness of her skin beneath my fingertips. I never wanted to let go again. Never wanted to stop touching her. "I'm not going *anywhere*."

Hold on. Don't let go.

I broke my promise the next moment as another body slammed into my side, sharp-edged shoulders knocking the air out of me as I toppled beneath her, my grip slipping from Irina.

"Shin! Don't you ever do that again," Aya sobbed into my shoulder as she crawled into my lap, her thin form shaking like a leaf while the words blubbered out of her. "You have to be more careful."

"I didn't exactly plan that." A frenzied, adrenaline-fueled laugh bubbled up from my gut as I squeezed my eyes shut again. I wrapped my arms tightly around her—for once not caring if she could handle it. I needed to feel her safe, feel her alive, to convince myself of my own corporeality. To remind myself why I still stayed.

Somehow, my sister and I were still here. Still breathing. Still fighting.

I opened my eyes again, my head spinning. How had I survived, exactly? The last I remembered, I'd been standing on the edge of the Current Chaser, stealing the air from the soldiers as they came within my range—

But we weren't on the river anymore. Instead, we huddled in a small nest of trees—Naveen next to me with Irina, Mal, Kas, and the twins a few paces away, watching me with worried gazes, thank the Breath. In the distance, orange and purple sunset flickered between tall trees—

No, not sunset. *Fire.* Still burning, devouring the surface of the river in strange, multicolored flames.

I gently nudged Aya off me, staggering to my feet. Naveen caught my elbow as I stumbled, his amber eyes scanning me like *I* was the patient for once. I swallowed back the bile that rose to my throat. "What happened?"

"Driss and Davke are dead, the soldiers too," Mal reported, but she stood eerily still as she watched me, her face flat and eyes bloodshot. Like she'd been crying. *Mourning.*

Like she was staring at a ghost, now.

I leaned a little more into Naveen, grateful for my tree-trunk of a friend. My skin itched all over, like it remembered the pain I couldn't, and I didn't want to imagine what'd happened. What the kids had seen. I looked to Irina—to the big brown eyes that'd pulled me back from the edge of oblivion, yet again. "How?"

"Davke took them out when she accidentally blew you half to the Breath," Ren answered instead, Kas sniffling tears into his side. "Herself, too."

His words were a punch to the face, my jaw clenched as I braced for impact. The pair had only tried to help us, and this was their compensation.

We were making a bad habit of leaving bodies in our wake. Soon— too soon, if I didn't change course—it might be one of ours.

I muttered a prayer that Davke and Driss could find peace together in the afterlife. Peace we'd stolen from them in this one.

Kas rubbed his eye sockets with the palm of his hand, lip wobbling. "What was that stuff?"

I looked to Mal again, waiting for my resident scientist's evaluation; but another voice answered, darker than I'd ever heard it before, laced with a vengeance that sent a chill down my spine.

"That was the Blight." Irina stepped forward, soil stare fixed on the burning river as her words scalded my newly healed skin. The healer that'd comforted me a moment ago was gone, replaced with a fury of war I'd never met before. "Nehir is behind *everything.*"

Horror shot up my throat with a jolt that left me breathless again, realization stealing the world from beneath my feet. My knees buckled, and Naveen caught me as I staggered.

I knew without a doubt Irina was right. Knew from the moment I'd laid eyes on those giant jugs that something was wrong about them, the wind screaming its warning cries in my ears.

But if that was the Blight...and if it was Nehir's doing...

We'd been running toward a mirage, a false oasis in a desert of pain. And I was working *for* the mastermind that had fucking poisoned my sister. Was about to hand-deliver the one woman who actually had any power to help us into her clutches.

I righted myself as quickly as I could. I had to be strong, had to lead the kids...

But where would we go? There was no way out of this mess. No easy roads that didn't meet dead ends, no solutions that didn't require one or all of us to sacrifice everything.

I'd known wickedness before. Had cultivated it, even, with the wind as my ally. But this was pure evil, a darkness that sent shudders running up my spine in furious waves.

Riku spoke first, gathering his things together with a determination setting his jaw in stone. "We have to run. Ecei will catch us—"

Irina's fists clenched at her sides. "But *Aya.*"

My heart ached like it'd been speared through. Even as she realized what this had to mean for her, as she uncovered the truth about what Ecei had done to her *brother*, the Princess was still focused on my sister's wellbeing. On finding an answer to extend Aya's time, even if it meant cutting hers short.

But there was no answer to this puzzle, no solution to the true Blight:

Ecei of Nehir.

A rueful, spiteful bitch who committed *genocide* without ever lifting a finger or drawing suspect to herself. She'd been poisoning all of Babylon for years, and likely would keep doing so if unchecked, to meet whatever sick, twisted goal served her. And if we handed Irina over to her—Irina, the only royal who gave a shit, the only girl in history with true healing powers...

We'd be cursing the population of Babylon to suffer the same fate as my sister.

As Irina's brother.

"There is no cure," I said aloud, hating how the others flinched at the words. I looked at Aya—at my sister's violet stare. At the soul-crushing knowing waiting there. "None that they'd give us."

She nodded, throat bobbing.

Irina had healed me, the last of my pain washed away by her touch, but there was no cure for this preemptive grief. No way to slow it as it hurtled toward me like an avalanche, ready to crush me one day. Maybe not today, or tomorrow even.

But soon.

Inevitably.

Aya would die. And if—*when*—she did, I would too, either on the path of vengeance to end Ecei, or squashed by the heartbreak that would shatter me in two.

I did not say it out loud, but Irina must have read my mind as her hand slid into my sister's. "We can go back to Dunyas. My parents will help us." She held her head high with all of the authority of the Queen she would one day become, her voice no longer a wobble, but a rock-slide of determination. "And I swear I will find a way to keep you alive, Aya."

My chest seized, lungs swelling so wide as I sucked in a greedy breath that I thought they'd burst.

I'd almost died today. Almost lost everything.

Still had so much to lose.

Hold on.

But Princess Catirina of Dunyas and my family would not sit by and idly watch. They fought. They stayed.

I would, too. Until my last breath.

Ren spoke next, his tone emboldened by Irina's as he held up a small metal flask—likely one he'd snagged off a patron at The Breeze Haven—and a sly smirk curled his lips. "I took a sample of the water."

The rest of us eyed the metal container—the *poison*—with disdain, fear rolling through me at its mere presence...as if we hadn't all been guzzling the stuff down for ages unbeknownst.

But Irina looked at it with something else in her gaze—something molten and bright that churned up long lost hope from my veins as she swiped it from Ren and held it like a precious gem in her fingers. The corners of her mouth twitched as she rolled her shoulders back. "Then we have our proof, and perhaps the start of an antidote."

If only it had been enough.

TWENTY-THREE

IRINA

With few options and even fewer resources, we made our way south toward my home on foot. It would take us seven days to reach the base of the Kawayama Mountains, at which point we'd be out of Sora territory and could find proper transportation across the plains of Dunyas. But unless we wanted Ecei to catch us, or to endanger more innocent civilians on the way, our only option was skulking through the woods like bandits on the run.

Which we were now, I supposed.

And with each step closer to Anastova, my dread grew, doubt circling my every thought like vultures. By the evening of the second day, they'd already started picking at my rotting sanity.

What if we couldn't find a cure? I'd examined the sample Ren had collected, the chemical compound so well dissolved by the water, it made sense that I hadn't discovered it before. But now that I knew it was there, I had already been able to identify it in Aya's blood—the inorganic compound a sneaky but distinctly different substance immune to my Qualification.

But facing it was different from *fixing* it, and I still hadn't managed a way to wrap my brain around that task.

Other 'what ifs' turned my mind to mush, trees and clearings and rocky crags blurring together as my thoughts tried to devour themselves with anxious churnings.

What if my parents didn't listen? What if the proof wasn't enough? They'd purposefully left me out of every decision since I was born, all in the name of protecting me, and they could just as easily ignore me like usual, writing this off as another one of my dramatics.

Or what if Drakkar and Ecei somehow beat us there before I could speak with them? Mother was close to Ecei, and the Ice Witch had a way with spinning things to her advantage. If I didn't get there first, it would be her word against mine, and they could ambush the Lost Ones before I could ensure their diplomacy.

What if someone got hurt along the way? What if I couldn't heal them again?

What if they all hated *me* for what Ecei dragged them into?

What if, what if, what if?

Lost in thought, I stumbled over a twig, the forest floor denser with greenery the further south we traveled. My gut lurched, the ground rising up to my face as I fell—

Muscled arms wrapped around my center before I could kiss the ground. My stomach jumped again, albeit for a different reason: Shin's fingers grazing across my ribs as he effortlessly righted me to standing.

His hand lingered at my side as hooded eyes scalded me like hot tea. "Watch your step, Princess."

I gulped, sure that he could feel my heart slamming a jig against my ribcage. "Thanks."

Something shifted in his gaze—like he hadn't been expecting gratitude—before his hand dropped and he walked away, continuing on at his brutal pace, leaving me behind.

I deflated. We'd barely spoken since I'd healed him. Since I'd watched as Naveen and Mal pulled his limp body from the river, deep, blistering burns covering his face, his arms, his chest in swaths of vicious red and rotting black. Since I'd been so *close* to losing him, his heartbeat a faint, fading thing that'd taken all of my strength to crescendo back into a steady beat. Since I felt *his* pain, searing and total, as I coaxed his skin back to life, since I begged the rotted, festered flesh to smooth again.

Since he'd held me as I had him—*close*—so close that any closer, and my power might have fused *us* together, two halves of a whole restitched by my magic's needle and thread.

But now, we were distant again—likely for the best, both for what came next and my dangerously quick heartbeat—each step of his putting a mile of space between us.

It took me a full moment to move my legs, the useless things still wobbling with his absence.

"'*Watch your step, Princess,*'" Ren mimicked Shin's deep timbre and light-footed walk with a wink at me, like he could tell I needed someone to diffuse the tension clinging to the humid air. "Why don't *I* ever get that kind of treatment?"

Shin spun, eyes narrowed, but before he could flay his friend, Riku chucked a twig at Ren, hitting him square across his breastbone. "Because no one likes you."

With an exaggerated stumble, Ren clasped his chest, crumpling his tattered tunic in his fist with a gasp. "You wound me, brother."

A laugh tumbled from my chest, "Well, *I* like you."

Ren stumbled for real, catching himself on a tree branch before he toppled entirely, fixing me with a smile that made his normally round eyes meager crescents.

"Hear that?" he bellowed, scaring birds from a nearby tree. The others all hissed and sighed at him, but he was undeterred as he smacked his hand across his chest again, this time in a salute as he straightened. "The Princess likes me! You may all now address me as *Sir* Ren, friend of Princess Catirina."

Shin's gaze flicked between Ren and I, filled with a twisting, burning thing I didn't want to name; but he said nothing, again choosing distance.

It was for the best.

I wished it didn't disappoint me.

"Get in line, Ren, I was her friend first," Aya teased; but there was a truth to her words, wrapped in a sweet sincerity as she fit her arm through mine—a tell, I'd realized, that she was getting tired, but was too brave to ask for support. I wedged my arm more securely beneath her pit and braced her forearm, stealing more of her weight for myself. And despite the added burden, my legs felt stronger and surer than they had in days. I was the one with life *Easinir*, but Aya had a way of levying the heaviness from my heart with her mere presence.

Dark 'what ifs' and lingering disappointments dissipated. I would walk a thousand miles if it got me even one step closer to a cure for this girl, and another thousand each for Ren and Riku and Naveen and Kas to be safe. My captors...my first real *friends*.

I cleared my throat of the phlegmy emotion coating my chords, letting my voice carry, more certain than I'd sounded in years. "Yes, *Lady* Aya gets first priority in all things."

She grinned as she leaned closer, resting her head on my shoulder as we walked. "Lady Aya. I think I like the sound of that."

I did, too.

"And I think all of us fancy lords and ladies need a break, Shin," Ren whined, dragging his feet through the leafy undergrowth. But I didn't miss the quick glance at Aya—all of the Lost Ones were attuned to her tells, but none brave enough to speak them into existence. As if acknowledging her weakness only made it grow, a monster fed on fear.

"We have to wait for Malina to catch up, anyway," Riku added, aligned with his twin in their act of distraction. Not that his excuse was untrue; Malina *had* taken a slightly separate route from us into the nearest village to send out ravens to those we needed to get messages to—Via, Madame Aheni, even my parents—promising to find us again before nightfall. She'd been quiet since we'd saved Shin, even more distant and grumpy than normal; and that was saying something, given the chilly reception I'd gotten from her.

Still, even shaken as she was, she didn't need us to slow our pace even a fraction to catch up. But if we didn't take our time—catch our breaths—there might have been one less of us for her to come back to.

Shin's full lips flickered into a frown for a breath, before a practiced annoyance stole his features once more. He tilted his head back, exposing the long column of his throat as he watched the sun dip lower through the leaves, the sky above already painted in streaks of purple and red. "Fine. It's getting late anyway, we might as well make camp."

Aya relaxed against me, her skeletal frame sinking into my ribs, but I didn't dare complain. She would never say it aloud, but her body spoke a language I was all too fluent in.

Exhaustion. *Pain.*

I spared her the embarrassment of naming it aloud, instead walking with her to a toppled tree trunk nearby and setting us both down on it. I slunk across the rough bark, exaggerating my soreness as I cracked my neck. "Ugh, thank the Mother. My feet are dead."

Aya raised a brow at me, but Naveen joined in before she could call out my charade, sitting on her other side and shucking off his boots, wiggling his toes through threadbare socks. "My blisters have blisters."

"My headache has a headache," Kas echoed, one-upping Naveen in both volume and exaggeration as he clasped his tiny head of curls.

The laugh Aya attempted to stifle blew through her nostrils on a shaky exhale, slim shoulders dancing.

Ren, refusing to be outdone, made a show of flopping face-first onto the log, his back end still sticking up in the air. "My hemorrhoids have hemorrhoids!"

"You need serious help," Riku groaned, smacking his brother's protruding ass with a satisfying *thwack* as he passed, so hard that Ren practically leapt a foot into the air on contact, a squeal blaring through the trees.

At that, laughter burst from me in belly-aching wrenches, my voice hoarse in my throat. And I was not alone—Aya clutching her gut as her giggles rattled her frame, Naveen cackling so hard that tears pricked the corners of his eyes. Even Shin, Mother bless him, chuckled, his straight row of white teeth flashing despite himself.

The sound, like nightshade and stardust, eased something in my core, and the last what-ifs died before they were born.

We would be alright. We had the best medicine in the world right here—heart, *laughter*—and I would find a way to use that and whatever else I needed to make it better. To make space for Aya—and Shin —to learn to laugh again until they forgot how to *stop.*

I didn't know why it was so important to me. So crucial.

But maybe that's what purpose felt like. Not something I needed for me, but a choice to do for others for the sheer *rightness* of it.

Naveen and Shin had camp set in minutes, a tent assembled from mud and twigs stitched together by Naveen's gift and tempered by Shin's soft wind. In another, Kas had a fire roaring over a few dry logs, the heat from the flames licking my face in coarse strokes as I set to making a tea—my unassigned, unofficial duty. I didn't mind—it was nice to have work to do for once, a sense of direction, as I crushed the leaves and berries we'd been gathering into something resembling flavor. Ren helped, drawing the liquid from it, and Riku heated it to near-boiling. It was a resourceful combination of tricks—all of the Lost Ones knowing their *Easinir* well enough to make the most menial tasks a flaunt of creativity.

It also made me question just how effective so many of the *Easinir* among the nobles were. How they hadn't used *their* gifts to solve so much of the lack I'd seen crawling through Babylon like a virus, infecting the hearts of the people.

My people.

Naveen took one of the newly made clay mugs of tea and sniffed, nose scrunching. "Do we have anything stronger than tea?"

I refocused, blinking up at him as he stood over me, eyes wide like a small puppy despite his staggering height. A mischievous glimmer nagged at the back of my mind, a secret from when Nikolaj and I were in our early teenage years aching to be remembered.

I'd only been thirteen, Nikolaj a few years beyond, when we'd started hoarding berries and fruits from our breakfast trays when the staff wasn't looking, storing them in a secret barrel in the back of his wardrobe. It'd been Nikolaj's idea, of course, his rebellion always stronger than mine, but it was a rare chance to use my *Easinir*—to practice my craft—and I'd savored the time we spent in our makeshift brewery, concocting the different flavors of our mutiny toward our parents.

Mother, of course, had it all set on fire when she found out. But oh, how colorfully it all burned, crimson and cerulean fireworks that scorched the memory across my soul.

I couldn't help my grin. "I actually think I can manage that."

Dropping the tea altogether, Naveen grabbed my face and smacked a kiss to my forehead, before throwing his hands high above his head in celebration. "Kas, get the woman more berries!"

Kas rustled through his pack, snagging another handful of indigo and black fruit—blueberries, raspberries, and juniper. "Got them!"

He poured them into the deep wooden bowl Naveen had whittled for us, eyes wide as he watched me work.

I shut my eyes, tunneling down into the pit of magic resting in my core. It was easier, with such small objects, to latch on to the threads. And though they'd already been plucked, life mostly drained from their tiny orbs...

Death had its stages, too. The same building blocks that I could use to heal, I could force to *break*.

The sweet smell turned acidic, and I opened my eyes as Ren again drew the liquid out, the bowl filled with a plum-purple juice that sloshed against the sides. "That should do the trick."

Shin perched across the fire, brows raised in surprise, grin flashing again. "Wine?"

I shrugged, my cheeks reddening—and not just from the fire. "Closer to a flavored gin, actually. I just sped up the fermentation by a few years."

At that, Naveen pounced. Scooping his cup into the basin and filling it to the brim, he took a long drag, a moan escaping as the liquid dribbled from the corners of his lips. "Mother Earth, *marry me*, Irina."

The others laughed with me, but I swore Shin flinched.

Or maybe that was just a trick of the firelight.

"Shin?" Aya inched closer, gaze flicking between the pool of gin and her brother's stony expression. "Please?"

Granite cracked with a slight smile. "Fine. But only a sip each."

Mugs filled faster than the light fled the sky, the sun disappearing as night reclaimed its throne.

And as everyone drank—aside from Kas—the tension recused itself, too, replaced instead with ruddy cheeks and easy smiles. The flames popped and crackled, chasing the chill, and for once, it didn't sound like snapping beams and breaking hearts—but an invitation, a gentle percussion that set the beat for a night of companionship around a campfire.

"How about a song?" Naveen said quietly after his fourth or fifth serving of gin, like he could hear the rhythm, too.

Aya curled deeper into her blanket, nuzzling into the log and giving me a glassy-eyed, half-tipsy grin. "Irina, what do people sing in Anastova?"

The question threw me off tempo, a wound pulling open in my chest that made my breath come short.

"We...we don't, not really." I racked my brain for any instance of my mother's voice, or even the maids and other servants, for any lullaby or lilt that might have soothed or stayed with me...but there was no well to pull from, that part of me as dry and seedless as the deserts of Jalta. Sometimes—rarely—Tasha would hum to herself as she cooked, but the notes were disjointed, senseless strings of noise, more of an aimless tic than a tune I could name. The only real music that ever played in Dunyas was during the Masque, when the performers from Sora made their way to our doorstep and brought life in their instrument cases and colorful costumes.

But that wasn't the only music I'd heard...

A distant, faded melody buzzed in my mind, the ghostly coo of a violin howling through me like a breeze. "But I do know one song..."

It had no words, but I didn't need them as I let my lips curl around the few gentle "oohs" and "ahhs," the song pouring from a long-ignored part of me that had always desperately wanted to join the chorus. To sing along, to let my voice fuse with and flit over the play-ers' instruments in harmony.

And for the first time in my life, people *listened*. Aya and Ren swayed along to the soft, melancholic tune. Naveen closed his eyes and nodded his head. Kas and Riku tapped their fingers in time with me, a steady drumming that let me know I was not alone. That I was *heard*.

Shin watched with a stillness that almost stole the breath from my lungs, honey eyes a deep amber in the firelight.

Almost.

Instead, I let it fuel me, let it carry me through, let it lift my song like wind beneath a sail.

I sang for the Opera House that taught me this music, for the boy and the violin that would never get to grace that stage with sweet symphonies ever again.

I sang for the people of Babylon, for the sufferers still fighting Ecei's Blight that didn't have many warm, peaceful nights like this left.

I sang for Driss and Davke, for the lovers that would have to meet again in Mother Earth's embrace, for the like-minds I couldn't save.

And at the very end of it, I sang for Nikolaj. For the brother who should've been here instead of me. For the mentor who taught me to sing.

Until my confidence dried up, the last bars of the music fading as my memory of them did.

I didn't realize the others had gone still—breaths held as mine blew out like a candle.

No one spoke for a long, full-bodied moment.

Until Shin's throat bobbed, his voice hoarse as he stared at me like I had done something worth looking at. "You've got a lovely voice. You should use it more."

The compliment was simple—polite, even.

But the light in my chest burned brighter than the campfire, a heat working its way across my skin like *I* was made of dry kindling.

You've got a lovely voice. You should use it more.

I tucked that sentiment away, storing it in a chamber of my heart where not even my mother could steal it from me.

I wouldn't let her take my voice ever again.

"But that song is a bore," Naveen lied through a bout of sniffles, wiping tears away with the back of his sleeve. "Let's pick up the tempo, shall we?"

Waving his hands, he swished away the heavy mood that'd befallen the group. He began a new tune, this one with lyrics that were vulgar enough to make a brothel-worker blush. By the second verse, he and Ren were both dancing as they sang, acting out half of the actions the story told with absolute debauchery.

And despite that fact my mother would've keeled over if she could see me, despite the fact the words made my skin crawl and their gyrating hips made my cheeks flare with crimson blush...

I let myself sing along, until my voice shook with violent laughter, until I could barely catch my breath as I cackled with everyone. Until a painful and perfect stitch pierced my ribs, collapsing my lungs in a fit of wheezing. Until I had to gulp down another glass of the gin-and-fruit medley just to soothe my hoarse throat.

A bittersweet revelation burned through my chest like the liquor.

I'd never had more fun in my life. Even as a kid, sneaking away with Nikolaj to the opera to hear the musicians...I'd never had this level of freedom. Of choice.

Of laughter and hope.

Of friendship.

Of *love.*

Well, *crap.*

I *loved* these people, flawed and ridiculous as they were. I loved this adventure, though long and treacherous. Loved the open air on my sweaty brow, loved the bickering and bonding, so much better than the horrifying quiet of my rooms at home. Loved Naveen's lazy, unassuming smile, and Aya's knowing stare. Loved Ren's bubbly laughter and Riku's quiet strength. Loved Kas's curious questions, and even Malina's unshakeable certainty. Loved—

No, I couldn't let that thought finish. Wouldn't.

Because I'd be home in a few days, and Anastova had a cruel habit of taking the things I loved from me and cutting them at the stem. And I didn't deserve to love these people. I had already burdened them, ruined their lives as they had mine, tearing down and cracking everything they knew and cared for in brutal, destructive chaos.

And yet, somehow, they reforged it all into something new. Maybe, just maybe, something better.

"Everything all right?" Shin asked—his voice a quiet breeze that cut through the noisiness—but still I startled, opening my mouth to respond—

But he was looking past me, Malina appearing between the trees again, her face somehow even stonier than usual, the furrow between her brows a cavern.

The song died in an instant, even Naveen snapping his jaw shut as he took in her grim expression.

"I'm fine," she clipped out, but didn't move to join us. "Ravens have been sent out to Via and the others, telling them to stay low or meet us in Anastova."

Her words slashed through any peace I'd stored in my middle, the reality of this situation an ever-returning ache that no medicine would cleanse until I got back to Anastova. Back home.

It didn't matter if I was happy here if the rest of the world suffered. If my joy was the price of fixing this mess, I'd pay it.

It's what Nikolaj would do. What I must, too.

I clutched the cup in my hand so tight, the feeble clay threatened to crack. "I will see to it they are taken care of, too. This is Ecei's fault, but it's Dunyas's, too. We've turned a blind eye for too long. I won't let any more Babylonian subjects suffer at her hands."

Malina scoffed, the sound shattering through me like the brittle kindling popping in the fire. "How noble."

Shame heated my already warm cheeks, but a different flame sparked in my belly, a flicker of something my brother might have left behind for me. I lifted my chin as he would have, defiant even at the end. "I'm not trying to be noble. I'm trying to be helpful."

Malina's tongue poked at her cheek, more venomous words begging to be unleashed, but after a moment, she swallowed. Rolled her eyes. Like sparring with me wasn't even worth her breath. "Sure thing, Princess."

She stalked away from the fire, snagging one of the bedrolls before she disappeared into the treeline again.

The Lost Ones watched her go, their gazes filled to the brim with a discomfort that set me on edge. This was not how they usually operated—this fractured disquiet. No, they had cultivated a team, a *family*, whose bond had weathered storm and siege, fire and fury.

A bond I had tangled and frayed with my presence.

Kas stood, offering me a sheepish grin that weighed too heavily on his young face, before scurrying after her. Part of my heart went with him—one younger sibling to another, wishing I could ease his burden.

Shin's back straightened like a blade's edge, conflicted thoughts warring in the divot between his eyebrows. I clasped my hands, hoping, wishing, that he'd choose this moment, just a little longer. That this didn't have to end just yet.

But when he followed them both, another piece of me hacked off and fell like an avalanche, my disappointment more forceful than I'd dared to admit—even to myself.

A throat cleared—Ren's—drawing me back to the campfire, to where the others still stayed, rigid and awkward though they all were now.

Riku's monotone voice finally broke the tension, the first stone skipping across the surface of the silence, rippling through the rest of us. "What will it be like when we get to Anastova, Prin—Irina? Last time, we only saw the outside."

"Warm." I smiled, grateful for the lifeline—even if it came with the reminder of home. A home that I'd get to invite them into, if I played my cards right. A home that would then rip them away again. Still, I pressed on, not wanting to add to their upset any more than I already had. "But it's nice. The gardens are remarkable, and the city is teeming with scholars. I think you'll like it. Dunyas is beautiful this time of year."

A tipsy snort from Ren. "Naveen says Dunyas is a hot waste of—"

Naveen clapped a hand over Ren's mouth. "Nevermind what Naveen did or did not say, okay?"

I raised a brow.

Naveen was Dunyasian, too. It made sense—his heritage had to at least in part hail back to the Motherland, his skin the same deep brown as mine, if not a shade darker. But he'd never spoken of it before, his attitude entirely built and burnished by the Hiku City air.

But whether he had run toward Sora, or away from Dunyas...I had no idea.

"Tell me about it?" I hedged, then added with a feeble grin, "No fighting, I promise."

Naveen shifted on the ground, tucking one long leg closer, his grip on his drink tighter. It all looked wrong on him, the nervousness a stark departure from his normally laid-back countenance. Hell, he'd almost died a week ago, and even in the moments after the life breathed back into him, he'd been smiling and laughing like the cat that caught the canary.

I braced myself as he spoke, his voice uncharacteristically low. "I can't speak about Anastova, since I only ever went there to make deliveries..." He paused, a deep inhale puffing his chest as he gathered his courage. "But the farms aren't all sunshine and flowers. It's hard work and high demand, and the labor is... intense."

I wriggled in my seat, my stomach squirming. "Intense?"

Naveen stared into the fire, watching the flames dance. "They'd make us work from sunup to sundown, and then when the Jaltans started sharing their lighting sources, the days got even longer. We'd keep working until we bled, and then they'd pump us full of Poppy Dust to keep us going longer and keep us too strung out to protest."

His eyes glazed over, like even the memory of the Poppy Dust was enough to drag him back beneath its haze. My stomach flipped, the gin souring in my gut as I processed his tale...

No, not a tale, a truth. A confession, a *reality* that peeled back layers of mine.

Anastova was a gilded cage, the vase atop the hill a pretty but lifeless place where flowers faded in a slow, dull ache.

But the farmlands—*right under my nose*—didn't just wait for the life to slowly dissipate. No, they tore it from their flesh, drained it from their blood and sweat, stole it from their opium-ravaged lungs.

"That's—" I swallowed the lump that choked me, made of guilt and grief and an anger I hadn't tasted in a long time. "How did you survive?"

Naveen tore his weary gaze from the fire, stretching his back as he returned to his body. "You mean how did I get out?"

I nodded, words too weighty to wield.

Aya crawled closer to Naveen, wrapping her hand through his as he took another shaky breath. He smiled at her, a heavy thing that didn't flash his teeth like it normally did, as he managed the rest of his tale. "The King was coming for an inspection, so they cut back the dosage of the opium that day so we'd look more alert. The...royals... well, they knew what was going on, but they didn't like to look at us when we were *bad*."

My lungs threatened to collapse, the air thin and burnt like ash.

The King.

My father.

My bumbling but kind, sweet but stubborn...

No, that's just the version of him I wanted to see. I didn't want to look at the greed and gluttony that sat at our table every night, or the shutdowns that silenced me time and time again, shoving me to the side of my own future. My own kingdom.

I did not turn from Naveen. Didn't balk, or protest, but instead made myself *see* as he finished, "Without the over-dosing, I had the clarity I needed...and that night, I don't know what motivated me, but I ran. From Dunyas all the way to Hiku City, where I knew I wouldn't be found. I lasted a week before the cravings got bad, and I crawled right to Madame Aheni's, stole some nobleman's purse, and spent it all on the Poppy Dust. And that's where Shin found me."

I imagined it: Naveen, a strung-out teenager, desperate and lost. Shin, the unexpected mother hen, taking him under his wing.

Lost, and found.

Just as Shin had done for me, in his own backward way.

This time, I wouldn't lose myself again, not to my parents' willful ignorance or to the compliance that had made me just as culpable.

Legs shaking, I stood...

And then bowed at the waist, my short curls curtaining my vision. "I am sorry for the complacency of my family, and for the system that has taken advantage of you." I raised my head, my declaration stiffening my back with the same iron I'd found that first night in Hiku City. "And I will be adding it to the list of things I will be changing when I take the throne. Maybe sooner, if I have my way."

And for the first time in my life, it wasn't a wish.

It was a *promise.*

Naveen's eyes misted as he clenched Aya's hand tighter, raising his cup with the other. "Then maybe Babylon isn't so fucked after all. Long live the future Queen, Irina."

Riku raised his, too, the ice in his tone no longer biting, but sturdy. "Long live Irina, friend of the people."

"And fighter for the little guys!" Ren tagged onto the end, hopping up on the log and lifting his glass high above his head so half its contents spilled out the side.

Aya chuckled, but there was only sincerity in her expression as she smiled, tipping her cup to me. "Long live Irina, finder of lost ones."

Something clawed its way up my throat, scalding and soothing all at once as these people—as my *friends*—offered me something more precious than all of the gold in Anastova. More valuable than every gem mined in the Jaltan passes.

Something that made kings and destroyed empires.

Something that birthed revolutions and exalted heroes.

Belief. Purpose.

Love.

"Long live Irina," another voice—a voice like nightshade and starlight—said from behind me, and I turned to a pair of tea-and-honey eyes that found me, again and again. He pressed a hand to his chest, a salute and a reminder of the life that still flowed through his veins—because of me. And then he bowed, head dipping low, even as those eyes remained locked with mine. "Healer of hearts."

And with his words, something I hadn't even known to be broken healed inside of me, too.

Twenty-Four

It was six days from the Black River to the valley of the Kawayama Mountains. Six days of walking until we couldn't, feet blistering and skin peeling beneath the wind's wicked gusts that bit our eyes teary. Six days of hungry bellies gurgling as we tripped over tree roots and picked at berries and mushrooms Irina and Naveen named safe, though never satisfying.

Days of huddling together in ramshackle camps when our legs gave out for the night, Qualified branches made into makeshift roofs and beds of leaves pretending as pillows. Days of huddling close around Kas's fire for warmth, hoping the light didn't attract predators…or company. Days of the kids' eyes going wide at every snapped branch and ghostly howl, days of reassuring everyone that it couldn't be Ecei; that we were fine.

Days of subtle touches between Irina and I, reminders that we were both here. *Alive.* Days of hands brushing as we roasted food or braided leaves into blankets. Days of stolen glances at each other across the fire, unspoken questions burning at the back of my tongue. Days of small comments that became inside jokes, days of little giggles and blushed cheeks that set my heart racing. Days of foolishly wishing that when we got to Dunyas, there might just be a place for me there, at least for a while.

Days of watching Aya fade.

Days of witnessing the limp in her left side grow more pronounced, days of marking the way the color bled from her yellowing skin. Days of tracing the bags beneath her eyes whenever she fell asleep, days of counting every bite she kept down and every rattling breath she stole back. Days of sitting on the sidelines and massaging her sore limbs as Irina did her best to coax life back into her dying heart.

Days of worrying in the recesses of my own nightmares, of keeping the mask up whenever the Lost Ones were around to spare them the same slow torture. Days of branches and mountains blurring together, the fickle wind an inconsistent guide as we tried our best to endure the wilderness.

Days of avoiding a certain blistering gaze whenever I could, too tired and burnt out to deal with more of the heat.

Until she cornered me the evening of the sixth day on my way back from a piss, arms crossed and a brow raised in the way that meant business.

Malina stepped in front of my path, blocking my way to the campfire where the others sang another lewd song Naveen had taught them the night before. "We need to talk."

I glanced past her shoulder at the merriment, the wickedness in my heart begging for *one last chorus* instead of this showdown, inevitable though it was. I pinched the bridge of my nose, scraping the bottom of my barrel for composure. "About?"

The muscle in Malina's jaw clenched and unclenched as she bit down on vicious words she didn't say, opting instead for, "About what happens next if the Princess doesn't follow through."

Maybe if I'd had a decent night's sleep or a meal that wasn't deer food or a proper shave in the last two weeks, I might have handled her with more care. But instead, frustration and exhaustion fought for dominance in my chest, both demanding the spotlight. "What does that even mean, Malina? She saved my life, and Naveen's. It's time to put the jealousy away."

Eyes blew wide as I crossed an unspoken line, but then narrowed again. She glared at me with the hastening heat of a volcano ready to blow. "*Jealousy?* Try *fear*, Shin. You almost *died* the other day, protecting her, when she's the reason any of our lives were at risk in the first place. And now we're throwing away Aya's chance at a cure on *her* orders? Do you not see how this could be a problem?"

"You know she's right about the Blight. Nehir tried to kill us for it." A sharp breath blew out of me as I placed a firm hand on her shoulder, attempting to soothe.

Malina swatted my hand away as her face contorted into a grimace. "And you don't think it's just a *coincidence* that we just happened to run into them, dressed in their Breath-damned uniforms, the same evening we were supposed to deliver her?"

For a brief moment, doubt and regret flickered through me, just a whisper of a breeze. I hated being at odds with Mal, and I trusted her with my life. But as I looked past her, at Irina sitting with Aya and Naveen and the others, a wide smile crossing her face as she sang and clapped along, a bone-deep certainty rooted me to my stance.

I stood straighter, my tone sharpening to a point I rarely used with Mal. "No. That's not a coincidence; that's *evidence*."

She stepped back like I'd slapped her, hurt flashing before her preferred rage took its place, her voice carrying through the open clearing to the other side. "No matter what, we are outmatched here. Our best bet is to finish this job, no matter what it takes, and then get as far as we can away from all the royals, including your precious *Princess*."

Heads snapped our way as the song died, the Lost Ones squirming as they overheard. I sucked in a deep breath, waiting for it to fill me up again, but I was empty. *Spent.* And if I was going to survive, going to get the rest of the crew to safety, I had nothing left to feed to Malina's ravenous anger.

So I sidestepped her, moving toward the fire and the food and the friends I needed. "I'm not arguing anymore."

I got five steps closer until Malina struck again, words slashing my back in vicious strikes. "And Aya? You're just going to watch her die?"

The air in my lungs burned, scraping up my throat as I struggled to keep the fire contained, wishing I could spew it at her in return. My hands shook with how tightly they clenched, holding back my anger with fraying threads.

I looked at my sister, sitting next to the Princess, the two of them acting as though they'd been friends since childhood. But two weeks ago, they'd been complete strangers. Irina hadn't even known Aya's name, never mind caring if she lived or died. And there was no telling if the rest of the Dunyasians would be willing to stick their necks out for her like the Princess had.

This was a risk. A leap.

But as a man who'd learned to make his own wings, I'd never been afraid of falling.

I spun on Malina, hands unfurling as a calming breeze coaxed down my spine. "Aya will be fine. I'm putting my faith in Irina and the medementals in Dunyas to come up with a cure."

"Since when are you a man of faith? Especially in nobles, after what they did to your mother?" Malina's throat bobbed as she stepped back, disappointment yanking her mouth into a frown. "Ecei is a bitch, but we have a contract with her, and money speaks. She'll want a return on her investment, and it would be stupid to screw her over now that we know what she's capable of. But the Dunyasians have no reason to help us, and we can't expect anyone's good will, or we'll end up like your mom did."

My heart threatened to stop in my chest, a long-lost ache twisting in my center. It was a cheap shot, and Malina knew it, knew *me* better than I'd ever let anyone else. And she was right; faith had done me no favors. Men were wicked, the nobility more than most, their greed and power corrupting their souls with the darkness that plagued Babylon worse than the Blight. My mother had learned that lesson the hard way when she died a beggar, and the streets of the city that raised me had made sure I hadn't forgotten it.

But if I didn't like the way things were, perhaps it was time to change them. To stay, instead of fly.

One last chance.

For me, and for Mal, whether she wanted to cooperate or not.

"Fall in line, Malina, or you're welcome to go your own way."

Malina staggered back as my words hit their mark. Thick lashes blinked away hot tears, but she swiped them away quickly before glaring at me with the heat of a thousand suns. "Fine. Have it your way."

She stalked off deeper into the forest, leaving a trail of ash in her wake as the tether between us went up in flames.

Regret and relief played tug of war in my chest, pulling and pushing in tandem. In the years I'd known her, neither of us had ever suggested parting ways. We were family, bound by something thicker than blood. But even the strongest bonds could wither over time, and as much as I wanted Mal by my side, I didn't have the capacity to let her keep sticking barbs in it.

She'd be back. She just needed to cool off and she'd come home, a stray that always found her way.

I should've gone after her, made it right. Or I should've gone to the others, given her some space and focused on the Lost Ones that needed me.

Instead, I sucked in a breath and let my winds sweep me up into one of the towering oaks. Through the branches, I half-climbed, half-Controlled my way toward the top, until I could rest in the nook of a sturdy branch.

From here, the world below was a small, insignificant thing, the air clearer as the moon greeted me with her wide half-smile. Settling more into the cocoon of the branch, tucking one leg beneath me, I let the cool breeze and the moonlight unwind the tension from my back.

It had been a long six days, and even wicked things like me needed to breathe.

But interrupting twigs crunched beneath me, and I peered down, leaves partially obscuring my view of the forest floor.

"Want some tea?" Irina called up from beneath the canopy of her curls, two clay cups in her hand—likely Qualified by Naveen—and her smile a match for the moon's.

Something eased within me, a breath I hadn't realized I was

holding finally squeezing from my lungs. I dangled over the branch, fighting my grin. "Hold on to your tea."

With a swish of my hand, a strong wind lifted the Princess, legs flailing beneath her as she squealed, and the tea spilled out over the sides of the cups. With another quick dance of my fingers, a second breeze caught the liquid, depositing it back into the containers as I lowered Irina to sit onto the branch next to me.

She swayed, eyes wide and cheeks flushed, as I steadied her with a hand at her back.

"Warn me next time!" she admonished as she caught her breath, but she didn't jerk away from my touch, instead leaning against my hand like it was an anchor.

"But this was more exciting," I chuckled as my free hand took one of the teacups from her. I sipped the still warm liquid—cooled only slightly by my breezy friend.

She stuck her tongue out, but didn't disagree, turning toward the moon and letting the blue-gray glow kiss her freckles. Her curls flickered in the breeze, eyes dark enough to reflect the evening stars just beginning to peek out, and my gut twisted again with a different sort of tension, one I'd been fighting since the Crescent.

Slowly—regrettably—I let my hand fall from her back, cupping my drink with both hands to occupy them instead.

Irina took a slow drag of her tea—the berry-flavored concoction probably also a brainchild of her and Naveen—before breaking the quiet. "I'm sorry. I'm guessing your...*conversation*... with Mal was my fault."

I shifted on the branch. Swallowed another sip. "No, it's mine. I should never have taken this job in the first place, and then we'd all be safe."

The truth slid from my lips easier than I'd imagined, my regret souring the fragrant air. I should've known from the beginning Ecei's cure was too good to be true. But I'd been blinded by false hope, so desperate that I'd been willing to drag my family and Irina into danger for a *lie* that a smarter leader would've seen through.

One last ruse.

"Did you really have a choice?" The question knocked my

spiraling thoughts out of loop, sucking me back to the moment. Irina stared into her tea like it held the answers. "We wouldn't have known what was happening if we hadn't been there."

"There is always a choice," I replied automatically as I aimlessly stirred my tea with a lazy breeze, but the words felt less weighty than they had before. Irina was right. If we hadn't discovered the Blight, Aya still would've died, and we'd all be ignorant as to why. Powerless to change it.

Now we had a chance.

"I don't regret it, you know," Irina said as she lifted her head, and stole my breath from my chest. Dark eyes sparkled in a veil of silver tears, thick drops that hung on her lashes like rain clouds ready to open up over dry soil.

My tongue went dry. "What?"

A bright smile captivated her face, appled cheeks crinkling her eyes and pushing the first tears off the ledge. "I wanted this adventure, even if I was upset about it at first. Scared. But I needed to get out and see the world. Needed to meet *you*, and the Lost Ones." Her voice quivered as her tears began their freefall, shaking her shoulders as she fixed me with a stare that pierced through my already waning defenses. "And even if this ends in...whatever...I am glad I know you all. I was *alone* for so long, and now...now you've added so much to my life."

Alone. Lost.

Found.

My hands acted on their own, discarding the makeshift teacup over the side of the branch and cupping Irina's face instead. Gently, *reverently*, my thumbs caught the drops before they could drip any further.

"Hey hey, shhh, no tears," I whispered, scanning her face as I cradled it. A breathy laugh escaped as I shifted closer, magnetized by her wide eyes. "All we've done is kidnap you and drag you through problem after problem. You're the one who keeps healing us, keeps saving me—"

"I only saved you once," Irina interrupted, soft palms wrapping around my wrists, and I let her lower my hands from her face. But she didn't let go, fingers lingering against my skin even as the deep blush pinched her cheeks. "But you technically saved me on the boat, so we're even."

Even. Clean slate.

Those had been my words. My terms.

But I'd been wrong. So blind.

Lost.

Found.

There was no erasing the history between us, the way the wind kept blowing her back in my path whenever I needed her most, the way my soul wandered whenever she was gone, wayward and wicked until she returned to set me right.

I pulled back, breaking her hold on my wrists, but quickly gathered both of her hands between mine, relishing their warmth. Because that's what Irina was; *warmth* and light in the darkness, the moon shining bright and round against an endless black sky.

"Twice," I finally murmured.

She stilled. "What?"

Rare anxiety twisted my tongue into knots, but it untangled as I stared at her, memorizing every inch of her face just as I had back then. Every freckle a spot where the sun kissed her bronze skin. Every stray curl a gift from the wild breeze that ran its fingers along her scalp.

She'd slipped through my grasp once before, a dream that disappeared on the back of a wind and into the recesses of my mind. But I didn't want her to disappear again.

I wanted her to *see* me, too. Wanted her to know.

"You saved me twice," I repeated, my thumb running across the smooth skin of the back of her hand in a shoddy attempt to soothe my own churning gut. "Once recently, and once...once during the Hiku City Opera fire."

I waited for drawn brows, for a demand of the overdue explanation she was rightly owed. But instead, her lips parted on an exhale, realization dawning across her star-speckled features. "The violinist."

A sheepish blush crept across my neck and face, hot despite the cool air this high off the ground. "I used to think you were a dream. But after Naveen...I remembered you. Remembered how you saved me."

"I remembered you, too." Her fingers filtered through mine as she sat closer, her smile stretching the ache in my chest so wide, I thought my ribs would crack. A half-delirious laugh bubbled from her, scrunching her nose. "I'd made my brother take me to the Opera six different times to hear you play. I was there that night for *you.*"

Something in my middle snapped in two, then restitched itself together out of stronger stuff.

She'd seen me. Heard me play.

Had been there for me, just as enchanted by my music as I was the song of her voice, calling me back to my body.

Hold on, don't let go. One more breath.

"I needed you then, and now, too," I blurted out, the words tripping over each other to exit my mouth, their tempo matching my racing pulse. Her brow creased, and I hurried on, clarifying before she could question my muddled intent, "Not just for your power, or for Aya. But because you don't give up even when I'm ready to."

The confession hung in the air for a long moment, pulled so thin and tight, I believed for a brief flash that perhaps I hadn't said it out loud at all. That maybe she was still a dream, just a figment of my imagination manifested by the wind and the moonlight and six long days of stress.

But finally, she spoke, her voice a quiet steady that set my blood on fire. "I needed you then, too. I needed something to dream about." She unchained one hand from mine, but I didn't have time to miss its absence as she replaced it on my chest, fingertips grazing on the thin fabric of my shirt—just above my heart—as if she could hear its dancing and decided to *join.* "And now...now you make me want to do more than dream. You make me believe that I can *choose.*"

The air between us thickened, electricity sparking across my skin and raising the hairs on my arms as if Irina had Qualified it. Or perhaps *I* had, the desire flashing through my core conveying my subconscious need as my gaze drifted to her mouth, admiring the way her full lips shaped around such marvelous words.

Choose.

The very thing I hadn't let her do at the start of this journey, but the one mistake I was determined not to repeat.

I wanted to choose her. But if she didn't want me in return, if she was ready to walk away—I'd not only let her, but I'd watch her go with my head held high and my broken heart full, happy as long as she was.

My knuckles rasped against the exposed skin of her forearm as I stroked a lazy line down to her elbow, a gentle invitation for all the desires I had yet to learn the words for, even as I braced for rejection. "And what is it you want to choose now, Princess?"

She shuddered beneath my touch, and I paused, afraid I'd crossed a line and made her uncomfortable. But the corner of her mouth tipped up in a smirk that made me dizzy, evaporating any lingering doubt. "I want you to call me Irina."

"Irina..." Her name sat deep in my voice, the answer to a question I'd been asking myself for over a decade. A promise of what I'd do for the next if she'd let me. My fingers wrapped around the crook of her arm, relishing the softness of her plump bicep. "What do you want, Irina?"

She answered in a language older than the wind, sweet, tea-stained lips skimming against mine in a first hesitant meeting that sent a shiver down my back. But then, something both familiar and entirely new took over as I tugged her close, my hand bracing between her shoulder blades as hers fisted in my shirt. Meeting again—as we always did—our mouths continued from where we'd left our first dance; sweeping and gliding together, keeping time to a music only we shared as the world drifted away.

And I kissed Irina until my lips were sore, until the smiling moon hung high in the sky, until I forgot all the reasons I shouldn't.

Twenty-Five

IRINA

Kissing Shin was like kissing a hurricane—a wild, awe-inspiring force of nature that both stung my lips to chapped and made me feel like I was *flying*. Unbridled parts of me swept into his embrace, my hands roaming his back, his chest—the surprising muscles hidden beneath his soft black tunic, the scarred skin that stretched just above his collarbone...the only evidence that he was still healing from the fire.

And he met me for every touch, every sweep of my tongue, every parting of my lips across his. Like he was just as voracious, just as *starving* for this as I was.

And when it ended—when we finally floated back to the ground a good while later, my curls a mess and his shirt a wrinkled tell—I was utterly storm-tossed.

It was a small victory that the others were all mostly asleep, only Naveen half-grumbling to himself like he was somewhere on the edge of waking, none of them alert enough to guess what had happened between us.

Malina was still nowhere to be found, but I didn't let myself dwell on that, my mind still too wind-battered to worry.

Luckily for my too-fast heart, after one last quick, breathtaking kiss, Shin set his bedroll in its normal place on the *other* side of the dying fire, giving me space to recover from the gale-force of his attention. And before I knew it, I'd drifted to sleep, too, a soul-deep, satiated satisfaction lulling me into the dreamworld within minutes.

And for the first night in ages, I did not dream.

The next morning, when the others roused—Malina returned to us again, quiet, but present—we packed up and set to walking. Despite only getting a few meager hours of rest, I had pep in my step. Like somehow, the wind was still carrying me on its back, an ever-present friend at my side.

Much like Shin's gaze, a near-permanent brand across my skin as we traveled, his focus unwavering as we made our way through the trees and took our first steps out of the Kawayama Mountains into the Anabrevi Valley.

Into Dunyas.

Though I'd never traveled this way, the shift in the environment was as clear as any map marker, the trees shrinking to bushes, the leafy underbrush fading to tall, reedy grass that licked all the way up my calves. Windflowers of every color peppered the rolling hills, their faces all turned to the sunlight. Here, its rays somehow reached further down, heat scratching at my neck and lower back within minutes.

It was beautiful, the sprawling, sun-loved planes even more stunning than the paintings hanging in Anastova suggested.

This was the world I'd dreamed of from my ivory tower, the visage of escape I'd always craved—and now, with the others keeping time and company with me, it was even more incredible than I could have ever pictured.

Not that I dreamed of escape, not anymore.

I had a far more potent, powerful goal.

Change.

But without the canopy of branches, the sun stole our breaths faster, sweat marring everyone's brows by noon, tongues parched as they stuck to the roofs of our mouths no matter how many swigs of water we all chugged down.

And Aya...

Flowers might have loved the sun, their life dependent on its gentle rays. But the same light that fed them also killed them, withering them to nothing when autumn beckoned.

Aya could not afford to wilt any further, even with my increasingly frequent boosts.

So when the lone, abandoned cabin speared the horizon as we crested a hill, its face more than a bit sun-bleached, the wood more than a little bug-bitten, we called it an oasis anyway, desperate for shelter sooner than expected.

Not that I minded. By tomorrow, we'd find our way into a nearby town—Brevos, a simple farming community—and strike a bargain for a wagon to take us the rest of the way to Anastova.

And though all the answers and solutions waited there, though I finally had a real purpose propelling me forward...

I wasn't ready to let it all go. Not yet.

One last night.

The inside of the home was less out of shape than the exterior, and larger than its illusionary face suggested. Dust coated the wooden table and the shelves of the first room—a dining space, it seemed, but the kitchen just beyond sported a wide stove and cabinets full of dry goods that somehow hadn't perished. It was abandoned, but not by too long, perhaps a few months of disuse etched into its crevices. In the next room, a wide sofa stood stalwart in front of the fireplace, logs stacked next to it ready to burn away the chill that'd settled into the floorboards.

The second floor had three bedrooms—each with soft beds that spoke of comfort despite the musty scent of the blankets—centered by a washroom with a deep porcelain tub, a *working toilet*, and a sink that still drew cold water, likely from a nearby well.

It was hard not to let excitement and exhaustion capture us all, this stuffy oasis more alluring than the most luxurious wings of Anastova.

"Everyone settle in and rest. We're only here for the night," Shin droned out—he sounded matter-of-fact, but I didn't miss the way his shoulders sagged or the way that his hands unclenched at his side for the first time in days.

Relief. Much overdue.

There was a spark to his step as he set toward the kitchen. "I'll make supper. Mal, do you think you can catch something before the sun goes down?"

Malina huddled in the doorway—half-in, half-out, even as the others all tore up the stairs to claim their rooms—glaring at the cabin as if it were one of the infamous Jaltan dungeons. Glaring at *Shin* as if he was her warden, not her dearest friend. "Fine. I'll be back."

Unease rocked my middle as she slipped out into the sunlight again, silhouette disappearing into the light like a fire pixie. It wasn't my place to fix their friendship. But I couldn't help feeling like it was my fault, even after Shin had reassured me last night. Even if there was a wedge between them already, even if this conflict predated my presence, there was no denying I'd deepened the chasm, cleaving through their bond deeper than I'd wanted to.

Perhaps they were better off without me. And after I got Aya her cure, after I made right the wrongs Ecei and my family had unintentionally levied upon these people...

Well, maybe I could get out of their way, and leave the mending hearts between Shin and Mal.

A braver person might have lingered, might have voiced my fears or worries, might have done something, *anything* to make it better.

I still didn't quite know how to be brave.

I cleared my throat, calling out so he could hear me in the kitchen, "I'm going to head to bed early, I think. Goodnight."

I didn't wait for a response, trudging up the stairs as fast as I could before my cowardice could catch up with me.

The furthest bedroom was empty, Riku and Ren claiming the largest and closest for themselves, Kas settling into the next—likely with Malina, when she returned. Naveen would most likely take the long couch downstairs, preferring to stay as close to a fire as possible, which left the last room for me—and later, Aya, who had made a bath up for herself and was busy merrily soaking like a fish in a pond.

Shin would probably sleep in front of the door or on the roof, the overprotective bastard always nodding off in the least friendly of places.

I shut those thoughts down as I shut the door to the room behind me.

I'd always had my own space to retreat to in Anastova, so I thought it would be nice to be on my own again, even for a few hours. But the second I crawled into the large, cold bed, an old, festering ache slithered through my bones.

I'd gotten used to it. To the constant, soft noise of the others breathing. To the gentle shuffling of bodies under blankets, to the little sniffles and snorts that let me know they were still there. That I wasn't alone.

I hated the quiet.

Hated the loneliness that crept back in, the emptiness that couldn't be filled.

So much so that I almost thanked the rain when it started pelting the windows in heavy droplets, a syncopated beat that helped me tune out the aching void in my chest.

Almost.

A new part of me—a part I didn't have a week ago—was worried for Malina, who still hadn't made her way back to the oasis, even as the sound of dinner being finished echoed from downstairs. Worried for Shin, who preferred sleeping on rooftops instead of beds.

I wished I didn't have to let them go. I needed my parents to hear me for the best of Babylon, but I didn't know if I'd survive them cleaving me from these people, these orphans and thieves that had given me more riches than any noble ever had. That had stolen my heart, too.

A knock at the door—three even raps—disrupted the rain's song.

Aya.

I forced myself to sit, to smile. I would not burden her with my privileged suffering. Still, my voice sounded softer—sadder—than I wanted it to. "Come in."

When the door opened, shock replaced all else.

Shin lingered in the doorway, one hand braced on the frame as he leaned in, his feet still waiting to cross the threshold. His arm flexed as his mouth pressed to a gentle frown. "You all right?"

I stilled, clutching the threadbare blanket like it was a shield, a blush automatically flooding my face. "Shin, I wasn't expecting—"

A tentative step into the room silenced me. Shin breathed—strangely hesitant—before saying, "Aya is going to stay downstairs, actually. Says she's cold after her bath and wants to warm herself up in front of the fire for a few hours."

"Oh." Disappointment twinged my sides. I'd miss my roommate, miss having another body in the room, but I couldn't hold it against my friend.

Though I suspected her change of plans had less to do with the fire and far more to do with a couch-dwelling, joke-cracking Dunyasian who she always watched with heart-filled eyes.

I smiled at the thought of both of them happy, if even for a night. "Good for her."

Shin took another step in, closing the door behind him, and green-tea-and-honey eyes softened. "You've been distant today. I hope I didn't...last night—"

I heard the words he didn't say, the apology I wasn't owed.

My heart both swelled and dropped.

"No, no, last night was lovely," I reassured him quickly, and I meant it. Still, my knees drew to my chest, as if they could brace against the ache that was carving me from the inside out. "I'm just thinking."

Shin took the invitation, perching on the edge of the bed, "About?"

I wanted him both closer and farther at the same time, two sides of me warring. The side that longed for the comfort of his embrace, the thrill of his touch...

And the side that knew that the longer I indulged, the harder it would be to let him go.

Braver parts won out as I scooted closer, fitting my hand in his.

"What would you be?" I mused, tracing shapes into his skin with my thumb. "If you weren't a thief, what would you do with your life?"

It was a question he'd asked me back in the garden, the first choice in the series of many, even if I hadn't realized, then.

Where would you go?

And the silent, less obvious...*is it with me?*

Shin thought for a long moment before shifting closer, taking my other hand, too, so our knees brushed together and our hands entwined.

"I'd be a musician." He smiled, just a small twitch of his mouth. "You?"

This was hard. *Intimate.* To be so close, to touch so freely...and to speak life into dreams and wishes I'd left to rot at the bottom of my heart.

But if the last few weeks had proved anything, it was that I could do hard things. That I could choose.

I spoke my first wobbling words, all of them as shaky as a newborn fawn learning to walk. To *run.* "I don't know. I always thought I wanted to study medementalism, or go live on a farm somewhere... somewhere like this... and just enjoy *growing* things." But even as I said it, the duty-bound part of me caged those daydreams again, replacing the narrative with what I had to do. "But those were fantasies, and after what Naveen said... I know I have to be a good queen. They all deserve it."

Shin watched me for a long moment, brows furrowed. Then, "Those other parts of you can still exist as a queen. In fact, someone who cares about healing and growing things is likely the best kind of ruler. One Babylon could desperately benefit from."

The lump that choked me was made of pure adoration and gratitude, both surging up from my deepest parts with renewed strengths.

Shin Koishi didn't just see me...he understood. *Uplifted*, like a wind beneath a leaf, carrying it on its back.

Just like he cradled me now, an unspoken shift drawing him closer as he tucked himself next to me, gently leading my head to the crook of his shoulder. I breathed him in—breathed in the windswept pine and musk of his skin, the warmth of his nearness—and wrapped my arms around his waist, like they'd always fit there.

It was new, uncertain, but right. *Natural.*

I didn't realize I was crying until I noticed the wet stains on his shirt.

Shin saved me from trying to articulate the madness in my mind. "Just because I don't play music professionally anymore doesn't mean I've lost my skills. Cooperation, creativity...they are still my weapons. You don't have to lose who you were just because you grew up."

I curled deeper into him, letting those words blanket me in a comfort I'd never know. And I wanted to return the favor. "Would you go back to playing?"

A sharp inhale. "Not like that."

His heartbeat ticked up beneath my ear, the steady rhythm now a race. "Why did you stop?"

I expected him to clam up again, to reapply his mask and leave me alone.

But Shin Koishi was nothing if not surprising.

He stroked an aimless hand up and down my back—like he was soothing himself with the touch—as he spoke. "My mother taught me to play. Her and my father...well, it seemed like for a long time they were in love, but the situation was complicated. He had other duties to fulfill, and sometimes, that got in the way."

I let his words hang, let myself picture it. It wasn't too far off from my parents' relationship—their love clearly there, but strained under the weight of their crowns.

I wondered what held Shin's parents down.

Wondered if all love had to be that heavy.

Shin continued, his breezy voice now just as burdened, "But things shattered when my mother got pregnant with my sister, and my father kicked her out because Aya wasn't his. Her father was a Soran merchant that never claimed her. My mother insisted that she was... forced...but he didn't believe her. He sent her to go home and live with the Koishis, but because of their shady business deals, they wouldn't take her back and risk the scandal on their name. So she was alone in Hiku City, trying to make money however she could."

My heart ached for the woman I hadn't had the honor to meet, and for the kids—for little Shin and Aya—who had to pay the price for such meaningless violence and betrayal. "So you played...so she would hear you?"

Shin's lips pressed against the top of my head as he inhaled, steadying himself. "It was the only place we could meet without raising suspicion. My father was a very important man, and I wasn't left to my own devices often. But the Opera was a safe place, one he let me travel to frequently. Or so we thought."

The dull ache sharpened into a piercing stab through my chest as I pieced together the end of this story. This *tragedy*. "Your mother was in the crowd that night."

"Yes." He swallowed. "She didn't make it."

"I'm so sorry, Shin," I whispered, and though I knew it was sometimes the worst thing to say to grief, a bandage that did little to stanch the festering wound, I meant it. Not from a place of pity, but one of understanding, of *recognition*, just as he'd given me.

Maybe love was destined to destroy, conditional and ruthless even in parents. Maybe only children could love purely, and suffered the most because of it.

Aya had just been a little girl, a baby, bearing the consequence of some grown man's treachery. Just as I had been a girl, desperate for affection my mother couldn't give because of her own self-loathing.

Just as Shin was still a boy, trying to reunite a broken family through his music. Trying to build his own on the fiery ruins of his first.

Fingers twirled through my curls, mimicking the tension that twisted in my gut as Shin talked on, voice hoarse. "I don't remember all that much about her anymore. But I remember the music. Tsojo and Aheni helped look after Aya and I for a while, and they let me play at their places to earn my keep. Music kept me *alive*."

I stiffened at that, realization dawning in my heart.

Maybe love destroyed, or could. But music saved. Shin's music, specifically. It had kept him alive, and had inspired me, too. Kept me company on my loneliest nights. Kept me fighting on my hardest days.

I sat up so I could look him in the eye. So I could *see* him. "Your mother is still alive in you every time you play."

Shin blinked, eyes glassy. His hand cupped my face, as he *saw* me right back. "And your brother, in you, whenever you heal and grow like the Queen you are."

A moment passed, as I let those words sink down into my deepest parts. Let them take root, new buds that I'd water with my every breath.

Then, I kissed him.

And he kissed me.

And I poured everything into the space where our mouths met, every word I couldn't say, every wish that I still clung to, every desire I'd long abandoned.

Every hurt we'd both suffered. Every broken part we'd both carried for so long.

But this time, I wasn't content to let myself get swept away by his hurricane. I wanted to *join*, to spin and surge and swirl with him, wanted to unleash myself just as much.

On instinct, my leg swung over his, and then I was perched on his lap, my thighs wrapping around him like thick roots of a tree that wouldn't be swayed despite the storm of our mutual desire.

His hands crept up my legs, kneading my soft flesh with a delightfully bruising grip as he rose to the challenge, his kisses even more desperate, more aching as his tongue clashed against mine.

This was reckless. *Wild.*

I didn't care.

If love destroyed, I was content to shatter. To *burn.*

I kissed him again, and again, and *again,* my hips rolling with my desire, unashamed and unbidden for the first time in my life. A dance that I knew in my basest parts. And as he always did, he met me step for step, grinding against me in ways that set every nerve I possessed on an all-consuming fire.

A moan broke free from his throat, deep and hoarse, and I stilled, concern dousing me out.

"I don't know what I'm doing." I pressed a staying hand to his chest as I mumbled shyly against his lips, worried that I'd done something to hurt him. That I'd gone too far, this unchained version of me too wild for even his appetite.

His face pulled back an inch so his hooded eyes could shoot me a look that challenged with an *"Oh, you know* exactly *what you're doing to me."* But instead of voicing that, his hands paused against my hips as he said, "Do you want to stop?"

He waited, letting me think. Letting me *choose.*

But there hadn't been a choice since the day we met. Back in the Opera House, when I was just a girl enraptured by his song. And again in the bar, when I was a stranger saved.

At the Masque, when I was captivated.

On the river, when I clung to his life with all my might.

No, there was no choice when it came to wanting him. More than want. Maybe even...

That word was so small yet too big all at the same time, too *destructive*, but it mattered not. My heart had already chosen a long time ago.

For once, I knew what I wanted.

And I was willing to let myself have it. Have *him*, if he'd let me. Even if I couldn't keep him for longer than tonight. Even if it hurt when it all ended.

"No, I definitely don't want to stop, it's just..." I let my forehead fall into his, dragging in a grounding breath as I chose my next words carefully. "Are you...is this your first time?"

He paused for a long moment, but his hands still held my legs in place. Bidding me to *stay*. Choosing me, too. "No. Is that...does that trouble you?"

It did, and it didn't.

It made sense that at least one of us should know what we're doing, should be able to lead this dance.

But that didn't stop the wriggling jealousy in my gut from clawing its way up my throat. "Who was it? A lover?"

His gentle laugh shook both of us. He shrugged. "Not quite. I used to help with the laundry at Tsojo's brothel to pick up extra coin. My *Easinir* let me dry the wash faster."

I waited, still in need of an explanation.

Not that he really owed me one—what did it matter what he'd done with his time and affection before we met?

But Shin pressed on, offering more truths. More *choices.* "But like I said, she also had a piano, and on nights when I didn't want to go home, she let me stay and play for a while. The ladies liked it, and so did some of the customers. I'd get tips."

Suspicion still clung to my frame, caging me in my own insecurity. "I see…"

The first signs of shame flickered across Shin's expression, a frown tugging his mouth. "Via…she particularly liked my playing. Said it made it easier for her to get lost when she…when she did what she did. Said it made her want to love again."

My stomach dropped.

Beautiful, effervescent Via. Slender yet curvy. Seductive in looks and spirit. *Free.*

Everything I wasn't.

There was no competition. I paled in grim comparison, and I could practically hear my mother's voice in my ear, reminding me of all the ways I'd never measure up and the ways I measured too much.

Via and her *Prince Shin.*

Words shook free of my trembling voice. "She felt that way about you?"

Unspoken words rang out, too. *Did you love her back?*

Shin brushed my curls from my face, fingers tangling at the nape of my neck. "Oh Breath, no, we didn't like each other like *that.* She was more interested in Mal, but she never gave her the time of day. Via enjoyed my playing, that's all. But one night, she offered to teach me some tricks if I taught her how to play. That way one day, we could both impress the ones we *really* were meant for. Make them feel *good.*" His voice dipped low, his thumb rubbing the tension away from my neck as his other hand trailed up my waist, desire burning away my lingering self-consciousness as his touch promised more. "I was a curious teenager, even though it was very much so based on learning how to please her."

Jealousy gave way to a curiosity that brought heat to my cheeks. "What do you mean?"

He pulled me closer again, so close that I could feel the evidence of his desire pressing against the most desperate, *needing* parts of me. A kiss grazed the hollow of my throat, and I shuddered as he mumbled against me, "There are ways to make a woman feel good that way that don't necessarily elicit the same pleasure from a man."

My thoughts drifted to books I'd read, to the romances the servants had lent me when mother wasn't looking. To the dozens of dirty, salacious things I'd only let myself imagine in the darkest, most private moments of my solitude.

But I didn't want this to be about me. To be one-sided.

I wanted a give and take. A push and pull, as we always did. A dance, two partners on equal footing, keeping time to the same song. "But isn't that not fair to you? I want you to feel…"

Feel good. Feel *seen*.

Feel like the whole world was burning, but it didn't matter as long as we were together.

Feel like his soul would cave in if we didn't have each other tonight.

"Trust me, Princess. I think I'll enjoy it just as much." A dark chuckle spilled out of him, stroking against the shell of my ear as his hands wandered up my waist, the calloused tips of his fingers scorching a line of fire across the sensitive skin beneath my shirt. "I've been dying to taste you since the moment I laid eyes on you in that bar."

I pulled back to look at his face, to see the sincerity and seduction written there. At the contradiction of themes, the hard and soft and light and dark that made up Shin Koishi. His round, bow-shaped lips, framed in coarse stubble from days on the run. His green-tea-and-honey eyes, set atop cheekbones sharp enough to wound. His night-shade laugh and silken dreams.

I'd wanted him before I knew what it was to crave. And now, I wanted to taste every contradiction he conceded, to feel every perfect imperfection of him. To learn what it meant to make love.

And for reasons I didn't understand, against all the messages I'd heard my whole life…

He wanted me, too.

"That makes us *even* again." I cradled his face in my hands, this man that had given me wings and freed me of my cage. This boy who deserved every happiness after all the ways he'd suffered. "I've wanted you since the moment we met."

At that, the hold on his restraint snapped. His mouth crashed into mine again, but hunger gave way to something stronger. Something deeper, a reverence I'd never know. A taste of the power that made the very world.

Faith. Love.

And as his mouth roamed, as the last layers between us slipped away, as our breaths synchronized and our dance sped up, I let myself fall into him entirely.

With only the stars our witness, only the wind to eavesdrop, the rain smothered the sound of our song as we joined together, singing an ancient harmony our bodies and souls knew deeply. As our melody, both rhythmic and soaring, crescendoed to its peak.

"Hold on." It was a husky demand, a promise made as he drove us to the very edge of the world. As he taught me all the tricks he'd learned, and I freed every part of myself to him.

I let those eyes, green-tea-and-honey, warm and nourishing, drown me as we both toppled over the edge, holding each other closer than I'd ever been held before. "Don't let go."

And he didn't. Shin Koishi didn't let go until long after our breathing steadied, until long after our muscles stopped trembling, until long after sleep dragged me into its deep embrace.

Shin Koishi stayed.

Twenty-Six

SHIN

I woke to warmth. Warmth, like sunlight through a window, somehow trapped in my arms. Like skin, soft as silken rose petals.

Memories of the night before finally floated to the surface as my mind shook off its dreamy haze.

Irina.

It was an effort to pry my eyes open, a satiated sleep still clinging to my lashes. I couldn't remember the last time I'd slept so deeply, so *safely*, but something about her in my grasp had lulled me deep into the realm of dreams.

Curls brushed against my chin as she unfurled from me. Deep bronze skin splattered in freckles—and lovebites—peeked from beneath *my* skewed tunic. She stretched and faced me, eyes like soil after rain nourishing my soul as they fluttered open.

My breath stole in my chest as she smiled.

Breath above, I wanted to freeze that moment forever.

One final touch.

One more kiss.

One last day at her side.
One eternal night in her embrace.

"Good morning." I brushed my knuckles against her cheek, already desperate to touch her again. To show her how she deserved to be *worshipped*.

A sigh tumbled from her as she nestled closer. Close enough that her nose brushed mine, her freckles blurring. "Good morning."

My fingers knotted in her hair, rooting her next to me. Wishing I could keep her here all day, not leaving this bed, not until she knew how crazy she'd made me. How foolish and free I felt with her. Not until I'd returned the pleasure tenfold. My voice dipped at the thought. "How did you sleep?"

"Terribly. You snore." A playful smirk flickered in the corner of her mouth—a mouth that I'd have to taste again, if she didn't stop teasing me.

"You lie."

She shrugged. "I'm learning."

A real laugh spilled from me as I pressed my forehead to hers. But with her nearness, her warm skin on mine again, the humor fled, replaced with something so potent, I could barely swallow back the wave of emotion that overtook me. "Last night—"

"No, it's okay." Irina pressed a finger against my mouth, and I kissed the tip. But she continued on, derailing my thoughts. "Listen, when we get back to Anastova, I would love for you to stay. But you don't owe me anything. I hope you know the choice is yours, and I respect it either way."

I inhaled, one more deep breath.

There was no choice I could make that didn't include her. Aya and I had lived so many years on the run, that when she first proposed the idea of us holding up in Anastova, I'd shot it down, fear fueling my decisions as it always had. Keeping me safe...and alone.

But I couldn't imagine prying Aya from her friend. From the girl who'd be her savior, too.

No more than I could imagine leaving her side. Her bed, if she'd let me. I had no claim to such honors, no merits that earned me a place in her life. I was unworthy. Intolerable.

But I would stay for as long as she chose me, in whatever way she wanted me.

And it was about time I told her.

"I—"

The wind's warning came too late.

The world exploded.

Instinct propelled me forward as the cabin rocked, light flashing. Was it a bomb? A *Controller*? I couldn't tell through the smoke that choked down my throat, stinging my eyes.

I covered Irina with my body, shielding her as she screamed. My vision blurred as the floor lurched toward me, my hands and knees scraping open as we skidded, coughs hacking out of us. I lifted my head, bile surging up my throat, trying to make sense of what—

A sharp sting hit the back of my neck, pain searing through the spot.

I grabbed for it, clasping around something small and sharp, and yanking it free.

My stomach dropped again, energy draining from my veins as my blood dripped from the end of the blue dart.

"What—?"

Clapping hands silenced the end of my sentence as Ecei—flanked by two broad guards—materialized through the smoke, the remnants of the cracked door hanging precariously from its hinges behind them.

"Well, I did not expect to see this." Ecei grinned, a wicked thing that twisted her whole face as her eyes darted between us; me, shirtless, and Irina, wearing my long tunic as a night dress. "Stealing hearts now, are you, thief? How sweet."

I took a protective step in front of Irina, but my legs wobbled, dizziness raking through me again.

What was in that dart?

"What are you doing?" I tried to keep my voice steady, my mask of disinterest tight, but I wavered anyway, unable to clear my head of whatever poison had set my skin to a fiery itch, unable to clear my lungs of the ash that clung to every breath. "This wasn't our deal—"

"Oh, our *deal*, hmm?" A brazen, shrieking laugh tore from her as she stepped forward, icy countenance melting when she bared her teeth. Smoke curled around her and frost gathered across her skin, a predator staring down her prey. "You think I'd still honor that after you killed a *whole squad* of my men and sent me on a wild goose-chase through Babylon?"

Horror lanced my heart.

Of course she blamed us, the witnesses to her treachery.

I had to get us out—get the others—and *go*.

One last escape.

I drew a deep breath, summoning the air around me—

Nothing.

Just another flip of my stomach. Another sway of my head.

Irina didn't hesitate to fill in where I faltered, raising her hands, her voice low and cool as she stood back up. "Let's talk about this. It's all a misunderstanding."

The Ice Witch narrowed her eyes, darkness tainting the blue in shadow. "Understand this, *Princess:* no one crosses me."

She snapped her fingers, and the guards moved.

One slammed full-force into Irina, the Princess crying out as he tackled her. Another breath, and I surged, launching myself at his back. But another set of hands grasped me, tearing me off him, my fingers fumbling for purchase as my head spun at a tornado's pace.

Arms caged me, and a hand grabbed the back of my neck, pressing the wound the dart made. Stars glimmered in my vision as the guard slammed me to the floor.

Right across from Irina, her cheek smashed into the splintered wood, tears puddling beneath her.

We had to get out. Had to *fly*.

Desperate, I dug deep, inhaling again, calling on my Control—

Nothing. *Nothing, nothing, nothing.*

No.

The dart, the poison...

"I can't—" I croaked, my strength draining as the wind withdrew further and further, as a hole carved so deep into my bones, I was convinced Ecei somehow sucked the marrow out with her brandishing stare. "What did you *do?*"

"Oh, that?" Ecei kicked the discarded dart so it rolled, stopping just in front of my face, the sharp metal-end glinting in the sun. Ecei crouched down, cocking her head to the side so she could gloat in my face, her goon still crushing me down. "It's another experiment I've been working on. Neutralizes *Easinir* for a bit. Handy, isn't it?"

My throat closed. Another malevolent experiment. Another act of Nehirite evil.

"My parents know *everything*," Irina bit through clenched teeth, rocking against the man's hold. But the guard was twice her size, and he merely laughed at her attempt. Still, she was undeterred, hurling her threats at Ecei with convincing force. "We sent them a raven with my seal. They know all about the Blight, about your *treason*, and they will not rest."

She punctuated each word, and for a second, I thought Ecei flinched.

But my hopes were dashed as another one of her wicked laughs tumbled from her.

"Oh, you poor thing, you don't *know*." Then she stood, snapping again at her guards. "Bring them downstairs."

My heartbeat was a wild thing inside me, aching to break from its cage, but my limbs, my *Easinir*...

I was numb.

Useless.

I could barely control my arms and legs, never mind my magic, as the guards heaved me up, my feet dragging in awkward limps as I fought to move them.

They let me tumble over myself down the stairs, the wood smacking against my back and head in more dizzying punches. A pop, and agony shot down my arm, my shoulder cleaving from its spot. I bit back a moan, the throbbing a death march as I finally hit the floor with a sick thud.

Acid rushed up my throat again, but I clenched my teeth shut, refusing to let myself heave. Refusing to acknowledge the pain as I blinked, struggling to make my eyes focus again. The guard dragged me up, tying off my arms, another wave of pain weeping through my battered shoulder.

I saw Naveen, Ren, and Riku first; tied and bound together in the center of the ransacked living room, bruises already forming across their jaws. But they were awake, thrashing against their ties, even as they gagged around Ecei's ice. Next to them, Kas propped against a guard, unconscious, a dart sticking from his neck, too.

My chest clenched around a terror that threatened to stop my heart's next beat. We wouldn't have our other Controller, either.

But fear turned into torrential rage, so potent it nearly doused the effects of the poison, as I saw Aya, bound and *bleeding*. My head cleared as my sister's name stormed out of my mouth. "Aya—"

"I'm fine, I promise." She shook her head, a warning for me not to get excited, even as she slumped against Naveen; even as the cut above her eyebrow spilled crimson life onto her pale cheek.

No, this was not fine. Everyone was tied up, injured, captive to this *psychopath*...

Everyone...

Everyone but Mal, who stepped through the door, unbound. Shifting her weight between her feet, her lip sucked into her teeth.

Dread dragged through me, hollowing out any hope I had left, as the puzzle pieces clicked together—and shattered me. "Malina..."

She didn't look at me. Wouldn't. Her back straightened as she stepped toward Ecei—

Her accomplice, and our captor.

"Cure the girl," Mal ordered. "That was our bargain."

A breath shuddered out of me. "You *didn't*."

Mal's gaze flicked my way for a second, and the shame swimming in her eyes was enough to confirm my worst fears.

She sold us out.

Mal, who'd been dodgy for days, who'd tried to rile me—no, *warn* me. About what she was doing when she snuck off.

Mal, who I'd trusted with my life. Who I'd pushed away, inch by inch.

"Oh, but she *did*," Ecei replied, pouring her sea-salt into an open, festering wound. She sauntered to Mal, fingers winding through one of her curls. But the fire pixie didn't fight back, didn't swat her away; her only reaction was a small flinch that slashed through my soul. Ecei sneered. "Your friend here is the only one with any sense out of you all. She turned the fae-stone back on a few days ago, helped me track you, and then she met me yesterday to renegotiate our terms."

Malina, who I'd found in the sewers, brave and sharp like a diamond in the rough.

Malina, who'd been the other half to every con I'd ever pulled.

I knew she was a liar. A thief.

I just never imagined that she'd ever lie to or take from me.

Broken pieces cracked through my voice. "How could you—?"

"We didn't have a choice. You almost died, Shin." Her throat bobbed, as if she didn't fully believe that excuse, either.

"The ravens," Irina snarled, her voice an uncharacteristically low rattle as she glared at Malina.

"Never sent." Ecei tsked, baiting the Princess. With her spindled finger, she squeezed and tilted Irina's chin upward, even as Irina jerked against her grip. "Not that it would do much. Your mother and I go back a very, *very* long time. And I doubt the Jaltans would be very happy to hear about *her* secrets, if she chose to spill mine."

Irina paled, and whether Ecei's threat was real or bluffed, it didn't matter. Because the light in Irina's eyes wilted, her shoulders slouching as she wrestled with her despair.

But there was no time to process, no time to breathe, as Ecei straightened again. *Smiled.*

Ready to deliver the final blow.

"Cure Aya, and let the rest of us go. You don't have to pay us the rest as collateral for the trouble. You take the Princess, and we all disappear," Malina spat, a hand on Aya's shoulder, drawing Ecei's attention again. "Those. Were. Our. Terms."

Ecei dragged her gaze over Aya. Curled a beckoning finger. "Fine, bring the girl here."

Aya's eyes widened in panic as the guards snagged her frail form, lifting her like she weighed nothing. Like she was no more than a feather.

I lurched against my restraints, toppling forward, but I didn't care, even as my head pounded and my heart threatened to stop. Even as my shoulder screamed.

I didn't care if I had to crawl over glass to get to her. If I had to roll through fire.

One last fight. One more escape.

Hands jerked me back just as the guard threw Aya down, her yelp fracturing through my ears. The others thrashed too, Naveen flexing every limb and muscle to break free, but it was no use.

"Don't you dare touch her!" I bellowed, a thunderstorm's call stirring in my chest. But my Control did not come, did not answer. My voice rasped out of me on a desperate, burning breath. "Hold on, Aya."

Shaking, Aya sat up as much as she could, her eyes meeting mine. Violet, like the first colorful rays of dusk. Warm, like a summer breeze dancing through a young girl's hair.

A trembling smile captivated her round face, those eyes crinkling at the corners like they always did. "Don't worry. Time to let me fly, Shin."

And for a moment, Aya *soared.*

A fierce wind exploded through the room, her Control unleashed as it tore the door off its hinges. It crashed into a guard, sending him flying into another, the garrison panicking as her *Easinir* roared like a triumphant tornado.

They'd all overlooked her, not bothering to shoot her with a dart, sickly as she was. None of them had seen her talent hidden beneath the bruises and pallor. Didn't see the butterfly just waiting to crack free of her chrysalis.

Just as I didn't see the ice shard until it jammed into my sister's throat. Until it tore out, a stream of gore flowing from its wake.

I don't know if I screamed or stayed silent.

Don't know if I moved, or went utterly still.

All I knew in that moment was my sister's last, gargled word as it coughed out of her, crimson staining her lips. "Shin—"

Then silence.

Eyes dulled. Frail frame dropped to the ground.

The wind stopped speaking.

And my sister's heart stopped beating.

"I—You said you'd cure her!" Malina shrieked as she fell to her knees, blood soaking her trousers. Soaking her hands, the guilt hers to bear just as much as Ecei's.

Just as much mine, for all the choices I made to get her here.

The universe tilted as a pain unleashed inside me, a force that crushed my soul to dust.

Aya was...

Aya.

Aya.

Everything honed to razor sharp focus, as if time itself slowed to honor the moment that my sister slipped into the next world.

And I watched in horror. In numb, endless shock, my ears ringing, my eyes blinking, as if my body did not understand. Couldn't.

As Naveen bit down so hard on his scream, blood poured from his mouth, tears streaming down his face.

As Riku and Ren moved in unison, tugging against their restraints, Ren even dislocating his arm with a sick pop as they tried to fight for her, tried to save her.

As Irina began to *glow*, a vile string of curses tumbling from her mouth while she shook with a primal, visceral rage.

But none of it mattered.

None of it changed anything.

Aya was dead.

My Aya. The girl who loved lavender tea more than she loved me, though she'd never admit it. The girl who sang back to birds. *"Because they deserve to hear some music, too."* The girl with my mother's smile and my broken sense of humor.

The girl who'd suffered before she had the chance to soar.

The girl who'd never complained, even as life dragged her down.

The girl who made me better. Redeemable.

Gone.

Gone.

Gone.

Gone.

Irina's sobs tore through my ringing eardrums, the sound deafening. "You will pay. She was my *friend*."

Malina snarled at Ecei, lunging. "You bitch—"

Ice snared her in her spot. Ecei wiped her blade with a handkerchief. "I *did* cure her. She's free of the Blight now."

The wind spoke the language of thieves, but Ecei wrote the book on manipulation. On pure, unadulterated malignancy.

With a smile and snarky remark, she'd stamped out a bud that hadn't even bloomed with her poisoned, wintry kiss of death.

"I'm going to kill you." My voice croaked out of me, and I must have been screaming with the way my promise scalded as I spat it out. "I'm going to see you hang."

Ecei didn't bother to look my way.

But if she had, she might have seen the truth in my words. The death threat in my stare.

Instead, her icy eyes settled on Irina. "Take her while I deal with the rest."

Panic rattled my bones, but I didn't have time to say goodbye as the guard pulled out a sack, strange green powder shimmering inside—

Fucking *fae-dust.*

Irina cried my name—once.

Then she *disappeared.*

No. No.

Not her.

Not her, too.

Not—

I launched to my feet, numbness giving way to something else for a brief flash. Something hateful and powerful. My sights set on Ecei, ready to strike. Ready to end her, and myself. To end the whole fucking world, because without Aya, without Irina...

"My Queen, we have company!" a guard bellowed as he burst through the door, sweat and ash staining his blue uniform, knocking me down again. "Jaltans!"

"How—?" Ecei whipped around, surprise lifting her brows. But with a grimace, she regained her composure, grabbing Malina's frozen arm. "No matter, that's my cue. I'll let the savages deal with you all."

I expected the green dust this time as she doused herself and Malina. As her guards all followed suit, flashing away in puffs of emerald magic, like they hadn't been here at all. Hadn't blown my whole life to bits.

Malina's teary eyes met mine—all the hurts and apologies she'd never get to say brimming in them—before she vanished.

And then she was gone, and I was lost again.

Irina was kidnapped. Malina was a traitor.

And Aya—

Gone.

Gone.

Gone.

Alone. I was *alone.*

It was all I could do to crawl to my sister's body as the Jaltan forces swarmed. All I could do to cover her, to shield her in death like I hadn't in life. To sob into her hair as I breathed in the last glimmers of her life—the freshly-washed scent of her hair, the final moments of warmth from her skin.

The others bellowed against their gags, but I didn't care. Not as red uniforms surrounded them, rifles cocked and seeking targets. Not as a man called their orders—*No one leaves!*

It wasn't until I heard my name that I looked up. *Turned.*

"Shin?"

Princess Naria of Jalta wore the same crimson uniform as her soldiers, the color matching the bright streak of hair in front of her face.

The color of her people.

The color I'd shed fourteen years ago.

The color of Aya's blood.

She stood stunned in the doorway, expressionless, a warrior surveying the scene of battle. Then she held up a hand, and her guards stood down. Started melting my friends' bindings, assessing them for damage.

Something softened in Naria as she looked my way again. As she knelt down next to me, biting the inside of her cheek, like she always did when she was worried, but didn't want to show it. "Shin, what *happened*?"

At that, the very last piece of my heart broke in two.

I clutched Aya's lifeless body as I stared into my other sister's eyes. One sister lost. Another found.

Fractured, and reunited.

Dead, and reborn.

Just as it had been when I was ten, when I ran and didn't look back.

"She's gone. They're both *gone.*"

Twenty-Seven

SHIN

The Soran blimp—powered by both Soran and Jaltan *Easinir* soldiers—buzzed as it moved, clouds misting past the wall of windows while sunlight warmed the metal sills to a branding heat. But even as I slouched against one, the glass and bronze burning the back of my neck, I barely felt it.

Barely felt anything.

Naria and Hana gathered all of us—except Kas, who slept in the chamber below between crying fits—in the Captain's bay, the large room full of whirring contraptions and blinking lights. All mysteries that might have previously stirred wonder and awe in my chest.

But I was hollow, everyone's voices distant as I succumbed to the nothingness.

Naveen, Ren, and Riku all huddled onto one of the plush purple couches, Ren clutching his injured arm in the makeshift sling the soldiers had wrapped him in. In a day, their faces had all aged years—eyes bloodshot and bleary, cheeks hollow and sunken, skin stretched too thin and blotchy from tears. Our *Easinir* had returned a mere hour after we'd been shot, the effect of the darts only temporary; but our magic's return did nothing to invite life back into our veins, all of us still empty and aching. Like without Malina, without Irina, without...

Without. We were truly, utterly *without.*

Lost.

They'd made room for me on the edge of the sofa, but I hadn't left my perch on the sill, watching the world shrink below us.

Feeling myself, shrink, too.

Irina was gone.

Aya was gone.

And I was in the clutches of the family I'd been running from since I was ten. At the mercy of more nobles that didn't give a shit about the death of a little girl who'd barely just begun to live.

Not that I needed anyone's mercy.

All I needed now was a stiff drink and the welcome of oblivion.

"So, Ecei is behind the Blight?" Naria paced the corner—away from the windows—a caged tiger, unused to the soaring heights.

I hadn't recognized her immediately that night at the ball. She'd been familiar, her swan mask a memory I'd tried to suppress, but I should've known that lethal grace and blunt voice anywhere. When she'd cornered us at the Opera, it had all clicked, my real name on her lips summoning memories I'd hoped dead and buried.

Memories of a sun-soaked palace tucked between two looming volcanoes. Memories of heat and discipline, of days training in the fighting pitches while the sun glared at us, and nights learning to dance and politick as the moon beckoned.

Memories of a sister, just a year younger than I, who met me step for step, always trying to catch up to the heir.

Memories of a father who'd loved me, once. Who'd been proud to call me his son, despite...

Memories of a mother who loved him. Who'd still chosen to protect him, even after...

Memories of when it all burned to ash.

I ignored her question for one of my own. "How did you find us?"

Dark eyes like hot coal shot to mine, her arms crossed. But it was Hana who answered—the mousy-haired little slip of a girl dressed in a frilly lilac frock that contrasted the soldiers' sharp uniforms—her voice high and demanding. "We'd been tracking you since the Opera House. We lost you a few times, but you left us a pretty messy trail of trouble to follow along the river. Then, when we figured out you'd headed to the mountains, I called the airship in."

I turned away again, back to the lazily drifting clouds and too-warm sun, as I heard the words she didn't say.

A messy trail *of bodies*. One dead and several injured at The Frog's Hollow. Davke and Driss gone from The Breeze Haven, never to return. An entire retinue of Nehirite soldiers blown to smithereens—along with the substantial evidence.

And my *real* sister, buried in an unmarked grave in some forgettable Dunyasian field, nothing to honor her legacy. Nothing to remember the life she lived. No title to pass on. No heirlooms to remember her by.

Then again, my sister wasn't in the body we buried. Her soul had already departed, mixing with the Ether and the *Easinir*, reacquainting with the Breath. It didn't matter where we laid her corpse or paid our respects.

I would not see my sister again until I crossed into the next life.

Now, she was one with the wind, just another whisper I'd have to listen for.

"What about the fae-dust? Do we want to know where you got it?" Ren asked Hana, finding his footing as I withdrew deeper into myself. Into the clouds, wishing I could float away with them.

Hana fidgeted with the ruffles of her skirt, a blush lighting her pale cheeks. "It was Prince Nikolaj's. He won a bet against Drakkar when we were younger. This was his prize. Nehir—"

"Must have been hoarding it for a long time," Riku sat forward on the couch, always step for step with his twin, "and *experimenting*. I wonder if they used it to create the Blight and those suppressants."

It was a grim thought, indeed.

It didn't matter.

Naria nodded along, nobles and Lost Ones united as they set their sights on the common enemy. As they gave their grief and rage a focal point, a target for their sharpened arrows to hit.

Hana stuck her hands to her hips, huffing out her breath like a girl who wasn't accustomed to not getting her way. "This is huge. We have to alert *everyone*."

But none of them would be winning this fight, try as they might. There was nothing left to do, only an acceptance that came with a lifetime of losing, of fleeing.

People were wicked because life was *cruel*. For every inhale, there was an exhale. Every boon, a drought. Every joy, a blight. And only fools bought into the wind's whisperings, believing that they were capable of *one last rescue, one final fight...*

Only to have victory slip through their fingers like a breeze through a wide net.

Like blood through an open wound.

Naria rounded on me, fierce determination written in her furrowed brows, like even after all this time, she hadn't given up on chasing my shadow. "Shin, we have to talk to Father—"

"I don't have a father," I hissed, the first smoke signal of the faint anger burning beneath my apathy.

My origins didn't matter. Hiku City was my home, the streets my tutor and guardian. The people my family. The wind my guide.

But when Riku's icy expression cracked, doubt worked its way through as he stared at me like he didn't know me. Like I hadn't been the one to pull him from the circus and give him a home. Like he was lost again, as he had been then. "We deserve to know, Shin."

My tongue went drier than the Jaltan deserts. I was still lost, too.

My friends deserved the world. Deserved better. They'd all been honest with me—let me find them at their most vulnerable, helped me through mine. Yet I'd kept this secret from everyone but Mal, had tried to protect them from the world I'd tried so hard to forget...

Only to land them right back in it.

Only to let it take Aya from me as punishment.

My friends deserved an explanation. But I had none left to give.

Naria stomped closer, rising to her full height like a swan craning its elegant neck. "Shin is a Koishi by his mother's line, but he was born Rashin of Jalta, son of King Odion."

Ren twisted toward me, jaw dropping. "*Prince* Rashin. Then you're the lost—?"

I winced at the name my father had given me. Rashin. *Morning sun*, in old Jaltan.

The world dawns with you, my boy.

Until it didn't. Until my whole world set in one sundowned evening of chaos.

"I *was* a prince," I snapped, the title nothing but a curse upon my loved ones. "But I was a bastard, born to the Queen's lady-in-waiting."

Ren, Breath bless him, shut his mouth and sat back for once, not willing to press that trap further.

Naria didn't have the same sense of self-preservation.

"I don't understand everything that happened, but I know our mothers...they had an... arrangement," she protested, fists clenched tightly. Her voice rose as she kept pushing, kept prodding, a ghost that would not fade. "You were always meant to rule. The Jaltans are your people, and they have been *suffering*."

Suffering.

No, my *mother* had suffered. *Aya* had suffered.

I'd had enough.

I jumped from my perch, the wind biting at my ankles like a rabid dog ready to attack. "But now I'm nothing to them, and they are nothing to me." I stared down at Naria, a stranger now, even in all the ways she was familiar. A phantom of a past I'd long mourned and forgotten. "*You* are nothing to me."

Her throat bobbed as the dismissal hit its mark.

"Shin," she said my preferred name like it was broken. Like *I* was broken, just a fragment of who I used to be. "You have it all so, *so* wrong. Father—"

"He *killed* her. He killed my mother," I fired back, the fury raging like an inferno now. If Naria wanted my Jaltan parts—if she wanted the flame of my father's people—she'd get it. I stared down my nose at her. "He sent those forces to the Opera House."

"That's—" she stuttered, a candle blown out by my gale force. Lips flattened into a frown. "Father sent the forces in that night because he received a threat. An anonymous tip off that they had you, and that they'd kill you if he didn't comply. It was a *trap*."

I paused, those words flickering through the old paths hope used to walk in my heart. Hope that it had all been a mistake; that my father never stopped loving me or my mother. That one day, we'd all be together again. That he and Mama would find a way to work it all out.

Hope that he wasn't a monster, after all.

But hope had long abandoned my life, and without Aya, it was utterly unattainable.

Naria's tale might have been the truth, or a version of it. But my father's intent did not weigh as heavily as his impact.

"He still kicked my mother out. He's the reason we were there in the first place." I stalked back to my window, the heat racing out of me, too. There were no justifications for any of this, no reason to fight her or argue about a past long abandoned. None of it changed the terrible, undeniable truth. "Now my mother is dead, and now Aya is—"

Gone.

Gone.

Gone.

It was Hana's turn to take a swing at me as she tilted her nose upward, a true-born noble throwing a tantrum. But her words held a sting I hadn't expected from the little gnat, waspish in her attack. "Don't you want the real killer brought to justice? Ecei killed Nikolaj. Killed your sister. Killed *thousands*."

The window beckoned again. The world below looked so small, so insignificant. Buildings were mere dots, the people working in the fields just ants to be squashed by Ecei's boot.

Like my sister had been. Like I would be too, when she found me. "What's the point?"

Naria flinched, and Hana looked away. The twins hung their heads, like my apathy had spread through the ranks, stealing their will as the last of mine died.

But it was Naveen, who'd always been three parts lazy and two parts cheerful, who leveled me with a glower that could pluck the tail feathers of a falcon. *Naveen*, who'd been quiet—and now finally spoke, his voice a parched rasp that scratched against my back like talons. "*Irina* is the point. She's one of us, Shin."

Her name cut me in two, and I winced.

Irina *was* the point. She had been since that day at the Opera, since the moment my eyes opened and only saw her. And it was that same desire, that tunnel vision, that had gotten her into all of this. That had ripped her life apart and ruined all that she could have had. *I* ruined her. I had selfishly used her for my own gains, and then to coddle my own wounded heart.

I hung my head in my hands. Holding on to Irina would only serve to hinder her growth. To chop her at the stem and force her into a life on the run. To steal her from the power she was meant to wield, for the sake of all of Dunyas.

It was time to let go.

"We have been fooling ourselves, Nav. Ecei won't kill the Princess. She needs her. Dunyas will find out, and they will take care of it. But as long as we're with her, she's in more danger," I croaked, offering my friend one honest thought. He could still be angry with me, but he would see I was painfully *right*. "I only bring misery."

But Naveen didn't back down, like he usually did. Didn't throw a snide remark and saunter away, all bark, no bite.

No, Naveen stood straighter. Stared down at me, a deeply rooted tree that would not be shaken by a whining gust of wind. "Aya didn't think so. She loved you more than anything in this world. More than herself. And you're just going to let her die for nothing?"

"Fighting won't bring her back," I sneered, but it lacked my usual conviction, my voice reedy and thin against his booming baritone.

"No, but running won't, either." He clapped my shoulder, his strength knocking me back; but he held me firm in place, refusing to let me flee. "Aya loved Irina. Are you going to abandon her? Is that how you want to keep Aya's legacy alive?"

My throat bobbed, tonsils swollen and useless as tears pricked my eyes. "You don't understand."

"*I* don't understand?" Hurt flashed across his expression before it was replaced again with that immovable stone certainty. "You act like Aya wasn't special to all of us. Special to *me*. Who was it that took care of her medicine for years, Shin? Who was it that was there to make her laugh and smile? I loved her, too. You don't get to own grief."

I tried to find a caustic excuse, or a witty retort...one that would absolve or absent me. One that would let me withdraw back to the window, or would chase Naveen away. One that would let me linger in anger or apathy, both of them easier than anything else that threatened to climb out of the void in my chest.

But none came.

I didn't realize I was crying until the tears hit my hands, heavy raindrops that finally fell from the too-full clouds. Didn't realize until it was a thunderstorm of shaking sobs, until Naveen grabbed my head and towed it to his shoulder, letting me collapse into him. Holding me upright, like I had held him through the years. Like we had done for each other.

"I'm—"

"You're sorry, we know." He saved me from saying it as he patted my neck, a sigh rocking through him. Rocking me, like the blubbering babe I was.

He let me cry another moment, let me pour it all out. Let the hurricane pass, withstanding every withering exhale and battering sob.

Then, he gripped my shoulders and straightened me out. "But we don't need you sorry. We need you *smart*."

I wiped my eyes with my sleeve and nodded, a *thank you* and a *sorry* mixed in one.

I wasn't built to lay down and take it. Wasn't built for a life underground.

I was built to soar.

And I had to, for both me and my sister now.

Riku stood at Naveen's side, a hand on his shoulder. His expression went cold, waiting for his next signal. Waiting for me. "What's the plan, Shin?"

Ren matched his twin like his mirror image, the sun to his moon. "We're still following you."

Before I could answer, Naria cleared her throat, taking charge like the leader she was raised to be in my absence. "We need real support.

We need Father and the Dunyasians and the Sorans. We need to unite against this. It's bigger than *all* of us."

She wasn't wrong.

But she wasn't right, either.

War was a game that nobles played, but peasants suffered. An ideal that only furthered the pain already inflicted across Babylon, that only dug the knife deeper into its bleeding side.

"We don't know who we can trust," Riku challenged, that ice clashing against my sister's fire. "Irina's family might be in on it."

"You can trust us," Hana countered, a hand over her heart, and something in the crack of her voice made me believe. "Trust that we love Irina as much as you do."

But belief alone didn't win fights. It was the energy, but not the tool, that created change.

We needed to be smart. Clever. *Careful*.

"We do trust you two. But we can't just alert all of the royals in the world, not until we know who is in bed with Ecei," I said, conviction finally lacing my words.

Hana opened her mouth, but shut it again, unable to contest logic. Naria huffed, but dipped her head in agreement. "Father—the Jaltans aren't on her payroll, not after the revolution. They've lost the most in this."

"Fine," I conceded; no matter how much I dreaded seeing the man who'd sired me again, the Jaltan people were also just innocent victims of Ecei's manipulation and ambition. People like Davke, who'd just wanted to make a life for herself and have a family. "Then we need more intel, first. We can't just ask Father to storm the Winter Palace and demand Irina back. And we don't want to start a war if we don't have to. Only the small people suffer, and Irina wouldn't want it that way, either."

No, Irina would try to save everyone she could, even if it cost her her own freedom. She'd think of a solution and use her warmth and light to guide her through.

I might not have been good for her. I might have been a curse. I might have ruined her life six ways to the Breath and back.

But it was about time I saved *her* for a change. Then, she could choose my fate.

Naria crossed her arms and tilted her chin, the soldier again, not the Princess—awaiting orders. *My* orders. "What do you suggest, then?"

One last heist. One last recon mission. One last game.

The wind spoke the language of thieves, and it had taught me its ways.

It was time I stole back what was mine.

My princess. My title. My life.

The sun set the small room in gold as I peered one last time out the window, a larger blob of color glimmering in the distance.

My home.

I smirked as the first stages of the plan clicked into place, the wind murmuring its suggestions in my ear. "Hana, can you get us clearance to land this thing in Hiku City?"

TWENTY-EIGHT

IRINA

Flowers bloomed even after the coldest of winters.

It was a lesson I'd heard daily. A platitude I believed.

But the Maesters of Dunyas must have never known cold like this.

It chilled from the inside out, stiffening my limbs and aching deep in my bones. It chapped my skin, peeling me back layer by layer, cracking me open.

The bars to my cell were coated in a sheen of ice, too frozen to touch, lest I risk sticking to it. So I sat along the wall, and my bare thighs burned—*burned*—where they touched the blisteringly cold stone floor of the dungeons, a frost creeping along the damp walls that I thought would consume me, too. They hadn't given me anything to cover myself with, not even a pair of pants. I only had Shin's shirt, the thin fabric my only salvation against the endless, taunting cold.

My breath misted in front of me in shaky plumes.

"How long has it been?" I asked aloud, the first words I'd spoken in hours—or days, maybe. It was hard to tell, when this far north, all that existed was light and cold.

Not a single bloom or petal, nor the deep red leaves of autumn. Not a single, riotous speck of color out of the small hole that served as a window.

Just white.

Just cold.

Just death, in its snow-covered cloak.

I hoped that whatever death claimed Aya, it wasn't cold like this. I hoped it was sunny and warm, with willow trees she could sit under for shade and windflowers she could pick to decorate her hair.

And I hoped she was not alone. Hoped Nikolaj was there to tease and laugh and watch over her. To tell her it would be okay. To welcome her home, one lonely big brother to a new little sister.

From the other side of the cell, the sound of shifting dragged my attention as Malina curled further into herself. The ice had thawed around her little patch of stone, the fire drake at least able to warm herself, even though she looked just as miserable as I did.

"It doesn't matter."

From deep within, heat surged, an anger that boiled my blood ever so slightly as I turned to face her. We'd barely spoken since we'd been dumped here. Barely even looked at each other, the bloodstains on her knees too hard to see, her betrayal too fresh.

But I'd had enough of staying silent. If I was going to freeze to death in this cell with her, I'd make her suffer, too.

"What, was this not what you expected when you chose Ecei?" I snapped, though the sarcasm I'd intended was diminished by my chattering teeth and hoarse voice. "Congratulations, Malina. You got exactly what you *bargained* for."

She bared her teeth at me, but pulled her knees closer to her chest, the bloodstains a mar against the endless gray and white. "Shut up. This is all your fault, if you hadn't—"

"*My* fault?" I spit back, for once in my life happy to be fighting. It beat sitting here and letting the cold sap the life from me minute by minute. Beat holding all my anger and grief like ingested poison, the caustic taste eating me from the inside. Instead, I let it all pour out. "You know, I admired you. I thought you were the most capable girl I'd ever met. Thought you were so smart and wonderful and *useful.*

But I realize now you're exactly what I first assumed. A selfish, foolish *thief*."

I expected Malina to fire back, for her to tell me all the ways I'd failed my friends, too. All the ways I was just as complicit in Aya's death.

But instead, her mouth fell open. Her eyes flashed wide. And *tears* lined the corners.

Before she could respond, clacking steps sounded from down the hall. Malina shrank back into her corner, her curls a veil as she hid her face.

Fucking coward.

"Now, now, ladies, no need to bicker," Ecei teased as she stepped into view. She wore another one of her frost-touched dresses, the Ice Witch of the North never deviating from her chosen element. One hand curled around the frozen bar as she dragged her gaze over us. "Don't waste your energy. It doesn't seem like either of you have much left."

My voice was rough, but biting. "If you keep us here, we'll die."

Ecei's long fingernails rapped against the bar, the sound grating down my spine. "I'm hoping for it."

I folded my numb arms across my middle, but forced a grin—one Shin would be proud of. "How does that work with your plan to use my crown, hmm?"

"Good point." Ecei tapped her finger against her chin with a smirk, a cat playing with the caught mouse. "Let's talk options, shall we?"

I didn't dignify her with a response, clamping my jaw shut so hard, it almost cracked my frozen teeth.

But Ecei didn't need an invitation to speak—she held the room, and she wouldn't let us forget it. "My son needs a bride, and despite this setback, I do hope it's you. So I will give you two choices: you marry Drakkar, keep your mouth shut, and I let you live. You write a letter to your parents and say that you're happy, and you're sorry you ran away, but this is your true home now. And you stay here, under my watchful eye. Then, when Drakkar begins his ascension to the throne of Dunyas, you play along nicely."

She rattled it off like she was simply asking for me for a small favor, not demanding my life and compliance in a royal coup.

Like her son wasn't pond-feeding scum.

Like she hadn't just killed my first friend.

The laugh that bubbled from my chest held no humor, a dry, rasping sound that mimicked the wind battering the dungeons' exterior. "What's my other option?"

Ecei's eyes narrowed to slits. "I kill you. And I make it look like this little Jaltan spy," she jerked her thumb to Malina, "was to blame. Your parents will be left without an heir, yet they'll go to war with Jalta. And then when they finally destroy each other, the only person left to reassert order will be me. Drakkar can marry that pretty little idiot from Sora, and we can rule all four kingdoms."

I couldn't help the way my jaw dropped.

Ecei didn't just want the quiet, biological warfare she'd already unleashed on Babylon. She wanted carnage. She wanted to water the soil with the blood of anyone who wasn't hers.

She wanted to rule on a mountain of frozen corpses.

And she didn't have to lift a *finger*.

A dark chuckle shook her shoulders. "You see, I actually like that plan a lot better. 'Ruler of all Babylon' has a ring to it. But Drakkar has a soft spot for you, Irina, so I will offer you the mercy of a *choice*."

A chill—not from the cold—ran down my spine.

A choice—between life in a frozen cage, married to the son of a psychopath, or war. A choice between forfeiting my life, or condemning all of Babylon.

My fists clenched, tears freezing on my lashes as they pricked my eyes. "And when the whole continent is dead to the Blight and your war, who will be left for you to rule, Ecei?"

At that, she cocked her head, like she hadn't considered it.

"The Blight does not attack indiscriminately," she mused, but there was an edge to her tone, like the pointed end of an icicle. "It's the worst for those with certain qualities and genetic codes. At least, *most* of them. We are still refining it, though I will say the batch you and your friends destroyed was some of my team's finest work."

My head reeled as I tried to make sense of what she was saying... what she wanted...

But it was Malina who finally sat forward. Malina, whose head shot up with such force, I thought she'd break her neck. "It's deadliest for Controllers," she hissed, realization brimming in her moon-wide eyes. A smirk carved her face, the pixie finding her fire again. "But not all of them."

Ecei stilled. Paused, before brushing it off with a scoff. "Enough of them. The *strongest* of them."

My head spun as pieces fell into place.

The Blight attacked controllers...like Aya, like Nikolaj...

"But not Shin," I challenged, pride puffing my chest. *Or Kas, Avi, or Naria,* I thought, but I didn't say it aloud.

And Ecei flinched.

Malina jumped in, "Is that why you picked him for this mission? Figured he'd get killed along the way?"

"I don't know what you mean." Ecei shrugged, but there was something off about it, her face too blank, her hands too tightly clenched.

"You didn't realize he was Jaltan nobility," Malina barreled onward, a half-wild laugh pouring out of her.

At that, I blinked, confusion flooding me. Shin was half-Jaltan? A *noble?*

My heart thundered in my chest, so many little hints and moments replaying in my memory...

Finally, it all made sense. His disjointed family history, and all of his formal skills. His hesitancy to give me details about his father...who must have been Jaltan nobility.

Which meant Malina was *right.* Naria, Avi, Kas, and apparently Shin...they were all Jaltan. It had to be the link.

But Malina didn't wait for me to catch on as she continued her jabs. "You still don't understand what makes them immune. Which is why you sparked the rebellion—"

A hand slammed against the bars with a boom.

"You two have dawdled *enough,*" Ecei slashed through Malina's explanation with brutal efficiency, her voice dipping to a wintry rumble. Her gaze tore from Mal and settled on me, just as biting as the frost. "I take your avoidance as compliance?"

If you don't like the way things are, change them.

I would never be compliant again. But I would be s*mart.*

"I will marry Drakkar." I lifted my head, hating as the words poured out of me, but I did not balk. Did not falter. "But Malina stays with me. And we need to be moved into proper rooms, otherwise I'll die before I can play any of your silly games."

Malina's head swiveled to me so fast, I thought it would pop off, but I ignored her.

I didn't want to save her, not after what she did to Aya. Not after the way she'd treated me. But her fate was not mine to decide. Her justice—or her forgiveness—belonged to Shin.

Ecei considered me for a long moment, drawing out each rattling breath I took against the frigid air. But when I didn't stand down, she let out a sigh.

"Fair enough." She waved a hand, sneering at Malina. "You can keep your pet. I do like to see the guilt on her face, and I could use some Jaltan blood to examine. I'll have guards move you later."

She turned to go, like we were no longer worth her time, her amusement over.

"Why not move us *now?*" I called after her as I scooted forward, my legs too numb to fully stand. I hated how desperate I sounded, but with every shivering moment, I could feel my heart slowing, each breath more painful than the last as my body shook.

Ecei's steps slowed. She glared over her shoulder. "You made me wait. Now it's your turn."

Each click of her heels across the stone was a punch to the gut.

"Bitch," Malina murmured when she was out of earshot. She paced the room like a caged animal, her hurried steps heating the stone.

I snorted, envy and anger still potent in my veins, even as my life force faded. "I thought you were best friends."

Her pacing halted. She huffed out a breath. "I was wrong."

I blinked at her. She worried her lower lip between her teeth, like there was more she wanted to say, but couldn't.

I had plenty to share. "Doesn't feel so good, does it?"

At that, she threw her hands up. "Are you going to rub it in all night? Because if so, I'll call Ecei back now and beg her to kill me."

I thought about it for a moment. Considered.

But if I didn't like the way things were, it was up to me to change them. And I would be dead in the water without an ally right now, even one I wasn't sure I could trust.

I chose my words carefully, slowly. "If you die, how are we going to plot our escape plan together?"

"What?"

"Isn't that what you do? Plot and plan and tinker?" I gestured toward her, my hands aching with the movement. I had to get warm, fast. Had to be clever. "I know I'm not your preferred partner, but if Shin and the others are alive, they're going to need us, and we all need to unite against Ecei."

I extended a hand.

A truce.

A deal.

Malina stared at it for a long moment, a war splaying across her expression. We couldn't be more different, two opposite ends of a spectrum. But she had a brother to get back to, and I had one to honor, and that made us more similar than we could have imagined.

Finally, she grasped my hand, delicious warmth running down my arm at her touch. She frowned, but it didn't hold the same vitriol anymore. "You have a deal, Princess. But don't expect me to braid your hair."

I smiled.

Flowers bloomed even after the coldest of winters.

And despite the frozen prison surrounding us, despite the river of bad blood between us...

Malina and I had planted the first seeds.

"Deal."

The glorified broom closet Ecei tossed Malina and I in that night wasn't luxurious, though it was a far step above the freezing dungeon, the unadorned stone walls and dilapidated cots at least *warm*. But the lack of windows and tight quarters were wearing, a trapped-in feeling that I thought I knew well now challenging the very limits of my resilience.

If Anastova was a vase, this room was a coffin.

Built for *two*.

Malina and I had agreed to work together, but that didn't make us friends.

No, my first friend was dead because of her. Because of Ecei.

In the frozen dungeons, it'd been easy to forget when my body was focused on surviving the cold. When my mind was trapped in its own pain, too numb to feel anything.

But as the ice thawed from my skin, as my limbs prickled with returned sensation...

The tidal wave of anguish I'd been avoiding crested in my chest, stinging the backs of my eyes.

Aya was gone.

Tears watered the dry plains of my cheeks as the truth slammed into me. I knew I didn't have much of a right to be hurt—I'd only known her for a few weeks, my grief a mere shower to the storm Shin must've been weathering.

But I cried for what might have been; for the tea-time in the gardens of Anastova we might have shared, both of us admiring the greenery. For the late nights we might have spent whispering away about secret wishes and boys who made us blush. For the things she might have taught me, experienced despite being young as she was, and the things I might have offered her in return once we'd found the cure.

Each tear expended moisture I didn't have, but I didn't care.

Laying on my cot, facing the wall with my back to Malina, I cried and cried and *cried*. For Nikolaj, for all the lives Ecei had cut at the stems....

For Aya.

"Are you crying?" A hiss from the other bed pallet interrupted my silent sobs, her voice cutting and brutal.

Sadness made way for something sharper, a bite that rusted my next shuddering breath. "Shut up."

We'd struck a truce, but that didn't mean I had to like her, and my patience was utterly spent.

That didn't stop the next bitter scoff. "Missing home? Is prison not up to your standards?"

I'd never quite understood my mother's behavior after Nikolaj's death. Never understood her jagged, serrated edges or her unquenched heat, not when I was tear-logged and soggy with my grief.

But now, as a fire surged up my throat, I recognized the parts my mother gave me in my acidic tone, a near match for hers. "Missing my *friend*." I sat up, glaring at Mal through the darkness with all of that scorching Jaltan rage. "The one you got killed, remember?"

I'd wanted my blow to land, but Mal dodged it, lithe and light on her feet as always. Instead, she lit like a dry wick, like she'd been waiting for a fight, for someone to light the match and burn us both. A sneer carved her face in the dull lanternlight, shadows eating craters into her already gaunt features. "She was not your friend. She was just a kind stranger who took pity on you."

Pity.

The word cracked in my chest, blowing a crater through it. Of all feelings—rage, regret, sadness and fear—pity was the most offensive, its taste like bitter ash on my tongue.

Maybe Malina was right. I meant little to the Lost Ones in the grand scheme of their dynamics, and Aya had likely just been kind. But that small kindness—pity-driven or not—had been dear to me. More luxurious than anything Anastova could buy, more decadent than any of Tasha's sugar-crusted creations.

And it was just the tip of the iceberg that was Aya, her worth far exceeding what she'd meant to me.

My voice was quiet, my anger now pulsing low beneath the surface like the tunnels under a volcano.

Aya deserved better.

And now she was gone.

"She was practically your sister. And now she's *dead*."

I was expecting—maybe even hoping—for Malina to lash back.

Hoping to spar and stab until we were both spent, until we found a release for this festering grief that lingered in the room like a bad smell.

I wasn't expecting the glimpse of what I'd seen earlier in the dungeons—that small flicker of regret—to erupt into a blaze. Wasn't expecting Malina's tears, spilling over like the dam had burst. Wasn't expecting her quiet, "I know."

My fire died, doused by each droplet that hit her hands. "Are you—?"

"She was more than a sister," Malina gasped between shaking breaths, each more agonizing than the last. "She—her and Kas and Shin—we were a family. The only family I've ever had...and I—I—"

The last truth caught in another awful, earsplitting sob that rocked her entire body.

I stiffened in my seat, equal parts dumbfounded and understanding.

I didn't get Malina, but I knew that pain.

Bodies were easy to heal—made of sinew and muscle and bone, there were tangible building blocks to mend and stitch. Visceral, observable wounds that made identifying the hurt clear.

But hearts were harder to reach—their beats containing secrets that operated under no rhyme or reason, their hurts the invisible sort. And as Malina's cries shattered through the room, as her heart broke, so did mine, not just for Aya, but for the girl that now had to fall asleep every night with her sister's blood on her hands.

There was nothing I could do to ease her pain, just as there was nothing I could do to bring Aya back.

What would Nikolaj do?

Even if I couldn't take away her anguish...

I could sit with her in it, trapped in this prison together, our only option each other.

"I'd never had a friend before, you know," I opened up, and her next sob was quieter. My hands fisted in my rancid shirt—trying to stay the discomfort from leaking out of me, more weaknesses that Mal could exploit if she wanted to. But I pressed on, unafraid of my own vulnerability. "Not one that didn't prefer my brother, sad as that sounds. So even if she was just being nice, it mattered a lot."

Malina was silent for a long time—longer than I liked, exposed and bare as I felt with my words still hanging around.

But then her eyes snapped up, bloodshot and hazy.

"She did like you," Mal sniffled, tucking her legs up to her chest as she pressed into the stone wall—guarded, but returning my peace offering. "She smiled around you more than she ever did with me. I was always too harsh on her."

I didn't miss the wince, even in the dark.

I gnawed my lower lip. "You did your best to protect her."

"Until I didn't."

There was no arguing with the truth, no asking it to change its face or pretend, so I didn't. Nor did I try to comfort her with useless platitudes.

So I just sat in the silence after, our breaths in tune as awkwardness shifted, our unspoken truce striking through it.

We were lost, both of us. Wounded.

But at least we weren't alone.

It was a far cry from the imagined tea-times and slumber-parties I'd dreamt of with Aya, but the companionship unknotted something within me all the same. "Tell me what she was like, when she was younger."

Mal waited, deciding. *Remembering*, as she stared blankly at the wall. "Before she was sick, you mean?"

"Yes."

A small smirk beat away a falling tear. "No one in Babylon could keep up with her, not even Shin."

"Really?" Despite the twist in ribs, I let myself dream of it.

Aya, running along jewel-toned roofs, a windswept giggle echoing through Hiku City. Aya, outpacing Shin as he trailed after her...as I followed them both, out of breath and full of joy, like when I'd used to chase butterflies in the conservatory when I was young. Clumsy, but *free.*

Mal's voice dipped to a whisper, like her stories were more for her, now, each memory precious and painful. "We were always chasing after her. Always trying to keep up with whatever trouble she got herself into. But she was smart as all hell, and always fooled us. And she was good, too. She never hurt anyone."

I didn't miss the hitch to her breath at the last part, that single inhale saying all the words she still couldn't.

It's my fault.

I'd told her as much twice already.

But that no longer felt fair, and if we were going to make things right, my grief did not need to be the dagger I used to cut her deeper. Instead, I'd opt to try for what I did best:

Healing.

"I don't know what Jaltans believe..." I hedged before diving off the deep end. Hearts were hard to reach, but not impossible. Just as the dead were not truly gone, their legacies intangible but ever-present. "But in Dunyas, we believe Mother Earth takes our dead and brings them to the next life, where there is no pain. Where there is nothing but open space and warmth."

Space and warmth...and hopefully, Nikolaj to guide her along. To sit with her, so neither of them had to be alone anymore.

Mal said nothing as another tear rolled slowly down her cheek.

One that matched pace with mine.

Malina curled deeper in her cot—her back facing me again, our moonlit companionship fading into the shadows once more. But to my surprise, she whispered, "I hope you're right."

I did, too.

Twenty-Nine

I didn't even need to ask Tsojo, Madame Aheni, or Via for their help.

They'd volunteered. For Aya.

For Babylon.

For the honor of Hiku fucking City.

Yet as we gathered in the Tsojo's kitchen to hatch our plan, despite being surrounded by riff-raff and royalty alike—

I couldn't help but feel like a king missing his crown jewel.

A diamond in the rough that I'd sharpened and polished.

A friend who I'd leaned on in all ways, the spine that helped lift my head.

A fucking betrayer.

Mal.

"Shin?" Naveen snapped his fingers in front of my face and I came back to earth, blinking away the haze. "Focus, man."

"Sorry." I cleared my throat, straightening as I surveyed the gathered. Naria and Hana sat to my right, Naria's head guard, Joval, stalwart behind her. All of them looked as out of place as a bird in a burrow, but to their credit, they hadn't said a word as they politely snacked on the various fruits and cheeses Tsojo had laid out. On my other side, Ren and Naveen huddled together, comparing notes on our target's movement while Riku ate pastries like it was his only job.

Kas was still upstairs.

He's barely spoken or eaten in days.

Barely looked at me, like somehow he bore Mal's shame.

"You were saying, Shin?" Via asked, leaning her hand on her chin. Like always, those gold eyes saw too much.

I flattened the wrinkles in my tunic—*when was the last time I'd changed or slept?* It didn't matter. I had to figure this out. Had to weave a tight plan, otherwise more people could get hurt.

But no matter how I shifted the shapes in my mind, they would not click together, a puzzle that was missing its centerpiece.

Mal. The liar to my lure, the devil and damsel in one. The most versatile and vicious of us.

Even when she was stabbing us in the back like a fucking coward.

"We have a limited window of opportunity," I said hoarsely. "And too many variables. Any ideas on how we tighten up our odds?"

The others lowered their heads like schoolchildren hoping I wouldn't call on them.

Naveen shrugged. "You know me, I always like the risky bets."

Too risky for my blood, now. We had too high of a stake in this to lose again.

Madame Aheni coughed from the doorway, offering the closest thing to kindness she could muster: "I think the trap is smart. That pest has made it his mission to smoke me out of a Den."

"Getting him there is the trouble," Riku voiced my thoughts aloud, his icy tone sending a chill down my spine.

He was right. Once we had the mark in our clutches, we could manage. Naveen would handle the extras, Via and I would manage the mark, and Ren and Riku would watch our flanks outside in case anything else went south. Both of the royals would then offer auxiliary support once we had what we needed.

But I was fresh out of bait.

Naria shifted in her seat. "I could distract—"

"Absolutely not." I ended her sentence before she finished it, knowing the Princess had a penchant for bold and blunt that did not serve our purpose. We needed stealth and subtly, not Jaltan blood-red sticking out like a sore thumb. "You're too recognizable."

Naria flopped back in her chair, crossing her arms. She wasn't used to taking orders instead of giving them. Hana patted her shoulder, but the tension still grated against my exposed nerves.

I wasn't used to doing this on my own.

A cavernous pit opened in my chest, anger and betrayal and a surprising *absence* echoing in my gut.

I must have flinched, because Via stood, tossing her auburn hair over her shoulder. "Why don't we all take a little break? Come at this again in the morning."

The others looked to me—their leadless leader.

I had nothing for them.

I ran a hand through my hair, like it could somehow untangle the knots in my stomach. "Fine. Everyone get some rest."

Chairs scraped and shoes shuffled across floorboards as they all filtered out, even Madame Aheni dipping her head and slinking through the door.

Everyone but Via, who saw too much. Knew too well.

Grabbing a pastry, she prowled closer, shoving the food into my hand with a raised brow. "What's got your goat, Prince Shin?"

I took the croissant and popped it in my mouth, happy to chew instead of talk for a moment. But Via—never shy—nudged my side, demanding an answer.

"Nothing. This job is just important."

Her teasing grin poked through my shoddy response. "Survival has always been important. But you're off your game."

There was no use playing strong and silent, not with Via. I collapsed into my chair, head hanging. "I haven't played solo in a long time."

The truth misted out of me, a lonely, feeble breeze that shook my frame.

I wasn't alone—no Lost One ever was. But I was missing pieces of me that I'd relied on for too long—people who I trusted too much, despite my better judgment.

Via perched on the arm of my chair, rubbing soothing circles between my shoulder blades. "You mean without Aya? Or *Malina*?"

My head snapped up—too fast, too telling.

And the cave in my chest devoured me whole.

Anger clogged my voice. "Both of them are gone. What does it matter?"

Via's lips pursed as she paused. Her hand stilled on my back. "What Malina did was wrong, Shin. There is no denying that," she said, slipping off the chair and standing over me. "But it's okay to miss her."

Miss her.

"You are blind when it comes to her, and you always have been," I hissed, projecting my fury outward so it stopped eating me from the inside.

Via shot me a dark look, but said nothing. She didn't need to, not when she was *right*.

I did miss her. Hurt as I was. Betrayed.

I fucking *missed* my best friend. The little fire drake that made this operation work. The girl that challenged my stupidity and called me on my bluffs. The brainiac that could tinker her way out of any mess, and could think circles around the whole world.

Until she hadn't.

Until she'd killed my sister.

"I do miss her," I admitted out loud, more for myself than for Via. "But I'm too fucking angry to care."

But Via wasn't done poking beneath my exterior. Wasn't done reminding me of who I was. "Be angry, then. Fight it out like you always do. But it's okay to want to save her, too."

Save her.

Malina was capable. Consistent. A diamond in the rough, since the day I'd met her in the sewers. Since the day she'd escaped a caravan full of slavers with her toddler brother, all on her own, another refugee from the Jaltan revolution.

But perhaps I'd seen too much of her potential. Put so much pressure on her to handle herself that I hadn't seen the forest for the trees.

Hadn't seen the little girl, lost and afraid, who'd needed saving.

Then or now.

When I didn't speak, Via ruffled my hair. "Madame Tsojo said she'd let Kas stay with us for a while...keep him out of trouble, if you want."

Kas. Malina's reason for breathing. It was what had united us, back then. Two older siblings responsible for toddlers that weren't theirs, learning how to survive.

I'd been so afraid for Aya, I'd forgotten that Mal might have been just as foolish as I had been when I'd accepted Ecei's deal. Just as desperate to protect Kas.

Kas, who had a knack for finding trouble and staying hidden.

Kas, who had all of Malina's stealth and strength. All of her fire.

Kas, who was always trailing at my heels, ready to prove himself. Ready to learn.

Kas, who had the stickiest fucking fingers in all of Hiku City.

Kas, who'd want a chance to save his sister, even if it was from herself.

"No...he needs some fire back under him right now," I said as I stood, the last lost piece clicking into place. "And I think I have an idea."

One that would hopefully save both Irina...

And my best friend.

Sadness clung to the room at the back of Tsojo's place like dust, a dry, aching aura that scented every inhale with the same heaviness. Still, there was no more putting this off, no more dawdling downstairs or up on the roof.

Lost Ones never suffered alone.

My knuckles kissed the door in three gentle raps. "Kas? Can I come in?"

Muffled sounds—a bed frame creaking and the brush of blankets being pulled higher—leaked through the gap beneath the door.

Then, a sniffled, "Go away."

A pang shot through my chest, but I pressed on. I'd already lost too many people in the last few days to let my littlest charge waste away.

"I have noodles," I said as I cracked the door, letting the smell of the savory pork broth and spring onions waft in and chase away the sadness.

Having Mal and I for role models had made Kas stubborn as he was sneaky. But no one could resist my noodle soup; it was a cure to all ills, and a rich bribe.

Kas sat up in the bed, eyes bloodshot and puffy, nose runny...

And licked his lips.

I took the win, stepping into the room with the steaming bowl and spoon before shutting the door behind me. Slowly, like someone might approach a wounded animal, I crossed the space, setting the bowl down on the small table next to the sad excuse for a bed.

Kas barely let it touch the wood before he snatched it up, forgoing the spoon and sipping directly from the side.

My heart ballooned in my chest as he sipped again, this time using the spoon to siphon noodles into the bite as well. He slurped the long strands up like a man starved—like the answers to all our questions waited at the bottom of the bowl.

Maybe they did.

I let him finish before I said anything, just in case; I didn't speak until every last noodle and bean sprout had been scoffed down, until he sat back against the wall with his stomach full and his shoulders eased.

"Ready to talk about it, kid?

Kas set the empty bowl back on the table and wiped his mouth with his sleeve. Brown eyes finally snapped up to me, tears welling in their corners. "Do you hate me?"

"*What?*" I scooted closer, resting my hand on his knee, but he brushed me off. Pain lanced my chest from the inside out. "*Kas,* why would I hate you?"

His throat bobbed, words breaking like glass against concrete as he clipped them out. "She's my *sister*. I should've known."

Sobs cracked out of him, each one shattering against my eardrums. His breath drew short—weak, shallow gasps that stung to listen to.

Kas, who had always been so small.

Kas, who had somehow grown when I wasn't paying attention, his limbs long and gangly as he collapsed into my side.

"Hey, look at me." I grasped both sides of his face, willing air into his lungs in slow pulls. In and out, slow and deep. "*Breathe*, Kas. This is not on you. Mal made a choice."

Another shuddering breath. "Mal chose them over *us*."

Mal, who'd always been my team, my family.

Mal, who'd been the spine of this operation, the backbone we all gained support from.

Mal, who'd stopped needing me a long time ago, yet still stayed because it was familiar.

I shook my head. "Maybe. But I think she was trying to protect us, in her own way." My voice was small, muted by the rage that still lived in my veins. Whether or not I could understand Mal didn't mean I'd ever forgive her for what she did. But it quieted Kas all the same, his next breath deeper. "It doesn't make it right, but it makes it under-standable."

At that—Irina's phrase, not mine—the shaking stopped. Kas exhaled, his last tear drying against his cheek, the little firecracker evaporating it with less than a thought.

Then, his head fell to my shoulder. And his arms wrapped around my middle.

I couldn't remember the last time I'd held him like this—perhaps a few years back, when his friend who lived down the street moved to Qara without a goodbye. Or perhaps the year after, when he and Mal had a spat and she'd called him a turd-eater, which hurt him more deeply than any of us anticipated.

But it didn't matter. No matter how old he got or how silly the problem was, I'd still be here, waiting with open arms.

I held him like that for a long time; long enough for the room to tint from sunset orange to twilight blue. Long enough for me to memorize the way Kas's overgrown form felt, my little brother not so little anymore. Long enough for Kas's next words to come out on a single, steady breath. "This is all so *fucked*."

I whacked the side of his head. "Hey, language."

"Oh, please." He snorted, but squeezed me tighter. "I miss her."

I winced, but didn't back down. This was what I came here for—the fire I needed this Pyromental to help me light. "What do you say we get her back?"

Kas shot up, tugging away. *"What?"*

"I have a plan." Or at least, the outline of one, though I didn't say that aloud. "But without Mal, I'm going to need a right-hand person. Perhaps a little firecracker."

Kas's eyes went wider than the moon gleaming outside, and his smile—the first in days—lit the whole room like daylight. "Really? You'll let me help?"

I pinched his cheek—something I'd never give up no matter how old he got. "I need you, kid."

Tears threatened to spill, but I didn't see them fall as Kas toppled me into another hug, his ash-and-floral smell clinging to his curls like the last tells of boyhood still lingering in that smile of his. "Thank you, Shin."

I hugged him back, not knowing how much longer he'd let me do it. Not knowing what else we'd lose to this brewing war, to the tasks we still had ahead.

But I would not walk the road ahead alone.

My family would be at my side, step for step.

The wind shifted, a hiss and a sniffle from outside the door alerting me to the other lost souls waiting beyond the threshold.

Pulling back, I winked at Kas; then, loud enough so the others could hear; "Are the three of you going to stand outside eavesdropping all night? Or are you coming in?"

The door flew open, Ren, Riku, and Naveen tripping over each other in a flurry of scuffs and curses as they toppled into the room.

I grinned despite myself. *Idiots.*

Ren stood first, brushing off his trousers. "Thank the Breath. Naveen was getting gassy out there."

"Don't blame me, you little shit." Naveen pinched Ren's side as he stood, earning a single-fingered salute from Ren before he dove onto the bed, shoving Kas.

"Scoot over, kid."

"Ohh, Ren, come *onnn*," Kas groaned as Ren wrapped himself around the boy, stealing more than half of the threadbare blanket. A whimper built in Kas's throat. "Riku, *help.*"

Riku offered a pitying grin, his hand splaying over his heart in false sincerity. "Wish I could, buddy."

But he instead perched on the end of the bed next to me, giving his twin a wide berth and leaving Kas to his mercy.

Kas shot Riku a look of pure betrayal as Ren's grin broadened, unopposed victory claiming his face as he snuggled closer. "You know I need cuddles to sleep."

A mistake.

"Good." Naveen wiggled his eyebrows. "Then make room."

And in a giant leap, Naveen tackled us all, the bed creaking under the added weight.

A chorus of groans punctured the quiet as the boys all kicked and adjusted, myself included, until we were a pile of limbs: Ren, wrapped around Kas like a second skin; Riku, back to his twin, wedged between him and the wall; Naveen, stretched across their feet with his hanging off the edge; and me, tucked into the uppermost corner, a crescent above them all.

Uncomfortable as it was, something eased in my chest.

The world felt smaller when I wasn't so alone in it. When I had warm bodies to elbow me in the middle of the night and soft snores to disrupt the uncomfortable silence. When I had my friends, my family, to share it with, triumphs and tests alike.

It didn't take long for us all to settle—for shallow breaths to drag deeper. For alert eyes to weigh heavy. For the moon to completely replace the sun with an easy, softer light, allowing us all a much-needed moment in darkness's gentle embrace.

"Let's get our girls back, yeah?" Naveen breathed, amber eyes locking on mine even in the dimness.

I nodded, a lump forming in my throat.

Our girls.
Irina...and Mal.

It should've been Aya, too, something I didn't know if I could forgive or forget. Something that still stung too deep to think about for more than a moment. But that didn't mean I would forsake the others just because I couldn't save her.

Mal would have hell to pay for what she did. For her fuck-up. But that was my debt to claim, not Ecei's.

"Deal."

And despite all that weighed on us, despite the things we were running from and toward, despite the people missing from our hearts and from the bed...

I slept like a baby, surrounded by the Lost Ones who always found me again.

THIRTY

It had been all too easy to lure Drakkar back to Madame Aheni's.

Too easy for Kas to corner him in the market just outside of Uma City—a seedy little sister to Hiku. Too easy, for him to slip the coupon for 'FIRST SIX PIPES ON THE HOUSE' into one of his bodyguard's pockets undetected–and steal the Prince's seal.

Too easy for Hana to send a missive to the Prince himself about perhaps visiting her in the famous Sora Sky Palace during his travels. Too easy, for her to give him an excuse to linger in Sora just a little longer.

Too easy for Naveen to forge a raven note with the stolen seal and send it to Ecei, informing her that his travels would be delayed by yet another few days.

Desire and duty. The vice and virtue that even a prince could never escape.

The two tools we used to snare him.

Of course, the princeling hadn't returned home to Nehir yet. Like many of the other young nobles, he'd extended his revelry on the way back from the Masque, letting his greed and gluttony take him on a slow crawl through Dunyas and Sora. And though he'd already blown past Hiku City by the time we formulated our plan…

Desire and duty.

He'd answered the call.

And so did we, our stage set and our music selected.

I watched from the corner of Madame Aheni's den, my senses on high alert as I listened to every shift in the wind's tune. The smoky haze hid me from view as I perched in the upholstered booth, a cloak pulled over my head, but my eyes keen as ever.

I wouldn't let my friends get hurt. Not tonight.

Never again.

The den was relatively empty tonight, thanks to Aheni turning away everyone except for her trusted regulars to avoid extras getting caught in the crosshairs. She'd even rearranged some of the gaming tables to create a makeshift 'VIP' section, cordoned off by deep red silks draped over gilded poles.

The perfect atmosphere for a princeling looking to shirk his duty and feed his desires.

Right on cue, Drakkar, one of the twin bodyguards, and the smaller redheaded fellow from our first interaction swaggered in with gleeful smiles on their faces—happy to let Aheni act as if the world revolved around them.

It was a challenge not to pummel him the second he stepped in the room.

How dare he enjoy himself while Babylon suffered? How dare he walk and talk and breathe when my sister was dead? When Irina was trapped by his mother somewhere, in Breath-knew what condition?

But my friends—*Irina*—were counting on me to use my head instead of my wicked parts. So I kept my rage on a tight leash, making room for my cleverest bits to lead.

Liar and lure. Damsel and devil.

The con written into the law of this city. Stitched into the fabric of my being.

Naveen was the lure today, a role he favored as he won hand after hand at cards—by cheating, of course—setting Drakkar on edge. The blond prince's distress grew as Naveen's smirk did, and when Drakkar slammed a particularly bad losing hand onto the game table, the curtain lifted.

Our signal.

One last ruse.

Via nodded from her position across the bar before sauntering toward the prince, her hips swaying like the smoke wafting from the Poppy Dust pipes. Her costume was well selected, the tight-fitting, Nehir-blue dress sharp against her warm skin and auburn hair. A true professional, she caressed her painted fingers across his back to get his attention. "Why don't you come play with me instead?"

"Not now." Drakkar waved her off, jaw grinding as he clutched another losing hand. "Not until I'm back up."

Via swiveled around him, planting her backside on the edge of the gaming table. "I can help—"

Her voice cut off as her back went stiff.

She went utterly still, until the redheaded man to Drakkar's left nudged her with his elbow, grunting something that sounded like 'get lost.'

She did, quickly scurrying away back toward the bar. And just like that, the wind's tune changed to a dangerous thrum.

Something was *wrong*.

I'd never seen Via drop her performance before, not even with the most vile, pot-bellied old farts that frequented Tsojo's brothel. Not even with the foul-smelling regulars that catcalled her with terrible words that made most people's skin crawl.

I was up in another second, hugging the walls as I threaded my way to her.

She fell into a seat at the corner of the bar, hands shaking against the countertop as she signaled the bartender for a drink.

My hand found her back—and she *flinched*.

The terror fled as she spun and recognized me, but her normally glowing skin still paled to corpse-gray.

I reached out again—slowly, this time—to rub her shoulder. "What's wrong?"

Her trembling hand braced my forearm, nails digging into the skin like the contact was the only thing stopping her from unraveling entirely. She looked past me—to Drakkar—and she somehow paled further, rivaling fresh snowfall. "That's...that's *him*, Shin."

My blood ran colder than the Nehirite mountains. I needed no clarification, the horror in Via's eyes telling a story no words could capture.

I swallowed back the ugly abuse I wanted to shout on my friend's behalf, my voice dipping instead. "Vox's...?"

Via forced her gaze back to me. A single syllable quivered out of her. "Yes."

Drakkar wasn't just the prick that hit on Irina. Wasn't just the bastard of the deadliest bitch in Babylon.

He was the one who'd left Via broken and bloodied in that room at Madame Tsojo's last spring. The one who forced himself on her, the one who took advantage of her in the most violent, *violating* ways...

The one that sired her son—and left them both to rot.

A dark, vicious thing grumbled in my stomach as the tether on my fury snapped. "I'm going to kill him."

Via's nails dug deeper, rooting me in place before I could rip Drakkar's lungs from his chest. "Don't you *dare*," she growled before sucking in a deep breath. Her shoulders straightened as the shaking stopped. "I can do this. I *have* to do this. I just need a moment."

I placed my hand over hers and squeezed tight. "But you don't have to. We'll find another way."

And I would, even if it cost me my life. Irina wouldn't want to be saved at the detriment of Via's wellbeing. Neither of us would ever ask her to face the monster that haunted her dreams.

Plans changed like the wind, and Via would not be Drakkar's victim ever again.

But steel lined her spine as she sat up. As her jaw clenched, and those molten eyes hardened to stone. "No. This is for Aya...this is for *me*." She lifted her chin, the shaking gone, replaced with an indomitable spirit that would not be stamped out by any man's lust. Snagging the shot glass from the bartop, she tossed back the liquid in a single swig, and stood. "I want this bastard to *pay*."

She didn't give me a chance to protest as she stalked back toward the table, giving Naveen the signal.

He raised a brow, but didn't object, purposefully folding his hand. "That's it, I'm out."

Liar and lure. Damsel and devil.

My pulse racing, I slunk back to my seat with the best vantage point, watching Drakkar with a new predatory focus.

"There we are!" He banged the table as he whooped his victory chant. "I won, *Kurniv.* Pay up."

Naveen faked a frown as he pushed his chips toward him. "All yours, sir."

Drakkar clapped his redheaded friend on the shoulder, before calling out to the bar, "Another round, wench!"

I watched Via take another deep breath. Watched her paint on a smile.

Then I watched her pounce, her weapons refined and deadly.

She ran a hand through his hair, leaning over him to emphasize her curves. "How about I tempt you with something sweeter?"

My stomach lurched as he ran his gaze over her, hungry and horrible. I gripped the edge of the table hard enough to crack it as he licked his lips. "You're hungry for it, aren't you?" He tucked an arm around her waist as he pushed back his chair, staring down at her with wolfish intent. "Fine, let's go have some fun."

Drakkar might have been a wolf, but Via was a snake. And she would sink her venomous fangs in with a blood-red grin if given the chance.

Via's throat bobbed, but she didn't drop her smile. Or her strength. "Follow me."

It took all I had not to leap after them as they wound their way through tables, headed toward Aheni's stock rooms. All I had, to keep my eyes on Drakkar's friends instead as Naveen tempted them into another round. All I had, not to end it all here, to watch with sick delight as Drakkar choked on his last breath.

But just as Via had managed her emotions, I checked mine. I *waited.*

Once Naveen flashed the signal, I chased after them, a breeze cloaked in shadows.

I gave Via fifteen minutes—the agreed upon time—to do her

work. And I counted every second, my back pressed against the stock room door, my breathing shallow and quiet as I listened to the mumbled voices within.

If there was any indication that he took it too far, even the slightest squeak or yelp from Via, I'd unleash hell.

But there was just muted conversation—some sloshing noises that turned my stomach—a chuckle here and there...

Until at minute thirteen, a thump sounded, and I moved, bursting through the door ready to kill. "Are you—?"

"I'm fine," Via held up a hand, a genuine grin breaking across her face—a snake well fed. I scanned the space—the small stock room empty save for the crates piled up along the sides, and small wooden pallet with a thick blanket draped over it in the center.

A blanket that wrapped around the very unconscious, half-naked Prince Drakkar.

Via—still fully clothed— slipped a tiny vial from her dress pocket, the red juice inside sloshing against the glass container. "Those drugs Naveen and Aheni cooked up are strong. He's out cold."

I took the glass, examining its half-empty state with a peaked brow. "Naveen said to only use a drop."

Via shrugged, her smile turning sinister. "He'll sleep it off."

It was a far kinder fate than he deserved, but it would work. I kissed her on her forehead, pride swelling through me. Though I'd always be there if she called on me, Via didn't need anyone to protect her.

She was a goddess of vengeance in her own right.

Breath above, I prayed Vox would take after her more than his father's side.

"Did you get what we needed?" I tucked the vial into my cloak, brandishing my dagger instead as I stared past her to the useless lump behind her. Drakkar's breaths were full and weighted—better than he'd earned. Better than my sister had. "If not, I'm happy to torture the rest out of him."

"You know me." Via tapped the edge of my dagger with her pointer finger, forcing me to lower the blade. She slipped her other hand into her cleavage and pulled out a small roll of parchment. "I don't fail."

I took the letters from her, sheathing my dagger so I could unroll the tight coil.

The first one—penned in elegant script—had my heart running in my chest.

Ecei was a terror to Babylon, but she was human. She had her vices that consumed her, had soft spots we could press. Desires and duties.

Her son.

And now I had the information I needed to make her squirm.

Tears lined my eyes as I glanced back at my friend. "You're a blessing from the Breath, Via. When this is over, I promise you'll be safe."

She stroked my face, her stare just as glassy. "Go get 'em, Prince Shin."

Thanks to her, I would.

"Get moving, boy. I'll deal with the prick when he wakes up." A voice like hurricane winds and poppy haze rumbled behind us, and I whirled to find Aheni standing in the doorway, her ageless form silhouetted by the lowlights behind her.

I dipped my head to the woman who had saved me from the streets, and who'd time and again let me bring trouble to her door. "I can't thank you enough."

"Hiku City looks out for each other." She gripped my shoulders, her hands strong for her age, before pulling me in for a quick, tight hug. "We all should've been more help to Aya."

I stilled for a moment, my sister's name a lance in my side.

But then my arms lifted, and I was hugging Madame Aheni back. Hiku City was my home, and these people were my family. More so than those waiting for me on the other side of this con.

"You did everything you could," I whispered before letting go, swallowing down the lump in my throat. Choking down my fear, instead rooting myself in something stronger. Something bolder and brasher.

Revenge. Retribution.

By the time I stepped back into the Den, both of Drakkar's men were slumped over the gaming table, drool leaking from their open maws, their cups spilled next to them as Naveen filched through their pockets.

My friend's smile was all teeth and dark promises. "Took you long enough. Ready for some payback, Prince Shin?"

Thirty-One

IRINA

Planning an escape was a lot harder than Shin made it look.

"You're pacing again," I snapped at Malina, which was admittedly impressive, given the space.

She huffed as she wore tracks into the stone. "It's good exercise."

"You're driving me insane."

"Good, welcome to the club."

I bit my tongue, the only measure to my swirling anxiety. We'd been at it like this for days—cooped up, our patience and sanity withering without sunlight or fresh air. Our tolerance for each other was just as frayed as the blankets on our respective cots.

And though we'd struck a deal to work together, we'd yet to strike gold, our ideas feeble at best and ridiculous at worst as we tried to figure out a way to climb out of our own tomb.

And we had to get out. Because I could not stay in much longer. Not with Mal, or with my own thoughts.

I fiddled with my dress—a plain, gray slab of fabric that Ecei had a maid bring in the day before when Shin's t-shirt had gone positively rank. Still, I'd cried when she took it from me, so much so that the poor servant promised she'd return it tomorrow.

It was the first bit of kindness the Winter Palace had offered.

Which sparked a half-formed idea.

"What if we pay off a guard or a servant?" I mused aloud.

Malina waved me off, her pacing unfettered. "Ecei probably has them all by the short and curlies."

"The what?"

At that, Malina stopped to glower. "Breath above, Princess, you need to get out more."

And then started again.

"I don't know, I'm trying!" I groaned, flopping back onto my cot and covering my eyes with my forearm, as if the pressure would chase the headache from my temples. We'd been down a hundred of these roads together already, all of them coming up dead ends. "It would be better if you let me in on whatever you're thinking, and we could—"

"No." She silenced me with a brutal slash, but when I shifted my arm to roll my eyes at her, the tears welling in hers stayed my retort. Malina shook as she inhaled deeply. "*No.* This is my fault. I have to do it alone."

The door banged opened before I could respond. Before I could tell her that neither of us had to be alone ever again.

And in sauntered Ecei with a look that could freeze hell itself. "Well, ladies, we need to have a *conversation.*"

I said straight on the edge of the cot, even as the knot tangled in my gut. "I have nothing to say."

"Then you'll listen," Ecei hissed as ice shot from her fingertips, snaring Malina and I by the middle. Cold bit through thin fabric, pinching and stinging, but it did nothing to freeze the dread that still sloshed through me as Ecei stalked to Mal, teeth bared while the fire user struggled against the restraints. Ecei's voice churned like an angry sea. "*Where is my son?*"

Shock smashed into me like a snowball to the face. What the hell did Drakkar have to do with this? I hadn't seen him since the Masque, and neither had Shin or the others. Was he missing?

Did Ecei think Shin had him?

"How the fuck should we know?" Mal spat, and for once, I knew this wasn't a bluff. Wasn't another ruse.

Ecei didn't seem to care.

Her hand lashed out, grasping around Mal's throat. "Watch your tone. You are not *necessary* to this, am I clear?" Mal coughed and sputtered, her face blotting red, as the Queen squeezed tighter. "Let me ask again. Where is my son?"

Panic flared in my hummingbird pulse.

I'd never seen war, but I'd seen death. And Ecei wore its face today.

If we didn't give her an answer, she would kill Malina.

I dug deep for my last brave parts, scrounging up the seeds of the rebellion my brother had planted in me. "Probably drunk and hitting on someone who doesn't want to talk to him in a bar," I sneered—drawing Ecei's attention.

Ecei whipped to face me, and her grip slackened, Mal wheezing in gasping breaths.

"No more jokes," Ecei growled, her full vitriol turned on me as she slipped a hand into her pocket and yanked out a crumpled paper. "I know your little friends have him. I received this by raven today."

Letting go of Mal, her fingers unfurled the note in aggressive tugs, until the writing inside was legible.

Just two lines of text.

Two lines that sent my heart fluttering.

A prince for the princess, and we're even.

Meet us at the border in three days.

I didn't need to have seen his handwriting to know who'd written it. He was there, in the direct swagger and the messy script. There, in the word *even*, a taunt of our promise that called to me.

That let me know he was coming. One rescue for another.

Even.

"We don't know anything about their next steps," Malina croaked as she found her voice again. "You took us from them, remember?"

Ecei didn't like that answer. She crumpled the parchment in her fist and pelted it at Mal's face as she prowled closer again, murder written in her features. "But you know them well enough to know where they would take him."

Mal's jaw clenched as she considered.

Decided, whether or not to betray the Lost Ones again.

But I wasn't giving her the chance this time.

"Dunyas," I piped up.

Ecei waved me off. "I wasn't asking you."

But I would not be deterred. I would not let Mal make the choice, or let Ecei pry it from her.

I would no longer be someone things happened *to*.

I would be the happening.

"I know better than the traitor. You saw Shin and I the morning you grabbed us." The memory was a punch to the lungs, but I pressed on, mixing truths and lies just as Shin would. "They're going to Dunyas. I told him if there was ever trouble, my parents would take him in. He has my seal to get in safely."

If Shin was smart, he wouldn't touch Dunyasian soil until he knew who his friends were. He'd be hidden somewhere in Hiku City, under everyone's noses, or even holed up in the mountains, waiting for this storm to pass.

Then he'd soar, far, far away.

Ecei scoffed, but I saw the faint glimmer of uncertainty that passed through her icy eyes. "Your mother would never—"

"Would never help because she betrayed the Jaltans?" I cut her off with a fake smirk I stole from Shin. Ecei's declaration in the cabin had rocked something deep within me—a reality I'd been denying for too long. My mother had an agenda that I would never understand, had likely been a player in the conflict that had begun the shattering of Babylon, and I knew better than most that she was capable of darkness. But I also knew how to lie now. New how to pretend I was in on the secret. I didn't need Ecei to believe me fully. I just needed her to *doubt*. "That just means she's likely willing to betray you too, you know."

Ecei inhaled sharply like she could smell the bullshit wafting off of me, her mouth curving as she stuck a hand to her hip. "Your mother was the one that let them in, you know. The Sorans that stole King Odion's little tramp. She's the one who led them to the Opera House. As a *favor* to me." She sauntered closer, leaning in so I could smell the peppermint on her breath as her voice rumbled like the low tide. "And *she's* the one who approached me with the deal that decided that you and Drakkar should be paired."

An ache that could have folded me in two hammered low in my gut.

She'd always been controlling. Bitter. Hot and oppressive, a sweltering presence that crept up along my back and weighed me down.

But apparently I wasn't the only one she wanted to tear up from the roots. Her vengeance started with her homeland, with the people that gave her the fire that ran in her veins and denied her a chance to use it.

I swallowed roughly, fear pricking up my spine as my ruse died before it had the space to fly. I might have been able to mimic Shin's snark and tone, but I didn't have the same mind for rebellion he had.

But his partner did.

Mal winked at me as she baited Ecei with a taunt. "But that was *before* Irina fell for the lost Jaltan heir."

A pause. Ecei went utterly still. "*What?*"

"You really didn't know, did you?" Mal cackled, the sound percussive and dry like logs snapping in a brutal fire. "Rashin of Jalta *lives*. And he's on the way to Dunyas with the Princess's seal, with your scoundrel son in tow, and a peace treaty signed by Princess Naria and King Odion."

I did everything I could to keep the shock from registering on my face.

Everything I could to keep my jaw from scraping against the floor, to keep my pulse from sprinting.

Shin...No, *Ra*shin of Jalta.

Not just nobility. Not just a forgotten son.

The lost heir.

The *Prince.*

At one time, the only rival to my brother's power in Babylon.

All at once, everything clicked together.

"And they have the evidence that you're in charge of the Blight," I piggybacked off Mal's declaration, using it to fuel my own. "If you think my mother is ruthless now, just wait until she finds out you *killed* her son. She might not love me, but she loved him."

I didn't mean for that truth to come rolling out, but it did.

My mother loved Nikolaj more than anything. More than herself, which was a feat. He'd had all of her attention, all of her praise. All of her doting affection and fierce protectiveness. I didn't know for sure, but I would bet all the gold in Anastova that she'd wanted Shin out of his way, the only other male royal Controller of our generation—too great of a threat to her son's future rule.

And she would not hesitate to take Ecei out too, once she found out about the Blight.

Ecei's face blotted red. Her fists clenched at her sides. "You both are bluffing."

Mal smiled at me—a coconspirator's grin that felt like the first stitch of a plan. "You *hope*."

"I've had enough of the games!" Thunder erupted from Ecei as frost burst from her palms, coating the edge of my cot in frigid cold. I flinched back, but Ecei marched for the door, snapping her fingers so the ice encasing us both puddled in an instant. "You both can rot here while I sort out this mess. And when I get back, you'll wish you'd cooperated."

The door slammed shut so hard behind her, the hinges groaned. But my quick heartbeat was not thrumming to the song of fear...

But of war.

Of victory.

I might have been a flower all my life, but I had thorns, too.

And I would stick in Ecei's side until it drove her to madness.

Malina stretched her chilly limbs, that grin unwavering. "Looks like we just found our opening, Princess."

This time, I couldn't help but smile back. "No; looks like we *made* it."

Thirty-Two

The black iron gates of Solyra Palace had been intimidating as a boy, but staring up at them as a man—as a prodigal son returned—I couldn't help but feel small. Built to face the setting sun, the early morning rise currently cast us in the palace's long, deep shadow, its carved face silhouetted against the harsh rays.

"Don't worry." Naria's hand squeezed mine, an equally tiny smile on her face that was meant to reassure.

It didn't.

If only it were as easy as worry. If only the jumbled pit in my stomach was just a case of nerves, the anticipation before a con or the held breath before a freefall.

No, this was deeper, something over a decade old and far more powerful.

Rage. Resentment. And beneath that...

Regret. For the way I'd left things.

Remorse. For the life I might have lived instead.

But I didn't have time for any of that, not with Irina's life in Ecei's hands. Not with Babylon in her clutches as well.

Leaving the others with Hana in the airship, Naria led me through the winding black-top path, but I needed no guide. I remembered every step of the stone road. Heat rose in hazy tendrils as it scorched through my soles, a brand on every pair of feet that dared walk along it, the sun beating down on us with equal vigor. Until the Solyra loomed above us, a fortress built of the same heat-trapping stone. Spiked towers jutted toward the sun in angry lines, like they were in constant contest with its jagged heat.

Home, sweet home.

But before I could truly stall and admire its...*beauty*...the metal doors swung open with a spine-curving creak, and out stepped the true monolith of the Solyra.

King Odion wore the same red and black uniform as his guards, except for the gemstone buttons that lined the front—mined from the Helsin Mountains—and the crown cut from pure rubies that sat heavy atop his head, just as it had when I was young.

But the man before me now held nothing of the General and King I'd once known. Gone were the smooth planes of his face, his skin sagged and sunken, wrinkles weighing his brow with worry. Gone was the dark, clean beard that framed his strong jaw, replaced by a ragged nest of hair that hadn't seen a trim in weeks.

Gone was the menacing hazel stare—instead, those green-brown eyes filled with tears as he beheld me.

As he took a single step, and let loose a *sob*. "*Rashin*—"

"It's Shin now," I interrupted. Because the scared little boy named Rashin was gone, too, cremated along with his mother in the fire.

Because I did not know the version of the man before me, as he knew nothing of me.

He held out a shaking hand, but then gathered the sense to drop it, letting it hang awkwardly against his side. He swallowed. "Look how you've grown."

A breeze cooled the back of my neck, the only temper to my growing discomfort.

"Fourteen years will do that," my tongue lashed before I could tame it. "You've aged."

The corner of Odion's mouth twitched—a dimple appearing in

the corner, one of our few similarities—like he was trying not to let himself smile, but failed. "Luckily for you, you favor your mother's heritage."

He turned, headed back for the doors, which was a stroke of luck for us both; because at the mention of my mother, my stomach turned to Jaltan stone.

The man before me might not have looked like my domineering, overbearing father. Might not have looked like the man who taught me to hold a sword and slash down my enemies. But he had been once.

And he was at fault for my mother's death.

Still, I followed him into the castle, the wave of nostalgia exploding through me like a wall of fire.

The halls I ran through as a child were colder now—fewer servants bustling about, fewer candelabras lit along the gray slab walls—but it still smelled the same, the breeze wafting the char-and-metal scent until it stung my nostrils. Our shoes echoed against the merciless flooring despite the deep red runners that led us to our destination—a sound that had often gotten me in trouble as a boy, until I learned to quiet my own footsteps with the wind.

When we made the left-then-right combo into the throne room, the familiarity drowned me.

Odion's throne terrorized the dais, the spiked metal chair forged in fire to match the Solyra's exterior, a hulking mass meant to intimidate. It was enormous, even when empty, just as it had been when I was young. As it had every time I'd knelt before it, apologizing for one failure or another.

Queen Katia sat on her throne next to it, a slightly smaller version made of the same material. Her black dress hugged her skeletal form— so much smaller now, like age and grief had eaten away at her from the inside. Gray streaked her dark hair, and her normally apathetic features —a flat affect that Naria shared—were twisted in a complex expression I couldn't name, some mix between sadness and fear that seemed entirely unbefitting of the Queen.

Instead of climbing onto the dais and taking his throne, my father stepped to the side, leaning against the presentation table they used for gifts and documents—and lowered his crown onto it.

I blinked as I registered the odd movement, but said nothing, the quiet stagnant and sour.

Naria coughed, clearing the awkwardness as she took the first dive. "Mother, Father, we must discuss some very serious matters—"

"Naria, a moment alone, please," Odion interrupted, jerking his head toward the door. He smiled—always soft for his precious girl—but it didn't reach his eyes.

I expected my sister to retaliate—always bitter when put out, always chasing my shadow and begging to be included. But Naria, for once in her life, bit her tongue. She bowed. "Yes, Your Majesties."

King Odion waited for the door to close.

There was no doubt Naria was listening on the other side—no footsteps signaling her retreat—but it didn't matter, because Odion just watched me for a long moment. Oppositely, Katia stared at anything but me, eyes darting from the floor to the tall windows that baked the room in gold.

Discomfort bit at the back of my neck, but I ignored the urge to make a comment or quip like I normally would. I would not rescue them from the silence, content to sit in it all day and watch them squirm.

But maybe if I had been the one to start the conversation, I could've better anticipated the next moment.

Odion stepped forward.

And fell to his knees, his forehead kissing the stone floor, as he *bowed*.

"I'm sorry," he blurted, then cleared his throat, raising just his head so I could see the tears budding in his eyes. "I'm sorry for what happened that day. For my part in it."

My mind warred with my eyes.

I'd never seen the top of the King's head. Never noticed the slight bald patch forming—or perhaps that was new.

Just as those two little words were new—*I'm sorry*. Words that sounded wrong in Odion's gruff voice. Words that I'd been desperate for since I first learned the taste of disappointment.

Shock was not a large enough word for the anvil that knocked me from my center, my breath escaping my mouth in a puff. *"What?"*

The King did not stand as he spoke; instead, each word shook out of him like it hurt to part with. "I know Naria told you our perspective —there was an anonymous missive that said they had you. That they were going to kill you, and I just *reacted*—"

"Get up," I breathed, unable to hear, to process anything while he stayed on the floor.

Odion lurched to standing with the warrior's grace he'd always possessed—grace I'd envied and tried my best to mimic—but his eyes sported fresh tears, his hands still *trembling*. "It was foolish. I should have sought more information first. But I was so *afraid*."

The King of Jalta did not tremble. Did not worry. He had been crafted of metal and solidified by fire. He was the eternal flame, an unwavering blaze that did not flicker or fear.

He acted. Decided.

Destroyed.

And I had a small part of his heat in my veins, a fire that scorched up my throat and spewed toward the King of the Pyre. "Like you were *afraid* for my mother when you cast her to the streets? Like you were *afraid* for me when you ripped her from my life?"

Odion winced—*winced*—like I'd slapped him. Like he felt the sting of those words across his skin. "I am so deeply *sorry* for that, too."

Katia stood, her hand clutched to her abdomen. "We both are. We loved her."

Love and apologies.

Useless sentiments, when Aya and I had been freezing and hungry in the streets. Useless, when she'd cried all night and I sat awake, begging for my mother to come back.

Useless, when my mother screamed as she burned.

Useless, when Aya choked on her last words.

"Fuck your sorry and your love!" I cried, the wind stirring like a tornado in my chest, fueled by pain and panic alike. "Your actions spoke for you."

Just as mine had.

But this time, Odion took my vitriol on the chin, tears still welling in his eyes but his feet planted firm. "Your anger is justified, and I will take it as my penance. I should have *believed* her." His voice broke, but he didn't crumple, his back straight and strong with his conviction. "I know I will never atone for that sin. The relationship was unconventional between your mother and I. Katia and I had an arranged marriage, and while we have formed a great friendship, there was never any real...attraction. And what your mother and I had—it was *special*."

Katia nodded sadly, no envy, only acceptance.

I'd known, at least in part, that things had been strange but secure between the three of them. Katia and my mother had raised Naria and I side by side, the best of friends, Katia never making me feel lesser despite not being of pure royal blood. In return, my mother was the only person I'd ever known to make Katia laugh, and she'd been the only person that Mama ever left me alone with outside of herself. They trusted each other.

Until they didn't trust her word.

And my mother loved Odion. Even after he'd banished her, even after everything, even when the only time we could meet was when I played at the Opera, she always left with a parting kiss to the forehead and the same message:

Tell your father I love him, okay? Tell him I'm not angry.

I wished I felt the same way. But my anger was unending, fed by the vat of hurt that still poisoned my bloodstream.

When I didn't respond—*couldn't*—Odion continued, wistfulness wrapping itself around his tone like a gentle wind. "But even though I knew she cared, even though I felt it—I was too insecure. I couldn't imagine that it would be enough for her to love in the shadows while I served my duty as King. To pretend to just be your nursemaid instead of live as your true mother. To always have to *share*."

For a second—just a single inhale—something shifted in me, a self-sabotaging part that could relate to the King's feelings. A part that always fled instead, a part that didn't know how to stay even when I so desperately wanted to. A part that let my fear and insecurity stand in the way of my own happiness.

A part I'd inherited, perhaps.

But the moment passed, and then I'd had enough.

I turned to go.

This was a mistake. There were no answers here, and there never had been. I'd been right to leave it behind, right to forget my fiery parts and instead let the wicked wind guide me home.

I would not forsake Irina. But I didn't need my father's help, not anymore.

It was Katia's voice that stayed me. Katia who cried out, so painfully that for a moment, I believed she'd been physically injured.

"Wait!" Footsteps rushed down the dais stairs as she ran, crashing into my father. Tears streamed down her cheeks, running her makeup in ugly, black rivers. "Please, wait. She was my best friend. We should have been there to protect her from the man who took advantage of her. We should have been there in Hiku City. And we should have protected you, and your *sister*."

I stopped. Breathed once, then again.

Aya.

My sister.

Fury fled as the only truth replaced it—the sadness that swallowed all else. The grief I hadn't had time to acknowledge, but that demanded to be felt.

They should've protected Aya.

I should've too.

Another breath, this one ragged and scraping. Then, "They're both *gone*."

I don't know which action happened first, or if it was some stroke of synchronous luck. But I pitched forward, legs buckling as my grief was too heavy to withstand—and then my father was there. My father caught me.

Gone was the whimpering, wallowing man who'd greeted me. Instead, my father stared back, strong and certain as he'd always been. Passionate as a burning torch, sturdy as mountain rock.

"They are not gone. Your *mother* named you. She chose Rashin. The sun still rises every day, and so do you. They live in both." His fingers gripped my shoulders hard enough to bruise—and to heal. "I am eternally grateful that you carry on her legacy. And even if you never accept me again—if you can't see me as a father...you will always be my son. My *heir*."

I didn't realize I was crying until my tears hit my palms—held in front of me, unsure if they wanted to reach out or push away. Until my voice quivered out in snagging breaths, "I don't want to be an heir."

I didn't want to be anything anymore. Not heir or thief, not prince or bastard. I was so fucking tired, my body trembling as the exhaustion finally leveled me with brutal blows.

I was tired of running. Tired of scheming and surviving.

I just wanted my family. Mama. Aya.

Naveen and Riku and Ren. Kas and Malina.

Naria.

Irina.

And...

Katia. Odion. My *father*.

Lost and found.

"Fine, no talk of succession." My father stroked my cheek, the action so gentle, so *soft*, it sent another wave of raw sobs tumbling out of me. He smiled, wrinkles crinkling. "You're safe now."

But I wasn't safe. I wouldn't be, not until Irina was in my arms again. Not until Ecei was dead.

"This...this is not what I came for." I fought my voice into submission as I grabbed my father's arm. I didn't need his help—but I wanted it. For Irina and for all of Babylon. For change. "You can't save Mama or Aya. But there is someone who needs my help. Someone I care about just as much as you claim to have loved her."

Odion glanced at Katia—a wordless conversation passing between the regents as they decided—and then to me, "Say the word, and whatever you need is yours. I have fourteen years of responsibility to make up for, and then some."

I didn't know how to forgive him. To let him atone. Didn't know how to sheathe my hurt or anger, to begin to repair those broken, wounded parts that still ached inside of me.

So instead, I told him everything.

I told him my account of what happened at the Opera House, of the little girl that saved my life. Of the one person who made this reunion possible.

I told him of Aya's condition, of the way it ate her alive. Of the way she fought until the end against the Blight.

I told him of Ecei's bargain, of the risky choice I made to save her. Of the kidnapping that really ensnared me, body and soul.

I told him of Irina. Of her gentle kindness. Of her saving power. Of her dedication to Babylon and her unwavering goodness.

I told him of Mal's betrayal. Of her friendship, too, and the looming questions between us I had to see answered.

And I told him of Ecei's Blight. Of her son's depravity. Of all of the evils Nehir has been weaving through Babylon for ages. Of their suspected part in the revolution.

And then, I told him of my plans. For revenge. For justice.

For salvation.

And for the *after*. For the maybes I held close to my heart.

When it was done, I cried until the salty tracks dried against my face in crusty lines.

Until my eyes were too puffy to properly see out of, my nose stuffed and my throat hoarse.

Until my soul was empty of all of its pain.

Until there were no tears left in all of Jalta.

And my father just sat with me, just listened to it all. All the hurt, all the anger, all the grief and joy. All of the still-stinging wounds and the still-breathing dreams.

Until I let him cradle me into his arms like I was a child, too exhausted and spent to protest.

After urgent business tore my father from our reunion—his role in the upcoming plan required immediate attention—I let myself wander through the Solyra, exploring the new version of the first home I'd abandoned. The layout was the same, even though furniture had shifted and swiveled in my time away—the table in the dining hall I used to hide under facing south instead of east, the bedroom I used to sleep in sporting a new grey duvet. But the grandeur of the rooms seemed to have faded—the once-roaring hearths now mere slumbering crackles, the glassy obsidian decor now matte trinkets.

Perhaps I was much harder to impress as a man—my eyes sharper and my head tall enough to see the spots of disuse and disarray.

That, or my tired feet were not up for exploring—too exhausted to really appreciate the rest of the changes. And by the time sunset tinted the gray halls in gold again, my legs tracked up the countless stairs, back to the one place in the Palace that'd always been mine. That I knew would be unchanged by time or taste.

The west tower had the perfect view of the horizon, the spire always warm this time of day. After catching my breath from the walk, I pushed open the heavy door. The dusty scent of parchment and jasmine hit me like a brick to the face, bringing me instantly back to the innumerable childhood hours spent hiding away here. Worn, sun-faded book spines cluttered the tiny room on mismatched bookcases, framing the small set of cushioned chairs in the circular space.

Chairs I'd picked with Mama, most of the others in the palace unwilling to climb this high.

This had been our sanctuary, once. And then, when she'd left...it had been where I came to cry, alone and afraid. As I was now.

I cracked the wide window before I plopped into the nearest seat, shutting my puffy eyes, the world blurring red. A breeze floated in, breathing life back into the musty room, back into my sob-wracked lungs.

But I was not alone—not when another set of steps crossed the threshold.

I turned to find Naria standing in the doorway, frame silhouetted in burnt orange. She'd changed from her uniform, instead donning a breezy cotton day dress that softened her sharp angles—still so small, despite her volcanic presence. She took a hesitant step forward, like she was still somehow the outsider even though I'd been the one to leave this place behind.

"I thought I'd find you here."

Though I hadn't asked for it, it was nice to have company. Nice to not be alone with my thoughts, not with the way they still churned and lashed against my skull after everything that'd happened today.

I patted the chair next to me—an invitation. "How did you know?"

Naria narrowed her eyes at the chair, like she could see the person who used to occupy it. But after a breath, she slid into it anyway, back rigid as always. Yet something eased in her expression as she looked at me, something that'd been shelved and hidden for fourteen years. "You always used to sneak off."

I curled further into the chair, one leg dangling. It had felt so much grander as a boy, but it was still as comfortable as I remembered —as safe.

Just as Naria's presence was. We were two adults now who didn't know each other outside of the faint outlines of the children we once were. But no matter how time had changed or life had aged us, there were pieces that remembered—that understood. "Thank you for looking."

Naria settled back into the chair—like it fit her perfectly.

"I used to come here a lot, too." She stared out the window, coal eyes lit afire by the light. Her voice hitched on something I couldn't name—a piece that'd she must have picked up in our travels apart. "After, I mean."

I heard the unspoken end to that sentence.

After you left.

After I thought you died.

I swallowed, Aya's death still fresh enough for me to easily imagine Naria's pain. What she must have endured, believing that her sibling was gone. How she must have lived with the ghost of me still lingering in the halls. In her parents' hollow stares.

How she might have grieved, alone and afraid.

Naria shrugged, a rare smile breaking her flat expression. "Part of me always knew you weren't really gone. I thought that one day, I'd come looking, and you'd just be here in your chair, waiting."

An ache throbbed through my chest, both soft and sharp at the same time.

Naria hadn't stopped waiting. Hadn't stopped looking. *Believing.*

But even though I'd made the only choice I could, even though I did my best to protect Aya...

I'd abandoned my other sister here. To her grief and her solitude, in a palace that had a knack for melting down the good in people.

"I'm sorry I didn't come back sooner." I choked back the bitter regret. "Or say goodbye."

Naria nodded, still enraptured by the sunset. Perhaps still waiting for something that might never come.

We sat in silence for a long moment—my apology hanging in the air until it blew out the window, carried on a gentle breeze.

"Your mother would have been proud, you know," Naria spoke first as she finally turned, tears lining her lashes. "Of the way you took care of your sister. I didn't get to know her...but your mother was family to me, too."

A piece of this puzzle that wasn't coming back, no matter how much either of us wished it. But still, something fit together with her words, the first stitches to repair this tattered family tapestry.

I reached across the chair to squeeze Naria's hand, long-buried memories of my mother's easy smile and Naria's wild laugh echoing through me. Memories of Naria climbing into Mama's lap with me, nodding off as she sang us both a lullaby. "She loved you. I remember that."

We'd been happy here, once. Whole.

But now, without Aya and my mother, there was no repairing the fractured bits of my soul. No happiness left, only half-formed mirages of it.

"I loved her, too...and you." Naria pulled me from those dark thoughts—or perhaps, sat in them with me, lighting the space with her fire. "And I know that if I had gotten to know Aya, I would've loved her just as much."

I let myself dream it for a moment.

What would have happened if I'd taken Aya back here? If I'd given her this sanctuary, too? Or better yet, if we'd never had to leave at all?

The dream took shape, spearing my chest.

Naria, teaching Aya to walk with her head high. Both of them teaming up against their self-important older brother.

Aya, laughing like a menace as she tore through the endless halls and up the unconquerable steps, Naria and I chasing after her before she got us all in trouble.

My mother and Katia, giggling to themselves as they watched us play. Or scolding us together when we took it too far.

Protecting us from forces like Ecei. From the very Blight that stole my sister from me. That cleaved me from the other one.

My voice sounded just as faraway as those fairytales, beyond a hazy horizon. "Maybe in a different world, we all could've had that instead."

Maybe in the next one, we would.

But that didn't change the world we still inhabited—the one that still needed saving.

"We have each other again, and that helps." Naria sat straighter, leveling me with her branding gaze. "I want to know you again—the real you."

I didn't know who that was anymore. Who was Shin Koishi, if not a runaway thief without a little sister to save? Without her smile breathing purpose into my lungs?

But as Naria looked at me, open and raw and expectant, I knew it was about time I found out.

"Tell me everything."

And she did.

She spoke of the struggles here in Jalta after I'd left, of the discrimination and destitution that plagued the desert sands.

Of my father's change of heart, of the softness she'd seen behind closed doors that contradicted the strong front he offered the other kingdoms; a performer like his son.

She exclaimed her wishes for the kingdom—the revolutionary changes she'd want to help see come to fruition one day.

And then she introduced me to *her*—to the way she drank her coffee black, but liked her cereal with extra sugar. To her passion for painting, trying every day to capture the sunrise in watercolor hues. To her insecurities, still fragile despite all the ways she'd proven herself.

And in return, she listened.

As I told her of the ways life in Hiku City had changed and challenged me. Told her of the nights gone hungry and the days filled with mischief and magic. Told her of Aya, of the girl I'd never get to hold again. Of the sister I failed most.

And as the last rays of sunlight fell beneath the Helsin Mountains like the embers of a dying fire, as the room chilled without its heat, I made her a promise.

"When I get back from Nehir, I promise not to leave you alone again."

Lost Ones were never alone. And Naria had been just as lost as I was, another silent victim of Ecei's.

Lost.

And found.

Naria grinned. Grabbed my hand. "Good thing I'm coming with you, then."

With her hand in mine, I stole one last look out the giant picture window, staring down at the kingdom of sand and heat beyond. From this vantage point, the world looked tiny. *Manageable.*

I'd been born to this land. To the fire and fury. To the sunlight and solemness. My mother had named me for it—Morning Sun, the first heat that touched the sky every day.

And with my sister next to me, with my father's forces at my back, with my Lost Ones near and departed at my side and in my heart...

I'd rise.

ICE

THIRTY-THREE

IRINA

It was my turn to pace the small closet of a room, my hands fisted in my dress as I strained, listening for movement in the hall.

Still nothing.

I worried my lip between my teeth as I turned to Malina, who sat on the floor, sharpening a wooden spoke with a screw—both of which she'd pulled from one of the foldable crossbars of the cot. "Are you sure—?"

"*Princess,*" she interjected before I could finish my question—for the thirtieth time in the last hour—a scowl on her small face. "We're as sure as we're going to get."

"I know," I reassured her—and mostly myself.

We'd been over the "plan" as many times as we'd could, until I could recite every step and possibility backwards and forwards and maybe sideways. Mal and I had stayed up most of the previous night ironing out details in whispers, only the shadows of our room around to eavesdrop.

Ecei would have left by now—either to chase Shin to Dunyas, or to meet him at the border—which gave us our window. But if we were going to escape, we had to time it right.

Wait for the maid to open our cage. Then, Malina would steal her clothes and find us a way out while I kept watch, knowing the guards would likely offer me more mercy than her. If we were caught, we had several tricks up our sleeves, but this would be a test of fate and quick-thinking no matter how much I wished I could practice and prepare.

It wasn't perfect, but it was a start.

Three raps against the door startled me. Then, a muted voice; "Excuse me, miss?"

Panic leapt up my throat, but I shoved it back, fighting for a casual tone as I stepped away from the door—and Malina flattened herself against the wall. "Come in!"

There was no more waiting and pacing. No more wallowing.

It was time to move.

The lock rattled as a key turned, and then the maid cracked the door and stepped through, a kind smile as she presented Shin's t-shirt with a slight bow. "Here is your—"

I slammed the door shut behind her, and we attacked.

Malina was silent as she leapt onto the woman, her hand clapping across her mouth as she screamed against it.

"Sorry!" I blurted, grabbing the maid's flailing hand. And my power burst forth, slowing her heart until her eyes shut and she stopped thrashing. It was a different sensation than healing–my limbs now awake and buzzing with excess energy instead of tired and sore–and I tried not to linger on the little bit of vitality I stole.

Malina caught the maid as she slumped unconscious, carefully lowering her onto one of the cots.

Life still thrummed in the poor woman's veins—the girl, really, younger than me, now that I looked closely—but her mouth hung open, drool pooling in the corner as sleep dragged deep breaths through her chest.

Still, it didn't stop me from muttering another thousand sorries as Malina quickly switched their clothes, tugging the deep blue dress over the woman's limp limbs and replacing it with her tattered tunic.

"Don't just apologize, *move!*" Mal chided, tying the maid's apron firmly around her waist, then dropping her stake into the large pocket.

I nodded—yanking the maid's shoes off and stuffing my bare feet into them—before pulling Shin's shirt over my head. If we made it out, we'd need to find better clothes to keep warm, but it was low on the priority list. We had to find our exit first.

Mal produced a second stake from beneath the cot...and handed it to me. "Do you know how to use this?"

"No?" I took it anyway, holding it away like it might bite. I'd never been one for swordplay or anything sharper than a dinner fork, my clumsiness already a danger in itself.

Mal rolled her eyes as she wrapped her hand around mine and shoved the stake closer. "Aim the sharp end at their soft parts."

I clutched the stake like it was a lifeline, nodding. I wouldn't slow us down this time.

Which was good, because Mal didn't wait for me as she fled through the threshold, head on a swivel while she surveyed the hall. Then, with a motion for me to follow, she was gone.

I scurried after her, breathing deeply as soon as I stepped into the wide hallway. After days in the dungeon and then in the closet, the long stretch of stone and crystal sconces felt cavernous—especially with the large, picturesque window that loomed at the end of the hall, the wintry weather swirling beyond it. This palace was beautiful for a cage, artwork hanging in gold frames on every wall, ice sculptures displayed in the alcoves.

But I couldn't relax, not yet. Not until we were out.

There were no guards immediately outside the door—Mal had noticed they stalked the halls in shifts instead of posted at stations—and based on the timing of the last pass of footsteps, we probably had a few minutes before they returned this way and found us gone.

So we had to act, and hope we chose right.

"Where now?" I whispered to Mal, who was already several paces ahead, prowling along the side of the wall with her stake in her hand. She dipped behind an ice carving of a swan, her head tilted with the same graceful stillness as the animal's.

She paused. *Listened*. For what, I didn't know, but I held my breath all the same, wishing I could quiet my heartbeat. Then, "Left."

She scurried down the hall and turned the corner, and I followed as quickly and subtly as I could, all the while trusting Malina's instincts. It was a leap of faith—to convince myself that she wasn't about to sell me out again. To know that without her, I had no hope. We were on a higher floor, given the window's north facing view; the giant springs that fed into the Black River pools of crystal blue tucked into the northern mountain beyond. It was beautiful and deadly, a frozen landscape of pure treachery.

So there was no other choice but to follow Malina's lead, or freeze on my own.

She veered left again at the end of the next hallway. This one was wider, a main connector based on the way the royal blue runners faded ever-so-slightly in the middle with frequent use.

But again, no one waited. Our pace hastened, Mal's steps sure and steady, mine scattered and struggling to keep up. But a beacon at the end of the hall kept us moving forward: a staircase, this one dark and slim, like it was meant for servants to pass through.

A way out.

Mal nodded, and we hurried down, my legs wobbling as we hurtled step over step. But even as they trembled, still sore from the cold and disuse, hope bloomed in my chest. I didn't know how this particular castle functioned, but I *did* know palaces. The servants' areas were usually far less guarded, and many of them couldn't bother to stick their nose in anyone else's business for fear of it hurting them in return.

Which made this the best option we had.

The bottom of the steps opened up into a wide hallway, labeled doors marked along the side, and that hope flowered into excitement.

Pantry.

Linens.

Laundry.

Everything we'd need to get out.

"Stay there," Mal whispered as she set her sights on the laundry door. She didn't need to clarify—we'd been over this plan. If we could both get a disguise, then we could filch some supplies from the pantry and find the exit.

I nodded, and Malina went first, slipping through the door with unnaturally quiet steps.

I stayed back as victory cried through my veins.

Until a voice carried through the door, stern and strong and distinctly *not* Malina. "You, there! You're not supposed to be here."

I rounded the doorway without a second thought, my fear springing me forward. Mal stood just past the threshold, the laundry room teeming with hanging, half dried uniforms and deep basins of water and suds that stirred themselves—

Likely thanks to the older woman standing in front of Mal, her arms crossed as she stared over the bridge of her pronounced nose. A severe blonde-and-gray bun accentuated the grimace she wore, tugging her skin back into a sneer.

But Mal didn't miss a beat, jerking a thumb at me and painting on a smile. "I have special orders to equip the new girl with a uniform."

This woman was a servant, not a soldier. And we could handle fooling one measly laundress.

Before I could think, I nodded, doing my best to play along and still my too-fast heartbeat.

But the woman's eyes narrowed as they dragged over us, cold and dark.

"I haven't hired anyone new," she hissed as she uncrossed her arms...

And revealed the gleaming bronze badge that delineated her rank in swirling, engraved script.

Head Maid Marriaj.

Well, *shit.*

Standard servants might have minded their own business, but this woman's job was to stick her nose in everyone else's.

Mal and I glanced at each other at the same time, and without a word—

We moved as one.

I scrambled to touch the maid's neck–to knock her out– as Mal flung herself onto her back, the woman crying out as the pixie attacked. But we didn't have the element of ambush on our side this time, and the first maid hadn't been an *Easinir*.

So with a flick of the Marriaj's hands, water rushed from the nearest basin, sending it and the cold contents careening toward us.

I slipped, my backside smacking against the concrete floor, knocking into Mal and Marriaj, toppling them both.

In a heap of limbs and grunts, all three of us surged in different directions, Mal and I both trying to grab Marriaj, who reached out for one of the basins...

And slammed her fist on a small red stone on the side.

Like the fae-stone Mal had swiped, this one lit the room crimson, the magic awakening from within...

In the next instance, a blaring whistle sounded throughout the whole hall, coming from everywhere at once.

An *alarm*.

We hadn't prepared for a freaking alarm.

"Shit," I cursed, and Mal's brows flew up—

I smacked my hand against Marriaj's, my power flowering as I called her heart to slow. This time, I shivered as I claimed her energy, relishing in my thievery. The old woman didn't have time to protest as sleep dragged her under, but the damage was already done. The alarm had been triggered, the fae-stone still glowing.

We had to move.

Mal jumped to her feet, grabbing a sack of folded clothes to her left, and then we both surged for the door, knocking shoulders as we squeezed through, our feet floundering for purchase over the slippery stone. But we didn't slow as we raced down the hall, desperate for an exit, panic blaring in my veins with each repeated ring of the ear-splitting alarm.

"There has to be a direct way out," I panted as we searched, the whole castle likely on high alert now. We had *minutes*, at most. "They don't want servants tracking through the main house."

At the end of the hall, we made a right, and an arched doorway beckoned a few dozen paces away.

My fear churned into anticipation, the end so near, so close...

"Stop right there!" A voice boomed behind us as four guards clamored into the hall, swords drawn and deep blue uniforms marked with silver bands.

Easinir.

Mal and I froze, just a few paces away from the door.

Just a few steps from freedom.

"*Shit,*" Mal hissed, shoving the pack of coats into my arms. Hands free, she drew the small stake again and dropped into a ready stance. Then she motioned to the exit, determination setting her jaw in stone. "Keep moving, Princess."

I blinked, my stomach bottoming out. "I'm not leaving without you."

No, I wouldn't leave anyone behind. Never again.

A stare hotter than lava flicked to me, burning in its intensity and demand. "I said *go*, Irina."

And something about the way she said my name—not my title—shifted the fabric of my being. Like she saw me, not my crown. Like she believed in me.

And I believed in her. Before she could protest, I flung my arms around her and squeezed. "You better catch up."

I was already running before she could hug me back. But as I glanced over my shoulder and watched her rocket toward the guards, a feral grin on her face and her stake at the ready, it meant more than any embrace.

I was at the door by the time I heard her collide with them. By the time I heard them yelp in pain, the little pixie faster and far more vicious than they'd anticipated.

And I didn't need to look back to know who'd be the victor.

So with a sharp inhale, I thrust open the door, pulled a coat around my shoulders, and sprinted as fast as my legs would carry me.

Winter wind slapped against my face—so much harsher than Shin's warm breezes—blurring my sight as I stumbled through the snowfall, my head down as I struggled to find my footing. But I ran on, one foot after another, because I was out.

I was free.

Mal would catch up, and we'd get out of here. We'd find Shin and the others. We'd expose Ecei.

And I wouldn't look back.

But I should've looked *up*.

I slammed into something cold and harsh...but alive. Strong.

The guard's arms wrapped around me before I could fight back, before I could fish for the stake in my pocket. I thrashed against the hold, but frost crept across my arms, spidery webs of ice stiffening my limbs...

As my eyes locked with a too-familiar shade of blue that froze my core with fear.

"I don't think so," Ecei tsked, her white fur coat blending with the expanse of snow around her. Tendrils of ice and frost swirled around the bottom of her dress, a menacing winter mist that churned in my gut.

And behind her, a dozen guards stood, swords ready. *Easinir* bands lining their arms.

My heart slammed against my ribs, panic working through my frozen limbs, but I inhaled deeply.

This wasn't the end. I couldn't let it stop here. I wouldn't.

Warmth spread through me like dawn spilling over the dawn horizon, sunlight pouring through my veins and heating me from the inside. "Let me go, Ecei."

"Or what? You'll make my leaves greener?" She sneered, and with a flick of her fingers, the frost bit deeper, my skin stinging as it spread over me like a tidal wave. "You are as powerless as you are *foolish*. You think I didn't see through your lies?"

"And you don't think I see through yours?" I spat back, dragging my eyes over her and the guards. It was an intimidating show of force —but a tell in itself. An overcompensation, a disguise stitched with shoddy thread. I grinned. "All of this, just for two little girls? You're only still here because your hands are tied. You don't know who you can trust anymore, and you can't find your son, so you're biding your time."

As I was biding mine. Waiting for Mal. It would be tough for her to get past this many guards, but if I could help, if I could just do *something*...

My power blossomed again, the internal warmth useless against the ice. If I could just hold on, if Mal could lend me some heat, I could break out. And if I could just touch Ecei's *skin*...

But Ecei's smile fell, darkness shadowing her expression. Whether her show of force was a ruse or not, her rage was real, its serrated edge aimed at me. "You can bide the rest of yours back in the dungeons. Take her."

I screamed as the guard hauled me up over his shoulder, ready to drag me back to the dungeon. To throw me back in the cage...

Two flashes of auburn and green blurred past me.

My guard grunted.

And I fell.

The ice rose up to my face, but with a splash, my ice bindings disappeared, just in time for me to brace. Pain shot through my hands as I caught myself, my wrists groaning even with the snowmelt to cushion my tumble. But as I scrambled up, my head spinning...

My heart leapt in my chest, threatening to break through my ribs and *dance*.

"Hiya, Princess. Were you all waiting for us?" Ren cracked a grin as he wiped the ice blade on the back of his gray sleeve, his auburn hair a match for the guard's blood that pooled at his feet.

Next to him, Riku twirled his matching daggers in his hands, staring down Ecei and the rest of the *Easinir* with a cold, calculating glare that warmed my soul. "Which one of you fuckers is next?"

The Lost Ones were here.

And I was found.

Thirty-Four

SHIN

The Northern wind cried the song of war as it stung our faces and eyes to numbness. It was not a friend, but a harsh, warning guard, a beast that survived at the edge of the world on its predatory nature alone.

But the wind was mine to command, to Control, and I would make that nature mine. Would let it fuel my breaths and steady my steps.

Would let it help me bring my princess home.

The Winter Palace wasn't the same hulking mass as Anastova or the Solyra. Instead, it sparkled like an ice-coated diamond in the blinding sun, delicate, swirling spires reaching skyward like icicles, designs carved into its face as beautiful and intricate as snowflakes.

It was breathtaking.

And it was a trap. A *lure.*

We'd been camped in the forest for a day, using the hot, swirling mist from the springs to mask our movements as we watched. As we planned.

As we noted the guard's rotations, and the entrances....

The Winter Palace wasn't a fortress, but it was a maze. It took Riku and Naria two whole shifts to track the basic routines and scout a plan of entry.

But the time for planning was long gone, and the wind trumpeted the revelry of action.

It was time to save our princess.

Ren and Riku were armed and ready, their green-and-white tunics blending perfectly with the tall pines that created a natural border to the Palace. I'd asked a monumental task of them, but like always, the twins did not balk, meeting each other and me step for step. Ren flashed a grin, pointing his favorite dagger—one he'd stolen from a Nehir nobleman—at the castle in a threat. "Operation Dazzle and Distract, at your service."

I rolled my eyes, reconsidering all of my decisions as I grabbed his collar before he could run off. "Subtle and stealthy. Get in. Get out."

Riku smacked his twin on the back of the head before nodding to me, his jaw set. "We'll find her, Shin."

I pulled them both in for a quick embrace, clapping them on the back. These two boys had been nothing but trouble since the day they leapt into my life, fresh off a circus caravan and straight under my wing. But through every headache and rough patch, they were there, ready to flow with me and clean up their own messes.

And mine.

The hug didn't last nearly long enough, and I shoved down the worry that it might be the last time.

We would make it out of this. We had to.

And then, with no more pomp and circumstance, they were off. The liars meant to sneak their way into the palace like running water through a cracked foundation. The Winter Palace was a maze, but they had a knack for twists and turns.

I watched them go, wishing I could follow. Wishing I didn't have to send them at all, that I had other options.

But we were out of choices, our duty clear ahead of us.

Throats cleared behind me, pulling me back to the task at hand. To the others still waiting on my word.

Kas practically vibrated next to Naveen, a frenetic energy buzzing through him. It was the most alive and alert I'd seen him in days—weeks, really. Like he could *feel* Malina, here somewhere, waiting to scold him—and me—for what he was about to do. What I—no, what *Babylon*—needed from him.

I looked over his head to Naveen, to my right hand and the only person I could trust with the task of keeping Kas safe. "I—"

"We know where we are going," Naveen rescued me from a mangled thank you, my anxiety likely written across my features in aggressive brushstrokes. A smile quirked at the corner of his mouth. "Right, firecracker?"

Kas nodded, a determined look that was all Malina capturing his small features. "We won't mess up, Shin."

I gulped down the fear that jabbed up my throat. I wanted to believe them, wanted to trust that this was the right choice, but after Aya... "At the first sign of trouble..."

"Get out," Naveen finished for me, clapping me on the shoulder. "No chances."

No, this was risky enough as it was. And even though we had other resources at our disposal now, it was also just as risky to not have my people take care of the most important parts. And I hated that choice. Hated chancing anymore of my family at all.

But if I was built to soar, they were crafted to survive. To run, if trouble came to chase them. To hide and lie and live, if all else failed.

If I failed.

I yanked Kas into my side, who groaned as I forced him into a tight hug, Naveen wrapping his long arms around us both. "Good. I need all of my brothers back."

Naveen pulled away first, amber eyes misting with tears he would not let fall; Kas next, a proud smile stretching his too-young face. And then, they were gone too, leaving me and Naria alone.

Leaving only one thing left to do.

Liar and lure. Damsel and devil.

It was time to make a scene.

My daggers were out in another flash, my black battle suit crafted from the most durable Jaltan soldier-silk, coated with thin links of metal that could withstand most blades. I'd only be vulnerable to

Easinir attacks, water molecules small enough to permeate the material. It was a gift from my father I wouldn't scoff at. Especially as Naria prowled closer in a matching one, her long blades drawn and sharp, glinting in the wintry sunlight. "Are you ready?"

Nehir had crafted a reputation of spoiling pretty, delicate things, often without sullying their own expensive clothes.

It was time to teach them the taste of Jaltan steel, and the mettle of a few nobles that weren't afraid to dirty their hands.

"Ready as I'll ever be." I smiled at my sister—as grateful to have her at my side as I was afraid of losing her. We'd barely begun to make up for lost time, to get to know each other again, and I wasn't ready for any of that to end.

"We have to watch for those suppressants." Her tongue poked the inside of her cheek, the only show of worry she'd let slip.

I shivered at the thought of those darts—of the numb, cold sensation that crept from the inside out as the poison leeched the Control from my veins...

Of the power it stole, my wind abandoning me.

Of the life it cost me, my sister unprotected with my body weakened and my power zapped.

I pitched a grin to mask the discomfort climbing my spine like a ladder. "I don't need to be told twice."

Naria gripped her daggers tighter. "But Father will be ready for us when it's done."

"I hope we won't need him."

It was a nice thought to know I didn't have to do this alone, that there was a squadron of Jaltan soldiers waiting for us if this went belly-up, but I still didn't know if I could trust my father. Didn't know if his penchant for war would consume him yet again. Didn't know if all of this was an elaborate, long-term plan for him to finally have a reason to march his troops across Nehir. And even though I wanted to see the Winter Palace topple, even though I wanted Ecei to feel the sharp sting of defeat and to pay for her crimes...

Despite the wind's incessant song, this excursion was not a declaration of war. This was a rescue attempt, for Irina and Mal, and for all of Babylon.

Salvation, not destruction.

Bait and steal.

I wasn't waiting any longer.

I marched over to the remnants of our camp—the fire already stamped out and the tent folded—to where my favorite part of the plan waited. Dried, caked blood smeared across his face from where it'd poured from his rebroken nose—a gift from Via, not me this time—yet he still glared through bruised-purple eyes as he wriggled against his restraints.

"Alright, bait," I sneered, sheathing one dagger to yank Drakkar's blond hair and tilt his head back, enjoying his wince a little too much. "You ready?"

He garbled against his gag, and I rolled my eyes as I used my other dagger to slice through it.

"Say again?"

He spat a wad of blood, wolfish teeth stained red as he bared them at me. "My mother will kill you. She will string you up by your insides and—"

I stole the air from his lungs to shut him up, and Naria snorted. "I'll take that as a *ready*." She grinned. "Let's move."

I let Drakkar breathe again, a coughing, sputtering mess as we dragged him from the treeline...

And marched directly toward the Winter Palace's main gate.

The swirling metal gate screeched as my winds broke the lock and shoved it open like an alarm. Dozens of white marble, frost-touched steps tapered up to the palace's ornate doors, and splashes of blue peeked out from the guard turrets as the people inside alerted to the intrusion.

While the others infiltrated like insects, crawling through the maze undetected, Naria and I were about to put on the performance of a lifetime, peacocks ready to squawk and dance.

I threw Drakkar onto the steps, a gauntlet that stained the pristine white marble crimson. An offering of blood, for what Ecei had taken from my family. From Aya.

I cleared my throat, my bellow echoing against the winter wind. "Anyone home? I've got a little present for Queen Ecei!"

A moment passed before blue-and-silver clad soldiers poured from the main entrance's mouth, orders ringing out and swords already drawn, Ecei not bothering with the ruse of diplomacy.

"Stand down and surrender, and we will spare your life!" an archer shouted from one the turrets, a blue-tipped arrow aimed at my chest.

I glanced at my sister, who met my gaze with a feral, unhinged grin.

It was time to dance.

Thirty-Five

IRINA

Ren and Riku were here.

Here, two mirror images, night and day, both ready to put themselves on the line for *me*.

It was a grace I had not earned, but gratitude swelled up my throat, clogging all the *thank yous* I wanted to spew at them.

And if they were here, Shin had to be...

No. I couldn't let myself think that.

Not now. Not with Ecei and her men circling us like a pack of wolves, ready to descend and pick us off, one by one.

Ren positioned himself in front of me, the sunshine fleeing from his expression as a darkness crept through it, intent and intensity sunsetting into lethal focus. "Irina, stay back."

Fear prickled down my spine, but I nodded.

Ecei picked her jaw off the ground and gritted out harsh words, spears of ice coating her fingertips like claws. "There is no escape from this."

A flick of her hand.

The guards surged.

And chaos erupted.

My head spun as I tried to make sense of everything, an onslaught of stimulus that blurred too fast to process.

Ecei rocketed a bolt of ice toward Riku, who melted it with a twist of his wrist, the Qualifier holding his own against the Controller's superior gift. But Ecei was relentless, throwing more and more at him, shards scraping across his cheeks, his hands. Scratches of red blood matched his hair as he lost ground. A guard circled his flank, ready to pounce as soon as there was an opening.

"Riku, watch!" I cried, and without missing a beat, he redirected Ecei's next ice shard over his shoulder, sending it straight into the guard's eye socket. Gore squirted, and the guard screamed as he collapsed.

At the same moment, Ren dove into the horde of guards. The snow rippled beneath their feet like waves as the Quantifier doubled its size, trapping them up to the waist as they scrambled for their footing. But in another breath, a staircase of ice jutted up from the ground, its formation a precise replica of the staircase in the palace. Several guards took advantage of the structure, propelling upward, the *Easinir* in their ranks just as equipped to handle this as Ren was. From their higher vantage point, their arrows rained down, so fast Ren barely had time to shield himself with another mound of Quantified snow.

The twins were forces of nature, clever as they were cutting.

But these guards and Ecei were trained for this, *bred* for it, and the boys were outmatched. Outnumbered.

Two guards shot for me, skidding across the snow as Ecei bellowed her next command: "Get the princess, kill the others!"

I ran, legs wobbling against the uneven ground—

A hand snagged my ankle, and I fell.

Agony lanced through my side as I collapsed, the frozen ground smacking against my ribs and hands. I groaned as I rolled, but a yank tore me back, my fingers scraping as I fought to catch myself. The cold numbed my fingers to useless, and I couldn't get a good grip, the snow too soft.

"Get back here," a guard growled as he crawled over me, weight pressing into my abdomen. I wriggled to free myself, but the snow dragged me deeper. Panic clawed up my throat, but the guard grabbed my wrists, cuffing them in his large grasp to subdue me.

His mistake.

I would not freeze. Not this time.

My finger grazed the skin of his wrist. "Don't you *dare* touch me."

And my power glowed as I sucked at the guard's life force, the same power that could heal and grow, set to take.

His head rolled, his heart slowing, as the euphoric electricity set my veins on fire. As my heartrate leapt, dancing in primal victory.

I jammed my knee up between his legs as hard as I could.

The guard rolled off me with a groan, clutching his crotch as he seethed, "Bitch."

I hurried to my feet, ignoring the ache that clamored through my body—and kicked again, my mark landing *twice*. "Dick."

The guard passed out, the whites of his eyes flashing before they shut.

I stood straight, triumph blaring through me like trumpet calls, my heart still drumming a furious beat. Life moved through my veins like lava, warm and *infinite.*

But it was short-lived as the ground beneath me rumbled and rolled, snow turning to mush and fluid water—

"Irina, get down!" Ren cried out, and I spun as the tidal wave of ice careened over his head. It darkened the sky above, hovering like a giant peering down, and then it rushed toward the ground, toppling six more guards, all too injured to stop it. It swelled again, set to crush them all, a merciless, overwhelming wall...

Until Ecei snapped her fingers, and the wave *evaporated.*

The world halted as both of the twins did, and my stomach dropped through my toes, my legs numb beneath me.

Ecei wiped the blood—whose blood, I couldn't tell—from one of her long, icy claws. They disintegrated too, droplets hitting the ground in angry thuds. Then, she raised a pistol—blue-tailed dart sticking from it—and aimed it at Ren's face. "Nice trick—did you learn it in primary school?"

My heart jolted.

This was the end.

She was going to take our *Easinir*, and then, Babylon.

We would not escape, not with her and the remaining eight guards ready to strike us down. The twins were more than capable, but even if we managed this batch, there would be more of them. Always more, an endless ocean of Nehirite soldiers that would never let us rest, never stop chasing us down and poisoning us slowly.

Yet Ren flashed a middle finger at Ecei, and *grinned*. "Joke's on you, lady; I skipped school."

He somersaulted into the air as the gunshot rang, the dart missing him by a breath. And in the second it took the guards to draw their shooters...

An azure-tipped arrow whizzed past my ear—

And embedded itself in the front guard's eye socket. He fell, dead on impact, his one good eye staring into nothingness.

"Sorry I'm late." Malina had the next arrow cocked and pointed at another guard's face as she jumped into the snow. Her maid's outfit was torn and bloody, her curls a wild mess, but the smile on her face spoke of feral glee. "Had to get supplies."

And Ecei paused, her guards freezing as we stared each other down.

Now, it was eight to four, and for some reason, I liked our odds.

My heart soared, beating like hummingbird wings as it lifted my spirit into the air. "I knew you'd come back."

Malina's lips twitched. "Don't hold it over my head."

Her next arrow struck a guard right in the throat, somehow cleaving between the small gap of his helmet and armor, his blood spraying as his gunshot went wide. The dart flew just over Ecei's head this time, forcing her to duck.

I scrambled back—knowing my limits. If anyone came for me, I could put them to sleep, but aside from my singular defensive strategy, I was not a fighter. And I was useless without skin-to-skin contact.

So I watched, waiting to heal if necessary, as Riku again shot for Ecei, a wolf on the hunt for blood. With every quick step he took, jagged spokes of ice dashed up from the snow—shards he broke off and hurled at Ecei with vicious speed. She gritted her teeth, waving her hands frantically to evaporate or redirect them, but Riku was faster, more and more of the spokes hurtling toward the Ice Queen.

But I didn't have a chance to watch the outcome of their standoff as a torrent of darts rained toward Mal, Ren, and I.

My hands flew up instinctively, my stomach knotting with fear as I ducked.

Until a flash of blue fire—its heat licking my face even from several paces away— burned them to bits mid-air.

The scent of ash stung my nose as Malina flicked off the lighter with another vicious smile. Where she'd gotten it, I had no idea. But while she might not have been able to produce her own flames, the Qualifier knew how to *burn*.

For the first time in my life, I welcomed the heat.

The guards attacked again, this time with their swords, the darts doing little if they couldn't get an accurate shot. Snow dipped and swelled as the water wielders all commanded it to their bidding. But Mal and Ren were ready, light on their feet as they tumbled over the banks and valleys, arrows quipped and daggers out.

This was a dance they knew well. One they'd perfected and performed, just like their demonstration in The Breeze Haven. Only this routine was lethal as it was lithe, their synchronization a murderous force. They somersaulted and flipped and danced, using each other to push up and over the unstable ground.

Ren sneered at Malina mid-slash at a guard. "So, you're on our side again?"

Mal shrugged before she finished the same guard off with a poison arrow to the knee, toppling him. "Irina and I had a plan—you two are just getting in the way."

Ren rolled his eyes, flipping over the next soldier and lodging his blade into his neck—then using his limp body as a shield against another oncoming guard. "We were heading in the servants' entrance when you two were running out, and if we hadn't frozen half the guards on your trail, you'd be shit out of luck."

He slammed the guard he held into the other one, sending them both hurtling toward me.

Swallowing down my panic, I leapt out of the way as the guard tripped over his dead dance partner. Then, with a quick touch to the forehead, my power enveloped him.

The guard's eyes shut as deep sleep dragged him under.

It wouldn't last long. But I didn't know how to kill. To destroy.

So instead, I'd do what I could. I would *fight*.

I smiled up at Ren and Malina, pride singing in my veins. I would not just stand around and wait. I would act, and even if my choices were foolish, they were *mine*.

I kicked the sleeping man in the ribs for good measure.

Five guards and one Ecei left.

But my celebration died before it could fly as the distinct sound of pierced flesh assaulted my ears, wet and tearing, as did the cry that tore from Riku's throat. "Agh!"

I whipped around.

Just in time to watch him fall to his knees, clutching his side. Crimson stained his hands, his body trembling in shock. Ecei drew back a dagger of ice, Riku's blood dripping from it. Raised to strike again.

Ren and I moved at the same time.

Before I could think, before I could understand, I tore through the snowbanks in clumsy, foundering jolts.

The first dagger flashed through the air as Ren hurled it at Ecei's hand, the sharp tip slicing at her wrist. "Don't touch him, you rancid bitch!"

Ecei yelped, clutching her arm to her chest. Her focus snapped to the sunny twin. *Distracted.*

I dove for Riku, my hand extended as he crawled over the ice, a river of red running from his side. So much blood. If I could just reach him, touch him...

A wave of snow rushed past us, blurring Ecei from sight. And Ren rode atop it, dagger drawn, vengeance written in blood across his face.

Riku lurched toward his twin as I reached him. "Ren! *No!*"

But I trapped him in my grasp, ignoring Ren's pursuit. I had to focus, *had* to stop the bleeding.

My magic flared, bright and hot, seeking and stitching Riku's side. Coaxing his skin back together. Stealing the energy from my veins, agony rattling through me as my power burned. I poured every ounce I'd taken from the others, every drop of excess I had, into his body.

I could do this. I could save him.

Hold on, don't let go.

Riku's side stopped bleeding. He sucked in a full breath, eyes wide.

The snow swell fell, crashing into the earth with a rumble. Instinctively, I grabbed Riku, holding on to each other as the snow-dust stung out eyes.

I blinked as it settled.

Ecei stood over Ren's limp form.

"It took me a minute to figure it out, but you're the Quantifier, yes?" She pressed her heeled shoe into the side of his face. Another smile. "Let's see how well your twin does without his better half."

The dagger slashed. Blood spattered.

Riku *screamed.* An inhuman, guttural sound deep enough to shake the mountains.

And I bit back a sob as the life blinked out of Ren's eyes...

As his head *rolled.*

Thirty-Six

Arrows rained from the skies.

But none touched us, my winds whipping them away, or Naria's flames burning them to cinders before they could dare sting us.

Just as we cut through the guards, slice after slice. Jab after jab.

Drakkar had scurried away already, likely holed up inside the castle as the guards did his work. But it didn't matter. The princeling was useless now, our task clear.

My legs ached beneath me and my chest heaved, my winds zapping my strength and stealing my breath as we fought up the steps, the soldiers surging and falling as we tore through their ranks.

Fire and air, feeding each other's gluttonous appetites. Waxing when the other one waned. When the *Easinir* in their ranks doused Naria's flames, my winds sliced through them with vicious power. When they managed to snare me, Naria melted away the icy shackles before they could even begin to slow me down.

We did not falter, our tempo racing like the build up to the final conclusion of a symphony. Did not yield, our backs together and our strikes coordinated as we gave no ground.

Another guard shot at me, a spear of ice in his hand—

Naria stepped in and batted it away with her daggers. A kick to the ribs, and he fell.

Slice after slice. Kick after kick.

Up the stairs.

Toward the palace doors.

But that was part of the ruse, the game we were playing. Naria and I didn't need to cross the threshold of the castle to win this battle. We didn't even need to make it all the way up the steps.

We just needed to take out as many of the guards as we could, and buy the others time. Wait for the signal.

Distract. Disarm.

So with each ragged breath, each heavy swing of my daggers, I stayed.

Even though it would've been easier for me to grab Naria and soar over their heads. Even though all I wanted to do was to have my sister melt the ice palace to the ground...

Kick after kick. Jab after jab.

More guards rushed at us, this time in a wave, all of them moving as one as the snow urged them forward. It was a well-coordinated attack, overwhelming in its breadth—

I stole the air from their lungs with half a thought, watching as they choked and crumbled, falling over each other like lemmings off a cliff.

"That was overkill." Naria smirked as she sent an arrow of pure fire through another soldier's shoulder. Then, a panted whisper that only I could hear; "You're *rushing*."

I sucked a deep breath, begging my heart to slow, urging my limbs to hang on just a bit longer.

This was not about winning.

Distract and disarm.

This was about *staying*.

I gritted my teeth together. Raised my blade.

Jab after jab. Strike after strike.

Sweat itched across my skin as my battle suit clung to every inch, as my muscles protested their repeated use. Yet I stayed, fighting alongside my sister. My sister, always chasing my shadow. My sister, always rising to the occasion. *Always* catching up. Catching *me* when I wavered.

But I didn't stop. Neither did Naria.

Not until a scream shattered across the world, the wind carrying it on its back as it stabbed through my very center.

The world paused. My breath hitched.

I knew that scream. Heard it in my worst nightmares, ones that had me careening from the bed to the basin to empty my guts. Ones that had me drenched in sweat and shaking for hours.

That scream belonged to a Lost One.

Riku or Ren. Which, I couldn't tell.

But there was no denying the tone, the urgency. Something was wrong.

Someone was *hurt.* Or worse.

I spun to Naria, panic digging its nails into my heart. My sister swallowed. Scanned the guards still rushing at us, the endless onslaught hemorrhaging from the castle.

She lifted her daggers. Coal-black eyes burned as they flicked to me. "Go, Shin."

Halves of my heart warred, yanking at each other. I couldn't leave my sister. Couldn't abandon her again, couldn't let her get hurt, too—not before I had a chance to know her again. "I won't leave you."

But the twins were my brothers. The Lost Ones my charges. And if they needed me...

Without my permission or opinion, Naria shot a flare into the sky, the red fire bursting into thousands of tiny particles, casting the world in crimson light.

A signal to my father for backup.

Naria's jaw tensed. "He'll come. Go save them."

Ideals of independence or cleaning up my own mess evaporated in that moment as the choice was made for me—and made well.

The Lost Ones needed me. And Naria needed our father. I had to believe that he would come.

With one last grateful look at my sister, I ran, headed for the north entrance of the castle where the scream had blown from. A swift wind spun beneath my feet with less than a command, an urgent song nibbling at the back of my mind.

One last rescue.

Step after step.

Breath after breath.

Until another sound boomed through the world, tearing it in two. The ground pitched, and I stumbled as the tremors rocked through the foundation of the castle.

An explosion.

My ears rang, head woozy as I wobbled to standing again. As pain thrummed in my skull and fear rattled my bones. If it was Naria, if something happened...

A plume of angry smoke expanded skyward, a beastly cloud of purple and black ash blotting out the sun as it devoured the light. Streaks of color rippled through its towering mass, like an unnatural lightning storm caught in its fiery fist.

But it wasn't billowing from the front entrance. Or the northern end of the castle.

It stemmed from the far side of the estate—from the abandoned guest houses that for some reason had extra security. From the one place in the Winter Palace's maze that truly made no sense.

From where I'd sent Kas and Naveen, their mission not to save Irina or distract...

But to rescue Babylon.

To destroy the Blight lab.

It had been just a hunch–a hope–meant to keep Kas away from the main fight, but to also potentially deal an unrecoverable blow to Nehir.

New fear threatened to noose me, tight and constricting around my throat. I squinted, searching for any sign that Kas and Naveen were okay. Any signal that my brothers had survived the blast...

A spark of orange soared through the black cloud—and my heart nearly burst.

There, in the skies, a kite made of makeshift canvas soared, propelled by bright flames, like a smaller version of a hot air balloon.

And on it rode Naveen and Kas, both covered in soot and smiling.

And even as the smoke stung my nose as watered my eyes, even as it stole the little heat from the sky, even as my panic still urged me toward the others...

It fueled my steps anew. Set my soul ablaze.

Babylon was free. Never again would we let little girls die from poisoned water. Never again would future kings fall to incurable illness.

The Blight was gone. Kas and Naveen had succeeded.

And it was time to avenge my sister and save the others.

THIRTY-SEVEN

IRINA

I had met Death before.

Seen him in his most subtle attack, as he stole my brother's last inhale for himself. As he silently, wordlessly dragged my sleeping, sick Nikolaj into his domain.

I'd witnessed his quickest strike, a single line of red across Aya's throat. As he snagged her from the world in a lightning flash, there one moment, gone the next.

But the scene before me now was not Death.

It was *carnage*.

Death's vicious, feral brother, a beast with no inhibitions that'd ripped Ren in two. That'd made a *mess* of him, savage and brutal and tactless.

My heartbeat deafened my ears. My middle clenched, bile rising up my throat. Gagging me. Choking me.

Ren was—

Ren was—

Mal spoke first, her gargled *no* stabbing me in the ribs. Riku stilled next to me, petrified. Stuck. Like without his twin, he forgot how to *breathe.*

I did too, gasps scraping down my lungs in sharp, punctuated heaves.

Ren's lifeless eyes stared blankly as his blood bloomed across the snow. As it stained the world—my soul—with the utter loss of him.

There was no healing from this. No urging muscle and skin and synapse together again.

No repairing what carnage had taken.

I tore my eyes away from the gore, tears blurring my vision as I gritted my teeth at Ecei—at carnage's agent. At Ren's *murderer.* "You killed him."

But Ecei simply glanced between Riku and me as she wiped the blood on her dress. And *snarled*, like *I* was the murderer. "Did you just *heal* him?"

Riku didn't move. Didn't respond, his mouth parted on his brother's last breath, his eyes just as unfocused as his twin's. Like he was waiting for Death to claim him, too.

My gut wrenched again, this time with a rage that begged to be unleashed. A rage born of hiding my gift for years, never given the sunlight to grow. A rage born of grief, old and new, for the blood brother I lost to *her* Blight, and the found brother who'd died by her blade.

A rage for all the suffering we'd endured. All the loss we carried.

Ren was dead.

Aya was dead.

Nikolaj was dead.

And Ecei would be next.

I trembled as I stood, angry bursts of power shaking through my fingertips. Power that craved death. Power that wanted to *take. "You killed him."*

"Not a medemental, but a true *healer.*" Ecei narrowed her eyes, a new dagger of ice forming in her palm. "No wonder why your mother hid you away for so long. But Drakkar will be disappointed. I can't let you live, now. You're too *dangerous.*"

Ecei raised her hand at me. Ready to snare and strike.

But I didn't respond. Couldn't.

Not as Riku lunged. Not as fury slowed his movements and tears stung his eyes. "You're *mine.*"

"Riku, no!" I screamed, stumbling after him. Reaching, again.

Mal got there first, planting herself between Ecei and Riku. Forcing Riku to skid to a halt. Wielding a sword she stole off a guard she'd ended. Slicing at Ecei's arm so fast, the Ice Witch almost lost her hand.

Almost.

She hopped back just in time, shock and rage painted across her grimace in equal proportions.

But Malina was all focus. All honed, sharpened anger. A weapon, forged in years of fire and survival. "My turn." She aimed her sword again at Ecei's throat. "I've been waiting for this."

Ecei's blade of ice lengthened as she gripped it with both hands. "Out of my way."

Ecei struck first...and missed.

Missed, as the ground *roared.*

No...it didn't roar. It *shook.*

Malina slashed, this time cutting into Ecei's cheek, but the earth pitched and rumbled so violently that she tumbled back, slamming into me.

I fell to my knees, the remaining two guards crying out as they toppled, too. I blinked as I tried to make out what was happening, but light fled from the day, darkness blurring everything...

Not darkness. *Smoke.*

A pillar of it, rising from the opposite end of the castle. So tall and wide, it sheathed the sun.

The Winter Palace was burning.

Fire.

Always *fire.*

Pale skin, blistered and charred to black.

Light; blinding, searing.

Eyes wide with terror, mouths set in disgusted frowns.

Panic roared in my deaf ears. Where was Shin? Was this his doing? Was he—?

Someone help!

He's just a boy!

No, he had to be okay. He couldn't—

"What was *that?*" Ecei hissed as she limped to standing, backtracking toward her guards, eyes wide and wild.

"Phase two," Riku spat as he fell to my side, an arm looping around my shoulders. Shielding me, protecting me, even now. But it didn't lessen his venom as he sneered at Ecei. "That was your precious Blight exploding."

Shock and victory cried through me. I glanced again at the smokestack, at the billowing clouds of black that were not loss, but triumph.

Fire burned. Destroyed.

But it also *saved.*

Babylon would not fall to Carnage's mighty sword. Would not succumb to Death's quiet torture.

Ecei's face fell. Her hands fisted.

Then ice shot from the snow, wrapping around Riku, Malina, and me like snakes. Squeezing the life out of its prey. The guards flanked Ecei, waiting for orders.

Something *cracked* in my side. I screamed as the agony bit into my lungs, my breath shallow and *burning* as the trap wrung tighter—

"You little *shits.*" Ecei stalked to us, and my stomach lurched again. She nudged Ren's head with her boot as she passed, my rage and disgust and dizzying pain all battling in each desperate inhale. "This one's death was too clean. Too *painless*. But I'm going to enjoy ripping you all apart...even you, Princess. Your power will never see the light of—"

The threats died abruptly in Ecei's throat as she clasped her neck. As her face went purple, and she collapsed to her knees, eyes bulging and red. As the two guards froze next to her–heads swiveling to find the unknown threat.

As they both crumbled, too, gasping and sputtering.

As the ice melted slightly around us, Ecei's Control faltering.

As Shin stepped around the corner, clad in nightshade black and standing tall like the noble-born street-rat he was. The Prince of Hiku City.

Shin, who *stayed*. Who came back.

Shin, whose gaze locked onto Ren's severed corpse. Whose expression fragmented like the pieces of my broken heart.

Shin, whose green-tea-and-honey eyes tinted pure, endless black.

"You took the words right out of my mouth, Ecei." A cruel smile curved his lips, disappearing the warmth I'd come to know. Vanishing all traces of mercy and goodness. He twisted his fingers again, earning another hoarse cough from Ecei. "Time for me to take the breath out of yours."

I'd met Death before, and today, Shin wore his face.

But this death was not an indiscriminate conqueror—it was a righteous thief. A vengeful king, taking for what had been stolen from him. An executioner, delivering justice.

A life for a life.

Even.

Ecei clawed at the invisible noose around her neck, and Shin's grin only grew.

He was going to kill her.

And I was going to *watch*.

Until the guard next to Ecei stumbled to his feet. Until he drew something blue from his pocket. Until I realized—too late—what it was.

"Shin, no!" I cried, just as the guard embedded the dart into the side of his exposed neck.

THIRTY-EIGHT

One moment, I held Ecei's life in my hands.

Perhaps this was what Irina felt when she healed—this power. This godlike, euphoric vengeance—and grief—that came with the weight of a life.

Not just one life, but several.

Aya's life. Ruined and then stolen, first by Ecei's Blight, second by her blade. Aya, who was made of butterfly wings and starlight. Who was goodness embodied, now just a memory on a breeze.

The breeze I used to rob Ecei of her next words.

Ren's life. Cleaved from his shoulders by Ecei's sword. Ren, who flowed and tumbled like an easy river, now stilled and dried up. His soul—only half of a whole—torn to shreds. Pilfered from his twin's side, like the sun snatched from the sky.

Like the light I'd snatch from Ecei's eyes, bulging with fear as she silently begged for air.

One moment, I had the choice to end her. To end all of this. To avenge my siblings, my mother, and all of Babylon.

But it was a moment I let carry on too long.

Irina screamed, and the guard's dart struck.

A mere sting against my skin.

Then the breeze abandoned me, just as I had Aya and Ren. No longer protected me, like I failed to protect them.

The dizziness was instant, a whirling in my head that blinded me as the winds died.

Ecei gasped a breath, dragging in greedy swallows of air that didn't belong to her. Air that should've belonged to Aya, to Ren...

I took a step forward, and my legs gave out. I crashed to the ground.

But I wouldn't stop. I unsheathed my dagger, the last of my strength focused on holding the hilt. My Control was not my only weapon, my body born and trained to fight and survive.

"Enough. All of this is enough," Ecei finally croaked as she stood, and with a swish of her hands, the ice around my family tightened again. Riku and Irina yelped, and Ecei scoffed. "This ends now."

All my strength, and I stood again. I raised my blade, fighting the wooziness sucking the life from my veins. "I don't need Control to kill you. I'm happy to make you bleed."

"You can try." Ecei twisted her fingers, and her icy hold squeezed again. "But you can't kill me and protect them."

I stole a glance at the others. At the fear and sorrow that doused Riku's face in numb horror. At Irina, whose warm skin was pale, her eyes wide with panic even as she stammered softly, "Shin, don't worry, it's okay. We're okay."

Breath above, she was a terrible liar, the pain written clearly across her face.

Don't worry. Time to let me fly, Shin.

No, no more veiled goodbyes. No more sitting and watching while others suffered.

No more lives sacrificed to Ecei's blade.

My gaze shifted to Mal—my best friend and betrayer—

Who blinked twice, then winked once with her left eye. Who scrunched her nose. A signal in the language only we knew.

Buy time.

The anger I carried onto the battlefield with me died in an instant, memories of all the jobs we'd pulled together blotting it out.

There was no time left. This was our final con, a soul-deep understanding passing through our shared look. We weren't going to make it out of this, not both of us. The game was up...we'd bet too high and would crash too hard.

But even if we lost, there were others here that we had to save. People depending on us to see it through, just as we had for the last fourteen years.

One last con.

Together, like we always were, no matter the pain between us.

I dove, my blade swinging.

Strike after strike.

But I was slow, sloppy. My limbs shaky and cold. My movements stiff and weightless. I slashed low at Ecei's legs, a move that normally would have knocked my opponent over with force alone, but it made no impact as she dodged easily.

Ecei met me blow for blow. She smiled as her sword of ice clashed against mine, her *Easinir* helping her move in fluid, dance-like strikes. On my better days, I'd have kept up, my winds faster and my limbs stronger, my being built to soar.

But now, the spinning made me dizzy, and I nearly missed the next block, her blade heavy as it swung for my head.

I dipped back, trying to catch my breath. Trying to find my feet, but they weren't used to standing on solid ground.

It didn't matter. I just needed one good strike, aimed at her throat like she had my sister's.

I feigned first, dipping low before jabbing my blade high–

And missed.

Something pierced my left side—just between the plates of metal of my battle suit. A well-placed stab, the water slipping through the cracks and then changing into a jagged, deep blade.

My lung punctured. Pain ruptured through me, whetting every jagged breath. My shins hit the snowfall as the world blurred.

"No, Shin—no!" Irina screamed, but she sounded so *far away.* "Don't you fucking touch him!"

"How does it feel?" Ecei twisted the blade, and black blotted the edges of my vision as searing heat burned through me. "To not be able to gasp your next breath? How does it feel to be *powerless?*"

My hands lost grip of my dagger and it clattered against the ice. A cold crept up my spine. Not the cold of a chilly, winter wind. Not the cold of a night on a rooftop.

The cold of death. The cold of endless oblivion.

But I had one job left.

One last ruse. One more feint.

One more minute.

"Almost as good as it felt to kill your son," I spoke around the blood coating my tongue, hot and metallic. Drakkar had scrambled away during the fight, but he didn't need to be here to be bait. To buy *time.* I smirked. "He begged for you the whole time. '*Mommy please, Mommy hel—*'"

Another twist, and my tease ended in a groan.

Ecei swore. "If you touched my boy—"

"You'll what, hurt me? *Kill me*?" I laughed, even though each shake of my shoulders was torture, the infinite cold settling deeper. Each breath, each word heavier. "Go ahead. My life is worthless anyway. But Babylon will know what you've done. The Jaltans are here, Ecei. Your son is *dead*. Your Blight is destroyed. This is already over."

One final threat. One more breath.

Ecei paused, fear flickering in her stare. "Then I will end you with me."

Liar and lure.

Devil and damsel.

Ecei inhaled, ready to drive her dagger home to my heart—

"Don't think so." Malina stabbed the blue dart directly into Ecei's neck, her clothes still dripping from the melted ice. Behind her, Riku held a knife to the last guard's throat—the same one who'd shot me. The same one who'd held both Aya and Ren captive in the Opera House—Sachir.

Ecei's ice dissolved from my side and she staggered back. The dizziness—born of her own poison—gnawed at her strength.

Mal gripped the back of Ecei's head, yanking her by her hair. "How does it feel to be powerless, Ecei?"

But even on her knees, even with the dart draining her, Ecei smirked. *One last jab.* "What do you think?"

The dagger–*my* dagger, lost in the scuffle–slammed through Mal's breastbone before I could stop it. Before I could do anything.

Mal clutched at her chest.

Fell to the ground.

I screamed.

"*No!*" It wasn't a plea, but a command as I crawled over the snowfall, my side stinging with every muscle moved, but I couldn't stop. I wouldn't.

Blood seeped from Mal mouth as she coughed, her whole frame shaking. "I'm sorry. I'm so sorry, Shin."

Our gazes collided like they had that first day in the sewers, hers wide and afraid, mine soothing and inviting.

"Shh, I know," I whispered through my sobs as I cradled her in my arms with the very last of my strength. As I brushed her mess of curls out of her face, like I had a thousand-and-one times.

Mal, my diamond in the rough. Mal, my hard-headed and iron-hearted friend.

But she wasn't unbreakable. Not all sharp and hard, not impenetrable.

She was just a girl. A scared, hurt, *fragile* girl, a feral thing that stood in front of her brother and snarled in fear's face despite her weaknesses. A marvelous, fiery thing that pretended to be strong for the people she loved.

Now, she was so tiny, so *cold.*

"How *tragic,*" Ecei laughed, a shrill shriek that wrenched down my spine. She took a teetering step toward us, tenacious as she was wicked. "Even now, you can't—"

A burst of light blinded me. I looked up, shielding Mal—

But this time, Irina didn't *give.* Didn't save.

Ecei's scream shuddered out of her as her skin waned pale and gaunt, as her hair bleached silver and straggly. Her bones crunched to dust and her eyes sank back into her skull, like Death sped up as her body decayed.

And Irina ended her life with one last touch.

Ecei's corpse crumpled to the ground with the most satisfying thud in the world.

One moment, she was there, the most dangerous person to walk the earth. The most wicked, vile person ever allowed to breathe.

And the next, she was gone, a pile of skin and bones.

But despite the victory singing through my heart, my vision faded at the edges again, my head spinning.

It was so cold.

"Shin, hold on." It was my name that dragged me back to reality. To the heat pooling across my fingertips—blood. Mal's and mine.

Mal smiled as she stroked my cheek, staining it with our combined scarlet.

I forced myself to smile back, to stay awake. To choke out a few more words, mumbling them as I kissed her forehead. "Hey, don't—"

"I love you," Mal interrupted, as she always did. So impatient, even at the end. Always one step ahead.

"I love you, too," I whispered, and it was true. I had been angry. Hurt. But none of it mattered. I loved her all the same. She was my family. The girl I ran to when I didn't know what to do. The sister who taught Aya to braid her hair. The accomplice who was willing to challenge me and compliment me in equal measures.

Family. Not by blood, but by choice, and somehow, that mattered just as much.

I didn't know whose eyes fluttered shut first, hers or mine. But if this was the end, so be it. We'd go out together.

Damsel and devil.

Liar and lure.

Always.

Coldness sank deeper, and my limbs went numb.

Not the cold of a winter snowball fight. Nor the cold of a poor man's bath.

The cold of weightless sleep. The cold of eternal rest.

So tired.

So heavy.

A flash stained my eyelids red. A voice like summer sunlight. "Let me heal you, I can—"

"Him first," a more familiar voice strained, and then went quiet. So *silent*, not even a breath escaped. So *cold*, her eternal flame fizzling out.

"Hold on, Shin." Sobs, so *sad*. So heavy. "Don't let go."

One moment—I tried to hang on. I really did.

But the next, I let go.

THIRTY-NINE

IRINA

Shin had not lied to Ecei.

The Jaltans came.

With nearly two hundred men, all poised to rescue us. A beastly body of scarlet and black, the ground thundered as they stormed the castle not long after Ecei fell, Naria and King Odion leading the charge.

And they were not alone. Hana's father, King Lin, sent along a small fleet of airships to retrieve us, carrying with them a missive from my parents that they too had sanctioned my immediate rescue and return. It marked the first tri-kingdom collaboration, all three countries unified as they occupied the Nehir Capitol.

It didn't matter.

They were all too late.

I couldn't save them both.

In the two days it took for us to travel by airship back to Dunyas, the reality hung over my head like a guillotine still waiting to fall. Even though Ecei and the Blight were gone, even though I was far from danger, even though my limbs were no longer half-frozen and numb...

Their names played on an endless loop in my mind.

Nikolaj.

Davke and Driss.

Aya.

Ren.

...Malina.

It was the same loop that moved in time with my heartbeat, in time with the breaths of the man lying unconscious on the soft medical cot before me.

Shin hadn't woken yet, but he'd survived. The last dregs of my power had been just enough to keep him alive. Just enough to keep him *breathing* until help came.

Now, despite the constant hum of the ship, my ears still strained to listen to every breath that rasped through his still-healing lungs. Every quiet beat of his pulse against the skin of his wrist.

But maybe it was better that he slept. When he woke, I'd have to tell him. Have to watch his face when he heard I'd chosen to save him over Mal. When he realized that if I hadn't spent so much of my already waning power on the guards and Ecei...

If I hadn't wasted my gift on *taking* a life...

I might have saved her, too.

But that was a truth I didn't have to face, not yet. Not while his eyes still stayed shut, long coal lashes resting against his pale cheeks. Not while the ship still brambled through the clouds, the night sky beyond a quiet cushion before dawn—and reality—crept back in.

A knock sounded at the medical bay door, and Hana popped her head in. She smiled—a soft, pitying thing—her voice low. "We're almost there, Ri-Ri."

I swallowed down the prickle of fear that stung the back of my throat. *There* meant Anastova. Meant *home.* "I know."

Hana popped her hip, round eyes giving me the once-over. "Come eat and freshen up. You don't want to see your parents like this."

Like this—in Shin's torn, dirty tunic, caked in blood and dirt and melted snow, short curls a rat's nest. Eyes bloodshot from lack of sleep —Mother Earth, lack of *blinking.* Smell about as fresh as the barn-end of a farm.

My parents—my *mother*—would probably pitch a fit if I showed up like this, filthy and downtrodden. If I dared embarrass her with such an uncouth appearance.

But for the first time in my life, I could not have cared less. My mother could throw a tantrum or hurl her insults my way. It didn't change a thing.

"I'm not leaving him."

I wouldn't, not until he told me to himself. Not until he chose something else.

Hana frowned—out of concern for me, not of what my mother thought. "How about a bath? It'll just be—"

"I won't go, Hana." My voice was firmer. Steadier.

Because when Shin opened his eyes, he would be alone in the world again. No Aya, no Mal, no Ren...just the weight of their absence. Just the duty to the other Lost Ones, still grieving and hurting in their own right, waiting for him to take care of them again.

Shin had come for me. He'd stayed. He'd *sacrificed.*

I would not leave him.

"Suit yourself." Hana blew out a sigh—the battle ended before it even started. "Naria said she'll take the next shift."

Which was fine. But both of my friends knew I wouldn't be leaving this small bay until we landed, whether Naria decided to join me or not.

I didn't pay attention to when—or if—Hana left, instead watching Shin's chest rise and fall. Sending my power out in thin, exploratory threads, checking that his soul still buzzed inside.

And I stayed that way for another few minutes—or hours, I couldn't tell—until another set of footsteps clanged against the metal flooring, not bothering to knock as they stalked up behind me.

Riku crawled onto the rigid windowsill, moonlight casting his face in pallor as he stared outside, slumping against the pane.

If I looked haggard, Riku looked half-dead. I had healed him fully, his wound from Ecei entirely erased, his body in perfect condition. But there were scars now that lived so deep, no power could mend them. No words could *touch* them. Like Ren's death had killed a part of him too, his expression unfocused and blank, his posture still as a corpse.

He didn't look at Shin or I as he spoke. "Still no change?"

Guilt bit at the back of my neck. Riku didn't need anything else to worry about right now. "No. How is Kas?"

He'd been the hardest to look at. The hardest to face, after...

"Sleeping," Riku offered mercifully. His voice softened by an impossibly small margin. "It's a lot to process. You know how much they meant to each other."

"I do." *Too well.* Just like Riku did, too.

Three little siblings, lost and alone. Powerless to save their own.

Except I'd been the one to choose which person I healed first. Who did—and *didn't*—survive.

Riku tore his gaze from the window, fixing it instead on me, like somehow he could read my thoughts. Or smell my guilt, the scent pungent and lingering.

"Kas will have all of us to get through it." His throat bobbed as he glanced down at Shin. "You made the right call."

I followed his gaze. Squeezed Shin's hand. "There wasn't a choice, not for me."

There hadn't been, not since the Opera House. Not since the night in the bar, or the Masque.

I would always choose Shin. Over my family, over my kingdom, over death itself if I had to.

Riku's mouth twitched—just a hint of a grin—the first signal of the life that still beat in his chest. "I know."

Another knock, and warmth wafted through the door, bringing with it the smell of blueberry and sugar. Naveen didn't wait for an invitation as he crossed toward us, a tray of muffins balanced in his hands. "You two look like you need something sweet."

I took one, gratitude taking root deep in my core. "Thank you."

I hoped he knew I meant it—for more than the muffin. Naveen had been the one to pull us all back, to gather us onto the ship, stepping into the role of leader as Shin healed.

"You look like you need something *strong*." Riku hopped off the sill, ignoring the muffins. "Come raid the stock room for some liquor with me?"

Naveen narrowed his eyes—still a con artist at heart that clearly smelled the bullshit on Riku's breath—but simply said, "Fine, but you're eating at least two of these while we're there."

Riku said nothing, moving for the door. But he paused in the threshold, dead gaze blistering, "We're glad you're okay, you know. We knew the risks going in."

I heard the words he didn't say—and maybe, didn't mean.

It's not your fault.

I forced a grin despite the guilt that tightened my windpipe. "I'm not sure that it helps."

Riku gripped the metal doorway, knuckles flashing white. "But it will. Ren..." he paused, his twin's name a cracked, broken syllable, "he didn't just like you because you gave him attention. He—*we all* believe you're what's best for Babylon. So make the changes they died for."

If you don't like the way things are, change them.

I would. So Aya and Ren and Malina would be the last martyrs. So we'd be the last mourners.

"You have my word," I swore, but Riku was already gone, his steps echoing down the hall.

Naveen offered another smile—and another muffin, placing it on the small table at my side. He winked, jerking a thumb at Shin. "If you want more lively company, come have a drink with us."

I smiled again. He knew I wouldn't come. But it was nice to be invited, anyway.

And then he was gone, too, leaving me to listen to Shin's breathing and the internal loop of names that would haunt my every thought.

Nikolaj.

Davke.

Driss.

Aya.

Ren.

Malina.

Over and over, until dawn came too early.

FORTY

IRINA

Alone, I stared up at the massive entry way to Anastova with a knot in my gut. Without my friends at my side—Naria taking Shin to be examined by the medementals in my quarters, Hana leading Naveen, Kas, and Riku to the guest wing where they'd be staying—loneliness clanged through me like a warning bell.

Anastova had never looked more foreign. Not that an inch of it had changed—not even the many hanging plants had wilted in my time gone, their green hues just as bright and healthy as I'd left them.

But *I* was irrevocably different.

I was not the same girl who left in a petal-pink, tightly laced dress that my mother chose. Not the same girl who stayed silent during dinners while her father 'handled it' for her. No, I didn't fit into the confines of the quiet, compliant princess anymore. I didn't match the image they had of me—not that I ever really had.

Now, I was a survivor. A fighter. A leader.

A killer.

Still, despite the dread weighing down my middle, I held my head high as I walked through the main doors, their jade green reminiscent of my favorite tea-and-honey shade...

If Shin could rescue me, I could do the same for him. No matter what my parents said or did. No matter the contempt or consequences I was about to face.

I had work to do.

Purpose.

But I wasn't expecting the crushing hug that wrapped around me the second I crossed the threshold. Wasn't expecting the slim, bony form that stabbed at my still-healing ribs.

I froze as my mother wrapped her arms tighter, staying silent until a jolt of pain twisted my side.

"Ow," I grumbled, wriggling with a discomfort that was both internal and external. My bones hurt, but so did the betrayal still waiting to be addressed. So did the novelty of this moment—my mother's preferred flavor of affection typically the reserved, absent kind.

Queen Vera didn't *hug*.

"Mother, I can't breathe," I gritted through clenched teeth, and her grip slackened. But she didn't let go.

"I thought I lost you," she mumbled shakily into my shoulder.

I stilled.

My mother, the volcano of a woman who melted down anything that displeased her. My mother, who trembled now like a pebble in an earthquake.

"I am so sorry, I thought you were *gone.*"

Things did not change in Anastova. The clay bricks all maintained their strength, the heat never cooled, and the leaves never shed their green.

But the emotion welling in my mother's voice, the desperation in her grasp—

Perhaps I hadn't been the only thing to shift in my time away. To *grow.*

"I'm fine." I did not know how to console her—how to bridge the distance between us. So I simply snaked my arms around her waist, holding this precious, liminal space as my mother hugged me for the first time in years.

Thank Mother Earth, she broke away first, eyes puffy with tears as she assessed me—but not with the stony contempt she usually wore as her favorite accessory. Instead, worry rested in her drawn brow, in her wrinkled frown.

Until her gaze snagged on my head.

"What happened to your hair?" She ran her fingers through my short curls like the motion could somehow coax them to grow again, her mouth dropping open.

I waved her hand away. Stood straighter.

If you don't like the ways things are, change them.

"I cut it."

My mother closed her mouth. Inhaled, shoulders slumping. Then, "It...uh..." She paused, then tried again, a small, hesitant smile spreading—like her mouth was still learning how. "It suits you."

I blinked away my surprise as my mother fit her hand through mine.

"Come on in, Ca— *Irina*," she corrected herself before my full name slipped, "your father is waiting for us in the dining room. We have a lot to discuss."

⁊

"You're *abdicating*?" I spat the word like a curse as my head swiveled between my parents, waiting for one of them to stand up from the table and yell 'just kidding!'.

But both of them remained seated across from me—next to each other, for once—their expressions matching in both severity and sincerity.

This wasn't a joke.

This was a declaration.

My parents were stepping down from the throne.

My father pushed the tray of Tasha's lemon tarts closer to me—a peace offering—his round face slimmer since I'd last seen him, like somehow worry had mangled his appetite—and perhaps his mind. But his voice laced with a grim authority I rarely heard from my jolly father, a gravity that dragged me down with it. "It's what we must do. Your mother and I made mistakes. We thought we were doing what was best, but we are partially responsible for what happened in Nehir."

My shock gave way to irritation.

What happened in Nehir, like it was a little miscommunication and a scraped knee. Like it was just a simple snafu that needed correcting.

Like it wasn't my friends' lives, forfeited to a dark, twisted queen that they had let into our home. That they'd let ruin her way across Babylon unchecked. That they had made deals with. *Plans.*

"*Partially?*" I challenged, staring at my mother. Sending her signature heat—a fire that lived in my bones, too—right back at her. "I know what you did with Ecei in Jalta."

I expected an eye roll or a dismissive quip. Or, perhaps a pinpricked insult, meant to disarm with minimal effort on her part.

But Vera's face blanched with shame. She gripped the edge of the table, knuckles ghostly pale.

"Everything I've ever done was to protect my children. To protect you and Nikki." Her eyes watered with tears, but she didn't look away. Didn't try to hide. "But that doesn't make what I did right. Which is why it's time for me to do some penance."

The intent doesn't lessen the impact.

I'd said it to Shin myself, back in Hiku City. And since then...we'd all made well-intentioned mistakes, our choices leading to unexpected outcomes that didn't lessen our well-meaning.

Nikolaj.

Davke and Driss.

Aya and Ren.

Malina.

But it didn't excuse my mother's years of selfishness. The decade of abuse of power, even if it was meant to 'support' us—

It had ruined Shin's life. Decimated Jalta.

Nearly destroyed all of Babylon.

I didn't know if *penance* and good intentions absolved the weight of her sins.

When I didn't respond, she continued, "After Nikolaj...I thought I was protecting you by trying to find you a suitable husband. The dresses, the hair, the bargains—I thought all of it would keep you *safe*, like marrying your father had done for me. But I was so wrong." She reached across the table to hold my hand, her grip soft, and her words softer still. "When you left...when they *took* you...I realized I couldn't go through it again. I couldn't lose you, too."

I stilled, my breath ragged in my lungs, the air too thin.

My mother had a penchant for overbearing. She was sweltering heat and oppressive attention. She was a crafter of gilded cages and gemstone disguises, always trying to keep me cinched and tucked *in*, to weigh me down...

To protect me. To keep the harsh world—the world that took her son—*out*.

Maybe she had done the best she could with the circumstances she had. Had coped the way she knew how, given all that had happened to her family.

But I was no longer content to let things just *happen*. And I wasn't lost.

"I'm here now." I pulled my hand away—not as a punishment, but a boundary I needed. An independence that I would have to carry moving forward—even though part of me wanted to sink back into the role of a little girl, to enjoy the safety my parents' embrace for the first time in a long time. But there was work to do, and I had promises to keep. "You can abdicate, but that's not real penance. That's avoidance. There are some things that need to change immediately, and if I'm going to make them happen, I'll need your full support."

Starting with a cure for the Blight, and then, a fix for the disproportionate suffering that still lingered throughout the continent. My head high, I listed my grievances:

The Poppy Dust epidemic.

The unfair working conditions in Dunyas and Sora.

The improper distribution of basic needs.

The pervasive mistreatment of the common folk by the nobility.

And as I spoke, my parents stayed silent—listening, instead of interrupting or dismissing for once, as I made my case. As I pled for the wellbeing of my people.

When I was finished, my father nodded, stealing a glance at my mother before turning to me. "It will be difficult. The nobility do not change easily. But the crown is yours once we step down, and we'll do what we can to help sway political opinions in your favor."

Like it had always been that simple. Like they hadn't spent the better half of my life telling me all the ways I was *lacking*. All the parts of me that were unfit to rule without a husband at my side.

"I won't marry Avi," I added—then, for good measure, "*definitely* not Drakkar, either."

My mother winced at his name, her guilt streaking across her features like a lightning strike across the sky.

He'd been spared, even as the Jaltans and Sorans occupied the palace—a show of mercy instead of war. A demonstration that none of the heirs would pay for the sins of their parents.

But he would not be allowed to rule—not if I had any say in it. Not until he faced trial for his own misdoings, his mother not here anymore to brush them all under a rug anymore.

And just as importantly—my heart was not for sale or bargain. I had already chosen to give it freely, and there was no returning it now.

"You don't have to choose anyone until you're ready." My mother cleared her throat, that same hesitant smile reappearing on her thin mouth. "We will be here to support you. But it's time we take a step back and reevaluate."

My father covered her hand in his—and for once, my mother squeezed back. He beamed. "And we both are proud of the Queen you're becoming."

Proud.

My head dipped so they wouldn't see the tears that sprinted to my lashes—ones I'd been holding for far too long—impatient to fall.

I couldn't remember the last time I'd heard that word directed at me.

No longer just my father's *good girl*, or my mother's *pretty doll*.

A proud queen.

That was what I would be. For Babylon, for Nikolaj...

And for them. For the people they were becoming. For the person I wanted to be, too.

Anastova had not changed in a long, *long* time; but it was about to, its foundation of stagnancy already shifting. The wind sang a new tune as a fresh bud bloomed in my heart, ready to finally take root and soak up the sun.

"Excuse me, Princess Catirina?" Gemma, one of Mama's head maids, bowed low as she entered, tearing me back to the moment. My head snapped up as she cleared her throat. "Your guest is awake."

I jolted from my seat.

Babylon would have to hold on for another night, because my Prince needed me first.

FORTY-ONE

IRINA

I ran as fast as my legs would carry me through the winding halls of Anastova, his name in my head keeping time with my furious footsteps.

Shin.

Shin.

Shin.

Like a heartbeat. Like the rhythm of my soul.

Shin.

Shin.

Shin.

And then, he was there, in the room I grew up in.

My breath caught in my chest as I took him in. The cherry-blossom-pink curtains swayed in time with his soft, dark hair, a warm breeze playing with both. His bare back faced me—carved in muscle yet smooth at the same time, always the contradiction—as he sat on *my* bed, the plush mattress dipping slightly beneath his weight.

Shin Koishi lived.

"Shin?" His name breathed out of me. "How are you—?"

He turned. Blinked.

And then he was up, devouring the room in three of his long strides.

He scooped me into his arms like I weighed nothing, despite the puckered, angry scar on his side. Breathed me in, like my unwashed scent was the most fragrant thing in the world.

Held me close, like he'd never let me go again.

His mouth moved against my skin as he buried his face in the crook of my neck. "I'm sorry for everything you endured. That I couldn't protect you."

My fingers laced through his hair as my legs wrapped around his trunk, tugging him as close as space would allow, ignoring the ache in my bones. Ignoring everything else.

Everything except the list.

Nikolaj.

Davke and Driss.

Aya.

Ren.

Malina.

"I'm sorry I couldn't save them."

Shin stilled. Lowered me back to the ground. "Don't be sorry. You saved my life *again*." He brushed curls out of my face with his wide palms as his eyes tracked over me. As that little dimple appeared in his cheek. "We're even."

I swallowed back the lump that rose.

Even.

If only it were true or that simple. I opted instead for the easier conversation, slipping back into my role as his nursemaid as I gingerly tapped the scar on his side. "How are you feeling?"

A smirk covered his slight wince. "Good as new."

But he was not good, body or heart. There, written across his face, much like the mark stretching across his ribs...

Evidence of all that he'd lost. Sadness, for the pieces of him that were amputated from his soul and couldn't be repaired.

Aya.

Ren.

Malina.

I shut their names out of my mind, all of them still too sore. Again, I chose easy, just for today. For this moment. For this breath where all that mattered was *Shin, Shin, Shin.*

"For a thief, you're a terrible liar." I quirked a brow as I ushered him back to sit, the mattress enveloping us both.

"I'm rusty," he chuckled, but the sound was off, its nightshade twinkle dulled. He sucked in a deep, shuddering breath as he sank further into the bed. Green-tea-and-honey eyes speared me with how *soft* they were. How *broken*. Then, "Can we maybe just—can we not talk, for a while? Can you just be with me?"

It seemed impossible—for us to just be here, *alive*, with everything that had happened. In my room, of all places, a thief and a princess in the heart of Anastova.

But today had already been full of impossible realities.

My tongue was lame in my mouth, but I managed a mumbled, "Of course."

It took a moment of adjusting—me laying on his left to avoid my bruised side and his, a pillow propped behind him, my head on his chest. But after a few moments, our breaths found a steady rhythm, the quiet music of our first easy moment together taking a hold.

And then, just like we had been in the bar in Hiku City and the cabin in Dunyas...

We were no longer princess and thief. No longer future queen and lost heir.

We were two people who had endured enough hurt to last lifetimes. Two people that needed to rest and heal, before reality came back in.

I don't know how long we stayed that way—limbs folded in on each other, fingers gently stroking over skin, unassuming kisses syncopating the quiet, a hummed lullaby soothing us both—but the sun had long vanished from my window by the time we spoke again.

"I was so afraid when they took you." Shin's voice was the first string of lyrics to our song, a quivering cello that vibrated through me. "You have *no* idea."

But I did know. Too well.

My hand drifted toward the vicious scar—tracing the evidence of how close it had been, even my power not enough to fully vanish the reminder. "I thought I lost you, too."

He sucked in a deep breath. Held me closer, strong arms bracketing me. "I'm right here. I'm not going anywhere."

But something about his voice was wrong—*distant*, like the memory of a melody, half-formed and fleeting.

Like part of him was already gone.

Forty-Two

The sunset blurred all else as it hung low in the twilight sky, dappling the garden in lavender and gold.

Aya would have loved this place. Would've stopped at every rose and tulip to sniff the fragrant air. Would have danced in the cool breeze, soaking up the last embers of the dying sun before night claimed it.

I held that thought close as we stood around the headstones Naveen had crafted with his *Easinir*, their gray-rock faces carved with the images of those we'd lost.

One for Mal, her wild curls and wicked grin immortalized with the version of her we'd loved best instead of the hurts that still ached.

One for Ren, his sunlight smile and gleaming gaze everlasting, even beyond the veil--his image still a twin for Riku's, but somehow opposite.

And one for Aya, smile bright and dark hair swaying in a phantom wind, freer in death than she had been in life.

Irina stood behind them—the rest of us too emotional to officiate, but the soon-to-be-Queen already taking the helm. Already helping to heal our hearts, as she had our bodies. Naveen, Riku, Kas, Naria, and I watched on, our breaths held in collective anticipation and anxiety. It was a small gathering—intimate—but it fit, the Lost Ones never alone, but always marching to the beat of our own drum.

Irina raised her hands, a warm glow emitting from her palms.

"Mother Earth, we ask you to accept these three lives into your warm embrace. We seek to honor their legacies here, but their spirits rest with you." Her voice floated on the ever-present breeze that kept the evening cool—and that soothed my nerves to bearable. But then she paused, nurturing tone hitching as emotion caught. "Does anyone have anything to say about them? Any memories or goodbyes to share?"

There was a long moment where none of us braved the chasm, avoiding the grief that brought us here this evening. This moment of mourning had been Irina's idea after we'd all settled in yesterday, and we'd wholeheartedly agreed; but now, the open invitation made it real, and all the more painful.

Mal, Ren, Aya...

They would not be joining us again.

Gone.

Gone.

Gone.

But one among us possessed the courage to light the wick, to leap into the flame and risk burning.

"I remember when you used to prank us all, but then you'd feel bad, so you'd tell us before the pranks happened." Kas stood with his back straight, but his bottom lip quivered over each word as he spoke to his sister's headstone—like somehow, she could hear him that way. "One time, you spiked my juice with prunes, but before I could take a sip, you downed the whole cup instead."

The memory speared me through my middle, chasing away the hesitation and springing fresh tears to my eyes. We'd made fun of Mal for hours after that one, all cracking jokes outside of the bathroom while she suffered, her pain her own doing. For the life of me, I could never understand why she hadn't just dumped the juice out instead.

Maybe that was her self-prescribed penance. Just as her death had been.

I offered a broken chuckle, a different memory shaking my shoulders. "One time after I screwed up a job, she put tacks in my boots, but then painted them bright green so I wouldn't wear them."

That was the Mal I'd keep in my heart—the one who saved me from Ecei, and herself. The one who was vengeful and vicious, but spared me from those parts for as long as she could, often by using my own vanity against me.

The liar to my lure.

The devil to my distraction.

Kas stroked the headstone, tears deepening the gray as they splotched against it. "I know you were a good person."

I smiled to myself.

Malina wasn't *good*. She was wicked and wild. But that was why we loved her—a diamond that would always be rough and uncut, but no less precious.

Riku stepped behind him, a hand on his shoulder—the warmest action I'd seen from him in days. "She was always taking lumps for us. Even at the end."

"Ren did, too," Naveen chimed in, wrapping an arm around Riku. For once, he didn't squirm, allowing our giant friend to envelop him as he spoke. "Not in the same way, but man, did that little shit know how to make us laugh. Especially when things got dark."

The breeze surged, the rustle through the hedges reminiscent of Ren's breathy chuckles—like he was ready to crack a joke even from the Ether's embrace.

But Ren had been more than giggles and sunshine. He'd been both fluid and constant—a river that ran along and adapted to its banks, but whose current always found its way back to us. Back home.

Riku stayed silent as Naveen continued, "He stayed with me for three days the second time I got clean. Through the shakes and the sweats, he didn't leave my side. And whenever I would howl in pain or beg, he'd crack a joke that made me want to punch him instead, until I forgot about how bad it was."

"When we—" Riku started, then stopped, a sharp inhale puncturing his sentence. Then, "When we were really young, sometimes he'd purposefully piss off the circus master just so he'd get more lashes than I would." Icy eyes melted, puddles forming across their lashes. "I never thanked him for that."

Irina's face pinched—one little sibling to another.

"He knows, Riku." She brushed a tear from his cheek. "He knows."

Riku nodded, wiping his face with his sleeve, reapplying his icy mask with the movement. But still, he stood taller, his gaze fixed instead on the last tombstone...

The one I'd been struggling to look at.

"Aya was the best of us." His voice was barely above hoarse a whisper, but it blasted into my chest all the same. "I think even Mal and Ren would agree to that."

Forcing myself not to run, to stay...

I looked at my sister's stony image.

Her hair and her smile were right, the stone perfectly capturing the angles of her soft face. But the eyes were wrong—too dull, too distant. They held none of my sister's grace and magnetic empathy. None of her charm.

"Aya was a breath of fresh air to everyone who knew her." Naveen's stalwart exterior cracked as his voice did, the pillar of support wilting into Riku's side as he stared at Aya's image, too. "I may have handled her medicine, but her presence alone was mine."

A universal truth. Aya was the heart. The lifeblood.

Without her, my pulse would forever feel foreign in my chest. Like it belonged elsewhere, beating like wings against an endless sky, my sister at my side.

"You were my first friend." Irina swallowed thickly, her palm flashing with light as she saluted the gravestone with a hand to the heart. "Say hi to Nikolaj for me."

Naria saluted too—a formal, Jaltan signal reserved for the bravest warriors. "I didn't know her well, but she took care of those most important to me when I couldn't."

It was the first time my sister spoke—and the last—for the little girl that should have been hers to claim, too. For the family we might have had in a different world.

"She made the best cookies," Kas piped in, then added, "no offense, Shin."

At the mention of my name, the others remembered I was there, attention swiveling to me, expectant.

I'd been quiet. Hesitant.

Like saying goodbye made it real. Like offering my last prayer to my sister really meant she was gone.

But there was a time for holding on, and a time for letting go.

Aya deserved to fly, without me holding her back any longer.

"I had the fortune of knowing her better than I knew most people." My voice cleaved from me as I cut the strings, letting my sister's spirit float on. "And there aren't words..." I stumbled, searching for anything that could encompass the magnitude of what she meant. Something that could begin to describe the vastness of my love—and my grief. "Aya knew how to make everyone feel like they could fly."

"She did." Irina reached over and grabbed my hand—warmth spreading through her fingers to mine. "She *does*."

And she always would. Her memory lived on, and would carry us all through until the Breath came to call for us, too.

Silence settled again, as everyone said their own prayers to themselves. As our hearts beat the rhythm of words we didn't know how to say aloud.

Until night closed around us, and one by one, everyone peeled off. Irina went first—called to a meeting with her parents to further discuss how she'd tame the nobility into accepting her rule—pressing a small kiss to my cheek before dragging Naria with her.

Sniffling Kas went next, solemn Riku in tow, the two brothers finding comfort together as their siblings accompanied each other to the next life.

Naveen was last—he said nothing as he stood next to me into the evening, as the moon climbed higher and higher, casting his bronze skin in a ghostly pale. But even he eventually sighed and retreated, long steps gently echoing against the stone until they faded entirely.

But even as the rest of the world slumbered, I stayed.

For all the times I hadn't. For all the ways I'd never get to again.

I stayed, until the sun once more peaked over the horizon, a new day dawning. Until the fallen Lost Ones all found their place among the fading stars.

Until a butterfly—white, small—landed on my sister's headstone, touching down for just a breath before it flew away again, tasting the skies on her behalf.

And then, because it was what I knew best...

I left, too.

FORTY-THREE

IRINA

Silence blanketed the dining room like a bad smell, invisible but cloying to all present despite the fragrant meal in front of us.

It'd been a bribe, Tasha's finest work to help me win over the royals and nobles from all three kingdoms seated around the table-- like medicine hidden in dessert to make it more palatable.

But as my declared plans for Babylon hung in the air like unpicked fruit, it hit me that perhaps I'd need more than some steak and lobster to overturn decades of tradition and corruption.

Seated between his brother, Lord Askil, and his son, Haro, King Lin frowned so fiercely his forehead crumbled like parchment, clearing his throat first. "Princess Irina, this is..."

"You will address her as Your *Majesty* now," my father's voice boomed, and Lin went silent again, the rest of the gathered staring down at their plates like scolded children; King Odion, Queen Katia, and Lord Hizan from Jalta, flanked by Avi and Naria. Lords Jakir and Lady Egrete, my parents' former advisors, next to my mother on my other side.

Of course, some were as highly ranked as I was; but as long as they were on Dunyasian soil, I held charge.

My hands shook at my sides, old nerves clawing up my back with vicious intent. It took all the courage I had, to lead. To speak up, instead of staying quiet. To shed my fragility in front of those who sought to only see me as meek and malleable.

But I had promises to keep.

Dead to honor.

Davke and Driss. Aya. Ren. Malina.

Nikolaj.

I offered my father a small smile—his support in recent days repairing more in me than I thought possible. But even with his backing, the rope I walked was thin. If I gave any ground now, the nobles would stampede, trampling me down before I could even stand. And I needed to stay strong if I was going to make this work.

I painted on the mask of a generous but detached regent, one I'd seen my mother wear a thousand times before. "You may continue, King Lin."

My mother squeezed my hand under the table—not her typical restrictive vise, but a show of solidarity.

"Your Majesty," King Lin grimaced, like the title tasted wrong, but he continued, "I see how well-intended these plans are, but you have to consider the implications. I know you are eager, but change does not happen overnight."

I set my silverware down, lifting my chin higher. A distant pang wished my brother were here—wished I could look to him for the answers, for the way forward.

But it was just me, now. And that had to be enough.

This time, it was Shin's smirk I copied. "Why not?"

Lin blinked twice, dumbstruck, like I'd just asked him to dance a jig on his hands.

His brother, Lord Askil, shook his head. "Well, there are procedures we have to follow—"

"And who invented those procedures? Who upholds them?" I sat forward, using their shock against them like the Lost Ones would. I was raised in this glimmering world, but I'd lived among the people, and I would not slow down just so bumbling fools like Askil could catch up. "We are the governing body. If we want to change things, we can. And all of Babylon does not have the time for us to sit here and bicker about bureaucracy."

My speech stole the air from the room, more acutely than even Shin's Control could.

I'd been silent for my whole life, a pretty flower in a vase. But now the nobles were truly speechless—trying to reconcile my thorns with my petals.

I didn't care. I was tired of being decorative and pleasing.

Babylon needed me to be *more*.

"Queen Catirina, you've only just been crowned. This is unconventional, and people will need time to adjust," Lord Hizan placated, a saccharine smile on his ruddy face. I'd always liked him the least—his eyes always lingering a little too long on places they shouldn't. They dragged over my chest now, and I stiffened as his voice cooled. "You don't want to ruffle feathers, especially as an unmarried—"

"Would you have made that comment to Prince Nikolaj or my brother, Lord Hizan?" Naria intercepted her uncle before he could finish, the Pyromental talented at turning up the heat in any conversation.

My heart leapt in my chest at the very mention of Shin, wishing he were here. But he needed his space to heal, to mourn, and I didn't want to interrupt that for him. Didn't want to burden him more than I already had.

Still, that truth didn't ease the ache of his absence next to me.

But I was lucky enough to have friends like Naria and Hana to uplift me, even when I wanted to slink down into my hair and hide from the world.

Lord Hizan sputtered at the question. "No, but—"

"Rashin is mourning his sister, and my brother is gone." My voice was a sharp-edged razor, and my mother winced as it cut. But I kept on, unwilling to be kind when I could be *helpful* instead. Like Nikolaj would. "I wish every day that it was him wearing this crown instead of me. But I'm what you've got, and I am taking this very seriously."

Hana and Naria both beamed at me, my parents nodding in quiet approval.

But the others at the table looked less thrilled...less willing to concede.

Lord Jakir, my father's long time financial advisor—and a major investor in the Poppy Trade— outright glared.

"Your passion is inspiring." The lie was as thinly veiled as his bald spot gleaming beneath the chandelier's lights. "But your experience is limited. We need to think critically. Everyone here has been in this business for a very, very long time, and—"

"And that makes you complicit," I finished his sentence, my own glower full of my mother's Jaltan heat.

My parents' abdication had only been the start. There was still justice that needed to be paid in every corner of this continent, and it was my penance for the mistakes I'd made to see it through.

"Excuse me?" Lady Egrete—another useless bystander to my parents' reign—clamped her hand over her chest as if I'd named her personally, exposing herself.

I sucked in a steadying breath—pretending it was one of Shin's grounding winds.

If he were here, he'd tell me to find their wickedness and exploit it. To use their desires against them.

But that would mean stooping to their level. Would further the cycle of blackmail and abuse of power.

So I would be better than them.

My voice was softer, but no less stinging. "Your policies and procedures did nothing to protect Babylon as Ecei poisoned us. You all let it happen, or squabbled amongst yourselves over money and power. My parents let unsafe farming practices run rampant through Dunyas and didn't bat an eye. Odion, you sanctioned a squadron of soldiers to attack an Opera House full of civilians, and now your people suffer for it. King Lin, don't think I don't know about your tastes for the brothels and smoking dens in Hiku City."

It was a risk, to lay it all bare. To call the shameful parts into the light.

But we had to acknowledge it all if we were going to fix it. To heal it.

As expected, the room went cold. King Lin shoved back from the table, his face blotting red. "That's an outrageous accusation—"

"It's not an accusation, it's the truth. We all played a part in this." My mother stood too, meeting him like steel against stone. But I noticed a tremble in her hands that hadn't been there before—a guilt that curved her normally proud back.

I stood next to her, fitting my hand through hers to ease the shaking. A show of unity. Of forgiveness and *change.* I cleared my throat. "We're all to blame, but we get to decide how our story is told from here on out. We can change this narrative and actually help the people of this continent. Or, you all can stand trial for your misdoings like Nehir will."

"Is that a threat?" Askil narrowed his eyes, his tongue poking the side of his cheek.

I shook my head. "No; it's a *choice*. I know that I'm asking for personal sacrifices and major changes. I know my agenda is as long as it is difficult. But no matter your pasts, I'm giving you all a choice now to either help me create a better future, or to answer for the failings that occurred under your rule."

It was a choice that had been denied our people for too long. A mercy that the everyday common folk hadn't been afforded.

But it was a bargain I was willing to make. To be better. To lead by *example.*

Lord Hizan remained seated, but his expression was no less caustic. He sneered, a sound somewhere between a snort and a scoff expelling from his overly large nose. "And who will preside over these trials if we decide not to follow an untested girl acting on her whims?"

I winced despite myself, the truth still harsh.

I *was* untested. Unsure. I had no idea how to lead or politic or write policy, no qualifications to back up my risky bets.

My mother went rigid at my side. "Watch how you speak to my daughter, Hizan."

Hizan leaned forward, ready to counter, but a dagger slashed into his steak, missing his big nose by a too-close margin.

"I'll personally officiate your trial, Hizan." Naria grinned as she stole his steak for herself, hefting it to her mouth and tearing a feral bite before plopping the rest onto her own plate. "Rashin and I both. We stand by Irina."

I fought a grin as Hizan paled, staring at the steak like she'd carved it directly from his ass.

"And if you don't comply, we'll usurp you," Hana chirped like she was simply admiring the weather, but her smile was all teeth as she nudged her father. King Lin blanched, but Hana pressed on, turning her candied attention toward the boys sitting silent at the table. "Right, Haro, Avi?"

Haro grinned, happy to be included. Avi blushed, but nodded with a chuckle, like Hana was just telling a joke to break the tension. The others laughed with him on shaky breaths, the potent density of the room dissipating with it.

But I knew my friend was not joking. None of this was funny, not anymore. She'd seen, too, what had become of our homeland. What happened to our people when power went unchecked.

King Odion stood, his expression unreadable. He'd been quiet this entire conversation, and I held my breath as I waited for him to speak, the King of the Pyre notorious for his branding stare.

But his gaze met mine—a familiar tea-stained shade—and warmed instead of burned. "Present us with actual plans, not just ideas, and we'll consider," he sighed, running a hand over his face. His wife slipped her hand into his, and he softened. "I want to support you, but I need clear cut objectives. Give us real documents and numbers that we can look over and negotiate, and Katia and I will do what we can."

I smiled, relief sagging through my middle, his commitment the first seed I needed for change.

I didn't want Babylon to run on just ideals or empty promises anymore. I didn't know what I was doing, but I was willing to learn. To grow.

To heal.

Reaching across the table, I shook Odion's hand. "Consider it done."

I barely touched my food at dinner, conflict souring my appetite, but instead of beelining for Tasha's lemon tarts or running back to Shin, I forced my feet toward the medementals' wing, in need of medicine and companionship more than I needed something sweet.

As expected, Naveen was already there, sitting in the closet he'd claimed as his office, poring over a book with worn edges as the single, flickering lantern lit his dark skin gold.

The very sight of my friend did wonders for the tension that stabbed at my back, my muscles unwinding as I slumped against the doorframe. "Tell me you have good news for me, Naveen."

I needed something to go right tonight.

Naveen's head snapped up, eyes bloodshot and bleary—either from crying earlier at the funeral, or from staring at faded pages...or both. But his smile still lit the small space, blindingly white teeth flashing. "Jaltan goats."

I blinked. "*What?*"

He pushed the book toward the edge of his desk, pointing to a drawing of a bearded, beady-eyed mountain goat. "Fascinating creatures. You've ever heard of them?"

"No. What...?" I gaped at him, reeling. Poor guy had absolutely cracked. "I meant about the samples..."

Naveen waved that off, flipping to the next page of the book with his eyes alight, pointing to a scientific rendering of berries. "Did you know that the national plant of Jalta is nightshade?"

I wilted further against the doorframe, resigned to follow wherever my friend led "Yes, actually." It was a declaration of Jaltan strength, that they held something so beautiful and deadly in such high regard.

"Morbid, I know. *Poisonous.*" Naveen shrugged, reading my expression. "But the mountain goats that live in Jalta *love* the stuff. Even though it's toxic."

Intrigue straightened my spine. "It doesn't affect them?"

"Nope." Naveen grinned, mischief and delight brimming in his gold-flecked gaze. "Do you want to know why?"

"If it will make this conversation begin to make sense..."

"Mineral licking." Naveen slammed the book shut, leaning back onto his rickety chair as his grin spread like wildfire. "The volcanic soil and surrounding rock is mineral dense, and those goats will lick those things all day, and it creates a barrier in their stomachs so the poison doesn't hit their bloodstream. The minerals have a compound that binds with the toxins and helps them excrete it safely."

A spark flared in my chest, realization dawning.

A compound that binds with toxins could mean a lot for our current predicaments.

I moved closer, examining the title of the book. *Jaltan Fauna and Flora.* "Mineral licking. Interesting."

Naveen continued, letting me in on the secret, "Why do you think the Jaltan nobility specifically were less affected by the Blight?"

I stilled, pieces fitting together, weaving it into something tangible. Something *understandable.* "Solyra is wedged between two volcanoes."

Naveen nodded, excitement shooting him out of his chair. "The soil, the clay, the palace itself...covered in the stuff. The pipes are built from it. The ground water is enriched with it. They've all been building their tolerance for *decades.*"

"So it's not a genetic superiority, it's environmental. The Blight doesn't enter their bloodstream as well." I exhaled on a shaky breath, hope and determination rooting in my gut. "If we could find a way for the compound already in the bloodstream to bind with the minerals..."

Naveen lifted the sample of the Blight from his pocket, the vial glinting in the lowlight. "It's a start."

A start. A plan.

I couldn't bring back those I'd already failed. Couldn't cure Aya or Nikolaj or save Mal and Ren. But I could offer Babylon more than they got, and I could use a cure to convince the stuffy nobles in my dining room that change—that healing—was possible. Necessary.

Hope blooming, I threw my arms around Naveen, smacking a kiss to his cheek. "You're a *genius.*"

Naveen chuckled, but his long arms wrapped around me all the same. "Don't thank me, thank the goats."

FORTY-FOUR

Word traveled at the speed of the wind, blowing through Babylon practically overnight.

Rumors moved even faster, propelled by man's wickedness like weeds in a garden.

By the time the dust settled in the few weeks after Ecei's fall, several rumors about what had happened had already spread through Anastova and beyond.

Some said I was the savior of Babylon—the lost Jaltan heir revived from obscurity to save the heart of the Dunyasian Princess and to stop the Blight. More ridiculous versions of the same narrative claimed that I had been a spy for years, faking my own death at ten years old to uncover the truth about the Blight. That I had risked my life and my title to personally bring down Ecei. It was a pretty fairytale that painted Irina and I as Breath-blessed saints.

As weeks turned to months, other tales—darker ones—claimed I wasn't the real heir. That I was an imposter, trying to use the situation to my advantage. Or that I was a pawn, hired by the Jaltans to reclaim their power now that Nehir was less of a threat. That Irina was using me as well to push her progressive agenda and seduce Jalta into Dunyas's pockets.

Better yet, some even claimed that the Blight was all Jalta's doing, and that sweet, innocent Ecei had simply been framed for the job, and that I was the traitor who'd tricked her.

But whenever I strolled through the plant-infested halls of Anastova, whatever rumors circulating about me died, the nobility all falling over themselves to get a look at me, or to personally *thank* me for my sacrifice.

Prince Rashin, back from the dead.

Prince Rashin, savior of Babylon.

Prince Rashin, the newest toy for them to ogle and gawk at.

None of them thanked Aya. Or Ren or Malina, the true saviors of Babylon. None of them *cared.*

Some of them, I recognized; patrons to the Crescent over the years, the same ones who'd scoffed or spat at us when we passed, sullied by our very existence.

Some of them, I avoided; their fake smiles terribly played cons, their jealousy and distaste thinly veiled like perfume over an unwashed armpit.

But Anastova was huge, which meant that even the Savior of Babylon could escape, my winds sneaking me away when I needed it most.

After all, I was ordered to rest. To recover, lying in Irina's cushy bed or sprawled out in the sunlight of the gardens like a cat on a windowsill. Or in the medementals' wing, speaking to the physicians about my aches, or my worries. My *grief.* It felt good to untangle the knots in my mind as they exercised my body.

Bit by bit, until my side was healed, and my range of motion was good as new.

And my soul was...not repaired, per se, but at least not hemorrhaging pain any longer. My mind not as addled by misty regrets and heavy sorrow.

Irina did not rest.

The moment her parents handed her the throne, Irina went to *work.*

Queen Catirina, the Blight-slayer.

Queen Catirina, voice of the people.

Queen Catirina, carrier of all of Babylon's worries and woes.

I saw her less and less, the moon already at its peak most nights by the time she crawled into bed beside me, tucking into my arms and passing out.

And by the time the sunlight returned each morning, Irina was already up and moving, save for a few brief, sweet kisses she'd spare me before she began her ever-growing list for the day.

Not that I could begrudge her—she did a wonderful job, despite the obstacles in her path. Change did not come easily to the corrupt, deeply entrenched nobles of Babylon, but that didn't stop Irina from trying, her light chasing back shadows that'd been present for decades.

Within the first month of our return, she'd gathered the royals of all four kingdoms and negotiated a deal to continue the occupation of Nehir and strip Drakkar of his title. After a grueling case, he was sentenced to house arrest and denied his birthright. His cousin Samir —the little blond whose arm I'd rearranged—was next in line, but as per the terms of Irina's proposal, he'd be supervised by delegates from all three kingdoms until he was deemed fit to rule on his own. And if he didn't stay in line, I'd personally be willing to snap his other wrist as a reminder.

By month two, she'd nearly made all of the nobles in Anastova shit their pants when she invited dozens of commoners to the palace, holding the first Summit of Commerce and Unity—an action meant to streamline the distribution of goods and create fair service agreements for business owners and workers throughout the continent. Madame Aheni, Madame Tsojo, and Sayeda had all been among the invited. And without a single noble present, Irina had crafted the Current Chaser Agreement—in honor of Davke and Driss—that opened new transportation channels and provided good job opportunities to thousands of Babylonians.

By month three, with Naveen's testimony and after inspecting the farms herself, Irina made the decision—against many of the nobles' wishes —to stop all production of Poppy Dust in Dunyas, and to form the first Farmer's Union to create safe working conditions. After many discussions, extra funds were allotted to the farms that needed to switch crops—incentivizing the owners to grow medicinal herbs or edible produce instead. With Hana's help, many of the smoking dens throughout Sora—Aheni's included—were given stipends to convert their businesses, making sure that as few common folk as possible suffered from the new policies.

And by month four, after countless hours in the medementals' wing with Naveen and Riku, examining the samples taken, after several failed attempts and nights where her power was utterly drained...

Irina announced the Aya Koishi initiative, a program that distributed the newly invented cure for the Blight to anyone affected for *free.*

It had taken Irina four months to change Babylon from the roots up, somehow accomplishing decades worth of work in a flash.

Less than four months, for her to cure the land of nearly all the disease and corruption that'd befallen it. For her to weed the garden and force long-standing tradition to bend to her will.

Less than four months for me to realize how truly unneeded I was. How little I belonged.

I'd been born a prince, but even as a boy, it felt ill-fitting. Untrue.

And now...

Now, I didn't know who I was. Without Aya and Mal, without the Lost Ones to lead, without something to run from...

I was just Shin.

And I didn't know what that meant.

But one thing was as painful as it was true: I wasn't going to find out by lounging around Anastova.

It was that uncomfortable acknowledgement that had me pacing outside of the council chambers, my steps silently wearing tracks into the clay flooring in the hall. My dress-tunic clung uncomfortably to my back—a second skin that didn't fit right, either, a uniform that itched and tugged in all of the wrong places—as I waited.

The doors opened, and just as I'd expected, Naria walked out first.

She rubbed the back of her neck, her primrose-colored day dress so out-of-place in comparison to her normal uniform.

Another thing we had in common, then.

"Meeting's out already?" I jerked my head at the doors she'd walked through when no one else came out, my anxiety a tangled ball of yarn in my core. This one had been something about Jaltan mining practices. I'd been invited to every one of Irina's summits—my new title as 'savior' and my former as 'prince' earning me a seat at the table.

But I'd stopped going in recent weeks—not fond of the reminder of how little my presence mattered.

Naria smiled as she glanced up at me, but it didn't meet her eyes. "It's just procedure now, and Father and I are heading home tonight." She hesitated, then carefully, "Are you coming with us?"

Her expression—flat and cautious—told me she already knew the answer. That she knew I didn't belong in Jalta, either—and hadn't for a long, *long* time.

I shrugged. "I'll visit."

And I would—I didn't need to be a Jaltan to be a brother. And the new friendship between Naria and I wasn't something I was willing to part with again.

"I thought so." Naria exhaled, her shoulders easing. But there was still a tension between her brows—a question we'd both been dancing around for weeks that would have to be asked aloud if we were to part ways without unresolved resentment.

Naria—like usual—struck first, blurting, "The title is yours, you know. If you want it. It was always yours."

I laughed—real and hearty, the first in months—at the absurdity of the statement. "No, it's not. You have *earned* it." My laughter fell away as the answer streamed out of me. I didn't need to list all of the ways Naria was more equipped, better-suited for the position—or all of the ways I was lacking. Anyone with eyes and a pulse could make out the difference; even my father, stubborn as he once was. Still, I added, "And if Father doesn't understand that, my next visit to Jalta will be to beat it through his skull."

"You sound excited," Naria snorted, but I didn't miss the proud tilt of her chin, or the joy that brimmed in her eyes.

She'd make an excellent queen. Her and Irina would do great things together, one day.

But if Naria was going to rule, I needed to be scarce, otherwise the old farts in Solyra would find ways to undermine my sister before she could even begin.

Though I knew she'd likely kill me for it, I ruffled her hair, tearing it from the careful braid she wore. "What can I say? I'm rooting for you."

As expected, she swatted my hand away—

And pulled me into an embrace.

"Don't be a stranger," she grumbled as she squeezed her arms around my neck—fast and hard, halfway between a hug and a choke-hold. "But be happy."

She let go, and before I could respond, she was off, strutting down the hall with purpose in every step—a classic Jaltan goodbye.

And with that—my first farewell was settled.

I stalked off before the others could filter out of the meeting room, a new wind nipping at my ankles.

❧

The trek to the medementals' wing was familiar now—a part of my daily routine in Anastova, for when I'd come to exercise my muscles and speak with Yurkov, the Medemental that'd helped me get my head straight.

But this time, I wasn't here for guidance or exertion.

I banked left at the end of the hall, to where Naveen's new work-room waited.

Like he had been nearly every day since we'd arrived, he was there, hunched over the cluttered desk, a magnifying glass in his hand as he examined a bottle of bright green liquid. Plants of every size and shape sat on the shelves, a tiny personal garden in this closet-sized room.

He didn't look up until I sat on the edge of the desk, knocking his glass trinkets to the side. He caught one as his head snapped up to glare at me. "Hey, watch the vials."

Challenge accepted.

I snagged the green-tinted mixture from his hand, swirling the liquid in its container, a brow raised. "Do I even want to know what's in this?"

He huffed back in his seat, stretching his long torso as much as the limited space would allow. "No, probably not."

"Are you training to be a medemental or a poisoner?"

A smirk, *finally*, as he snatched it back from me—my friend ready to play. "Maybe *both*, if you keep acting like an ass."

But the mischief was short-lived, as he examined the bottle again before scribbling down notes in his journal, one finger held up as if to tell me to be patient.

I swallowed back my frustration. The urge to run, to flee.

It was strange, to see my lazy friend disappeared. The lounging, wayward version of him vanished entirely, the obsessed—*consumed*—man before me both completely foreign...

And the happiest I'd seen him in years. The most self-assured.

Something I secretly envied, if Yurkov was to be believed.

"Where is Riku?" I changed the subject, the game no longer fun without a playmate. I was stalling, anyway—a bad habit that none of the medementals in all of Babylon could cure me of, it seemed.

"Already packing for Nehir," Naveen sighed, shutting his journal as he realized I'd pester him until he gave me the attention I needed. He rubbed a hand over his face, worry nibbling at him as he frowned. "I can't imagine what the hell is there for him in that frozen wasteland, but he seems motivated."

It had been a shock to us all, that when Nehir offered free housing and *Easinir* education to any water-wielders willing to return to the motherland and help them rebuild, that Riku was the first to sign up. That his mind hadn't shifted an inch in the weeks since, unmovable as an iceberg, no matter how many times Naveen, Kas, and I had tried to convince him otherwise.

"Training and opportunity," I answered Nav, sheathing my personal disappointment. "Closure, maybe."

Riku hadn't been himself since Ren. Likely wouldn't be for a long, long time. And since he refused to talk to someone like Yurkov...

Perhaps being in Nehir would help him feel closer to the part he missed. The part buried there in the snow and ice.

Naveen nodded, amber eyes misty. "At least Via and Vox will be there to look after him, too."

Another deal Irina had worked out, when Via had agreed to testify against Drakkar in the emergency trials. Protection, for her and Vox, and compensation for the years they'd spent suffering. Official acknowledgement of Vox's heritage, his status secure no matter what happened with the Nehirite succession disputes.

Via was richer than all of us now. And Vox would grow up with his mother, and with all of the education and resources he needed for when his *Easinir* presented itself.

So Riku would have friends with him, too.

And I'd have a few good reasons to visit the frozen shit-scape... whenever I was eventually ready.

Naveen coughed, bringing me back to the moment—to where the mist had condensed into full-bodied tears as he watched me. As he swallowed hard. "This is goodbye for you too, isn't it?"

This was what I'd come for—the permission I'd needed. The last of the Lost Ones that I had to let go of—a man with his own destiny, now. With a future he found all on his own.

It still hurt like a punch to the gut anyway. "Don't go all sappy on me."

His shoulders shook as he laughed through the tears. "You know I can't help it."

I hopped off the edge of the desk just as Naveen stood, years of synchronicity propelling us forward at the same time. Years of having each other's back, of calling each other's bluffs. Years of brotherhood forged in sweat and survival. Years of laughter and pain and everything in-between.

I yanked him into a quick, fierce hug. "This isn't goodbye. It's a see-you-soon."

"Good." He clapped my back twice before letting go. "Because I can't lose you too, brother."

Riku was where Naveen had said he'd be...in his rooms, stuffing his whole life into a few small bags. Preparing to flee again, but this time... for the first time...all alone.

Not that he had much to pack anyway—Irina, of course, had gifted him with an entirely new wardrobe, but he'd done very little to decorate the rooms and make them his in the four months we'd been here. Like from the beginning, he'd known he wouldn't be staying long.

I knocked three times, but still waited at the threshold before entering. Even if he'd done nothing to claim the room, it was still so evidently his—the hollowness speaking volumes of the young man who inhabited it. Nothing dwelled on the fine furniture, the bedding and couches all clad in the same drab gray that was standard for guest rooms in the palace. The curtains stayed drawn—blocking out the colorful landscape and warmth beyond.

An icy, voided gaze looked up, meeting mine. I cleared my throat, painting on a smile. "When do you go?"

Riku shoved one last item in the canvas bag before tying it off.

"Tonight," he said sharply—the word piercing through me even though I knew it was coming. But Riku looked me up and down once as he slung the sack over his shoulder, eyes narrowed. "How about you?"

"How did you—?" I blinked, surprise registering. Vacant as he was, Riku always *saw*, always anticipated the next move.

I hoped that instinct would keep him safe in his next venture. He'd need it, if he'd survive the icelands.

I swallowed, rocking back on my heels as the truth poured out of me. "Dawn."

By tomorrow, the Lost Ones would be scattered across Babylon. And though I knew I'd see Naveen again...I didn't know where the wind would carry Riku. Didn't know if it would ever call him back.

He didn't let me linger in the melancholy for long, a snort that was eerily reminiscent of his twin's breaking the tension. "Good, I'm gone first. Glad I won't have to watch that sad scene, then."

I smirked, grateful for the momentary ease, even if it was just a rare parlay from a time passed. "I'll make sure to write you all about it."

Riku chuckled, but it died in his throat. He shifted his weight between his feet as his lips pursed, false cheer giving way to something far more uncomfortable for us both.

"Thank you for taking care of us for all these years," he finally said, and somehow, that was worse. Quick blinks dusted away his tears before they could fully form. "I hope now...now you have some time to find what you're really looking for."

My heart shattered.

In a breath, I was on him.

I didn't care that he went stiff as a board as I tugged him into a tight embrace, my hand anchoring his head to my shoulder. Didn't care that he grumbled something inaudible, the sharpest of my Lost Ones always trying to slice his way through life and keep us at arm's length.

Maybe he wouldn't come back. Maybe he'd find something else out in the ice that would help him soften and heal.

But he would always, *always* have a home with me waiting for him. Always have a place under my wing if he wanted it.

"Living with you all *was* what I was looking for. It was a joy, not a burden," I spoke against his hair, conviction steeling my tone as I kissed the top of his head to the chorus of another groan. I pulled away, but didn't let go, my hands trying to hold him for *one last breath* before he could slip away into his future. "But I realize now that it's time to let you all fly, too. I hope you figure out what gives you purpose, because that alone will make my life worth it."

Riku couldn't blink fast enough this time to bat away the torrent of teardrops that ran down his cheeks—rivers that his brother would've swam. "He wanted to be just like you."

The words battered me like a storm against a window, both watering and weathering.

Riku and I would both have to carry the weight of Ren's death wherever we went. There was no setting the burden down. We would just have to learn how to manage it.

But even if we were kingdoms apart, we would always have each other to help us lift the load.

"No, he was better than me." I wiped his tear tracks, my own vision blurring. "So are you, Riku. I have no doubt you're going to make something special of yourself."

He would. And no matter how far he went, I would be rooting for him.

Ice cracked, giving way to a long pent-up tidal wave.

"I'll miss you." Riku trembled through the downpour, head falling back onto my shoulder. "But if you tell anyone, I'll kill you."

A real laugh sputtered from me as I cradled him. "Fair enough. Your secret is safe with me."

Riku let me keep his secret until the sun set. Until he couldn't put off his trip any longer.

Until he left the room—and Anastova—even emptier.

I saved the hardest for last.

It was evening by the time I made my way back to the room, a bit tipsy and bleary-eyed—thanks to one of Naveen's elicit concoctions that Riku had left behind in his room, stuffed under the bed—and dreading what came next.

I didn't have to wait long.

Like usual, just after supper, Irina fluttered into the shared room like a hurricane on a mission, a flurry of frantic movement as she hurried around the space, tearing open drawers and cabinets—

Not noticing the bag next to me, already packed.

Not that I blamed her—she had more important things to attend to than my whims and worries.

"Have you seen my book?" she asked, acknowledging me for the first time as she ripped through the wooden desk next to her vanity— one she'd had the servants drag in from the study so she didn't have to go as far between the two. "I left it somewhere in here...it has the notes I need for later tonight."

"I haven't." I tried to keep my voice strong—sure.

It faltered anyway.

Irina didn't notice as she searched through her closet. "Maybe it's under the—"

"Irina?" I tried again, her name cracking in my throat as the anxiety I'd tried to stay broke through the shoddy dam I'd built.

"Yes?" She whipped around—

Her face fell as she spotted the packed bag. Her shoulders slumped.

"*Oh.*"

She took a hesitant step closer. Two. Like she was afraid she'd scare me off, a bird on a tree branch.

When had I become so meek in her eyes?

Not that she was wrong.

I inhaled—gathering my resolve. She had been nothing but steady for me, and for the continent. I could give her this. "I don't know how to start this—"

"You need to go, don't you," she finished for me, her voice miles away even as she closed the distance between us, taking a seat next to me.

Parts of me already wanted to take it all back. To slurp the words back into my mouth and throw the bag back in the closest. To wrap her in my arms and tell her I'd never let go ever again.

But it would be a lie. And though I had a talent for tall tales, Irina deserved the truth. "I don't know *what* I need."

It hung there for a moment as she blinked away tears. As it settled into our lungs, both of us breathing it in. Letting it sink deep into our bodies, where it couldn't be taken back.

I didn't know what came next. Didn't know how to heal the hurt or find my way again.

Didn't know how to ask Irina for help without dragging her down with me.

She smiled, like she knew all of that, too.

"You were built to soar. It's not your fault." Irina's hand slipped into mine like it belonged there. But she was right—I didn't fit *here*. I was meant to ride the breeze and devour the skies.

I squeezed her hand, rubbing small circles against her warm skin. "I don't want to leave you."

The truth of one statement didn't minimize the validity of the other.

I needed to find what was lacking in me. Needed to take Riku's advice—needed to find my purpose outside of the Lost Ones. But so much of me wanted to stay. To be the man she needed. To hold her close and not let go.

"But I'm needed here." Irina leaned in, her forehead pressing to mine, as her next words shuddered out of her. "And you're not happy as a bird in a pretty cage. You need to find somewhere where you and Kas can start over and explore and play music and *heal*."

Tears streamed down my face before I could stop them, everything I'd pent up spilling over. Irina saw me, even the parts I'd hidden from myself. The things I'd been denying for too long, air trapped in a balloon ready to burst. "I don't know if that will be the answer..."

Her lips pressed against mine for a brief, fleeting moment, as she quieted the storm. "But it's a start."

The last floodgate unlocked—the last truth I'd been avoiding. Running from, since the day I found her in the Crescent.

I loved her.

I loved her empathy, her grace. The way her freckles danced across her face, the way her nose scrunched when she was thinking hard about something.

I loved her unintentional eloquence. The way she always knew the right thing to say—and to do.

I loved the way she could heal me, even when her heart was breaking.

And because I loved her, I had to leave.

Because my bad mood would become a poison to her new reign. Because my wickedness would change us both for the worst. Because my grief would fester into resentment she didn't deserve. Because without the Lost Ones to scurry after or Aya to treat, I had no idea how to spend my time.

Because she loved me, too.

And if I stayed, I couldn't be happy, and that would hurt her just as much. Because she'd notice. Because she was good and kind and always focused on everyone else's needs before her own. Because if I asked her to leave with me...she would. And Babylon would suffer for it.

"I love you, Irina," I said aloud—because she deserved to hear it. Because it was the truest thing I'd ever said. Then, "But you need a prince, not a thief."

Irina sniffled as she curled into me, shifting so her head was tucked beneath my chin and her arms wound around my trunk. "I needed *both*, and that's why I met you."

Gripping just below her chin, I tilted her head back, forcing myself to meet her gaze. The deep earthen brown that nourished and saved. The soft, round eyes that I wanted to bury myself in. "I needed you more, and I always will."

Our mouths crashed together, nothing soft or sweet about their union. No, this kiss—this dance—was a swirling symphony too fast to stop. A crescendo of everything we'd ever meant to each other. A culmination of every moment we'd spent together.

Our meeting at the Opera House.

Our reunion at the Crescent.

Our first joining in the cabin.

I savored every moment of it. The lemon-and-rose taste of her mouth. The supple press of her body against mine. The silken strands of her hair that knotted in my hands.

And when we parted again, breathless and crying together...

She said it back.

"I love you too, Shin."

For one last night, I let myself hold her.

Let myself be that man—the thief and prince combined. Let myself sleep, safe and warm in her embrace, comforted by her steady breaths and her even more secure presence. Let myself dream of petal-pink kisses and of futures that would not see the morning light.

And when dawn broke, I slipped from the room quieter than a flower on a breeze.

I was ready to leave by mid-morning, my belongings few and my plan simple: head to Hiku City and then let the streets tell me what came next. They'd taught me everything I knew, and I was in need of another lesson.

Irina didn't come to say goodbye. Not that I blamed her for that, either—I didn't have the heart to wake her this morning and manage another tearful farewell. And she had a kingdom to run, everyone still relying on her even though I was abandoning her to it.

But I wasn't alone—Lost Ones never were.

Kas had his bag slung across his back—likely full of things he'd stolen from the castle, the sticky-fingered twit—as he stared down the steps of Anastova like they were a dare to be conquered.

"Ready, kid?" I tucked him closer to my side, a breeze lifting his hair in wayward sweeps. "It's just you and me now."

Two Lost Ones without their siblings to fall back on. An older brother in need of someone to look after, and a little one in need of someone to set his course straight.

I didn't know where we were going or what we would find. But I knew Kas needed it just as much as I did.

Still, his weight shifted between his gangly limbs as he glanced back at the castle, fingers twitching at his side. "You know, we can stay. I like it here, and Irina—"

"Don't you want to see Hiku City again?" I derailed that train of thought before I lost my nerve, grabbing his head and turning it toward the steps again. Toward the horizon, and the waiting adventure. "We've got some rebuilding to do."

Kas set his shoulders back. Grinned. "I'm good as long as I have you."

And we would be good.

I nudged him in the ribs and took the first brave step. Then, the next. "Come on, then. Let's see where the wind blows us."

Step after step, we set down the stairs, my gaze focused on the road and the life ahead. On the possibilities opening before me, given life by all that I'd lost.

But a warm breeze wrapped itself around my neck, a gentle, quiet tug that urged me to turn.

One last look.

And there she was, on the balcony of her room, one hand on the rail as she watered her flower box with the other. As tears watered her freckled cheeks, her sorrow gave way to growth. To life.

Queen Irina, holder of my heart. Love of my life.

I didn't think she could see me, not from this far down.

I blew her a kiss goodbye anyway.

I used to think that people were inherently wicked. Used to think them weak—bowing to the wind's whimsy, to the darkness within.

But there were some who were just *good*. Some who were untouched by the gray, seedy desires that consumed most. Some who could not be swayed by the wind's coaxing, no matter how strong it rattled their branches and tore at their roots.

Some people—like Irina and Aya—made me believe in something better. Believe in a world where even a wretch like me could be better, too.

One more adventure.

The wind sang the melody of change, and Kas and I set out to find our own goodness.

And for once, I didn't look back.

FORTY-FIVE

IRINA

Flowers bloomed even after the coldest of winters, and by the time the following spring rolled back in, seeds of hope bloomed through all of Babylon.

It was a slow bloom—watered with trust and time—but I'd never seen anything more wonderful. Nobles offering up resources to aid the less fortunate. Workers from all four kingdoms volunteering their skills and effort to the many restoration projects throughout the continent —including the Hiku City Opera House. Jaltans and Sorans sharing transportation tips over dinner. Dunyasians and Nehirites exchanging recipes for medicines over drinks.

It was cause for celebration. For laughter and dancing and joy.

For a party; this time, for all of Babylon, not just the elite few.

Invitations for Prince Nikolaj's Masque were sent wide and far, a call for the masses to celebrate the spring and newfound abundance. To celebrate unity and change.

Not that Babylon was a perfect utopia.

There were still lingering pests and weeds in the garden—like Drakkar up north, still fussing in his house arrest and claiming he'd take back his kingdom one day. Though if Riku's reports were accurate, the new King Samir wanted very little to do with his cousin's ramblings and ravings these days. Or like the opposition in Jalta against Naria's upcoming succession, many of the old-school Jaltans still opposed to a woman's rule, even with Odion backing her entirely. Though I had faith that my friend would prevail, especially since the other Jaltan heir was conveniently *lost* again.

There was still work to be done, to maintain prosperity and peace. To turn it into something perennial and lasting.

If you don't like things the way they are, change them.

I would...in due season.

Tonight was a night to *enjoy.*

The Masque had always been my favorite, after all. And this time, the champagne and revelry felt far more deserved.

"Excuse me, Your Majesty." Gemma bowed as she entered my chambers, her sunset-yellow gown puffing up with the action—the old maid unused to moving in anything other than her normal uniform.

"It's just Irina," I corrected as I gave myself one last look-over in the floor-length mirror. The chiffon gown was my favorite yet; my mother ordered it specifically according to my taste this time, the bodice not too tight or restrictive as it flowed gently over my hips instead of in spite of them.

The color, however—a sage green with gold accents—had my heart in my throat, the shade so close to one I was trying desperately to forget.

One that hadn't written or visited *once* in nearly a year.

I shoved all thought of him aside as Gemma said my name, still awkward in her mouth, "*Irina.* It's time."

I turned, the skirts breezing around my ankles, and snagged the floral mask from the vanity, completing my attire. "How do I look?"

Gemma smiled. "Like a queen."

An absent hand touched the gold, pointed crown atop my cropped ringlets.

Queen.

Even after the year since I'd taken the title, I still didn't quite understand what that meant. Because even now, I did not intend to rule or roost.

I was a servant—just like Gemma was—to my people.

Still, I held my head high as I exited my chambers. Queen or servant, I'd earned a night of dancing and fun just like the rest of Babylon.

"What's taking so—" Naveen whined from the hall, but stopped short as I turned the corner, his amber gaze sweeping over me as his jaw dropped. "Oh, Irina! You look absolutely lovely."

I raised a brow—taking in his finely tailored, *very purple* tux. It was a far cry from his normal herb-stained, wrinkled tunics and plain-as-crackers-trousers. "As do you. Who are you all dressed up for?"

Naveen shrugged, but the color in his cheeks deepened as he offered me his arm. "Hana said she'd save me a dance."

I looped my hand through, letting him escort me down the hall, my grin unleashing. "You two have been spending a lot of time together."

A lot was an understatement. My friend had been back in Anastova for three weeks, and I'd barely seen her except during meals, after which she'd rush back to Naveen's workroom to help him with his research.

Which was hysterical, considering Hana's idea of research included a lot more giggling than actually reading or experimenting.

Not that I could begrudge either of my friends. Naveen had made his name here through his handwork and grit, his skill blossoming under the proper tutelage, but his work-ethic born of his own experiences. And Hana had always been too kind, too selfless for her own good. It was time she enjoyed something, too.

Time she moved on.

"We have a lot in common," Naveen said, and in it, I heard other things he couldn't say out loud, unspoken pieces that united him and Hana more than I could understand.

Loss. Futures taken before they could even be dreamt.

Part of me hoped that Nikolaj and Aya were watching them from the world beyond, conspiring together on how to push them closer.

I believed in my heart that their spirits—and the others'—would be here tonight, too.

I decided to give my brother a hand as I dragged Naveen along. "Well then, we better not keep her waiting."

Naveen and I wove through the halls, headed not toward the grand staircase, but to the main ballroom doors—another symbol of unity between commoners and nobility. I wasn't interested in having my own special entrance, and all the same, I didn't need my first Masque as Queen to start with me tripping down a flight of stairs.

My heart skipped as the music met my ears, soaring from the ballroom beyond. The string orchestra we'd hired, the Soaring Stars Symphony, had been quite popular lately, their reputation quickly working through the continent in a matter of months. And with just a few bars of the crooning violinist's bow work, I understood why.

I hadn't heard a sound that rich and sweet in years.

Not since...

Tears pricked at my eyes, but I blinked them away—along with the misplaced hope that beat through my veins—as the doors to the ballroom opened, the music fading to an intentional pause.

So much for avoiding a special entrance.

My father stood on the other side of the door in a ridiculous orange-and-mint tux, his chest puffed with pride as he bellowed, "Introducing Queen Catirina of Dunyas, first of her name, savior of the people."

Heat flooded my cheeks as I clung to Naveen's arm just a little tighter. "I hate when they call me that," I muttered through a forced smile.

A deep chuckle from Naveen. "It's the truth."

Together, we wound through the crowded room—more so than it had ever been, the gardens beyond also likely teeming with guests. But for once, the stares tracking my every move didn't burn or blister, but warmed, especially as I spotted not just nobles like Hana and Naria and Lord Avi...

But my people. Madame Aheni, dressed in a poppy-red gown that made her seem even more ageless and lovely. Riku—standing next to the young King Samir—in a silver tux that looked like the glowing edge of a crescent moon, his smile just as slim and telling. Kas, who'd arrived this morning on his own, somehow already a head taller than he'd been last I'd seen him, his curls tamed by Naveen's expert assistance.

Sayeda and her husband, next to my mother. Tasha and her two daughters, Miri and Lilah, sandwiched between King Odion and King Lin.

My heart swelled as the music kicked back up, the sound matching the symphony in my soul. This was what it was all for. All of the pain and suffering, all of the stress-filled days and too-brief nights.

Even though I couldn't find the one face I wanted most in the crowd.

This was enough.

But a figure stepped out of the mix, a kind smile on his face as he walked toward me.

Lord Kai, a friend of Hana's from a prominent manufacturing family in Sora. He'd been helpful in the last year, frequently committing his family's airships to help with distribution channels and job creation, though we'd only met in person once before, during a meeting where I'd barely been able to pay attention to the quiet man in all my overwhelm.

But today, he demanded to be noticed, the soft beige-and-amber of his unassuming tux highlighting his warm skin, his upswept brown eyes shining from beneath wisps of his silky russet hair. He bowed, taking my hand and pressing a chaste kiss to my knuckles. My stomach did a flip I didn't realize it was still capable of. "Your Majesty, would you care for a dance?"

Part of me instinctively wanted to say no. To spend the rest of the night either dancing with friends, or hovering around the buffet tables so I could snack as I made small talk with everyone. To recluse myself—like I had for nearly a year—my heart a clammed up, guarded pearl.

But for the first time in a long time, parts of me *did* want to dance. Wanted to laugh, to feel someone's arms around me, even if they weren't the same fit. To celebrate, even if there were still parts of me in mourning.

Naveen held up a hand with a polite smile—always the protector. "Her Majesty doesn't—"

"Why not?" I stayed Naveen with a squeeze and a reassuring glance. Then, to Kai, "I'd love to."

A smile lit Lord Kai's face, and it almost was enough to clear the clouds still lingering in the back of my mind.

Almost.

Still, I let him lead me to the dance floor as the musicians resumed their playing, a delightful waltz bursting free as the lead violinists' melody tore through the room.

And to the tune of that soulful cry, I danced.

Kai was a competent partner, matching the tempo with both skill and grace. But his feet never strayed from the structured steps, the distance between us never succumbing an inch.

This was not the whirling, all-consuming storm of my previous dance partner, but the practiced, metered machine of a technician.

Maybe that's what I needed. Predictable. Choreographed. *Safe.*

"You look wonderful in that color, Your Majesty," Kai's voice was warm but formal, a mechanical contrast to the violin's expressive song.

"You as well." It wasn't untrue—and still, the compliment felt forced. Polite.

Kai seemed to catch my shift, a sigh rolling out of him, "You know, your mission has been most inspiring. The way you have shifted and healed so many lives in the last year is impressive." His next step brought him closer, the hold suddenly more intimate, his smile less practiced. "I hope there are people tending to your happiness, too."

Again, a flutter in my stomach—still pale in comparison, but *there*. Reminding me I was still alive. That I still could feel.

Digesting his words, I thought of the many, *many* reasons I had to be happy.

A growing, plentiful Babylon. A close, treasured group of friends.

A celebration for my people.

A beautiful symphony to listen to.

A reason to dance with a stranger.

And it didn't matter if I'd tasted the euphoria of a tree-topped kiss once, or the forbidden delight of an intimate night running from danger. Breathtaking, *heart-stopping* as those moments had been, they were unsteady. Unreliable.

Perhaps content was enough. Consistent.

My smile was less polite as my hand drifted lower down Kai's bicep—letting him in. "Thank you for the reminder."

Kai's gaze dipped—just briefly—to my mouth, before he cleared his throat. "If it's not too forward, I'd love for us to become better acquainted. I'll be in the area for a few days...perhaps we could dine together one night?" He leaned in, his breath tickling against my cheek as he whispered, "There is a rumor going around that you have a sweet tooth, and I happen to know a wonderful bakery I'd love to show you."

A giggle worked up my throat, the prospect of a baked good and a kind man to share it with watering something deep within that had wilted too long without sunlight. "That sounds—"

"May I cut in?" A voice dark as a moonless night interrupted, silencing all else.

I hadn't noticed the violin stopped.

I spun, nearly knocking Lord Kai over.

Dark hair hung down to his shoulders now, brushing the plain black suit he wore—a match for the other performers—his mask a familiar ebony silk across his face. But even in the lowlight of the chandeliers, even with a new uniform, there was no mistaking those eyes anywhere.

Green tea and honey, a laugh like nightshade.

Breezy dizziness, rooftops like sparkling treasure.

Air rushed into my lungs as I took a deep breath—my first in a year—and my gaze locked with Shin Koishi's. "You're *here*."

Kai's hand found the small of my back—protective and gentle—as his brows knotted together, wrinkling his fabric mask. He dragged an appraising gaze over the violinist turned pursuer, before he looked at me, expression softening. "Is everything alright, Your Majesty?"

I barely heard him over the deafening drumming of my pulse. Both nothing and everything was alright.

Shin Koishi came back. He was here.

"We're old friends," Shin explained, a smirk dimpling his cheek. "I'll take it from here."

Kai narrowed his eyes, but when I said nothing, he bowed and stepped back anyway—ever the gentleman.

The other musicians kept playing, a deep cello and a viola singing a familiar tune, one I could hum from memory. One that I'd sang before, in a forest with captors-turned-friends.

And just as he did at the last Masque, Shin took one hand, his other brushing against my waist. Breathed me in, and swept me along to the tune.

"You're back," I finally blurted, the motion unlocking my tongue from its cage.

Shin was back. Was dancing with me, our steps in unison like we'd never missed a beat together.

A laugh like nightshade. "I am."

Shin was laughing, like nothing had happened. Like he hadn't left, taking fragments of my broken heart with him.

I stopped, halting us both before he could fly us away. Before he could make my heart soar, only to let it crash again. "And you just interrupted a *wonderful* conversation."

Bowed, cherry blossom-stained lips pursed. He glared over my shoulder at Kai, who'd wandered back to the refreshments table, still watching us with worry. "Did I?"

"Yes."

"*Good.*" Green-tea-and-honey eyes scalded as they flicked back to me. As they poured down my frame, drinking me in. Then, "You're stunning."

"That's *it*?" Anger—rare and raw—reared its head, as it often did when I was dealing with Shin. As it had many nights in the months he'd been away, a placeholder for my grief. "I haven't seen you in a year, haven't heard a word, and that's all you can *say*?"

How dare he just waltz back into my life without warning? How dare he dance with me like he'd never left at all?

How dare I *let* him? How dare my stupid, silly heart race at the slightest hint of his attention?

He hadn't let go of my waist. But he did now, ripping his mask off in a swift tug. He flattened me with the most soul-shattering, earth-ending look I'd ever received.

Anger gave way to something else. Something stronger—and all the more painful. Something that both glowed like starlight and burned like fire.

"I went and did what you said. I played music, I forgot, I *ran*." His throat bobbed as the words spilled out of him, both honeyed and hoarse—a lesson in contradictions, like every other part of him. Parts I still, despite my better judgment, *loved*. Parts I'd missed. He continued, a breeze unfettered, his hand cupping my cheek. "And I looked. For something, anything that gave me purpose. For something that made me feel *alive*. And every time, the wind kept blowing me back here. Back to *you*, Irina."

The world fell away, melting like snow during spring's first balmy day. The music, the chandeliers, the gathered masses...they all faded to nothing, my awareness solely focused on the space between us. On the face that I'd imagined night after night, real and smiling in front of me.

Shin came back. Shin was *here*.

I leaned into his touch, my body disobeying any commands to the contrary. Forgetting my reservations. Still, I managed to croak, "But you *left*."

Shin nodded. His thumb swiped away tears I hadn't even noticed falling.

"I came back. Several times, actually," he chuckled, resting his head against mine. Breathing me in. "But each time, I stopped at the door. Convinced myself you were doing just fine without me."

I let myself imagine it—Shin in some disguise, finding one way or another to sneak back to Dunyas unnoticed, just as he had tonight. Torn between wanting to stay, and his instinct to flee. Between his desire and his guilt.

"I *was* doing just fine," I said, pride lifting my chin higher as I pulled away. Somehow, I'd managed, even with my heart in tatters. Somehow, I'd healed. And yet, "But I could've been better. You *left*."

Left me cold and alone, harsher than the ice of Nehir. Left me to grieve on my own.

Left me to heal himself, after all he'd suffered through because of my involvement. Left me to *grow.*

"I did. And I don't regret the choice I made." He stood taller, his truths both hard to swallow and refreshing to hear. Then, his hand found mine again.

And in front of all the guests—now gathered and staring, enjoying the spectacle—in front of our friends new and old...the lost Prince of Jalta dropped to one knee.

"But if you'll let me, I'll spend the rest of my life making it up to you."

Flowers bloomed even after the coldest winters, spring forgiving the frost before and offering second chances at life to all. At love.

And hope had already taken root in my soul, a knowing that even when we were the most lost and afraid...

Shin would always find me again.

I breathed in. Then, "I suppose I technically told you to go, so we're even."

Even. His terms.

But mine, too. Another word for equal. And that's what he was... my equal in every way. One I'd never find a replacement for, even if I'd learned to be content with something lesser.

He raised a brow—somehow both tentative and playful. "Is that a yes?"

Worry slammed through me...fear that he'd run again, once the pressure resumed. Once the overbearing, overheated weight of the crown and Anastova rested on his shoulders again, caging him like a bird. "I thought you didn't want to be a king."

But Shin Koishi was built to soar above, and even now, he managed to transcend my concern, his voice carrying through the open ballroom.

"I don't care what my title is." It was a declaration of both love and loyalty as he rose, his head high, his back straight despite the heaviness of the promise he bore. "All I ever want to be is *yours.*"

"I can't do this again, Shin," I warned, my breath a shaking, quivering thing, like a violin's bowstring ready to snap. The last fearful, doubtful parts of me whirled like a gathering storm. "I can't fall and believe and then lose you all over again."

Shin smiled—that ever-loving dimple sucking me back in.

And a wicked wind blew me forward, sending me stumbling into his arms.

Shin caught me, his broad hands capturing my waist, green-tea-and-honey stare watering my soul. "Then hold on," he whispered, his voice a soft, breezy melody against my ear.

And as the Soaring Stars Symphony struck up their song again, as our hearts beat in time with the cello and the crowd erupted in cheers, as the chandeliers sparkled like stars watching over us...

Shin and I danced, and didn't let go.

THE END

Acknowledgments

Flowers cannot bloom without sunlight and water, and I could not write without the vast support network that has carried me through to the end of this standalone. Gratitude is etched into the beginning, middle, and end of this book, but I hope to be more specific in my immense thanks.

To Renee, my fearless critique partner, editor and stalwart friend. This book would not be here if you were not there writing along side me. Thank you for telling powerful stories that give me purpose and make me want to keep writing mine.

To Cass, my alpha reader, who gave me that push through self doubt before I could set this book on fire and start over. Thank you for encouraging me to hold on just a little longer, for always inspiring me with your feedback and creativity, and for your shared appreciation for Irina's thighs.

To Cassidy, my fabulous proofreader and friend. Thank you for teaching me yet again how to properly use em dashes, and for participating in our mutual love for traumatized ginger siblings.

To Saint Jupiter, my brilliant cover artist. Thank you for capturing the whimsy and wonder of this book in such a stunning display, and for putting up with my numerous and increasingly confusing emails.

To my Beta readers, Alexandra, Alina, Camilla, Cassidy. Cassandra, Cayla, Chelsea, Jennifer, Kelly, Kellie, Lucy, Molly, Maxine, Maddie, Maddy, and Tanvi. Thank you for your time and energy, for your fantastically constructive feedback, and for watering my dead heart with your many, many tears.

To my Street Team and ARC readers, thank you for taking a

chance on an odd pitch, and for helping me get this story out in the world.

To my therapist, who probably won't read this, thank you for keeping me sane, and for allowing me the space to go to the places within myself that I needed to write so many parts of this book.

To Alyssa and Edward, for being my similar monsters. Thank you for giving me a place to fully belong as my authentic self, for sticking with me through my wild years, and for loving me even though I'm objectively boring now.

To my family, for your unending support and love. Thank you for letting me poorly explain the plot of every random idea that comes into my head, and for buying more copies of each book than you'll ever need, just because it makes me smile.

To my husband Armand, thank you for showing me what a soft love could look like. For growing with me as we move into the next season of our lives, and for telling me to hold on, even when letting go feels like the only option. No love story I write will ever hold a candle to ours.

And to you, dear reader, for sharing in this book. For connecting with these characters, for feeling along with them, and for letting yourself believe in magic again, even if just for a little while.

Growing up on the east coast in small-town New Jersey, Lina spent her early days playing pretend and making up stories for her friends and family. Little did they know, that pastime would soon turn into a lifelong passion for storytelling in all of its forms. While she's a couple's therapist by profession, she's a writer at heart. When she's not scribbling ideas about fictional worlds into the margins of her notebooks, Lina spends her time reading anything she can get her hands on, driving her husband crazy with her wild daydreams, and snuggling her adorable pups.

Lina founded Silver Wheel Press in 2020 as a publishing label for her own debut NA Fantasy novel, Daughter of the Deep (an IndieBrag recipient), first in the Children of Lyr Series. However, in 2021 the project expanded to include other authors, creating a hybrid publishing group designed to uplift and inspire independent storytellers. Silver Wheel Press remains dedicated to supporting quality stories told with authenticity, creativity, and just enough fantasy to keep the daydreams alive. You can find her on Instagram @Lina_Amarego_Writes or www.silverwheelpress.com.

Also by Lina C. Amarego

The Children of Lyr Trilogy

Daughter of the Deep

Sister of the Stars

Mother of the Moon

The Elysian Saga

This Eclipsed Crown (Summer 2024)

Other Works

Of Fate & Fury; A Deadly Sin Anthology

www.ingramcontent.com/pod-product-compliance
Lightning Source LLC
Chambersburg PA
CBHW022017300726
48970CB00003B/934